A Leaf in the Wind

As usual the strange calm passivity held her still, closed her ears, so that she heard nothing, and saw nothing but Harry's mouth working as he hurled abuse, first at her, then inevitably at his wife. She told herself that soon it would be over; when the worst of his anger was spent he would flop down in his chair, tear off his muffler, lean his head back and close his eyes. Then with the closing of his eyes would come blessed release from what she knew was not the behaviour of a normal man, but invective from the mouth of a madman.

Also in Arrow by Marie Joseph

Emma Sparrow
Maggie Craig
Footsteps in the Park
The Gemini Girls
The Listening Silence
Polly Pilgrim
The Clogger's Child

Non-Fiction

One Step at a Time

A Leaf in the Wind

Marie Joseph

ARROW BOOKS

Arrow Books Limited
62–65 Chandos Place, London WC2N 4NW

An imprint of Century Hutchinson Limited

London Melbourne Sydney Auckland
Johannesburg and agencies throughout
the world

First published by Hutchinson 1980
Arrow edition 1981
Reprinted 1981, 1982 (twice), 1983, 1985 and 1986

© Marie Joseph 1980

Printed and bound in Great Britain by
Anchor Brendon Limited, Tiptree, Essex

ISBN 0 09 927220 2

For
Kathryn Louise Hampton

I

'I'm half an hour late anyway, so there's no point in moithering myself, Mr Waring. I might just as well be hung for a sheep as a lamb.'

Jenny Macartney laughed, and as she laughed Bob Waring was struck with the fanciful thought that if he put his hands towards her, they would be warmed in just the same way as if he held them out before a fire.

That was the effect the tall smiling girl walking by his side had on most folks. Jenny Macartney was all youth and freshness, as bonny as a spring-lit day, with her dark brown curly hair, her red cheeks, and a mouth that always seemed set to smile.

He knew also that they made an incongruous pair, or what would be called in that part of Lancashire a *right* pair, the thirty-one-year-old widower with his gingery brushed-back hair, and the seventeen-year-old shop girl.

She turned to him suddenly. 'It's good of you to walk home with me, Mr Waring, but I'm not frightened, honest I'm not. I've got a spare hat pin ready in me pocket. A long one with a point on it as sharp as a dagger.'

Jenny patted the pocket of her long brown coat, and he nodded, wishing he could think of something funny to say. They were there all right, the smart replies, the witty remarks, but he could never quite put them into words.

'Aye, well, I'll come just the same,' he said, and fell into step beside her.

They walked down the cobbled street away from the red-brick Sunday School building, past the terraced houses, already showing yellow lights behind their upstairs blinds. When mill workers had to be up at five, they were in bed by ten, sometimes even earlier than that.

Bob Waring often watched this girl's face from his seat in the choir stalls on Sunday mornings and evenings at the Chapel adjoining the Sunday School. It was what he called privately a *thankful* face, even when she was supposed to be praying, and the minister was preaching about the fires of hell. A hell that awaited most of his congregation, judging by the deeds he categorized as sins.

Bob inclined his head gravely. 'You make a gradely Mary Magdalene in the play,' he told her as they turned the corner into Whalley Street. 'I thought you were very –', he searched for the right word, 'very moving tonight when we did the last scene.'

Jenny nodded, wishing with all her heart that this funny little man with his protruding eyes and bobbing Adam's apple would stop insisting on seeing her home. She could have run all the way if she had been on her own, and more than that, she could have gone over and over in her mind the beautiful words she had to say. She could hear them like music in her ears as she tried to imagine how it must have been all those years ago. Nineteen hundred years ago, which wasn't long if you said it quick.

'They have taken away my Lord, and I know not where they have laid Him. . . .'

She was going to wear a red tablecloth draped round her before she was converted, then afterwards a white sheet coming up and hiding her hair. And she was going to cry if she could manage it, and she would manage it or bust. Really cry with tears running down her cheeks.

She could work herself up into a mood of anguish and sorrow before it was her turn to go on. She could be practising right now if only this little man would leave her alone. If he would only stop staring at her with his face that reminded her of one of the pet rabbits in a cage in the shop where she worked. He was supposed to be Pontius Pilate in the play, but trying to be dignified only made him look ridiculous. No wonder the man taking the part of Jesus had looked at him with such scorn.

Jenny bit her lip, aware that her thoughts verged on the blasphemous, knowing that often her thoughts were far too frivolous for such a sacred subject.

To her, Jesus and God were real persons, and God was a loving father she felt she could call on at any time, even chivvying Him up a bit when things were going wrong.

'Come on, then, God,' she would say when her mother whined more than usual, or when her step-father went into one of his frequent rages. 'Come on, God, let's have a bit of peace round here,' she would say.

But as far as peace went, her step-father, Harry Howarth, did not seem to know the meaning of the word. It was as though he was angry with everybody, all the time, forever shouting and swearing and sweating, his big face puffed up with temper so that the veins stood out on his forehead like purple tramlines. He hadn't even had a good word to say for the old Queen Victoria when she had died last year.

'Right old misery she was,' he'd said, shocking his wife into stunned silence.

Jenny turned to smile at the earnest little man trotting beside her. 'We're nearly there now, and thank you for walking home with me. See you on Sunday at Chapel then. Ta-ra!'

The door of the dingy terraced house, a house built at the time of the Industrial Revolution for the town's mill workers, was on the latch, but Bob Waring waited at the corner of the street until he saw that she had opened it and gone inside.

Jenny knew that he was standing there on the pavement, raising his billycock an inch or so above his head, managing somehow to bow from the waist at the same time. And the

9

image he conjured up in her mind would have made her smother the laughter, if she had not heard her step-father's voice booming out from the living-room.

'Oh, flipping heck,' she sighed. She was in for it again, and if she could have gone straight up to her bedroom she would have done so, but the stairs went straight up from the living-room, so there was no escape.

Taking off her coat and snatching the tammy from her head, she laid them over the horse-hair sofa in the darkened and never used parlour. She smoothed down her unruly hair, tucked her blouse more firmly into her skirt-band, then parted the curtain dividing the two downstairs rooms. She would brave it out, she decided. This time she was not going to apologize. She had done nothing wrong, and there was nothing to apologize for. Nothing.

'It's turned proper cold outside,' she said, in what she hoped was a light conversational tone. 'It wasn't too warm in the vestry neither. John the Baptist said his chilblains would give him what for when he got home in front of the fire.'

Mollie Howarth stared at her daughter through eyes swollen with weeping, then weakly turned her head away and stared into the fire.

Small-boned and fat, with flesh that seemed to lie in loose folds beneath her dress, she had married Harry Howarth five years ago, not long after her first husband Jack had died of consumption.

Jack had been a good husband to her, always kind and thoughtful, and she had taken it for granted that her second marriage would be as tranquil. She stared at the dying embers of the fire until she felt her eyes ache with dryness, then as she heard Jenny's voice, they filled and swam with ever ready tears.

A persistent and habitual crier was Mollie Howarth, and always had been, even when she was reasonably happy. When her Jack had been alive he had always been ready with softly spoken words of comfort, his quiet voice soothing and placatory. Not a bit like this great hulk of a man who terrified her with his rages, reducing her to a quivering mass of jellied nerves and emotions.

Harry Howarth was standing with his back to the fire, and she did not need to look at him to see that his flat mottled face was scarlet with uncontrollable rage. She knew that his fingers were on his wide leather belt, itching to remove it, and give this step-daughter of his a right good leathering.

One of these days he would do just that, and then Jenny would go. Mollie knew that for a fact, and the tears flowed afresh at the thought. She raised a corner of her pinafore and wiped her eyes on it.

'Oh, Jenny, love,' she pleaded silently. 'Why do you have to rile him so? Why can't you come in at half-past nine like he tells you to? Is this extra half-hour worth all the bother it causes?'

'What time do you call this, you young devil?'

Harry's head was back, his mouth wide as he stared at the girl standing straight and tall with the length of the table between them.

'Five minutes past ten, Father,' Jenny answered politely, so politely that the big man immediately construed her tone as insolence.

He moved, and for a terrifying moment Mollie was sure he was going to hit out with his clenched fists. She risked a quick glance at her husband and saw how his face was suffused with hate. She could feel his anger, and tremulous and helpless, she bowed her head before it, and began to moan softly to herself.

Jenny, with a tremendous effort, kept her voice low and her tone reasonable. 'The rehearsal went on a bit later than we thought it would, and if I had come away it would have spoilt the scene for the others.'

She tried to smile, but all the shining happiness was wiped from her features, as if someone had taken a damp flannel to it. She held her head high as she told herself that she would never be afraid of this bully of a shouting man with the veins standing out on his forehead, and spittle glistening at the corners of his mouth. He was nothing but a big shouting wind-bag, and she would tell him so if it wasn't for her mother cowering on her chair behind them. He could rant and rave and she could shut herself right off from him, just as if she had suddenly gone stone deaf, but it was her mother she worried about. Somehow Harry always managed to take it out on his wife.

The beautiful words of the scene she had recently taken part in, flowed through her mind unbidden, and Jenny found she was comparing their serenity with the coarse language being hurled at her. She felt she hated her step-father so much she was sure her flesh crawled with the despising of him.

He thumped on the table so that the teapot rattled its lid, and the two pint pots actually rose an inch into the air. 'When I says half-past nine, I means half-past nine, not five-past bloody ten!' he roared. 'And take that look off your face, you cheeky little sod! While you're living here you do as I say. D'you hear me?'

There was for Jenny, a strange and unadmitted excitement in standing there watching this man disintegrate as he lost control. Over the years she had taught herself to keep quite still as she watched him go to pieces and saw his eyes bulge out of their sockets like chapel hat pegs. His thick-set body swelled as if he were actually going to explode.

What might have struck an onlooker as insolence on Jenny's part was in reality a carefully monitored fear. Not of what he might do to her, but a fear that she herself would lose a grip on her slipping control, and find herself shouting back at him.

And that in itself was funny, because her fat sloppy little mother screamed back at him sometimes. So why couldn't she?

Maybe he would shut up quicker if she did, but her

habit was to stand her ground, her expression non-committal, and her eyes weighing him up as if she found him wanting.

Harry's throat was swelling now, puffing like a bull frog's, and as always, when he was more than usually angry, his Irish accent became more pronounced:

'No decent girl walks the streets alone at this time o'night. I'd have come a-looking for you, that I would for two bloody pins!'

Jenny blinked mildly without changing her expression. 'I did not walk home on me own, Father. Mr Waring brought me home almost right to the door.'

'Mr Waring?' Harry's contempt seemed to spatter the walls of the room, so that Jenny imagined the gas lamps dimmed in their brackets. 'Who for the love of Mary and the angels is Mr bloody Waring when he's at home?'

Jenny sighed and shifted her weight from one foot to the other. If only it had been a Friday instead of a Thursday, then her step-father would have had a belly full of beer, and his thoughts would be blurred. Nasty, but blurred.

As it was she guessed that with no money in his pockets he had been forced to stay in, giving him time to work himself up into a lather before she came in.

She sighed. 'Mr Waring is a good man. He sings tenor in the choir. His wife died two years ago having a baby, and he lives now with his sister and his father up Park Road. His father got his leg caught in a machine at the paper works, and it went worse and won't heal, so he stops in bed all day. He's an old man now . . .'

She was gabbling and she knew it. She was trying to interest her step-father in something other than the fact that she was late in, but it was hopeless. The only thing that had registered with Harry was that Mr bloody Waring was a Methodist, and therefore to him, a non-practising Catholic, the scum of the earth.

'Aye! One of them Methody buggers!' he roared. 'I know his sort. All mealy-mouthed and down on his knees of a

13

Sunday, then getting a girl with her back up against a wall of a Monday. I know his sort!'

'Harry!' Mollie's protest was a thin wail. The tears gushed from her pale eyes and ran in full flow down her flabby wobbling cheeks. 'We ought to be glad that Mr Waring brought our Jenny home. We ought to be glad there's some as are gentlemen.'

She began to rock herself backwards and forwards in the chair, head down, chin folded over chin, swollen ankles hanging over the tops of her threadbare slippers. 'They're a nice family the Warings are. He's got a white collar job young Mr Waring has . . .'

At last Mollie had done what Jenny had failed to do. She had drawn her husband's fire to herself, and his immediate reaction was to lumber over to her, place his hands on the chair arms to still its rocking. The next move was to bend down and leer into his wife's petrified face.

'Stop that bloody rocking, can't you! And stop interfering too! So Mr bloody Waring's a gentleman, is he? Like your precious Jack was, is he? And I'm not, am I? I'm good enough to pay the rent, but not good enough when it comes to a bloke what sings in the choir and wears a blasted stiff collar!'

Quietly Jenny tiptoed to the foot of the stairs. She gave a last despairing glance at her mother cowering back in her chair, then ran swiftly up the flight of uncarpeted stairs.

There was no point in staying to defend her mother. On more than one occasion she had done that, and only made things worse. In the end they had both finished up shouting at her, united for a brief moment. Married couples were like that, Jenny had decided.

She shuddered. But if what she was hearing downstairs was what marriage was all about, then she wanted no part of it. Ever!

Groping for the candlestick on the table at the side of the bed, she found the matches and lit the candle. Then she closed the door and started to undress, ignoring the hollow feeling at the pit of her stomach. Going straight from the cat-meat shop where she worked to the rehearsal had meant that all she had eaten since twelve o'clock was a bun, with the mug of tea brought to her by the proprietor's wife at five.

'But I'm not going downstairs again. Not for nothing!' she told herself firmly.

There was a swing mirror on the top of her dressing-table, and by sitting on the bed, there was just enough space for the drawers to be pulled out, whilst over in one corner a curtain wire stretched from the picture rail, forming a wardrobe of sorts. Jenny unbuttoned her navy blue serge skirt, let it drop to the floor, then picked it up and folded it carefully over the bed-end. Then taking off her blue knitted jumper, she held a fold of it between her finger and thumb and sniffed.

'What a pong!' she said aloud, and wrinkled her nose in disgust.

In spite of the cotton overall she wore in the shop all day, the smell got through to her clothes. Huge slabs of horse-meat cut up and boiled in the copper in the backroom, then weighed out for the dog owners who came to buy it and carried it away in newspapers. Why they didn't call it a dog-meat shop Jenny did not know.

She peeled off her black stockings and sighed at the chilblains discolouring the backs of her long slim legs. Even in summer they were pink, and when the weather turned cold they changed to purple.

'Who *wouldn't* get chilblains, dear?' the minister's wife at the chapel had remarked. 'Standing like you do on your legs in that cold shop for twelve hours a day? Surely there could have been something better?'

'Me mother didn't want me to go in the mill,' Jenny had told her, and the minister's wife had rolled her eyes upwards and said no more.

In spite of the wooden wedges Jenny had used to fix the frames of the sash window, the wind was rattling them as if they would fall out any minute. Jenny pulled her long flannel nightgown down over her head, and with frozen fingers tried to fasten the row of tiny buttons down the front of the yoke.

'Right, God,' she said out loud. 'I'm going to say me prayers in bed tonight, that's if You can hear me with all that row going on downstairs.'

The hardest part was pretending she didn't care. Most of the time it was true, because there was always something you could laugh at if you tried hard enough. Even when the laughter had to be bottled up inside her like a corked bottle of sarsaparilla for most of the time.

She could remember a time, when her real father had been alive, when the little house had been filled with laughter and teasing, when Jack Macartney, with his dry humour, would say something dead-pan and leave Jenny and her mother helpless with giggles.

'You should be on the Halls,' Jack's friends would say, but they were wrong. Jack's humour had been the gentle sly observance of his fellow-man's idiosyncrasies, not the coarse jokes spawned out by the comedians of the day, in their too small bowler hats and their vividly striped suits.

Jenny got into bed, pulling the flannelette sheet with its greying bobbles up round her chin. Before she stretched out a hand to snuff out the candle she stared for a while at her father's photograph, as he smiled with his kind dark eyes into the lens of the camera, the deep lines on his thin face settled into a kind of melancholy good humour.

It was nice to lie there in the darkness, warm, but not yet warm enough for her chilblains to start itching, just thinking about her dad, and how it might have been had he lived. Now she had to look at the photograph before she could remember what he looked like, but every single night, closing her eyes, she could see him, small and dark, the bone structure of his face forming a skeletal-like frame for the sallow skin, exaggerating the deep lines running from his nose to his mouth.

'Look at that little lass and the way she's growing,' he would say. 'Stand up, Jenny-wren, you are going to be bigger than your old dad.'

And she was too. Taller, and with the roses and cream skin of a girl reared, not in the closed-in streets of the mill town, but in country lanes, with hedges growing greenly, and primroses lifting mud-splashed heads after a shower of softening rain.

She was more like her Grandma Macartney who lived in the next street, Jenny told herself, clinging to the meandering pattern of her thoughts as she heard footsteps on the stairs. Her father's mother had been born in a country village, in a sturdy stone-built cottage flanking a green, with the village pump set squarely in the middle.

Superstitious, unable to read or write, Grandma Macartney had managed somehow to rear six children, even after her husband had died of the same choking disease that had claimed her son Jack. Politics, distant wars, and indeed any form of violent protest were unknown quantities in the quiet village, and though the villagers respected and worked for the owners of the big houses, they kept their own fierce independence. Kowtowing to nobody, as Grandma Macartney would tell her granddaughter.

Jenny could never hear her fill of the stories of how it had been in the village. The stories transported her from the clinging dirt of the streets, with their houses built either back to back or with a narrow ginnel separating them from an identical row in the next street.

Even Mollie had tales to tell of jam-jars filled with sticklebacks and red-throats; of after-school raids on turnip fields and rhubarb crops. Of times when the high-piled logs outside the cottage were frozen into a solid mass, and of when the lamp was brought to the table as they worked on the cut-rugs to be sold to summer visitors from the neighbouring towns.

Now Grandma Macartney was old, and wrinkled as a

prune, with a crab-pink scalp showing through sparse white hair. Her terraced house in the next street still retained its country air with newspaper packets of dried herbs hanging from the ceiling, and the pot of goose grease in the cupboard ready to deal with the first sign of a wheezy chest.

'God bless Grandma Macartney,' Jenny said, and burrowed her face into the pillow as she heard her mother's footsteps on the stairs, followed by the heavier tread of Harry Howarth.

The upstairs rooms were separated by a wall so thin that when Harry snored it was as if he were lying in the same bed as Jenny. If the wall had not been there she could have put out a hand and touched the iron bedstead of the double bed set at right angles to her own.

'Please God, let me go to sleep before they start,' she whispered, but even as she prayed she knew that sleep would elude her until it was all over.

Was this a part of marriage too? The shouting rows followed by noisy love-making that creaked their bed springs and even jangled the iron bedstead against the dividing wall?

Jenny put her fingers in her ears and felt she could die of shame for both of them. More than once she had crept downstairs, to huddle in her coat over the dying fire until it was all over, and she could creep back to bed.

She saw her sleep-dazed mother yawn her way downstairs next morning, hair in uncombed disarray, as she groped on the mantelpiece for the matches, before she slumped on her knees to rake out the ashes and stuff the grate with crumpled newspaper.

Ordinary everyday habits as if nothing had happened the night before. Jenny, busy at the stone sink splashing her arms with cold water, saw Mollie crouching there with the shovel propped up and a paper spread across it, as she coaxed the fire into life.

'Your father's not going in to work today. His back's

bad again,' she said, then she snatched at the paper as it burst into flames and pushed it into the grate. 'He says it's with all the lifting he has to do down at the wood yard. He's talking about giving it up and looking around for something better.'

Jenny rubbed at her arms with a coarse towel, grey from infrequent washing. She could hardly bear to look her mother in the face. It wasn't that she was a silly prude or that she did not understand about such things. She had been well informed about things like that by a sharp-nosed girl at school.

'What I cannot understand,' she told herself as she pulled the blue jumper over her head, 'is how she can let him touch her just after she has seen him staring at her with hatred in his eyes. It's awful, that's what it is.'

Mollie was putting the kettle directly on top of the flames, bending down with her hair wisping round her face.

'Sit down, love, and I'll cut you a slice,' she said, reaching into the bread crock for a loaf and taking the knife from the drawer set into the side of the square table.

Jenny knew that her mother had come downstairs without washing; that she had used neither the jug of water on her wash-stand, nor the cold tap over the stone slopstone. It wasn't that she was obviously dirty really, just that she was never particularly *clean*.

She averted her eyes as Mollie pulled the loaf towards her, resting it against her drooping breasts, and holding it firmly with her left hand.

'I like it when my . . . my father doesn't come down in a morning,' she said, then to avoid watching her mother she bit her lip and stared round the room, fairly tidy on the surface, but with dust clinging to surfaces, and crumbs swept underneath the cut-rug on the hearth. With piles of newspapers thrust underneath the chair cushions, and crocheted chair-backs that were never washed from one year to the next.

Grandma Macartney's house was never like this, even though the old lady had already suffered one stroke, and used one hand only with the greatest difficulty. In that neat little house in the next street, the fire brasses glittered, the fireplace was black-leaded, and the cut steel fender burnished till it reflected the light from the fire.

'I sometimes think it would be better if I lived with Grandma Macartney,' she said suddenly. 'She could do with someone living in with her, and I only make trouble between you and my . . . my father. You know I do.'

She took a slice of bread, put it on a plate, then going over to the fire held the butter dish out in front of her so that the leaping flames coated the hard yellow slab of margarine with oil. 'It was my fault that he shouted at you last night. It's always happening. First he loses his temper with me, then when I won't retaliate he takes it out on you.' She turned round. 'It's not fair.'

Mollie, without answering, came round Jenny to rescue the kettle before it spluttered onto the coals. She poured a stream of boiling water over the tea in the pot and stirred it round and round with a spoon. She sat down at the table again and pushed a half empty jar of red jam across to Jenny.

Her movements were slow and lethargic. She always felt like this first thing in the morning, as though everything was too much trouble; as though nothing mattered any more.

But what her daughter had just said mattered. She lowered her head, and felt the hard knot of tears in her throat well up to spill out from her eyes.

Jenny spread a slice of bread with the over-bright jam, and cut the slice of bread into two pieces. She wished with all her heart that she had left unsaid what she had just said. She felt sometimes that if her mother wept just once more she would do something unforgivable, like slapping her face.

'Mam. . . .' Jenny took a bite of the bread and jam then

immediately felt as if it would choke her. 'Please, don't cry. I would only be in the next street, and I would come and see you every day. It would only be for the best, you know that.'

But it was no good. Mollie was crying in earnest now, fumbling in her pocket for a frayed grey handkerchief, and holding it to her eyes, shaking her head as she wept, then lifting her head for a moment and staring at Jenny with accusation swimming in her pale eyes.

'How can you talk like that, I don't know! You know I couldn't manage without your money, no matter how hard I tried. Even when he's in work . . .' she jerked her head upwards, 'he doesn't give me near enough, not now the rent's gone up fourpence. Then there's the clothing club, and the doctor's man to pay, not forgetting the insurance. . . .'

All the time she was talking Mollie had been pouring herself a pot of tea. She heaped three spoonfuls of sugar into it and stirred it round as the tears dripped from her quivering chin.

'Your grandma likes living on her own. You know what she's always saying about shutting herself in of a night and pulling the blinds down. You know what she's like. . . .'

The tears were flowing in earnest now, running in rivulets down the fat cheeks as Mollie held the pot of hot tea to her lips, agitating it so that the tea slopped out onto the table.

Her whole attitude was one of such despair that Jenny's thought now, her only thought, was to comfort her, to promise *anything* if only she would stop crying. It seemed to her that most of her life had been spent in watching her mother weep. Besides, now that the tears did not make her afraid as they had when she was a child, Jenny thought there was something grotesque in this fat mother of hers sobbing into a pot of tea, but still remembering to take a sip between sobs.

She pushed back her chair so abruptly that it almost fell over.

'I won't mention it again then,' she said quickly. 'I just thought that me being out of the way might help, that's all.'

Then she patted her mother's shoulder, and took her coat down from the peg behind the door. Her face above the high collar was sharp with exasperation and worry. Worry because she knew she was committed to staying with her sloppy little weeping mother, and because she could see no chance of happiness for either of them whilst she shared the same roof with the uncouth snoring bully upstairs.

'I'm going to be late for work, and as it is I'll have to run all the way, or else Mr Pearson will be docking coppers off me wages again. Mean old skinflint. He wouldn't give the skin off his rice pudding, Percy Pearson wouldn't.'

Mollie's bottom lip dithered as she tried a wan smile, and Jenny went to stand by her mother's chair for a brief moment, trying not to mind about the musty smell coming from her body and clothes.

'I'm sorry, Mam. Honest I am. I'll try not to rile him again. I know last night was my fault.' She squeezed Mollie's shoulder, then parted the curtain between the living-room and the parlour and let herself out of the front door.

Then with the heavy morning mist bedewing the nap of her coat, she began to run up the street.

Mr Percy Pearson, the owner of the cat-meat shop in a side street tucked away from the centre of the town, had been up since half-past five. A veteran of the Boer War, he had lost his left arm below the elbow as the result of a Boer's bullet. Every morning his wife Nellie would pin the empty part of his jacket sleeve neatly into place.

With the small legacy Nellie had come into on the death of her father, and Percy's pension, they had bought the shop.

'It doesn't do no more than keep the wolves from the

door,' Percy would tell anyone who cared to listen. 'But I don't owe no man a single penny, and that's all what matters, I say.'

Nellie Pearson suffered badly with her chest, and with dropsy in her legs. For the last three and a half years, since Jenny had worked there, she was only rarely seen in the shop. A childless couple, they loved the few white rabbits, the moulting canaries, the occasional puppy with devotion, preferring them to humans, as Percy was fond of saying.

'An animal never lets you down,' he would say, holding a kitten in his hand. Without any training whatsoever, he had become the unofficial 'animal doctor' of the district.

Small boys would come into the shop, holding a mouse carefully in cupped hands before handing it over with touching trust. One such boy was leaving school at Easter. Already Percy had promised him Jenny's job.

'She's good with people, Mother,' he told his wife. 'You know that. She gets stuck into slicing the horse meat up, and she is willing and cheerful, but her heart isn't with the animals. I can see her holding her nose when she cleans the cages out, and she never talks to them like what you and me do.'

'I know, love.'

Nellie Pearson smiled on her husband with love. 'You are right as always. But what will the lass do? If she had gone in the mill she would be on two looms at least by now. I'm not all that happy about you sacking her. From what I have heard her wages are needed at home, badly needed. They say that Irishman her mother married lifts his elbow a mite too often. An' I don't think she's good with her fingers or anything. What will she *do*?'

Percy shook his head, and leaning across the table, patted her hand.

'Now, Mother. You know as well as what I do that sentiment and business never go hand in hand, but I'll tell you what I'll do, if it makes you feel any easier. I'll be straightforward with her and tell her what I have in mind.

If I tell her now it will give the lass a chance to look around a bit. Now that's fair enough, isn't it?'

Nellie's small eyes crinkled into slits of love, as she smiled on her husband.

'You always were a fair-minded man, Percy. None fairer. The world could do with more of your sort, and that's a fact.'

When the shop door-bell jangled Percy had already made up his mind that today would be the day. He would tell Jenny right off, no beating about the bush, just a straight-forward talk explaining that both he and the missus thought she would be better off working somewhere more suited to a girl. In a haberdasher's maybe, working with lace and ribbons. Working with women's bits and pieces instead of with slabs of horse meat and animals what smelled. In a way he was doing the lass a good turn. She would turn round and thank him some day, he didn't wonder.

He lifted the flap of the wide counter and nodded at Jenny.

'Bit parky this morning, love,' he said.

Aye, but she were a bonny lass all right. Out of breath with running all the way, her cheeks were shining and rosy like two red apples, and because she was a few minutes late she was out of her coat and into her brown cotton overall before you could say Jack Knife.

'Have you got the copper going, Mr Pearson, or shall I get on with the rabbits?'

Percy hesitated. It wasn't going to be easy, but he had promised the missus, and what was to be said was best said quickly. He opened a cage and took out a puppy of indefinite parentage, the runt of a litter found in the canal by a boy on his way home from school.

'Me mam won't let me have it, but I knew that you wouldn't turn it away,' the small boy had said, producing it from inside his jacket. 'Me mam let me give it a saucer of pobs and it made short work of 'em, so it's old enough to feed itself.'

24

Percy felt it would be easier to talk with this little chap cradled in his hand. His fingers stroked the soft pulsating spot between the floppy ears. Aye, you could always find a bit of comfort from a soft warm body with the tiny bones moving skeletal-like beneath the soft fur. Animals understood, animals did.

'I'm takin' somebody else on at Easter,' he said.

Jenny completely misunderstood. She rolled up the sleeves of the brown overall and smiled. 'Oh, that's a good idea, Mr Pearson. You'll be able to spend more time with Mrs Pearson in the back then, won't you?'

Then cheerfully, feeling that her boss wasn't a bad sort after all, she knelt down by a cage and pulled out a tray littered with droppings.

Percy's voice came out louder than he had intended.

'Jenny! Put that back! What I am trying to tell you is that I'm takin' somebody else on *instead* of you. A lad straight out of school.'

And he had read in books where the colour drained from faces when folks had a shock, but he had never seen it happen before. For an anxious moment he thought Jenny was going to faint, but then she stood up, and her head went back as her chin lifted. Her eyes seemed to be blazing at him with little shafts of light. Percy took a step backwards.

'Do you know, love. I thowt as how she was going to dot me one,' he was to say later. 'I've never seen anybody lose their temper as quick.'

Jenny's voice had a slight break in it, but what she said went straight home:

'So you're taking a lad on so you can pay him less money than what you give me, Mr Pearson? Less even than what you pay *me*?'

He decided he did not like that remark. It stung, and was cheeky as well. Percy felt the place where his left elbow should be start to throb the way it always did when things got difficult. He saw the way Jenny's face seemed to

25

have sagged into chalk-white hollows of despair and disbelief, and he wished with all his heart that his missus would appear, breathing noisily, standing on swollen legs as she leaned for support against the wall. Nellie always could smooth things over.

He tried a bit of bravado. 'Now there's no call for cheeky remarks. This is my shop and if I want to make changes then I will make them.'

'But not without telling me why, Mr Pearson.'

The colour was flooding back into Jenny's face, and she knew that she was angry, humiliated, and sick with worry at the thought of finding another job in a town where girls went into the cotton mills straight from school, or if they were lucky *trained* for something like a machinist or a packer. At seventeen she knew nothing. Nothing, and all because her father had died and Mr Pearson who was supposed to be his friend, had offered a job straight away.

Jenny turned away from him, unwilling to even look her employer in the face. She could actually feel the disgust welling up inside her.

'Because you knew my father,' she said slowly, 'and because he was your friend, you came to see my mother and offered me a job, and because my mother did not know which way to turn she took me out of school that very day.'

Jenny felt tears misting her eyes and shook them angrily away.

'I've been here a long time, Mr Pearson, and all that time I've been trying to forget that if my dad had lived I might have been doing something far different. I was a good scholar, Mr Pearson, so good that my teacher went to see my mother when I started here and told her it was a crying shame. Did you know that? But I came here on account of it being steady and safe, and because we needed even the few shillings you gave me to try to pay our way.'

She turned and stared with loathing into Mr Pearson's astonished face.

'An' now it's too late. I haven't even been able to work

on anything in the evenings for stopping on here so late. You've kept me here even when there wasn't a single customer after seven o'clock.'

Jenny realized for the first time that she was taller than Mr Percy Pearson, and even in the middle of her distress, the thought was somehow cheering.

'When do you want me to go?' she asked, and the way she said it sounded as if she would be doing him a favour of her own choosing, not the other way round.

'Easter, Jenny. I thought . . .'

But what he thought Jenny did not want to hear. Turning on her heel she walked quickly away from him through into the back place to the smell of horse meat and the big waiting copper boiler.

At twelve o'clock she was handed her dinner as usual. A mug of strong tea and a plate of bread flanked by a hunk of cheese. There were eight hours before she could take off the brown overall and go home, and as usual, because it was a Friday, Mr Pearson placed her wages on the counter beside her.

'Look here, Jenny,' he began, then hesitated. He had talked it over with his wife and she had agreed.

'I'll tell her she can go at once,' he had said. 'After all, fair's fair, and I can manage on my own till Easter. It won't be easy, but I'll do it.'

Nellie had been lying down upstairs, and she patted the bed for him to sit beside her. 'You're a good man, Percy, none better. That young lass will thank you one of these days for giving her the chance to better herself, and don't you go fretting that you only took her on because you were in the Odd Fellows with her father. Kindness has a nasty habit of rebounding, I am always telling you that.'

So it was with his prickling sense of guilt assuaged that Percy Pearson explained that Jenny could leave any time she liked; that she would not be upsetting him if she left at once.

27

'Fair do's,' he said, then with a jauntiness he was far from feeling, he walked over to the far side of the counter to arrange one-handedly a hanging display of dog-leads.

'That's very good of you, Mr Pearson.'

Jenny was staring at him with those dark eyes of hers, and without daring to meet the stare Percy knew it was saying everything his young assistant wanted to put into words.

It was saying she knew she had been dealt a dirty trick, that never once in the whole time she had worked for him had she had a single day off sick. That she had done all the filthy jobs without complaining, and even cleaned their living-room at the back and done the washing when his missus wasn't up to it. The look reminded him of how he had promised Jack Macartney that he would keep a fatherly eye on his daughter when the cough had taken him off...

Mr Pearson suddenly allowed the clasp of a leather dog-lead to drop from his fingers with a clatter before he scurried back to his wife and her unstinted admiration.

For the rest of the day Jenny worked automatically, stopping herself from thinking by saying the words of the Easter Play over to herself. As she cleaned out the canary's cage she was Mary Magdalene, serene and beautiful after her conversion; eyes which had once invited men into her home, downcast with pious devotion. As she cut and weighed great slabs of horse meat, she was in her imaginings telling the Disciples that she had seen their Lord, and when they did not believe her, she was the epitome of all the suffering women in the world as she raised anguished eyes to their bearded faces in supplication.

She was only seventeen. She was a bright curly-headed big girl who had been born to be happy. She was the kind of girl who had time for the old and the tiresome, and she was beautiful mainly because she had no idea that she was even remotely beautiful. There was gaiety and affection in the smile that she thought was too wide, and there was hope and a quick wit that had so often turned her mother' tears into smiles. In her own eyes she was too tall, and to her own ears her voice was too deep. It was a dark brown voice that when she was angry came out louder than she expected, and in spite of her easy-going nature she was often angry about so many things.

She was angry about the poverty she saw all around her. She was angry about the lack of opportunity for girls born into her own kind of situation. She hated the way not one of THEM seemed to care. She was not very sure who THEY were, but to her way of thinking they were a composite figure of wealthy people concerned only about their own well-being.

Injustice she could barely tolerate, and for the moment she was defeated with a heavy listlessness she could not seem to shake off.

When the shop door-bell jangled she was sweeping the dirty sawdust from the corner where the moulting canary sat on his perch. Leaning for a moment on the broom handle so that the first thing the man coming in saw was her profile, made sweet by the rounded curve of her forehead, and the slightly uptilted lift of her nose.

Accustomed to immediate attention from shop assistants and their like he rapped on the counter with his fingers.

'Could I possibly trouble you for a moment, Miss?'

Jenny turned round, startled, propped the broom against a wall, wiped her hands on the strip of material looped over the belt of her overall, and smiled.

'I am so sorry, sir. I didn't hear you come in. . . .'

It was a dark February afternoon, with wet pavements made greasy with the day's unending fall of rain. The interior of the little shop in its undistinguished side street was dark too, cold and dank with the smell of droppings which made the man wrinkle his nose in distaste.

His ride into town had been a wasted one, and he was

fuming inside at the incompetence of a wholesaler who could promise something and then have the effrontery to tell him to come back the next week when there would be more chance of delivery. He hated incompetence, did not suffer fools with even a pinch of gladness, and was vaguely depressed, then angry with himself for being so uncontrolled as to allow himself to be depressed.

On leaving Cambridge Paul Tunstall had joined the army, and without any active service experience had been gazetted to the rank of Captain straight away. He topped six feet by two inches, and since leaving the army where his orders had been obeyed without question, had retained a commanding air, of which he was not entirely unaware.

The lamp, swinging from the ceiling, threw shifting shadows onto his face, and because his errand embarrassed him, he stared straight ahead at a point well above Jenny's head.

'I would like a collar for a dog. A small dog. A Pekinese. First choice red, and second choice blue.'

He rapped out the request as if he were giving an order; as if he wanted it carried out at the double, and Jenny immediately recognized his sort. He was one of the rich nameless ones who did not care. He would see to it that the little lap-dog was well fed, whilst children in the streets went without even a scrape of margarine on their bread. He was not the usual type of customer, not at all, and she could only guess that he had been unable to find what he wanted in the town, and had called in the cat-meat shop as a last resort.

'Yes, sir.'

Her voice was cool and distant, without warmth, completely alien to her normal way of speaking. She rummaged in a drawer beneath the scarred counter and produced a clutch of collars. 'Would you be requiring a bell on the collar, sir? They come in handy if the little dog tries to run away.'

For a moment he guessed she was laughing at him, and

his mouth tightened. This girl had the husky voice and the insolent amused tolerance he had so often found amongst her like. Working-class inhibition, a deep-rooted sense of unadmitted inferiority. He had come across it in the army, and was meeting it now amongst his housemaids and the field workers at the farm. Newly back from the war, he had once tried to buy one of his men a drink in the village pub, only to have one bought back with a speed bordering on the insolent.

'No bell, thank you.' He pocketed the collar, handing over the money and striding from the shop, his military bearing apparent in the set of his broad shoulders, and the swing of an arm.

'Thank you, sir.'

Jenny narrowed her eyes, taking in the good cut of his jacket, the good cut of his fair hair, thick shining hair that had never been trimmed by his wife, she guessed, as he sat by the fire with a towel round his shoulders.

This man was one of the powerful group, the shadowy group who were never really to be trusted. A *gentleman*, as her mother would say, and likely to do you down as soon as look at you.

Only five more hours to go and she would be free to go home and tell her mother and her step-father that she had lost her job. Only five more hours of thinking what to say, and of how she could nerve herself to stand the sight of her mother's tears . . .

Jenny gathered up the collars, pushed them away and dismissed Paul Tunstall from her mind. A rude and arrogant man like him wasn't worth a second glance anyway. . . .

2

At ten-past eight Jenny banged the shop door behind her and set off to walk home through the streets, with the gas lamps throwing shadows onto the shiny wet pavements. The rain was so heavy that it bounced up from the cobbles and streamed down from broken gutterings.

When she let herself into the house her coat was black-wet, and the tammy she snatched from her head was as sodden as if it had laid for hours in a puddle. Mollie was sitting at the table, giving the impression that she had not moved since early morning, but when she heard the front door bang she roused herself, pushing herself up from the table with her elbows.

'Your grandma's not well,' she said. 'I've been round there all day, and the doctor thinks she has had another slight stroke in the night. She won't get into bed though, not her. She's just sitting there in her chair, staring into the fire. As soon as you've had your tea I'm going back to see her into bed.'

As she walked over to the fire-oven her movements were as slow and laboured as if she was forcing herself through waist-high water, and Jenny knew this was not the time to tell her about losing her job.

'Grandma must be bad if she would let you fetch the doctor,' she said. 'Grandma doesn't trust doctors. Is she real bad, Mam?'

Mollie took a steaming dish from the oven, and nodded.

'It's hard to say, love, but at her age every setback is serious.'

Jenny removed her wet coat, shook her tammy over the slopstone, and turning a chair round, set them to dry before the blazing fire. Her mother was wearing the same blouse and skirt she had come downstairs in that morning, and the only concession she had made to tidying herself up was that the slipping bun of hair was now festooned with hairpins sticking out like quills.

As Jenny sat down at the table Mollie slid a kipper onto a plate and pushed a plate of bread and margarine close to it, but before Jenny started to eat she handed her wages over.

'Grandma can *afford* to have the doctor, can't she, Mam?' she wanted to know. 'Because we can help out a bit, can't we?' She raised her eyes ceilingwards in a gesture that Mollie interpreted at once.

'Out.' Her mother's face crumpled as her lower lip wobbled. 'He got up at dinner time, then went down to the mill to line up for his money, then they told him he wasn't needed any more.' She groped in the pocket of her apron for a handkerchief. 'What can you expect when he spends more time in bed than what he does at work?'

Jenny drummed with her fingers on the table. She was so hungry that the smell of the fish made her mouth water, and yet she knew that if she had taken a single mouthful at that moment she would have choked.

'What I would do without your money I don't rightly know.' Mollie put the coins into the table drawer, and from force of habit pulled the knives and forks over them. 'The rent man's been, but I told him I'd give him two lots next week. He was very nice about it, considering.'

Completely oblivious to the fact that Jenny was sitting still without attempting to eat, she took a plaid shawl down from the peg behind the door, and draping it over her head and holding it close beneath her chin, went out without another word, leaving Jenny staring after her with an expression of dismay.

'You've got to eat,' she told herself out loud. 'Otherwise you'll be looking more like a bean-pole than ever, won't you? But oh, dear dear God, what a mess. Him and me, the both of us out on our heels.' She glanced up at the clock on the mantelpiece and forced herself to swallow the steaming fish, washing it down past the lump in her throat with the hot scalding tea.

After she had washed up she went through the parlour and shot the bolt on the front door. Then she half filled the enamel bowl on the stone sink with cold water from the tap, and setting it down on the rug in front of the fire, topped it up with boiling water from the kettle.

Laying a clean nightdress to warm over the guard, she undressed quickly and stood in the bowl, wincing as the warm water splashed the chilblains up the backs of her legs. It took less than five minutes to soap herself all over, and then after she had pulled the flannel nightdress over her head, she emptied the bowl and drew the bolt on the front door.

When Harry Howarth came home, reeling down the street worse for the drink he had consumed, she would be in bed, with the chair pushed up against the door . . .

'God bless Grandma,' she prayed, 'and if she has to die soon, let it be quick. She could not bear to be a burden. You know that.'

She closed her eyes, and felt the familiar agonized itching begin as her body took in the warmth of the piled blankets. 'An' I'll tell them tomorrow about Mr Pearson giving me the sack. I will, honest I will.'

Then before she slept she remembered for no reason that she could fathom, the tall young man with the brown jacket with its leather patches on the elbows, the man who had looked at her as if she was nothing, so far beneath his contempt that she doubted if he could have told whether she was young, or old like Grandma Macartney in her chair by the fire and staring at the wall.

There was a rehearsal for the play on the Monday of the next week, and still she had not told her mother about losing her job.

Again Bob Waring insisted on walking her home, and before they had turned the corner from the steep street, she found herself telling the strange quiet little man all about it.

'If I could find myself another job before I let on, it wouldn't matter, but how can I begin to look around when I work such long hours? And besides, I'm not *trained* for anything, you see.' The tammy had dried into a peculiar shape, and she gave it a little impatient tug as it slipped to the back of her head. 'I'd be better off if I had gone into service when I was thirteen, but my mother needed me, and she needs me more than ever now. At least she needs the money I take home on a Friday.'

She was walking so quickly that Mr Waring had to take little skipping steps now and again to keep up with her, and under normal circumstances she would have seen the funny side of it, and when he spoke she realized with a start of surprise that he hadn't even been listening to her properly.

'My wife died in childbirth, Miss Macartney,' he was saying. 'And our baby died with her.'

'How dreadful.' Jenny tried to be suitably sorry. She *was* sorry, but with one rehearsal behind her she was rehearsing another scene in her mind. This time she would have to tell them, this very night, when she got in, in fact, and her mother would cry and her step-father would rant and rave, but it had to be said. Somehow she had to find the courage to say it.

'Yes, the Lord giveth and the Lord taketh away.'

Jenny glanced sideways at the man trotting by her side. His bowler hat was pulled down over his ears, and as they walked past a lamp she saw the way his Adam's apple was bobbing furiously above his high starched collar.

This man was kind. He was peculiar and strange, but he was kind, and once, years ago, he had been married to

35

a girl who had died trying to give him a baby. Losing her job was nothing compared to a tragedy like that.

'I'm truly sorry, Mr Waring.'

Jenny squeezed his arm in sympathy, and to her surprise he covered her hand with his own neatly gloved hand, holding on so tightly that there was nothing she could do but carry on walking, linked to him as if they were walking out together.

'I live with my father and my sister, Miss Macartney. My father stops in bed all the time now, and Agnes is good to him. She is good to us both, but it's not the same. Not at all the same.'

'I don't suppose it is, Mr Waring.' Jenny tried to disengage her hand but he held on.

'Once you have been married you can never be the same.'

'No, Mr Waring.'

Linked together they turned a corner, and passing another lamp Jenny saw that in spite of the bitter cold of the winter's night, Mr Bob Waring's face was beaded with perspiration.

'I'm thirty-one years old, Miss Macartney, but I am already senior clerk at the iron foundry up Dartwell Street. You know the place?'

'Just past the Bank,' Jenny said, trying to be helpful.

'Built during the cotton riots in 1878,' Mr Waring said, and she nodded.

'Terrible times, Miss Macartney.'

Jenny nodded again, wriggling her hand once again but to no avail. It was like a conversation from a book she had read recently called *Through the Looking-Glass* by a writer called Lewis Carroll – quite sensible taken a sentence at a time but nonsense when strung together.

'Agnes is ten years older than me, you've seen her I'm sure at the Chapel services?'

Jenny immediately saw a picture of a kneeling Miss Waring, hands clasped in pious devotion, mouth working rapidly as she added prayers of her own to those the minister was intoning. Always in black, with tufts of gingery hair sticking out from an old-fashioned bonnet Jenny was sure must have belonged to her mother years ago. And she was only forty? She could have been taken for at least twenty years older than that. Why, she even talked with her eyes closed as if she was praying underneath the words she was saying.

'I've seen her, yes.'

They were passing a public house when a man reeled out much the worse for drink. He was so far gone that he could only make progress by walking with a kind of keeling run, his long arms flaying as he fought for balance.

'Oh, no!' Jenny's protest came out as a smothered moan. She clutched Mr Waring's arm with her fingers digging into the nap of his overcoat, and with a feeling of protectiveness, a feeling he had felt for his own young dead wife years before, Bob Waring gave the hand three reassuring pats.

'It's all right, Miss Waring. He won't come near us. All he is thinking of is getting home all of a piece, and judging by his condition he will be lucky if he manages even that.'

But Harry Howarth *had* seen them. As Jenny closed her eyes in horror, praying in vain that her step-father would let them pass unnoticed, he lurched over, grabbing Jenny by the arm, leering into her face, his eyes narrowed into red slits, and his foul-smelling breath blowing into her horrified face.

'So *this* is where I find you is it? Walking the streets with a man old enough to be your father by the look of him, when all decent girls are at home in their beds!'

He stumbled and would have fallen but for Bob Waring's instinctively outstretched hand, a hand he knocked rudely away.

'Keep your filthy hands off me, you . . . you Methody bugger! And sod off . . . now, before I knock tha blasted block off!'

It was like something out of a penny melodrama, with

the three of them swaying in the light from the street lamp, with Jenny pushing Bob Waring away, forcibly, pleading with him to go. Just to go, and leave her to deal with the huge unshaven man with the grey-white muffler wound round his bull neck, and the red veins standing out on his cheeks.

'I'll see to him. He . . . he's my step-father,' she whispered, her voice ragged with shame. 'Please, Mr Waring. Just go . . . Please!'

'Aye. Go . . . go away you mealy mouthed sod. . . .'

Jenny took her step-father's arm, and with her heart banging like a sledge-hammer inside her buttoned-up coat, with tears stinging at the backs of her eyes, half led, half dragged the drunken man down the street. When at the corner, she risked a quick glance back over her shoulder Mr Waring was picking his hat up from where it had rolled into the gutter and was dusting it off with the palm of his neatly gloved hand.

'Walking the streets like a night woman . . . cracking on he was just seeing you home. I saw you. With me own two eyes I saw you. . . .'

Harry mumbled, stumbled, regained his balance and mumbled again. Now that she was sure Mr Waring was no longer there, Jenny withdrew the support of her hand and began to run. Snatching the tammy from her head, she ran, feeling the cold air lift her hair away from her neck. She had only one thought in her mind – to get to the house, to close the door behind her, to run upstairs and wedge the chair against the door of her room. To close her heart and her mind against what had just happened.

'I'll show you up in the street!' Harry Howarth had promised. 'One of these fine days I'll show you up proper, that's what I'll do!'

And now he had done it. Now Mr Waring would know she lived with a man like that. Now he would know that she wasn't fit to play the part of Mary Magdelene in the play, even *before* she was converted. He would realize from

38

now on why the minister's wife had provided Mary Magdelene with a sheet from her own linen cupboard, because girls like Jenny Macartney lived in houses where there were no linen cupboards, where sheets were left on the bed till they were mucky enough to crawl off. Where men came home night after night, too far gone in drink to know what they were doing or saying, and where wives waited by the fire with tears running down their cheeks.

Before the terrible scene had taken place she would not have cared what Mr Waring thought about her. He was nothing but a kind soft nothing, but now he knew. An' he would tell his sister with the carroty hair peeping out from her black bonnet, and she would stop praying for a minute in Chapel, just to open her fingers a little and stare through them at Jenny Macartney whose father was a drunken uncouth bully.

Sobbing uncontrollably Jenny lifted the latch, banged the front door to behind her, and rushed through the darkened parlour into the living-room.

From her position by the fire, Mollie Howarth twisted round in her chair and nodded with satisfaction.

'You're home before him, then. Praise be to that.' She nodded towards the knife and fork drawer set into the side of the table. 'He found the money, what there was left of it after I'd been up to the shops, and if I was you I'd get straight off to bed. I'll bring you a pot of cocoa up when he goes out to the back. *I'll* deal with him tonight.'

For once Mollie was taking the initiative; for once she was trying to be strong, and it was too much for Jenny. Snatching off her tammy and throwing her coat over a chair she went to kneel down by her mother's chair, and raised her anguished face.

'He's coming now, Mam. He would be right behind me, but he's too far gone to stand. But even if he's fallen flat on his face he'll be here any minute, and he showed me up, Mam. I was with Mr Waring from the Chapel and he grabbed at me and told Mr Waring to bugger off. He was

39

walking me home and telling me all about his wife dying and his baby dying, and we were having a proper conversation when he . . . oh, Mam, why did you have to go and marry him? Why?'

Immediately, as if a tap had suddenly been turned on, the tears gushed from Mollie's pale eyes. And as Jenny saw them her own tears stopped as if the same tap had as suddenly been turned off.

'I'll stop down here, Mam. I'm not letting you take the blame this time.' She stood up, her eyes going to the brown curtain dividing the living-room from the front parlour. 'But blame for what? What am I supposed to have done? I went straight from work to the Sunday School, and then straight from there to here. I'd never let a boy be cheeky with me or nothing.'

'All I've done,' she thought with despair, 'is to get meself the sack and not find the courage to tell. An' if he makes me lose my temper tonight then I might blurt it out, and he'll blame me. He'll· say I've done something when I haven't . . . he will, I know he will.'

They were very different, the two women in the small over-heated room, so different that it would have been impossible for them to be taken for mother and daughter. As Jenny stood straight and tall, watching the door, eyes wide and cheeks flushed, so her mother crouched on the chair, her head down and the stuff of her skirt falling down in between her clasped hands as they hung uselessly between her knees.

When the front door crashed open they stared at each other, like two defenceless animals cornered and terrified with no hope of escape.

'We're behaving as if he can kill us,' Jenny thought, 'and when he sees how truly afraid we are, he will know he has won again.'

She straightened her shoulders, and with her heart hammering in her breast, she waited trembling for what must be.

And as usual the strange calm passivity held her still, closed her ears, so that she heard nothing, and saw nothing but Harry's mouth working as he hurled abuse, first at her, then inevitably at his wife. She told herself that soon it would be over; when the worst of his anger was spent he would flop down in his chair, tear off his muffler, lean his head back and close his eyes. Then with the closing of his eyes would come blessed release from what she knew was not the behaviour of a normal man, but invective from the mouth of a madman.

Jenny covered her ears with her hands and found that they were damp with terror, and when she lowered them again, clasping them together she could feel the perspiration tingling in the palms.

Harry picked up a pint pot and crashed it down onto the table. His scarlet face exploded with fury as the pot cracked into splinters and flew in all directions. Mollie, with her hands over her head, was moaning softly to herself, and from the house next door came the sound of knocking on the wall as the neighbours tried to show their displeasure at what was going on.

'Stop that bloody whining, or do you want me to land you one?' His raucous voice at one with his almost primitive brutality, Harry Howarth raised his hand as if he would knock his wife forcibly from her chair.

Jenny stepped forward to stand before Mollie's chair, her arms spread wide in unconscious protection.

'Hit my mother and I'll go for the police!' she heard herself saying, in a flat calm voice with a ring of authority that drained the terrifying purple from Harry's face, leaving him swaying on his feet, his slack lips open as he tried to believe what she had just said.

After what seemed to Jenny like an eternity he did the last thing she expected of him. He threw back his head and began to laugh. His mottled face exploded into gusts of hiccuping laughter that left Jenny trembling with renewed fear as she wondered what he was going to do next.

41

'So you're goin' to get the police, are you now?' His voice dropped to a sly cunning, and Jenny saw the blood leave his face, showing grey patches over his high cheekbones. He looked spent and suddenly very ill.

He nodded his head three times in terrifying deliberation. 'Aye, well it makes sense that it does. You would think nothing of turning on your own, would you, you young devil you?'

Jenny clenched her hands so that the nails dug into her palms. 'But you're not my own, are you? You are not my flesh and blood, thank God. My *real* father would never have come home in the state you are in. He would never have walloped my mother, or opened a drawer. . . .' She nodded towards the knife and fork drawer set into the front of the table. 'And taken the only money in the house left there for buying food.'

To her own amazement she heard herself saying: 'And soon there won't be my wages there for you to steal, because I have got the sack. Yes, it's the two of us now without a job to go to, but with one difference. I am going to move heaven and earth to find meself another place, and I'll tell you something. When I do it won't be to provide you with drink. So now you know.'

Harry raised an arm, and Jenny flinched, anticipating the blow that never came. Instead Harry dropped his head forward on this thick neck, and hissed the words at her.

'To be sure I am not your real father either, am I? Aye, there's no dis . . . disputing that, is there, Mollie?'

Jenny held her breath with a sudden sinking premonition of danger, as behind her, Mollie gave a low moan of pain.

Her voice rose in a thin wail. 'No! No! You swore on the Holy Mother you would never . . . never . . .'

Harry spoke with a softly vindictive sneer of satisfaction.

'And nor was Jack Macartney your father. He married your mother when she was five months gone; when she was chucked out of one of the big houses with nowt but

42

the clothes she stood up in, an' I kept it to meself when I thought that you and me might click.'

He lumbered over to his chair and sat down. He had reached the maudlin stage now, and was staring at Jenny with his mouth working convulsively, his big hands tearing ineffectually at the buttons on his waistcoat, all anger spent.

Jenny tried to move and found she was rooted to the spot. She turned her head and saw the truth written on her mother's anguished face, and it was all more than she could bear. Moving slowly, dragging one leg after the other, she left them there, and climbed the stairs to her room, her head spinning.

Sitting on her bed she stared at her reflection in the swing mirror. She put up a hand and touched her face, running a finger down a cheek. She was too numb to cry, too numb to do anything but stare as if the face she saw belonged to anyone but herself.

'But he *was* my father,' she whispered. 'I am dark as he was dark. We were alike in so many ways.' She glanced at the photograph on the bedside table, and lit the candle so that the whippet-clean lines of Jack Macartney's features were thrown into wavering focus.

She ran a hand over the unruly curls of her tumbled hair, and little things, stupid things came into her mind. Mollie's hair was straight, as straight as a drink of water, as Grandma Macartney often said. Mollie was tiny, no more than five feet tall, and her father . . . her so-called father had been small, a pint-sized man who had teased her when it became apparent even before he died, that his daughter was going to be able to look down on him some day.

'We was never good scholars, your mother and me,' Jack had teased when she came home from school to tell how she had been moved up a class to sit on the back row where all the clever pupils sat. 'I can see you being a teacher some day, and coming home and looking down your nose at me and your mother,' he had said, the pride shining in his kind dark eyes.

And somewhere there was another man who was responsible for her sitting here on the edge of her bed, a man from whom she had inherited so many things. His height, there was no doubt about that. His eyes? Jenny widened her dark eyes at herself, but got no answer. Her quickness of mind? Her addiction to book learning, a thwarted addiction that had been nullified by her long hours in the dark little shop.

'Who *was* he, Mam?'

Jenny asked the question without preamble as her mother came into the room to sit beside her on the bed. 'You have to tell me. I have a right to know.'

Mollie's eyes were swollen and red with weeping, and Jenny took in her ravaged face in a strangely detached way. So used to her mother's tears, to the endless source of dripping flowing tears, that their power to move her was almost gone.

'I am not *blaming* you. I just feel heart sorry for you and the way it must have been. But who was it, Mam? And why did he not want to marry you? Was he married already or something?'

'Harry should never have told you.' Mollie lowered herself heavily onto the bed by the side of her daughter. 'I only told him one day when he goaded me into it by criticizing your father.' Her bottom lip quivered as if some external current had set it going. 'There was no need for you ever to know, not the way Jack took to you.' More tears gushed from her pale eyes, and she made no attempt to wipe them away. 'He was that proud of you, and you brought him such joy.' She nodded towards the photograph. 'What difference does it make after all these years? He was your *father*, Jenny love. He held you when you was first born, and you loved him too. You used to wait behind the door for him coming home, like a little dog waiting for its master. You *loved* him, you did, you know you did.'

Jenny put an arm round the plump shoulders, and drew her mother towards her, so that Mollie's head rested on her shoulder, and even in that instinctive gesture of sympathy she could not prevent herself from seeing how their reflections differed in the mirror. She realized then, even in that first hour of discovery, that she *wanted* to look like the stranger, the unknown man who was her father.

'Who was he?' she asked again.

But it was no good. Mollie was too wrapped up in her own unhappiness to even begin to understand its importance.

'He's sleeping it off in the chair. He ought never to have . . . it's not true, love. He's a wicked man and that's just the thing he would say when he's in drink.'

'No, Mam. He was speaking the truth. He's not clever enough to make a thing up like that.' Jenny, still holding her mother close, leaned forward and took a clean handkerchief from the drawer underneath the swing mirror. 'Here. Don't cry, Mam. I don't hold it against you, honest. I'm just sorry that you must have been so very unhappy when it, when it all happened. But I'm not a child. I deserve to know.'

'I thought because I had had one good husband, the next one would be the same, an' Harry was at the first. He was always laughing, and he promised to look after us both, an' it wasn't till he had got his feet under the table that he showed his real self. Oh, Jenny, love, what would I do without you? How could I manage? What would I do?'

The sobs started again, and as Jenny rocked the fat, sloppy little woman in her arms she knew she would never get away. Even Grandma Macartney wasn't her real grandma at all, and when *she* was dead there would be nobody to run to. She was trapped. For ever.

3

The next day, to Jenny's surprise and Percy Pearson's obvious delight, the tall fair man came into the shop again to buy canary seed, and this time, because his business in the town had been concluded successfully, he smiled at Jenny.

It was a wide smile showing strong white teeth, changing the arrogant set of his face into lines of boyish mischief that made his light grey eyes twinkle as if he savoured some private joke.

She could see the high trap outside, with the horse tethered to the iron stoop in the narrow street opposite to the shop, and because the air was light and clear after a night's rain, she could see the dark brown mottles on the horse's coat. Dappled marks as if the horse stood underneath a tree whose leaves shifted in the pale sunlight.

Mr Pearson had taken his wealthy customer's order and gone into the back of the shop for a special bag of grain, so that Jenny was alone with him. Again, she was strangely on her guard.

Paul Tunstall was staring at her with open and insolent admiration, slapping the sides of his breeches with a riding whip. 'I have to pass this way,' he said suddenly, as if explaining that in the normal run of things he would never have put one highly polished boot over the threshold.

Jenny nodded. 'Yes, sir.'

Her eyes were suitably downcast as she wondered if getting on with feeding the rabbits would be construed as rudeness. You never knew where you were with THEM. Her mother had drummed that philosophy into her long ago.

'You live here?' Paul Tunstall's tone was that of an employer interviewing a prospective employee, and as her sense of humour asserted itself briefly, Jenny wondered if a curtsey might not come amiss.

'I just work here, sir.'

'Hm? I must say that surprises me somewhat. Are you fond of animals then?'

The whip was pointed towards the muddle of cages, the sloppily piled bags of grain, and the dirty sawdust covering of the sloping flag floor.

'Not particularly, sir.' Jenny faced him with her head held high, telling herself that as she was living on borrowed time anyway as far as her job went, she might just as well speak her mind. 'You might as well be hung for a sheep as a lamb' had been one of her father's favourite sayings. Then she remembered that Jack Macartney had not ever been her father, and her eyelids came down over her eyes like a shutter coming down on one of the built-in market stalls at night.

'I hate the smell if you really want to know, sir,' she said, miserable in her futile defiance.

Paul Tunstall laughed, throwing his head back so that a yellow silk cravat moved against his strong brown throat. 'That's honest, anyway. Well, tell me then. What is a damned pretty girl like you doing working in a place like this if she doesn't like animals? Or their smell.'

'Needs must, sir.' Jenny's voice was demure, but her direct glance owed nothing to servility. When Mr Pearson came in from the back she moved gratefully over to the rickety cages and knelt down on the stone-flagged floor.

'Needs must,' she heard the gentleman customer repeat as if she had said something funny, and she hated him so much that she kept her head down until he had gone out of the shop, closing the door none too gently behind him.

47

Mr Pearson's voice held a quiver of pride. 'That was Mr Paul Tunstall, Jenny. I'm glad to see you were talking polite to him. That's twice he's been in here lately.' He held the coins for the seed in his one hand as if reluctant to slide them into the drawer with the coppers from his ordinary customers. 'He's a gentleman farmer is Mr Tunstall, ever since his father died. You must have heard of his father, Jenny? He used to be a big man in the town, but they say his son doesn't go in much for politics.' Percy jiggled the coins up and down in his hand, completely unaware of Jenny's lack of interest. 'It stands to reason though. I don't think as how a soldier what's seen service on the battlefield can have much respect for the big noises what stay at home on their backsides and tell fighting men what they should be doing or who they should kill next.' He opened the drawer and dropped the coppers inside one by one. 'Did you see his trap, Jenny? I don't remember seeing a trap so well set up afore, certainly not round these parts. Did you see it, Jenny?'

'I saw it, Mr Pearson.'

There was a lonely droop to her shoulders that smote Percy's conscience with an almost physical twinge. There was no doubt that she'd taken it badly about his replacing her. He fingered his chin thoughtfully. Young Mr Tunstall had looked at Jenny with a gleam in his eyes that any man with red blood in his veins could recognize, and for a fleeting moment he wondered if perhaps he had been a bit on the hasty side in getting shut of his bright and comely assistant.

Then he reminded himself that customers of Paul Tunstall's station in life weren't exactly popping in and out of his shop every day of the week, and went through into the back to tell the missus about the pride he had felt on seeing the shiny trap in the street right outside his shop.

At eight o'clock when Jenny went out into the darkness

of the empty street it was to see Bob Waring waiting patiently in the shadows thrown by the overhanging eaves of the house opposite.

He stepped forward and raised his hat. 'Good evening, Miss Macartney. I have been troubled all day about . . . about what occurred last night, and I hope you, I hope you didn't get into too much trouble with your step-father? I couldn't rest till I had another word with you. He wasn't himself. Not at all himself.'

He fell into step beside her, and Jenny subdued a sudden urge to stretch out a hand and push the little man away from her. He was only trying to be kind, but the shame was still there, the knowledge that this well-respected funny little man knew now how she lived, knew that her step-father sometimes fell down in the gutter to lie there till he came to enough to stagger on, weaving his uncertain way home.

'He's no blood relation at all. I *hate* him,' she added defiantly. 'He makes my mother cry and he makes me sick, and if I had the courage I would kill him. Stone dead, like squashing a blue-bottle. So now you know.'

There, that was two men she had put in their place in the space of one day. Three if you counted Mr Pearson. And all because her mind was filled with loathing for the unknown man who had got her mother into trouble, then rejected her. All day long she had been thinking about him, though she could not have admitted it even to herself till now. An' he must have been a horrible sort of man because that was the way she was feeling now. Horrible, inside and out, and if Mr Waring did not stop trying to be kind to her she would tell him what she was really like, then see if he would keep pestering her, walking along with her and telling her things about himself that did not interest her.

'I'm not without a bit put by, Miss Macartney,' he was saying, panting a little with the effort of keeping up with her long anguished strides. 'My wife's father owned two houses down Mill Lane, and after he died they reverted

49

to her, and when she passed on they reverted to me. They bring in four shillings a week each, and there's never any problem about the rents because they're let to decent Chapel folks. It's a nice little street is Mill Lane.'

'I've lost my job, Mr Waring,' Jenny said, entering into the Alice in Wonderland kind of conversation, neither expecting nor getting a reply.

'My father has a pension, albeit a small one, and Agnes takes in crochet work from Mason's fancy goods shop, just off Town Hall Street, you know the one? She has always been good with her fingers.' He paused suddenly, checking his skipping stride. 'For what reason have you lost your job, Miss Macartney?'

Jenny read his mind like an open book. 'Not for putting me fingers in the money drawer, Mr Waring. It's me step-father who does that. He pinched me last week's wages to spend on drink, that's the sort of man he is.'

Bob Waring suddenly put his gloved hand on Jenny's arm and pulled her round to face him. Then, staring into her astonished face, he swallowed hard and managed to blurt out his proposal:

'Will you marry me, Miss Macartney? I've been praying for guidance for many a while now, and no, don't stop me saying what I must. I told myself you were no more than a child, and I told myself you would never look at the likes of me, but you're a good girl, Miss Macartney, I've watched you from the choir seats and you love your Saviour as I do, I've seen it on your face.' He put up a hand as if to clamp it over Jenny's open mouth so that she backed away. 'And then last night I knew you needed looking after. When I saw that dreadful man I knew I would have to take you away from him, and now that you affirm he is not your father, it makes me all the more determined.' He lowered his voice to a hoarse whisper. 'You could be in moral danger living in the same house with a man like that, though in the purity of your innocence I don't expect you realize . . .'

'Mr Waring! Stop! Please stop. You don't know what you're saying.' She shook her head from side to side. 'I can look after meself, honest I can. If he ever tried to touch me I would take the poker to him, an' he knows it. He's only tried to touch me once an' he'll never try it again. I told him I was going for the police, Mr Waring, but when I got to the top of the street I waited for a bit then came back. I would never fetch the police for me mam's sake, but he wouldn't understand that. Not him.'

'Oh, Jenny . . . Miss Macartney.' Bob Waring's voice was ragged with embarrassment. He wet his lips, then stroked his small moustache with the back of his thumb. 'Do you think I might call you Jenny?'

She nodded, trying not to look up and down the deserted street in case . . . you never knew with Harry Howarth. He might just take it into his head to come and fetch her, especially if the money was all gone, especially if he suspected that Mr Waring might be meeting her. And she couldn't bear it, not again, not after what he had told her last night. She snatched her tammy from her head, and stood there twisting it round and round in her hands. If she was going to run, and run she must, she wanted to have it safe, not slipping from her head like it was always doing.

'Mr Waring. I'm sorry, but I have to go. He might be out looking for me. You don't know him, really, you don't know him. When he can't get money for drink he takes it out on me. Most of the time on my mam, but sometimes on me. And now that he knows I have lost my job he'll give me hell till I find another. You don't know about men like him, Mr Waring. You live in the same town but you live in a different world. Honest.' She hesitated for a moment, backing away, then coming forward with a little rush to stand beside him. 'And I think it's very kind of you wanting to marry me, an' I'm not refusing you because you're too old or nothing like that. It's just that I can't marry you or anybody. Ever.'

She saw the drooping bereft look on his long and melancholy face, and even in her distress and anxiety to get away, remembered that his wife had died along with his baby. 'The Lord giveth and the Lord taketh away' he had said. Oh, the poor little man, the poor, sad and lonely little man.

Lowering her head slightly, Jenny brushed his cheek with her lips, turned on her heel and ran, leaving him standing there rubbing the place where her lips had touched with a kid-gloved finger.

By the time she reached the house she was completely out of breath, and when she closed the front door behind her she leant against it for a minute, her hand rubbing at the stitch in her side.

Casting her eyes upwards she uttered a fervent prayer: 'Let him have gone out, please God! Let me have me tea and go upstairs before he comes in. *Please?*'

Then she parted the curtain and went through into the living-room, saw a covered plate on the table, and a note propped up against the brown teapot.

'Grandma worse. Back soon.'

Working at speed Jenny pushed the kettle-stand over the coals, took a loaf of bread from the crock and cut a crooked slice. The lifted covering plate revealed two slices of tripe, cut from the seam, and she wrinkled her nose. Good for you it might be, but she could never prevent herself from thinking where it came from. A cow's stomach she'd heard, and even her griping hunger could not make her fancy it.

Still, needs must, as she had told the fair man with the riding crop, and the twinkling grey eyes, that had laughed at her and not with her, so she took the vinegar bottle from the dresser and doused the revolting white slippery mess, and sitting down began to chew and swallow automatically, trying to think of other things.

Mostly she thought of her grandma who was not her

grandma, the little independent woman with the bird-bright eyes living alone in the next street, sitting in a chair and refusing to get into bed and be decently ill like other folks. When she had finished her tea, Jenny decided, she would go round and see if there was anything she could do. She would stay all night if needs be, and sleep in the rocking chair by the fire and be on hand if the old lady wanted a drink, or needed helping out of bed to the commode. Jenny smiled to herself, as she thought about the commode, remembering the fierce arguments there had been before Grandma Macartney would even give house room to it.

'I can still get down the yard,' she'd protested, and for once Mollie had been firm.

'And what happens if you fall down the steps and have to lie there all night? Stop being so flamin' independent, Ma,' Mollie had said. 'There comes a time when we all have to realize we can't go on as before.'

'When that day comes I'll just lay me down and die,' the old woman had said. 'When I can't see to meself, then I'm off.'

And now it looked as if that time had come. . . . Jenny pushed her chair back so sharply that it made a squeaking sound on the oilcloth. There was only one good thing to be said about tripe, and that was that it went down almost without you noticing. She took her plate over to the stone slopstone and rinsed it under the cold tap. She left it to drain, then turning round saw Harry Howarth framed in the doorway.

For the big Irishman it had been a frustrated wasted evening. The little money in his pocket had run out early on, and the very men he had treated when he was flush, over and over again, had turned their backs on him. He was drunk, but not quite drunk enough, and now he was home and his wife was out – he glanced at the peg behind the back door where her shawl always hung – and for once he was alone with the girl who had, overnight, or so it seemed, changed from a thin gangling child into a woman of such glowing beauty that he could not take his eyes away from her. He looked hard at her now: at the tumbling waves of shining brown hair, at her big dark eyes, watching him now with that calculated criticism in their depths. At the firm high swell of her breasts, and the tilt of her head as she waited to see what he would do next.

There was a viciously cruel streak in Harry Howarth's make-up. He had lived his forty-five years not by his wits – he had never learned to read or write – but by his physical strength. He had come over from Ireland with his parents as a child and had been reared in the Liverpool slums, living in the overcrowded teeming streets where he soon earned the reputation of a bully. He was clumsily built, but strong and powerful; horny-handed and bull-necked, with shoulders as broad as those of the fabled Atlas. He had married Mollie Macartney for the simple reason that he needed a roof over his head, and because at first her tear-drenched eyes had sparked off a certain responsive sentimentality inherent in his make-up.

Now, because of what he had blurted out last night, he was in a quandary. Now he knew that any lingering respect his wife had for him had gone. She would never forgive him for betraying the secret of her daughter's birth, and last night for the first time since he married her, Mollie had left him to sleep it off in the chair downstairs. Normally she would have come downstairs in the early hours, helped him off with his shoes and led him up to the warmth and comfort of the double bed in the front room. But not last night. . . .

And it was all Jenny's fault. It was all the fault of this girl standing straight and tall before him, her head held high, but the wariness in her eyes betraying her fear of him. As he stared at her she raised a hand, to try to still the beating of her heart, he guessed, but the innocently provocative gesture drew his attention to the sweet swell of her breasts, and desire flared in him like a lick of flame.

She wasn't such a little innocent either. Oh, no. Hadn't he seen her with his own eyes walking out late at night arm in arm with that mealy-mouthed little sod from the Chapel? He lumbered round the table towards her, then as Jenny started quickly towards the back door, he lunged forward and caught her by the arms.

'Come on, now,' he muttered thickly. 'All I want is a little kiss. Just one little kiss, that's all. Come on!' He caught her then by the throat, one big hand encircling her neck so that he was staring straight into her wide-open terrified eyes. He could feel the softness of her straining against him, then as he lowered his head she jerked her knee up and got him full in the groin, so that he gave a loud shout of pain, and doubled up for a second with the agony of it.

But years of street fist-fighting had quickened his reflexes, so that as she ran round the table he was after her, catching her by the arm and pulling her close to him. He had not seen her pick up the heavy poker lying in the hearth, and staggered for a moment as a blow took him full on the shoulder.

'You little devil!' he roared. 'You filthy little bastard!' And even though the pain roared through him he still kept his hold on her, wild now with fury, beside himself with rage. With his free hand he grabbed the neck of her jumper, pulled until the stitches gave, and bared a white shoulder.

With the instinct of an animal, he bent his head to sink his teeth into the white flesh, then fell like a stone as Jenny raised the poker and hit him with all her strength.

She stood there for a long moment, staring down at the man lying still across the cut-rug, blood slowly seeping from the back of his head. Red sticky blood, matting his jet-black hair and trickling down his neck into the off-white muffler.

The poker dropped from her lifeless hand as she knelt down, and putting out a finger touched him gently, hoping, praying for a response that was not there.

She was sitting there, whimpering with fear when Mollie came in, her eyes swollen with weeping, holding the plaid shawl tightly underneath her chin.

'He's dead,' Jenny moaned, rocking backwards and forwards on her knees. 'He's dead, Mam, and I killed him.' She jerked her head towards the poker. 'I hit him with that, and now he's dead.'

Throwing the shawl over the back of a chair, Mollie knelt down awkwardly and lifted the unconscious man's head onto her lap. There was nothing of tenderness or even sorrow in the movement, just a doing what had to be done.

'He's not dead, see, he's coming to already. It would take more than a clout on the head to finish *him* off. Why, lass, I've seen the doctor come and stitch him up while he sat in his chair and never moved a muscle. Get me a bowl of water and a clean cloth.' She raised her head and saw the torn jumper slipping down from Jenny's shoulder. 'He's not? Oh, my God, he hasn't been trying it on with you, has he?' The slack mouth started its familiar wobble as the tears rushed into the red-rimmed eyes.

'No, of course not, Mam.' Jenny told the lie without flinching. 'He just went on at me again about losing me job and about oh, everything, and I lost my temper and went for him. It was what he said last night, an' it was seeing him drunk again and knowing he'd been out spending the money we needed to live.'

She ran water into a bowl, rummaged in a drawer for a teacloth washed to a sketchy grey and passed it over.

'Your grandma died just after I got there,' Mollie said, dabbing at the cut on her husband's head, wiping away the blood, and unknotting the scarf from his throat. 'It was very peaceful, she just closed her eyes and sighed and that was that. I sent for Mrs Ormerod to lay her out, and she looks lovely; you would think she was just sleeping except that her nose looks more pointed.' Harry grunted, and with a purely automatic motion Mollie patted his cheek. 'Your dad was the same. *His* nose went proper peaky when he was in his coffin. Mrs Ormerod says she has seen it happen more times than she can recollect.'

Jenny hid her face in her hands then slowly drew them down her cheeks. She had known her grandma would have to die some day; she had even known it must be soon, but the shock of what had just happened and what her mother had just told her, drained the colour from her face and took the use from her legs so that she had to grope for the nearest chair and sit down.

'She's gone to a happy release,' Mollie said, wringing out the cloth and holding it to her husband's head once again. 'She'll be with your grandpa now, and her laying-out gown and her sheets were just where she'd always said they were, all folded up neat and tidy with little bags of lavender in between. I'll walk round with you so you can see her if you like after we've got him to bed. Mrs Ormerod seemed to think I was being a bit callous coming away, but it's not her lying there. The real her is up in Heaven with Grandpa and my Jack. Aye, all her troubles are over now, God rest her soul.'

Jenny's gaze was fixed on the man lying on the floor, narrowing with fear as she saw the way his nose twitched and his eyelids quivered as he recovered consciousness. The tripe she had forced herself to eat lay heavy in her stomach, and she hoped she wasn't going to be sick. Grandma Macartney was dead, lying on her bed between clean lavender-scented sheets, organized in death as she had always been in life. She was lying there with her little snub nose gone all peaky as it pointed up to the ceiling, and he, Harry Howarth, was alive, opening his eyes now and putting a big hand up to his forehead, then sitting up and staring straight at her.

'What the 'ell?' he muttered. 'What happened? An' don't say it was the beer because I only had half a skinful.' His eyes narrowed, and Jenny gripped the wooden arms of the chair, waiting, mesmerized for him to remember.

'You come over a bit faint,' Mollie said quickly, then with an arm about his shoulders she tried to pull him to his feet, but as someone had once said, it would take a crane to lift Harry Howarth to his feet once he was down.

Slowly, pulling himself up by the table edge, he forced himself into an upright position, then growled like an angry bear as pain shot through his head.

'You'll be right as rain after a good sleep,' Mollie said. 'You must have struck your head on the fender . . . aye, that's what you must have done, and don't go feeling sorry for yourself because the cut at the back goes no deeper than a whisker, and don't let that basin worry you because a bit of blood goes a long way; it's mostly water.'

Then to Jenny's relief the big man allowed himself to be steered towards the bottom of the stairs, shaking his shaggy head from side to side as he went, muttering and cursing, snivelling and groaning, but doing as he was told.

'Come up behind and give him a bit of a shove,' Mollie whispered over her shoulder. 'He's concussed, that's what he is. I've seen him like this before after a fight. He'll be all right when he's slept it off . . .'

Between them they got him to the side of the bed, then drawing back the blankets Mollie gave him a push which sent him sprawling flat on his back at his side of the bed.

'Get his boots off, love.' She spoke in a decisive tone, her tears forgotten for the moment. This was the man she thought she had married at first. Down on his luck, humble even, needing her, as Jack had needed her all through the last months of his long illness. This man she could cope with, even love if he would let her, but to-morrow he would wake up and remember and with the remembering would come the shouting and the cursing, and she couldn't stand much more of it. . . . The tears flowed as Mollie leaned over the pillows and her chins quivered with self-pity as she manoeuvred his head into position. And now that Jack's mother had gone, there would be no one to go and sit with of an afternoon; no one

58

to listen when she told how it was. It had never once occurred to her how ludicrous it was her going on about her second husband to the mother of her first, but Grandma Macartney had listened and said nowt. Said nowt, but listened with her head on one side and her bird-bright eyes shining with understanding.

So overcome with her own grief was Mollie that she failed to notice her daughter, picking at the knotted boot-laces with fingers made stiff and red with chilblains.

'Here, let me have a go,' she said, and wrenching off the boots, she pulled the covers up over her husband, and left him, fully dressed beneath the blankets to sleep it off.

'Now then,' she said. 'We'll go down and have a pot of tea, then you can go round and see your grandma. You know where the key is, and I've left the lamp burning, it didn't seem right to leave her there in the dark, even though it's not really her, not her at all.'

'I don't want to see her.' Jenny sat huddled down in the chair by the fire, shivering and aching as if she was coming down with a chill. 'I want to remember her as she was, not see her lying there. I don't want to go, Mam.'

Mollie swung the kettle over the fire and took two pots down from the dresser. She was still weeping, crying with silent tears that ran from the corners of her eyes in a never-ending flow. She glared briefly at Jenny's bowed dark head, then looked away again.

'I think you ought to go. Just to pay your respects. They'll be putting her in her box tomorrow and then it'll be too late.' She reached for the big glass sugar-bowl and heaped three spoonfuls into her own pot. 'She thought a lot about you, your grandma did. She couldn't have thought more even if . . . even if you'd been her own flesh and blood.'

Suddenly it was all too much for Jenny. The tears, the great hulk of a man upstairs who would wake up remembering; the realization that she would never see Grandma Macartney ever again, her mother's tears, and the poker still lying there on the floor where she had dropped it. She put up a hand to the torn jumper and pulled it up over her shoulder.

'I am not going to see her,' she said loudly. 'I loved her and she loved me, in spite of knowing that I was nothing to her.' Jenny raised her head to stare straight at her mother. '*Did* she know about me? Or was she kept in the dark like me? Did my father know, or did you deceive him as well? Did you pretend I was a six and a half month baby like Mrs Carr over the street?'

For a split second Mollie saw in her daughter's flushed and angry expression the face of the man she thought she had forgotten. It was all there, the same proud stare, the lift of the head, the glowering look when things weren't going quite the way he wanted them to. She thought she had forgotten him, because Jack Macartney had wiped the memory away, but there he was, angry and defiant, staring at her.

She raised the hem of her apron and dabbed at her eyes. 'I never thought to say it, but there's one thing you've inherited from him, your real father, and that's his temper.' She nodded at the poker. 'Taking that to Harry just because he went on at you for being late.'

'Who was he, Mam? Does he live in this town? I have a right to know.'

Mollie whimpered, and turned her head away. 'I was hardly more than a child, when he flattered me and told me I was beautiful.' She put up a hand to the slipping bun. 'Oh aye, I was as innocent as a new-born babe when he flustered me with the things he said, then when I told him about you he didn't want to know, Jenny. He gave me money and sent me away, and if it hadn't been for Jack I would have had to live with the shame. That's the sort of man your father was.'

'Was he married?'

'I'm saying no more.' Mollie lowered her head and began to fold the brown wool of her skirt into tiny pleats over

60

her knees, and Jenny got up from her chair and walked to the foot of the stairs.

'All right then, he was married, and he had a bad temper.'

She turned and with a sudden rush came back to her mother's chair and knelt down on the floor. 'I'm not blaming you, Mam. I know how men can be, but I can't stay here. I can't live with him upstairs no longer, and with me out of the way there might be a chance for you and him.' She caught her mother's fidgeting hand in her own. 'And when I've gone, try not to go on so much about my father, about Jack. It will maybe be better now that you're not round at Jack's mother's house quite so much. Settle for what you've got, Mam. It's the only way. Honest.'

Mollie's breath caught on a quivering sob. 'But where will you go, love? There's nowhere for you to go now that Grandma Macartney's dead, and besides, how will I manage? What you brought in made all the difference between getting by and going under. What will I do without your money?'

Jenny shook her mother's hand gently. 'He'll *have* to provide for you, Mam. He's like that, all shout and bluff, but when he knows that the alternative would be the workhouse he'll buckle to, you'll see.' She sighed deeply. 'Mam, tonight Mr Waring asked me to marry him, and though I refused him I'm going to tell him I've changed my mind.' Her eyes were very dark, very clear. 'He's a good man, you know that, and I'll try to make it up to him for losing his first wife and his baby. I will, I know I can. If I try.'

She tried not to see the dismay that clouded her mother's swimming eyes. Dismay followed by a kind of shamed relief. If she kept on talking, Mollie would see that it was all for the best. She was like that, harbouring no strong convictions of her own and ready to absorb other people's opinions as if they *were* her own. In that quiet moment as the fire crackled and the black kettle started to hiss as it came to the boil, Jenny knew that her mother would never change. First she had allowed herself to be seduced by the unknown man who was her father, then she had willingly and gratefully enjoyed Jack Macartney's cherishing and now in a strange way she would survive on Harry Howarth's domineering ways. Always led and never wanting to be the leader, that was her sloppy untidy little mother. . . .

'Mr Waring is *kind*,' Jenny said. 'He's so polite it makes me uncomfortable. He'll look after me, Mam. You know that.'

'They're a nice family the Warings.' Mollie nodded. 'His father was a big noise in the Oddfellows before his accident, and they say his sister dusts the coalshed she's that particular.'

'There you are then.' Jenny stood up and taking the kettle-holder from its hook on the wall, lifted the kettle from the fire and brewed the tea.

'Oh, please stop crying, Mam. *Please*. It'll all be the same a hundred years from now. Dad used to be always saying that. Don't you remember?'

Then as a loud and furious bellow spiralled downstairs from the upstairs room their eyes met and mirrored the other's terror.

'Oh, my God, he's coming to,' Mollie said, but already Jenny was flying up the uncarpeted stairs to shut herself in her room with the chair firmly wedged against the door handle.

As the sound died away, to be followed by loud snores, she lit a candle with a hand that trembled and pulling out a drawer, she started to pack her few belongings in a sheet of brown paper spread out on the faded quilt of her bed.

And that night, in spite of her chilblains, she said her prayers kneeling down, with her hands clasped tightly together:

'Let Mr Waring be there waiting for me tomorrow after work,' she prayed, 'because it wouldn't be right me having to go knocking at his door to ask him to marry me. And forgive me for taking the poker to him in bed in the next room, instead of turning the other cheek, like You said we must. There are times when you have to stick up for yourself, God, surely?'

She squeezed her eyes tight shut. 'And if there's a Heaven, and Grandma Macartney's up there in it with you, let there be fields for her to walk in, and flowers for her to pick, and explain to her I could not bear to go and see her dead. For the sake of your son, Jesus Christ. Amen.'

She lay awake for a long time, listening to the sound of her mother's slow tread on the stairs, hearing the bed in the next room creak as Mollie's weight jangled the springs into noisy protest. She trembled a little when her step-father's snores seemed to waver and stop, and she prayed that the chair would hold the door fast.

4

At half-past five Jenny awoke to the sound of the knocker-up coming down the street, rattling his long pole topped with umbrella spokes against the windows of the sleeping neighbours. Barmy Billy, with his slouching walk and his cap pulled down over his low forehead, living with his mother who never failed to rouse him from his bed in time to make his rounds. Jenny lay there, half asleep and half awake till the clatter of clogs and the slamming of doors told her that the mill workers were leaving their houses, shawls over the women's heads held close against the chill cold damp of the February morning.

She lay there until the murmur of voices from the next room made her sit straight up in bed, hugging her knees and listening with an intensity that made her ears ache. Her step-father seemed to be doing most of the talking, his low rumble interspersed by her mother's petulant whine. If he was remembering; if the blow to his head aided by the drink he had consumed, had healed during the night, then he would be fumbling to remember, and when he remembered . . .

Jenny's glance was caught by the brown paper parcel on the floor where it had slipped from her bed, and pushing the clothes back she got up, pulled on her clothes, and tiptoed downstairs. Without bothering to light the gas, she splashed cold water over her face, ran a comb through her hair, took her coat and tammy from the peg behind the door, and let herself quietly out of the house.

It was coming light as she stepped out onto the pavement.

A woman late for work scurried by, her clogs clattering as she went. The cobbled street glistened like oil, and the huddled terraced houses showed mellow lights behind their yellow blinds.

There were two hours to go before she could go to the shop, and a soft drizzle was falling, chilling her bones and clinging damply to the nap of her long brown coat. She ran up the street, going nowhere in particular, then she thought of her grandmother's house, with the key hanging on a string through the letter-box.

Her grandmother was dead, but the little house still remained, a haven of refuge, a place she could shelter for the next two hours. Jenny stood still for a moment. The sight of Harry Howarth lying on the floor with blood matting his thick black hair, his eyes closed and his face the pale pallid shade of putty was like a picture held deep in the recesses of her mind. She shifted the paper parcel to her other arm and hurried on.

She came to the house, glanced quickly up and down the street and reaching through the letter-box withdrew the big key on its length of string. She opened the door and stepped inside the front parlour and saw from the back living-room the soft glimmer of light from the lamp.

Slowly, she forced herself to go forward and there on the bed at right-angles to the fireplace lay her grandmother. With her heart beating with dull heavy thuds Jenny walked to the bed.

Grandma Macartney looked as if she was fast asleep, so fast asleep that she was removed from the little room with its knick-knacks along the mantelshelf and its clean clothes airing on the rack. The sleep she was sleeping seemed to have removed every wrinkle from her face so that her skin glistened like white wax just beginning to melt. Her small mouth with its gathering thread of wrinkles was lifted at the corners into a tiny smile, and her brown-spotted hands were crossed over the starched cotton of her laying-out gown.

There was no pain in that tranquil face, no pretence at hiding the arthritic pain she had suffered for the past few years. The eyelids were closed against the world, the bright eyes blind beneath the shuttered lids. She was far, far away from all hurt, her struggle to retain independence over, and when Jenny touched her crossed hands they had the texture of frozen marble.

Backing towards the old lady's rocking-chair Jenny sat down to begin her lonely vigil. There were no tears, not even in her heart, because this, she felt, was how death was meant to be. A natural ending to a long and industrious life, a gentle relinquishing of all sorrows, all burdens, to sink into a sleep where nothing mattered any more.

What would her grandma have said when she told her she was going to marry Mr Waring?

'Do you really want to marry him, or is it on account of you wanting to get away from that man your mother married on the rebound from my Jack?' She would not ask if Jenny *loved* Mr Waring, because whilst love was there, as it had been from the beginning of time, it was rarely talked about. 'He's a good man my husband,' the women from the narrow streets would say, never 'I *love* him'. Love was never put into words.

But what *was* love? Jenny wondered, sitting quite still with the parcel clutched to her chest. She leaned her head back against the crisp cleanliness of the old lady's chair-back cover.

If love was being married to a man like Harry Howarth, then she wanted none of it. If love was being married to a man like Percy Pearson, with his sly ways and his terrible meanness, then she wanted none of that, either.

'Mr Waring is *kind*,' she told the still figure on the bed. 'You once told me that kindness was all that mattered; that if a man was kind, then all the rest fell into place.'

She whispered the words aloud, resting her chin on the top of the parcel. 'You would have liked Mr Waring, Grandma. Honest you would. He's not much to look at, but he keeps raising his hat to me, and sometimes he gives a little bow as if I was royalty, an' I'm not all that keen on ginger hair, not when ginger eyelashes come with it, but it's a case of beggars can't be choosers. You would have said that, wouldn't you?'

Her head drooped as the realization that she would never again hear the trilling sweetness of the old lady's voice, or listen entranced to the tales of a country upbringing, hit her. And there, as the morning light seeped through the lace-edged blind at the window, dimming the lamp set high on the pedestal table by the bed, Jenny wept, and weeping fell into a brief but soothing sleep.

Bob Waring was there, waiting goodly outside the shop when she closed the door behind her, and he listened with his small head on one side as Jenny told him that never again could she go back to the house to live under the same roof with her step-father.

'I went for him,' she explained, omitting any mention of the weapon she had used. 'Went for him with the poker' would, she felt, have offended Mr Waring's sense of decorum. That was the sort of behaviour common to the streets at the end of the town where she lived, and certainly not the way of life up at the park end of the town.

She knew in her heart that she was taking an unfair advantage of the little man. She was throwing herself on his mercy, but she guessed that he wanted her so badly that he would think of something. She read his desire in the way he ran his tongue over his lips and the way his eyes shone wetly when he stared at her.

'Then we'd better get off home,' he said, and the way he said it, and the way he phrased it made her feel that she would do anything in the world to make him happy. She would see to it that he never regretted what he was doing; she would have his babies, as many as possible to make up for the one that the Lord had taken away. Her whole body relaxed as they fell into step together. She smiled at him as he drew her hand into the crook of his arm, and she tried not to mind that she was almost a head taller. If she bent her legs a little as they walked along, it would not show all that much, she felt.

He had taken the parcel from her, and that small gesture made her feel cherished and better already. Harry Howarth would never have lifted a finger to help her mother, even on a Friday when Mollie filled the zinc bath with buckets of cold water from the tap, before pouring the boiling water from the kettle and a pan into it. And Percy Pearson would never have stretched out even the one arm he possessed to help her lift a sack of grain in the shop.

'We'll get married as soon as possible, Miss Macartney, and perhaps the time has come for me to call you Jenny, and for you to call me Bob. Do you think you can manage that?'

His face was young and eager, and the bouncy springy-ness of his step made it difficult for her to keep in rhythm, but she said:

'Yes, Mr Waring, I mean Bob.'

'That's better, *Jenny*.'

There it was said, and all the way across the market place, and up Steep Brow he behaved as if he were a lad, talking in short and smiling sentences and squeezing her arm closer to his side with excited little movements.

The thought popped unwillingly into Jenny's head that acting like that only made him seem *older* and not younger; silly really in a sort of pathetic way.

But she firmly in her mind told the thoughts to go away, then was irritated with them when they lingered.

Agnes Waring had once, in one of her extremely rare flashes of humour, described herself as one of life's unwanted blessings. She had inherited the red hair and freckles from her mother's side of the family, but the freckles sat ill on her long melancholy features, and the straight gingery eyelashes stuck out from puffy white eyelids which she lowered frequently as if her every other thought was interspersed by prayer.

For the past three years she had insisted on holding a prayer meeting round her father's bed, with Bob at one side of the quilted counterpane and herself at the other. The prayers she prayed were without fail impassioned pleas to keep them from temptation and sin, and Albert Waring, the father, sometimes wondered drily what chance any one of the three of them had to even consider straying from the straight and narrow.

But he put up with Agnes's ways because he was, above all, a tolerant man. His kindly tolerance and his acceptance of his disability showed in his smooth unwrinkled face, and the twinkling good nature in his deep-set eyes. Agnes kept him clean and fed; she changed the dressings and packed the gauze into the hip wound that would not heal, and he had the good sense to realize that without him to minister to, Agnes's life would be empty indeed.

His son Bob's brief and tragic marriage had long been forgotten by Agnes, and now that she had her two men to care for, her days were filled with a kind of grim satisfaction that the good Lord was working his purpose out. As far as Agnes was concerned the good Lord in his infinite wisdom had showed her where His purpose lay, and she was busily working and fulfilling His plan for her with rewards to come in the glorious life that lay ahead in His kingdom beyond the skies.

It was the first time that Jenny had actually walked the length of Park Road, but her mother had often spoken of the neat respectability of the terraced houses set back from the pavement by a strip of garden, with a short flight of steps up to their front doors.

'That's where I would like to live,' Mollie had often said. 'And if my Jack hadn't died that's where we might have finished up one day.' Once when Jenny had been a schoolgirl, a young and enthusiastic teacher had taken her class on a 'nature walk' in the Corporation Park, and they had passed the end of Park Road. Even then Jenny had been impressed by the fact that there were no children playing bare-bottomed in the wide street, and no women gossiping on doorsteps with arms folded over flowered cross-over pinafores.

Some of the bounce seemed to have gone out of Bob Waring's step as they drew near the house, and as they climbed the three steps to the front door he turned to Jenny and spoke quickly:

'My sister might . . . you might come as a bit of a shock at first.' He dropped his arm so that her hand fell to her side. 'It might be as well if we kept it dark for a day or so about us getting married, just till she gets used to the idea of you being there. Agnes is a bit set in her ways, but she can't do nothing about it, not with me paying the rent and my wife's bit of money putting the jam on the bread.'

'You mean you've never told them about me?' Jenny's hand crept to her mouth. 'Oh, you ought not to be bringing me here, Mr Waring,' she added, forgetting that she was supposed to be calling him by his Christian name. 'They'll have a pink fit, with me turning up like this.'

Bob stepped into the wide vestibule with its black and white tiled floor and its ruby-red panels of glass in the door, and gave Jenny a little push into the hall.

It wasn't much of a hall, more like a long passage really, but to Jenny, used to stepping straight from the street into a front parlour, it was immediately as if she was stepping directly into another way of life. She took in quickly the gas bracket set high in the wall, and the length of red patterned carpet, with a closed door to the left, and two closed doors straight ahead.

'Put your parcel down on there.' Bob pointed to a hallstand, remembered he had taken charge of it and laid it down. He took off his gloves and opening a drawer put them away, then as he took off his coat and bowler hat he motioned to Jenny to do the same. There was a small mirror set into the wood in the middle of the row of pegs, and she fluffed anxiously at her hair, and tucked her blouse more firmly into the band of her skirt.

The room at the back was a large high-ceilinged living-cum-dining-room, and as Jenny followed Bob Waring nervously inside, she saw Miss Waring sitting in a winged chair by the fire with her carroty head bent industriously over a piece of sewing.

'This is Miss Macartney, Agnes.' Bob pushed Jenny forward. 'She's a member of the Chapel, and a good worker for the Sunday School. You must have seen her at the meetings?'

Agnes Waring laid the sewing down on the round wine table by her side and stood up. Jenny held out her hand, then when it wasn't taken let it drop to her side again. There was no welcome in the long face with the brown freckles standing out on the white skin.

'I found her in grave moral danger.' Bob's voice was curt and sharp, and Jenny looked at him with surprised respect. Miss Waring might be a bit of a dragon, but she hadn't got the upper hand of her brother. Not quite.

'Moral danger from whom?' Agnes's pale, heavily shuttered eyes closed as if in prayer. In the middle of her nervousness Jenny found herself wondering how Miss Waring managed to make her front lie so flat. Even strategically placed darts in her bust bodice would hardly have had such an obliterating effect.

Bob was staring straight at his sister, never once taking his eyes from her. 'From her step-father, Agnes. A man much given to drink and violence. A man who attacked Miss Macartney last night so that she could not risk going back home after she had finished work this evening. The Lord showed me clearly where my duty lay, and I knew you would respond in exactly the same way.' He drew out a stand chair from the polished table set in the window, and motioned to Jenny to sit down.

'I'll go up and see Father, then when I come down we'll

all have a nice cup of tea,' Bob said, and left the room.

'What are your plans, Miss Macartney?' Agnes spoke the words even as the door closed behind her brother. 'If you feel you cannot live at home, where do you plan to go?' She raised her head and closed her eyes, and Jenny looked towards the door and wished with all her heart that Mr Waring had not said what he had said on the steps outside. Now she was in a very difficult situation and it was all his fault. He was making her out to be a stray dog or cat he had found on the way home, in need of shelter for a night or so till somewhere permanent could be found.

'I have no plans, Miss Waring,' she managed to say after a lengthy pause during which Agnes picked up the sewing again and took a dainty running stitch.

'I should think a living-in job would be the answer. Some of the houses up at the top end of our road have one living-in maid. There are three bedrooms, you see.'

Jenny fidgeted on the edge of the chair with embarrassment. Three bedrooms meant Mr Waring in one, old Mr Waring in another, and Agnes in the third. She closed her own eyes in a moment of sheer horror. Oh, dear, dear God, what had she done. In her terror she had grasped at the only straw that seemed to be floating towards her and in her stupidity she had imagined being shown into her own room, however small, however humble, and now she would be expected to share a room, even a bed, with this prim, thin-faced woman with the ginger hair pulled so tightly back from her forehead that it looked agonizing.

'You're not involved with the police, Miss Macartney?' Agnes's voice was low and soothing, but there was no kindness in it.

Jenny felt her face flame and wished she could be rid of the habit of blushing when she had nothing to blush for. Swallowing hard sometimes helped, but this time she had had no warning.

'I've never had nothing to do with the police, Miss Waring. That's a terrible thing to say.'

Agnes shook her head slowly from side to side. 'You are very, very young. Sixteen? Seventeen?'

'Nearly eighteen, well eighteen in August, but I've been working for five years.'

'Where?'

'In a cat-meat shop.'

'A cat-meat shop.' The way Agnes said it made it sound worse than if Jenny had confessed to being a night woman. She wrinkled her long nose as if the smell had suddenly hit her. 'And you can read and write, Miss Macartney?'

Suddenly Jenny's hard-fought-for control snapped. She was nervous and she was tired. She had slept hardly at all the night before, and she had spent the early hours sitting beside the bed of the dead. She was convinced that if she went back home her step-father would set about her, if not exactly kill her, and Agnes was right, she *was* young, and scared, and craving kindness as a dried-out plant craves water.

'I *can* read!' she cried out. 'I'll show you whether I can read or not!'

There was a Bible on the table by her side, and she took it and opened it at random, the pages falling at the Book of Revelation, Chapter Three. '"Behold, I stand at the door, and knock, and if any man hear my voice, and open the door, I will come into him, and will sup with him, and he with me. To him that overcometh will I grant to sit with him in my throne, even as I also overcame, and set down with my Father in his throne."'

'There! Who says I can't read, Miss Waring?'

The tears were there, in her voice, and trembling on the tips of her long eyelashes. Agnes got up from her chair, and crossing the strip of carpet took the Bible from Jenny's hands and closed it reverently, laying a long thin hand on its black cover.

'Kneel down, child.' To Jenny's dismay she felt a firm touch on her shoulder, so that hardly knowing what she was doing, she fell to her knees and covered her face with her hands. She heard the rustle of a starched petticoat as Miss Waring knelt beside her, then felt a shamed embarrassment all through her body as Agnes began to pray:

'Turn this child from her wickedness; rid her of pride, pour oil on the troubled waters of her evil temper, and make her able to accept with meekness the road thou hast planned for her . . .'

Agnes droned on, but now that Jenny's tears were falling in earnest, she heard nothing more than the whine of a voice coming from the other side of the chair. Miss Waring was right. She *had* an evil temper. For two pins she would have *thrown* the Bible instead of merely reading from it; she would have let fly in just the same way she had let fly with the poker the night before. Something in her had snapped right from the time Percy Pearson had given her the sack. She was spoiling for a fight with anyone who crossed her, and even her mother had admitted that it came from her father, the unknown man whose existence she had been in ignorance of till just a few days before.

What would Miss Waring think if she knew she was praying for a girl who was illegitimate? A bastard? Or was that word unknown in a house like this, set in the middle of a respectable street? And what would she think if she knew that her brother wanted to marry her, that in a short while she could be her sister-in-law?

'And now we will have that pot of tea,' Agnes said in a matter-of-fact voice, and getting up from her knees walked with her flat-footed walk out of the room.

Jenny raised her tear-wet face, her mouth a round O of astonishment as she found herself alone. Miss Waring had switched off that prayer like turning off a tap. She was barmy, that's what she was, getting down on her knees to pray right there in front of the fire, then going through to brew up. She was making out that Jenny was a heathen too, as well as wicked, and nothing could be further from the truth.

Jenny took her handkerchief from the pocket set in the

74

side of her skirt and wiped her eyes. She happened to have a God too, but it seemed he was a very different kettle of fish from Miss Waring's. Jenny's God, when she had pictured him, was a kindly old gentleman with a long white beard, not someone always going on about the sins of the flesh. And where was Mr Waring? Bob? It was taking him a long time to say goodnight to his father in bed upstairs. Perhaps they were praying too? Perhaps this strange house rang with prayer from morning till night? It was all very well being taught at Sunday School that Jesus was a real person who lived in the house, but from what she had just experienced, He was almost a member of the family!

For a second Jenny smiled as she imagined telling her grandma all about it, saying what she had just said, and making the old lady's little round face crease into laughter. Then she remembered that Grandma Macartney was dead and would not laugh at her jokes any more.

Miss Waring came back into the room carrying a tray set with a teapot, sugar bowl and milk jug and three cups and saucers, all matching with tiny wreaths of blue and pink flowers round their fluted sides. It was all so perfect, so civilized, that in different circumstances Jenny would have been impressed, enchanted even, but just then she longed to be back at home, sitting round the square table with her sloppy snivelling mother, drinking tea from pots with brown thread-veined cracks decorating their insides. And she *would* be there, but for him, but for Harry Howarth, the man she had hit with the poker not twenty-four hours ago.

'Have you tried praying with your step-father, Miss Macartney?' Agnes set the tray down by her chair, and began to pour. 'If every morning, first thing, before you eat your breakfast you knelt down together, along with your mother, I'm sure he would see the error of his ways.'

For a moment, a wild hysterical second, Jenny saw in her mind's eye the burly unshaven Harry Howarth, getting down on his knees on the cut-rug and clasping his big hands in prayer.

'He's hardly ever up first thing in the morning for one thing, and for another he's a Catholic. An Irish Catholic, Miss Waring, though not a practising one.' Jenny turned with relief as Mr Waring came through the door. 'He isn't very often sober enough to pray, and when he's sober he's not fit to live with.'

'Poor child.' Agnes spoke directly to her brother. 'You did right to bring her here for the night. I'll get her settled in a place first thing in the morning. Top end of the road, a Mrs Ellis. She needs a living-in maid, she was only saying so at the sewing-class last week.'

'Agnes. Show Miss Macartney upstairs. She looks all in, then I want to talk to you.' He came over to Jenny and took her hand. 'It's all right, lass. I've told Father all about it, and he wants to meet you, but not tonight. He's in a fair bit of pain.' He let go of her hand and patted her cheek, and Jenny felt rather than saw Agnes's gasp of surprise. 'Good night, dear, you're quite safe here. You need never be afraid any more. You are safely gathered into the fold of His abiding love. Isn't that so, Agnes?'

There was a terrible sense of tension in the room, made all the more terrible because there was a deep grinding bitterness in the religious atmosphere. Jenny followed Agnes upstairs picking up the brown paper parcel from the hallstand on her way, and was left alone without a word.

She took off her skirt and jumper, then washed her arms and face in the cold water poured from the jug on the wash-stand into a large china bowl trimmed with flowers like the cups and saucers. There had, she felt, been enough praying for one night, so she climbed into the high double bed, lying as near the edge as was practicable without actually falling out, and closed her eyes.

The room, at the back of the house, was directly over the living-room, and she could hear the voices seeping up through the floorboards. They were angry voices, made all the more menacing by the fact that they were not raised. It was like being back home with her mother and Harry Howarth rowing away, except that it seemed that in this quiet respectable road folks rowed in whispers.

When at last Jenny heard footsteps on the stairs, she crossed her arms over the front of her nightdress, holding herself in, pretending sleep. She heard the rustle of petticoats as Agnes undressed; she heard the splash of water as Agnes emptied the water *she* had used into the slop bucket underneath the wash-stand, followed by fresh clean water being poured into the china bowl.

Opening her eyes a fraction she saw the pale gingery hair being tortured into two long plaits, then she waited, holding her breath, for Agnes to get into bed by her side and blow out the candle.

'Get out!' The command, given in a low throaty voice, startled her so that her eyes flew wide as she clutched the bedclothes closer round her chin.

'Get out!' This time the blankets were wrenched from her grasp as Agnes motioned to her to get down on her knees on the cold oilcloth by the side of the bed.

Agnes Waring spoke to her, not directly, but through prayer. Bowing her head over her clasped hands, she began:

'Oh, Lord, Thou has seen fit to bring into this household this child who is to dwell with us and be a comfort to her husband and assuage the weakness of his flesh.'

Jenny felt a chill run down her back as if the door had suddenly been opened, but felt it was more than her life was worth to turn round. So Mr Waring, Bob, had told his sister that they were to be married. She had guessed as much from the whispered anger taking place downstairs, and now Agnes was venting that same anger on her, but clothing her anger in a conversation with God. She shivered, a long shuddering shiver as if someone had stepped on her grave. . . .

'Mould her into Thy likeness. Subdue her wicked ways, tame her into submission,' Agnes was saying, spitting each

77

word out with fury. 'Destroy her pride, and make her ever mindful that Thy word is the only law worth heeding. . . .'

The tight, barely controlled voice went on and on, until Jenny's knees ached with the stinging cold, and she could actually feel the goose-pimples crawling up from her skin. Five minutes passed, then ten, until the words became a meaningless jumble; till she stopped trying to make sense of them, and merely buried her face into her hands willing them to stop.

She flinched as a bony elbow was prodded into her side.

'Amen,' said Agnes.

'Amen,' Jenny said back, then pulled herself up only to find that her knees, frozen into the kneeling position, gave way underneath her.

'No decent girl goes to bed with her hair hanging loose like that. No decent girl *ever* has her hair hanging loose like that.' Agnes pulled her bodily over to the dressing-table set in the window, and taking up Jenny's brush, dragged its bristles through the long wavy mass of hair with such ferocity that Jenny's eyes watered in protest.

'Hair must be plaited, like this.' Agnes made a parting down the back of Jenny's head then plaited the hair so tightly that Jenny saw in the candle-light her eyebrows ascend almost to her hair-line. With each tug her scalp twinged in agony, but pride stopped her from crying out, though she sighed with relief as the second plait was secured at the end by a fiercely tied length of narrow black ribbon.

Then when they were in bed, with Jenny almost hanging over her side, the candle was blown out and darkness filled the room.

In an almost unbelievably short time Agnes was asleep, leaving Jenny staring up into the gloom. Someone coughed on the other side of the wall, and bedsprings creaked as if sleep eluded more than one member of the strange household.

She would go away in the morning, Jenny decided. She did not know where, but anywhere away from this mad woman lying asleep in the bed beside her. Tears spilled from her eyes to run sideways down her cheeks into her pillow. She had thought . . . oh, what had she thought? That through the kindness of Mr Waring she would be lifted out of her environment into a better life? That she would be the well-respected wife of a Chapel man?

Well, that might still come to pass if she stayed here, but what she had not bargained for was his sister. She had known that Miss Waring was a bit barmy, but had thought it was in a *nice* way, a religious way, not a bitter jealous woman who mouthed her evil thoughts in the singing language the minister used when he stood up in the pulpit.

Jenny moved her leg quickly away as Agnes stirred in her sleep. Tomorrow she would go. She would go somewhere; she did not know where, but somewhere. She was young and healthy and strong, and she wasn't afraid of hard work. God always helped those who helped themselves – everybody knew that to be a fact.

But the next morning she met old Mr Waring, and what he said convinced her that maybe, just maybe, there was a chance of happiness if she stayed.

'You must not take too much notice of Agnes, lass. She's a strange girl,' he said, speaking about his daughter as if she was a child and not a grown woman of forty. 'There's bound to be some awkwardness at first, seeing as how she has been the only woman round the house these past years.' The old man raised himself on an elbow and peered at Jenny through rheumy blood-shot eyes. 'Bob was telling me last night that he is going to hurry the wedding on as quick as he can. He *needs* a wife so bad, and I'll tell you why. Would you like to know why?'

Jenny nodded and pulled the hard-backed chair closer to the bed. Oh, but she trusted and liked this frail gentle old man lying back on his pillows, with his snow-white hair fluffing up round his strangely unlined face. He was kind, as his son was kind, and once she had got Agnes's measure she would be all right too. It was only natural that Agnes felt the shock of her brother turning up like that with a strange girl and announcing that he was going to marry her. No wonder she'd acted funny . . . Jenny touched her head where it ached just as if her hair was still dragged back from her forehead in the two heavy plaits.

Mr Waring smiled. 'He's a good lad, Bob is, but he's a lonely man, so lonely it makes my heart ache sometimes to see him come home regular from work, eat his tea, then either sit by the fire reading, or go out to one of his meetings at the Chapel.'

'He sings lovely.' Jenny smiled at the thought. 'You can hear his voice above all the others.'

Mr Waring moved and winced as if the movement pained him. He was all white, Jenny thought. White face, white hair and white pillow. Only his eyes seemed alive, bright blue beneath surprisingly black eyebrows.

'Aye, it's a singing faith Methodism is. Have you been saved, lass?' There was a twinkle in the blue eyes as he asked the question. 'Aye, I know. There's too much praying goes on in this house, but Bob tries to put his faith in the place of his dead wife, and Agnes, well, she prays because she has nowt else to do.' He put up a hand. 'Nay, I'm not against religion, far from it. If I hadn't had a God to turn to I don't know where I would have been these past years, but I can tell you, it will be nice to have a smiling face around the house, and you and me, we're going to get on all right, I can see that.'

Jenny looked down at her hands clasped together in her lap. If she hadn't done that she might have cried, and that would never have done when this dear kind man wanted a smiling face around the house. For him she felt she could put up with anything. Kindness had that effect on her.

'Mr Waring – Bob, is very kind to me,' she said when she felt her voice was under control. 'He said he was going down to the shop this morning to tell Mr Pearson I wouldn't be going in any more. I'd been given the sack anyway,' she admitted, 'but we thought my step-father might go down and make trouble.'

'And Agnes won't let you help her downstairs?'

'No.' Jenny's forehead settled into anxious lines. 'She says she has her own way of doing things, and that I would be more bother than I'm worth.' She glanced round the room, at the tall chest of drawers, the wash-stand with its marble top, and the row of books on top of the drawers with a china spotted dog at each end to keep them in place.

'Would you like me to read to you, Mr Waring?'

The thought had come to her suddenly, and when he smiled and said that would be very nice, she got up and traced her finger along the bindings.

'I used to read the *Weekly Times* to my grandma, an' I always had to start with the bereavements.' She turned round with a book in her hand, and flipped over the first pages, sliding the tissue-paper from the illustration. 'This one's by Sir Walter Scott. *Woodstock*, a tale of the year sixteen hundred and fifty-one. Would you like this one?'

'One of my favourites, lass,' The old man crossed his hands on his chest, closed his eyes as his face took on a listening look. Jenny sat down again and began:

' "There is a handsome parish Church in the town of Woodstock – I am told so, at least, for I never saw it, having scarce time . . ." '

Her voice was low and sweet, and as she became engrossed in the story, it rose and fell giving the words the right poetic emphasis. She read on until she could see by the old man's deep breathing that he had fallen fast asleep, then she read on to herself till the chiming of the grandfather clock in the hall downstairs told her it was eleven o'clock.

It was the strangest thing she had ever done. There she was, sitting like a lady, turning the leaves of a book instead of serving in the shop, cutting up the horse meat in great

81

slabs and dropping them one by one into the copper at the back. There was no fire in the room, and her hands were turning blue with cold, but old Mr Waring looked warm enough, lying there with the blankets round him. Jenny got up and gently pulled them up to his chin, then she walked over to the window and lifting the lace curtain looked down into the road.

It was very quiet apart from the clip-clop of a shire horse pulling a cart piled with sacks of coal. The driver wore a sacking apron shiny with coal dust over his clothes, and a peaked cap pulled down over his eyes. Once, a long time ago, Jack Macartney had taken her down to the staithes and pointed out a boy of about ten or eleven years old dragging a heavy barrow loaded with massive slabs of shiny coal across the muddy yard.

'What chance has he got in life, poor little bugger?' he'd said. 'Now you, me little lass, things is going to be different for you. You've got a head on your shoulders you have, and one of these fine days you're going to be a teacher, that's what's in store for you.'

'Jenny?'

Agnes's voice spiralled upstairs. 'Come down here a minute.'

Jenny felt her heart give a little jump. Then reminding herself of what old Mr Waring had said, she ran down the stairs, eager to help, eager to do anything that would make things right with the hard-faced woman standing in the hall with one hand on the balustrade.

'You can help me carry the things up for Father's dressings,' she said, and Jenny followed her carrying a slop bucket and a roll of gauze.

'I won't be sick,' she told herself. 'I won't even turn pale,' but when Agnes peeled off the soiled dressing to reveal the gaping hole in Mr Waring's hip wound, then told Jenny to hold one end of the gauze as she packed it neatly inside, she had to swallow hard against the bile rising in her throat. He was so wasted, so painfully thin, so brave, and so dependent on the woman working over him with her sleeves rolled up to the elbow.

'The nurse comes once a week, but this has to be done every day.' Agnes laid a pad over the wound then bandaged it into place. 'Did you watch how I did it?' Her eyes were suddenly sly.

'Yes, I watched how I did it, Miss Waring.'

'Agnes.'

'Agnes.'

'Then you can do it yourself tomorrow. If I'm to be nothing but a skivvy from now on, then this is one job you can take off me.'

Turned on his side, with his face pressed into the pillow, the old man raised his head. 'Nay, she's nobbut a lass, Agnes. I can't let her do that for me. I won't let her do that for me.' His voice rose in a pitiful show of strength.

'I don't mind doing it for you. Honestly.' Jenny clenched her teeth, and bending over the wound, its sticky stench rancid in her nostrils, forced herself to watch carefully, trying to remember every detail of how it was done.

5

On the day that Jenny married Mr Waring she sat drinking
tea with Mr Hobkirk, the minister from the Chapel, with
Agnes presiding as usual over the flowered teapot. Her
husband of an hour was upstairs seeing to his father, and
though Jenny had said she wanted to show the old man her
new shiny wedding ring, Agnes had made it quite clear
that her duty was to stay exactly where she was.

Mollie Howarth had refused to come to the wedding,
dissolving in floods of tears in front of an embarrassed Mr
Waring, and telling him between sobs that her husband
had forbidden her ever to speak to her daughter again.

Embarrassed to the point of incoherence, Bob Waring
had passed her a clean white handkerchief. 'I will always
take care of her,' he had promised, his horrified gaze
taking in the untidiness of the undusted room, 'and some
day, when things have blown over a bit, I know she will
come down to see you.'

'Not while he's anywhere about.' Mollie had wept into
the handkerchief. 'He'd kill her if he gets his hands on her.'
She raised her face, swollen into ugliness with the flood
of tears. 'He's had to shape himself and get a job now that
Jenny's money isn't coming in any more. He's been taken
on as a loader down at the Co-op warehouse, and he says
it has made his back worse. Harry's not a good sufferer,
Mr Waring.'

'More tea, Mr Hobkirk?' Agnes unbuttoned her small
mouth into the semblance of a smile, ignoring Jenny as if

84

she was of no consequence. When she discovered that the milk jug needed filling, she turned to Jenny as if suddenly remembering she was there. 'If you please,' she said.

Jenny left the room at once, tall and somehow vulnerable in her brown skirt and jacket, with her curly hair wisping down from the bun pinned high at the back of her head.

Mr Hobkirk shook his head and tightened his mouth into a thin line. It was right, he supposed, that his Sunday School Superintendent should marry one of the younger faithful members of his flock, especially when the first marriage had ended so tragically, but there was something very wrong in the dark over-polished atmosphere of this house. His wife had told him that Miss Waring worked her fingers to the bone looking after the house and her sick father upstairs, but the thought of that young girl living here made his flesh crawl. It was like putting a flower on a muck-midden, he decided, then blinked furiously at the very idea. What was he thinking about? Agnes Waring was a good and devout woman who lived by the Good Book, her every action a sacrifice to the God she worshipped each minute of the day. So why did he feel this sense of unease settling in his stomach along with the hefty slice of seed cake baked by Miss Waring's own capable hands? And why, when he came to call, did he feel this irresistible urge to get away?

'Is there perhaps a chance some day that you might get a place of your own, Mr Waring?' he whispered, surprising himself by his own boldness as he said his goodbyes to the happy couple on the doorstep.

'My responsibilities include not only my wife, but my sister and my father,' Bob Waring told him, his small head nodding emphatically. 'There would not be the money for my sister to retain this house if I took my support away.'

Mr Hobkirk shook hands with both of them, and hurried away down the road, a stout bothered little man, with his plump cheeks creased up into little red mounds of anxiety.

'May the Lord have mercy on that bonny little lass,' he muttered, giving his long woollen scarf an extra twist round his throat. 'Comfort her and keep her, for Christ's sake, Amen.'

And the way he said it made it sound more like a threat than a gentle wedding-day prayer. . . .

When Bob went up to bed as usual at ten o'clock that night he found his bride sitting up in bed, clutching the neck of her nightgown, her dark eyes wide and terrified. He closed the door behind him and walked with his soft tread over to the bed.

'You must be the most beautiful girl in the world,' he said quietly, then as he took her hand, she felt him tremble. He was trembling all over, and his eyes were wet and shiny, and there were two hectic patches of scarlet high up on his cheekbones.

Jenny tried to pull her hand away from his hot clasp, but he held on tight, the way he had held onto her arm when he had walked her away from the shop. He was a small-made man, but he had a grip of steel, and when with his free hand he began to stroke her long hair she had to will herself not to cringe away from his touch.

'It was a nice wedding, wasn't it?' She wanted to talk to him, to hear the gentleness in his voice, but with a sudden sharp tug he pulled her towards him and began to kiss her with open-mouthed wet kisses that made her shudder and push at his shoulders in a vain attempt to push him away.

'Jenny!' His voice was a moan as he tore at the neck of her nightgown, and when she fell back she saw his eyes. They were Agnes's eyes, light and almost transparent with the blue shining through as though someone held a candle behind them.

'That's right!' he groaned. 'Fight me! Try to stop me! Oh, that's right, that's how I want it. Jenny . . . Jenny, my love.'

She tried to wriggle from his grasp, but he held her fast, covering her with his shaking body as he tore at his own clothing. She felt him claw her nightgown from her, then a sharp pain as he bit into her shoulder and squeezed her breast with a rhythmic motion. His fingers moved downward and he straddled her with his bony knees so that she moved her head from side to side on the pillow, struggling to get away.

Even in the midst of her terror she was remembering the sounds that had come from her mother's bedroom, so that a deep ingrained sense of shame stopped her from crying out.

'Please, please. No. Not like this. Please, Bob!' She whispered and pleaded but he held a hand over her mouth and nose so that she felt the blood pounding in her ears.

'Yes! Yes! That's the way. Kick me! Go on kicking me. Oh, you're so wonderful. Jenny! You're not fighting hard enough. Stop me. Stop me, please!'

She felt the hardness of his fingernails as he violated her, and as she twisted and writhed, he took her savagely, hurting and wounding, sending sharp shafts of burning pain through her.

'Now lie still!' he ordered. 'Now you must, you *must* lie still!'

As he sweated and groaned above her, thrusting, shattering, she began to cry soundlessly. She had not known exactly what was going to happen to her, but in her wildest stretches of imagination, she could never have dreamed it would be like this.

So she lay still as he commanded. She was too shocked to do anything else but lie still. Then, when she thought she must surely die of pain and humiliation, he gave a shuddering groan, and rolled away from her, leaving her bleeding and torn.

Then he turned over onto his side with his back to her, and fell immediately into a snoring sleep.

For a long time Jenny lay there, not daring to move in case he should wake and begin all over again. Then gingerly, aching and shivering as if she was in the throes of some tropical fever, she slid out of bed, and going over to the washstand, sponged herself all over, wincing as the cold water stung the places where his sharp pointed teeth had broken her skin. Then picking up her torn nightgown from where it had been tossed to the floor, she pulled it over her head, and got back into bed.

So this was what old Mr Waring had meant when he had said that his son was a lonely man in desperate need of a wife. But how could that be? The old man was gentle and kind and could never have dreamed that his only son, a pillar of the Chapel, had the instincts of a maniac.

Jenny lay on her back, her eyes wide open as she thought about the wife who had died giving birth to her child. 'She was a fine healthy woman,' Bob had told her. 'There was just no reason why she should have died, that was why the shock was so terrible.'

'The Lord giveth and the Lord taketh away. . . .'

The words rang like a muted peal of bells over and over in Jenny's mind. She put a hand up to a throat that ached as if she had screamed aloud and gone on screaming. *Had* she screamed? Was Agnes lying now in her wide bed across the landing, her eyes with that strange light behind them, shining and gloating on what she had heard? Was that patient, suffering old man listening too? Listening and glad it was all over?

Bob sighed in his sleep and Jenny clutched the sheet up to her chin, forcing herself to lie like a log in case he turned over and reached for her again.

If he reached for her again she would go for him, and go for him proper this time. Not fight him as he had urged her to do. Jenny felt the tears slide from the corners of her eyes and run sideways into her pillow. Why had he wanted her to fight him? She couldn't understand it, but even in her innocence she knew that his coming at her like that had been perverted. She had never known even the rudiments of love-making. No boy had ever trailed his finger down her cheek or kissed her, or caressed her, but she had read books where eyes looked into eyes, where bosoms heaved and cheeks blushed rosy-red at the sound of a lover's endearments. She tried to blink the tears away, afraid to put up a hand in case the man by her side should wake.

She wanted to pray but somehow the God in this house had got all mixed up with the God she knew, and if it was true that He listened to every prayer, what had He made of her own incoherent pleas of less than an hour ago?

There was no answer. And if there was no answer to that, Jenny felt there never would be an answer to anything any more.

When Bob Waring heard his sister's light tap on his door the following morning, he opened his eyes, twisted round and saw that Jenny was so deep asleep that she might have been dead. The soft pink colour had drained from her cheeks; there was a purple blood blister on her lower lip, and her torn nightgown had slipped from a shoulder dark with finger bruises.

The sight excited him, racing his pulse and making him run his tongue over dry lips, but this was the time Agnes tapped on his door to tell him breakfast would be ready in ten minutes sharp, and there were morning prayers to be said round his father's bed before he left for work.

The clerks in the iron foundry up Dartwell Street started late – half-past seven, as against the workers early start of six, but Bob always left the house well before seven, liking to be at his high desk in the outer office well in good time. He walked quickly down Steep Brow, past the stone houses set back from the road, down past the row of shops, to where a huddle of men waited for the Corporation horse tram. He always timed his arrival to the minute, and as he joined the short queue he saw the tram approaching with its driver muffled against the cold, but still wearing his round billycock set squarely over his head. The two horses quiet in their shafts needed no more than a flick of the whip and a shouted 'whoa there' to stop, and Bob climbed aboard, the coin for his fare already tucked neatly into his gloved hand.

There was nothing in his demeanour to suggest that the day before had been his wedding day. Nothing in the melancholy set of his long features to betray the wild dissipation of the night. The conductor, his leather bag slung low round his waist, bade him a good morning, and Bob acknowledged it with a nod of his head.

Leaving his coat and hat in a small overcrowded cloakroom, he went into the big outer office, took out a pair of celluloid cuffs from a drawer, slipped them over his own shirt cuffs which in their turn had been starched to perfection by his sister, drew a thick ledger towards him, and began to write.

If he stood up on the rung of his stool he could see down into the foundry where men and boys in overalls had been hard at work for an hour; if he turned his head to the left he could see the manager's glass-fronted office, where Mr Hargreaves, the son of the owner, was already dictating letters to the only lady clerk, a Miss Warburton, well-practised in Mr Pitman's shorthand method of writing.

But Bob Waring kept his head down, writing neatly with a new Waverley nib in his pen, too engrossed in his work to even begin to overhear the conversation going on behind the wide glass panel.

Mr Hargreaves stared into the outer office over the tops of his spectacles, then turned to his secretary.

'I heard that Mr Waring took the day off yesterday to get married. Was that so, Miss Warburton?'

She coughed discreetly. 'Yes, so I believe, Mr Hargreaves. To a young girl from Mosley Street Chapel. All done in a great hurry, and total surprise to everyone.'

'Hm . . .' Mr Hargreaves had lost his train of thought,

and rubbed his chin thoughtfully. 'A bit of a dark horse our Mr Waring, but then they're often like that these devout little men. I wonder if I ought to have him in and congratulate him? Do you think that would be in order, Miss Warburton?'

She fingered the black velvet bow at the neck of her blouse. 'In order, sir, but hardly necessary. Mr Waring doesn't encourage intrusions into his private life.'

'The best clerk I have, and I can't stand the sight of him.' Mr Hargreaves picked up a letter and pushed the spectacles back up the bridge of his nose.

'I wonder why?'

Bob Waring worked all day, stopping for an hour from twelve till one to eat the sandwiches Agnes had prepared for him. There were facilities down in the works for a pot of tea to be brewed, but he preferred to quench his thirst at the cold tap in the cloakroom. Usually he stepped outside to walk briskly for twenty minutes or so, but not today.

Only the day before it had seemed that spring was not all that far away, but today the sky was the same metallic grey of Miss Warburton's scragged-back hair. She did not like Mr Waring either, but she considered it very ill-mannered of her boss to have spoken in that indiscreet manner. She hoped of course that Mr Waring had found true happiness, but she remembered that he had taken only one day off work for his first wife's funeral, and she considered him to be a strange and melancholy man.

'How on earth had he ever got round to proposing?' she wondered, then as she flipped over the pages of her lined notebook, she dismissed Mr Waring completely from her tidy mind.

It was a hectic busy day at the foundry, and when Bob stepped outside into the short street leading to the road served by the horse trams it was as dark as any night he could remember. Even the gas lamps were shrouded in dank black mist, and before he had taken more than a few steps the nap of his velour overcoat was beaded with drizzle. He stepped into a doorway to turn up his collar and snap the fastener of his gloves together, turned round and came face to face with a big man with a cap pulled low over his face.

'Mr Waring?'

The man reeked of drink, and to Bob's horror, actually put out a hand and gripped his arm.

He felt his heart begin to pound. He looked around to see if anyone had seen what was happening, but as usual, because he had stayed a few minutes later than the rest of the office staff, preferring to make his way alone, the short street was deserted.

'I don't think we are acquainted,' he managed to say in a voice that even to his own ears sounded stiff with fear.

The pedantic phrasing seemed to rile the big man further as he pushed his unshaven face closer.

'Oh, it's like that, is it, high and mighty Mr bloody Waring? Well let me tell you, I know *you* all right. You're the man what took me step-daughter away from her mother without as much as a thought as to how we were going to get by. An' I'll tell you something, Mr bloody Waring. You are welcome to her, and much good may she do you.' His voice dropped to a low whine. 'An' it's not much I'm asking for. Just a little in the way of compensation, that's all, and don't go telling me you haven't got it because I checked, and today's the day you get the little envelope with your wages in.' He let go of Bob's arm, gripped the lapels of his overcoat and jerked him even closer.

'C'mon now, Mr Waring. Me wife has it that you're a kind man, so let's see if all that praying has made you mindful of the needs of others. Right?'

'You'll get no money from me.'

Bob could hardly believe what was happening. This sort of thing did not happen, not in the tight little Chapel

92

circle he moved in. He glanced round wildly and saw the light was still burning in Mr Hargreaves's office. He considered shouting for help, but he knew that his cries would never be heard, not in this little street of no more than four houses either side, a street where the night-women lived. Even in his distress he remembered a night of more than a year ago when he had merely passed the time of day with a woman standing on the doorstep, and found himself inside without hardly knowing how he had got there. But the Lord had forgiven him for all his following indiscretions, and the same Lord would help him now.

'You'll get no money from me,' he said again in a louder voice, then the brave words died in his throat as Harry Howarth hit him. Just once, a stinging blow to the side of his head, taking him by surprise so that he fell back, striking his head on an iron upright foot-scraper set by the front step behind him.

He saw nothing, heard nothing, felt nothing as Harry Howarth bent over him, swiftly. He lay there, still and bleeding as the big man lurched away from him, falling over his boots in his frantic haste to get away. And neither he nor his assailant saw anything of the woman with a raddled pock-marked face, who appeared briefly at her front door, glanced swiftly up and down the darkened street, then went back inside, closing the door firmly behind her.

It was after seven o'clock when the police came and knocked on the house in Park Road. One was dressed in his uniform, and the other in plain clothes, and the latter was the one who knocked on the vestibule door till the ruby glass panels shivered in protest.

'See who it is.' Agnes had been telling Jenny that there was nothing unusual in her brother being as late as this. 'He often stays on by himself. He's not afraid of hard work.' Her sharp voice had been full of bitterness as Jenny gazed at her in despair.

'I've offered to help, over and over, and you won't let me do nothing,' she said.

'You don't look fit to do nothing,' Agnes had retaliated, her pale blue eyes sly.

So, grateful for having been allotted even the small task, Jenny walked down the hall and opened the door.

'Is this where Mr Robert Waring lives?' The man in plain clothes doffed his hat and stood there with the rain plastering his sleeked-down hair even closer to his head.

'Yes, but he hasn't come home from work yet.' Jenny stepped back instinctively, knowing it was not done to have the police standing on the doorstep, even on a night as dark and wet as this. When the police called down the street where she had lived, it spelt trouble, and trouble was private, everybody knew that.

'You'd better come in,' she said.

The policeman in uniform was very young, and this was the first time he had been briefed to do a job like this. He stared at Jenny then looked quickly away. Even though she looked pale and ill she was still a very pretty girl, and married at that. His quick glance took in the wide gold band on her wedding finger.

Jenny walked down the narrow hall and opened a door on the left. 'Agnes, it's the police,' she said, and Agnes got up from her chair by the fire and with the characteristic gesture that Jenny was beginning to know so well, tilted her chin and closed her eyes, as if in prayer.

'Yes? What can I do for you?' she asked quietly.

'You're Mrs Waring?' The man holding the hard hat asked the question, but the young policeman looked over to where Jenny stood by the door watching the older woman as if she expected to be sent from the room at any minute.

'I'm *Miss* Waring. That is Mrs Waring, and if it's about anything unpleasant I would rather the three of you went through into the kitchen.' Agnes's eyes blazed a message of disgust in Jenny's direction, and the curl of her lip said that she wasn't surprised in the least to find the police calling on her sister-in-law, even as quickly as the day after the wedding.

The young policeman looked at the floor, but his superior came straight to the point. He turned to Jenny.

'I'm afraid I've bad news for you, Mrs Waring.' He walked over to the table and pulled out a chair. 'See here, lass. Come and sit down. That's better.' He put a hand on Jenny's shoulder and pressed her down into the chair. 'It's about your husband, Mr Waring. Mr Robert Waring.'

'Yes?' Jenny looked up at him trustingly, her eyes wide in the pallor of her face.

'He was found lying in the street just outside Hargreaves's iron foundry. With his head split open. He was dead, I'm afraid, lass.'

'Murdered?' Agnes's voice rose in a thin high scream, as Jenny buried her face in her hands.

'This is what you've done!' She made a grab towards Jenny, but the young policeman stepped forward and held her arm above her head. 'I knew you would bring trouble the minute you stepped over the doorstep! It's one of your sort that's done this! Coming from where you come from. He was always a fool when it came to a young 'un with a pretty face. Look at her. Just look at her! She doesn't look pretty right this minute, does she?'

'There's never been no mention of murder, Miss Waring.' The older man spoke quietly but firmly. 'Your brother's wages packet was found in his pocket, and there was no noise of a scuffle according to the testimony of the neighbours we questioned. Have you any reason to suspect . . .?'

'She's responsible. I tell you she's responsible!' Agnes opened her mouth and screamed, loud piercing screams that brought the sound of anxious thumping from the room above.

All four faces turned upwards to the ceiling, Agnes stopping in mid-stream as if someone had slapped her hard.

'It's Father.' She took a step forward, groping with her hands in front of her face as if she was blind. The young policeman led her gently back to her chair. 'I'll make a pot of tea. Yes, that's what I will do,' he said. Jenny got up and showed him the way, but when she tried to open the tea caddy she found that her hands were shaking so much she could not get the lid off.

'Agnes? Jenny?' Old Mr Waring's voice spiralled downstairs, and Jenny thrust the tea caddy into the policeman's hands.

'I'll see to him. I'll go.' She ran along the passageway, then up the stairs, holding up her long skirt with one hand as she hauled herself up by the banister rail with the other.

The old man was sitting on the edge of the bed, his stick-thin legs protruding from his nightshirt, his eyes wide and terrified.

'What is it? What's going on down there?' He held out his arms to Jenny and she sat by him and pulled him close.

'Now you've got to be brave. You have to be very, very brave,' she said before she told him that his son, his only son, had been found lying dead in the street with the rain falling down onto his upturned face.

The days before the inquest passed without Jenny realizing that they were passing. The coroner's report stated that Mr Robert Waring had died of a fractured skull, caused by slipping on a wet pavement and striking his head against an iron stoop. The report was printed in the *Weekly Times* and went on to mention a heart condition, a diseased valve that could have ended the victim's life abruptly at any time. The coroner put on record his condolences to the young wife, who, he said, had tragically become a widow before she had known what it was to be a wife.

Agnes spoke to Jenny only when it was necessary, treating her with a studied coldness even in front of the Chapel folk who crowded the front room after the funeral. Old Mr Waring lay in his bed, submitting to having his dressings changed, and sinking into an apathy that was as profound as a coma. Jenny watched him grow more frail with each day that passed, and one day when she was trying to spoon thin gruel into his mouth, he opened his eyes and stared up into her face.

'You must go back home, lass,' he whispered. 'This house is no place for you now. When is the . . . the funeral to be?'

Jenny mopped up the gruel dribbling down his chin and laid the bowl aside with a sigh. 'Tomorrow. It's tomorrow, Mr Waring. I haven't been able to get any black clothes but the minister's wife says my brown will do.'

'Mrs Hobkirk? Aye, she's a good woman, and she knows, she knows what Agnes can be like.' He tried to push himself upright then fell back against his pillows. 'You must go back home, lass,' he repeated. 'Agnes is only biding her time. When all this is over and folks stop coming to the house she will crucify you. Not with nails and a wooden cross, but with words.' He moved his white head from side to side. 'I see her do it to that other little lass Bob brought home, though Bob himself had a part in that. They're my own flesh and blood, lass, but they – Bob was unstable in some ways, and Agnes, well hers takes a different form.'

'He guesses about the night of the wedding,' Jenny thought and turned her face away as shame flooded her whole body with the memory of it.

'Violence doesn't have to be physical, tha knows.' The old man's eyelids drooped as he lifted a thin hand and waved the gruel away. 'Get rid of that muck, lass. It's babby's pap, that is.'

He watched Jenny go from the room, her head down, the back of her neck vulnerable beneath the high-piled mass of dark hair.

'She's nobbut a child,' he muttered, 'a child what needs her mother as bad as if she were a babby not yet breached.' He closed his eyes. 'Go home, little lass. Go on home. . . .'

Then with the next breath he took he was asleep.

One rainy afternoon Jenny took her coat and tammy from

the hallstand and left the house. She did not trouble to tell Agnes she was going out, knowing that she would merely have met her sister-in-law's blank stare of indifference.

Where she went, what she did, was of no consequence to Agnes, and the sooner she accepted that the better.

It was more than possible that her mother had never heard of Mr Waring's death. Jenny still thought of her husband as Mr Waring now that he had gone. She hurried along, head down against the driving rain. Yes, it was possible, because Jenny had been the one to buy the *Weekly Times* each Friday, to read it in snatched moments behind the counter at work then take it straight round to her grandmother's house at the weekend.

Mollie glanced at the headlines on occasions, but Harry Howarth would use it to make into long spills for his pipe whenever he got his hands on it.

'Why can't he admit that he can't read or write?' a younger Jenny had asked more than once, only to be answered by the trembling of her mother's lower lip.

'He can't help it if he got no schooling in Ireland. It's cruel to bring it up like that. Can't you see that's one of the reasons you and him have never hit it off? You make him seem small. In his own eyes you make him seem small.'

Jenny turned the corner of the street she knew so well, turned it, walked down past the first three houses, then stopped. She almost expected to see the familiar door open and Harry Howarth lurch out onto the pavement, with his hands sunk deep in his pockets and the off-white muffler knotted round his neck. A woman standing on her doorstep across the street saw her, recognized her and called out, and the sound of the shrill voice gave Jenny the impetus to keep on walking. If her step-father was in, then she would just have to open the door and face what would surely happen. He couldn't *kill* her; at the worst he could only shout and at the moment, after the last few days of Agnes's stony indifference, even his drunken bawling would come as a relief. She put a hand out to the latch, lifted it, and opened the front door.

And oh, dear God, but he was there all right. She could hear him; she realized now that she had heard him even before she had reached the house. His deep voice was booming out, slurred with his own particular mixture of anger and drink, and the raucous sound was interspersed by the noise of Mollie's plaintive whining.

Jenny stood listening, and it was like listening to a play from the wings of a theatre, a play that had run for months with the words the same and the voices the same.

'Get up from your backside you lazy slut! Is that all a man can expect when he comes in from his work? A pot of tea and a bloody piece of bread and scrape?'

'You're home too soon, Harry. I never expected you as soon as this. . . .'

A plate smashing in smithereens on the cut-steel fender, the back door almost pulled off its hinges as Harry clattered down the steps into the yard, her mother's loud sobs as she picked up the broken pieces of crockery and dropped them into the pail underneath the sink.

Then the smell of a not quite ready fish tea as her mother opened the oven door. Jenny saw it all as clearly as if the dividing wall had suddenly fallen down. Saw the way it would be when Harry stumbled back up the steps, his braces dangling round his overhanging paunch. More shouting, more weeping, more insults, more whining, until unbelievably the two of them sat down together and ate their meal as if nothing had happened. . . .

She took a step backwards, then another, closing the door softly before setting off back up the street.

There was no way she could ever be a part of that again. There was no way she could live with Agnes for much longer, not even for the sake of the old man lying uncomplainingly in his bed upstairs. Jenny walked quickly, feeling in her mind a kind of shamed relief at the realization that

99

there was no obligation for her to suffer either the one or the other.

She was seventeen, that was all. She was strong and she could still laugh. She wasn't quite clear at what as yet, but she would think of something. That very night she would tell Agnes she was going to take the advice she had been given on the night Bob Waring had brought her home. . . . She would look around and find a living-in job.

'I've had no experience, but I'm willing,' she would tell her prospective employer, and then she would be shown up to her own room, high at the top of the house, a tiny room with a sloping roof and room for no more than a bed and a washstand. It would be a family where the praying and rowing weren't overdone, a *normal* household where she would become almost as one of the family, keeping her place of course, but belonging. And *respected*.

That was what she wanted above all else, Jenny decided – to be respected for herself alone. . . .

Darkness was falling as she climbed the steps to the house on Park Road, and she was surprised to see that the big front door had been closed, knowing that usually it was left open into the vestibule until time for the bedtime ritual of locking up took place.

She raised a hand to the knocker, then before she let it fall against the door glanced down and saw a brown paper parcel on the step almost hidden by the leaves of a stunted hydrangea bush.

There was something vaguely familiar about the shape and size of it, even the feel of it. Jenny held it for a moment in her hands turning it round and round, the frown in between her eyes deepening as she tried to understand. Her head jerked up swiftly as she heard Agnes's voice from behind the closed door.

'Aye. Your things are all there, madam. Just as they were when you first came here thinking you had found yourself a nice soft place for the rest of your life. But you was wrong, wasn't you?'

For the first time since they met, Agnes had forgotten her impeccable way of speaking. Jenny clutched the parcel to her, and with her free hand pounded on the door.

'Agnes! Let me in! It's raining. It's raining hard. I promise you I'll go just as soon as I find somewhere. Agnes! Your father? He will be very angry with you when he finds out what you've done.'

Agnes laughed then, a trilling laugh that made Jenny's blood run cold.

'But he won't *know* what I've done, will he, madam? I'm here in the vestibule with the door closed behind me, and he can't hear me, not from upstairs. I'll tell him you've gone home to your mother.' The laugh came again. 'I heard him telling you to do just that earlier on, so he'll just think you have taken his advice.'

'But he will *know* I wouldn't go without saying goodbye. He knows me better than that.' Jenny lifted the knocker once again. 'I will keep on knocking till he's bound to hear, an' he'll know it's me. . . .'

'And upset him all over again?' Agnes's voice was strong. 'After what you've done already? Oh, yes, you would do that, wouldn't you?' The voice broke. 'We was all right, the three of us, till you came along! Now go off somewhere else and find someone else's life to muck up, and make sure it's a man, because women can see straight through you, just as I did. And I was right, wasn't I? Just go on knocking if you want yet another death laid at your doorstep, you little heathen!'

Jenny took two steps backwards down the stone flight of steps. She looked up at the windows, at the front window of the bedroom where on her wedding night her husband's kindness had disappeared as if it had never existed, where with that strange blue light shining from behind his eyes he had demonstrated that in his own way he was as mentally unstable as his praying sister. And old Mr Waring, lying in his bed at the back of the house, he had known and tried to warn her.

'Go back home, lass. Go back home. . . .'

Jenny turned her back on the house set back from its respectable neat little paved garden. She walked away along the respectable road, but when she came to the corner leading down Steep Brow, she turned right instead of left.

She was going nowhere; not back to her mother's house. Just nowhere.

6

Walking away from the town Jenny passed the straggle
of buildings leading to the outskirts. On past the Corn
Millers, the Silversmiths with its bow-fronted windows, on
from one flickering gas lamp to another, the shops now
interspersed by rows of terraced houses, their front windows
dark and shuttered, blinds and curtains drawn against the
cold winter's night.

There was an Eating House at the end of one street, and
in the light of the lamp suspended from the corner of the
building, Jenny read the sign 'Oysters', with a second
neatly printed sign underneath 'Careful Removing Under-
taken'. This shop too was closed, but the oysters were piled
high in one corner of the window, with the weighing scales
to hand. Jenny walked on, trying not to remember the day
Jack Macartney had taken her down to the market, and
fed her with the slippery sea-tasting shell fish, swimming in
vinegar and trickling down her throat with nauseating ease.

Then they had made her feel sick; now she would have
savoured their taste on her tongue, and even chewed them
on their way. Teatime had long since been and gone and
there was a cold empty feeling inside her. As Bob Waring's
widow she supposed she was entitled to some of his money.
Or was she? Jenny knew nothing of solicitors, and all the
law represented to her was a Bobby standing at the door
bringing trouble of some kind or other.

One thing she knew for certain and that was she wasn't
going to go back and ask Agnes for anything. She would

starve first. The bit in the paper had been right. She was a widow before she had known what it had been to be a wife, and now she did not feel like a widow either. She was Jenny Waring, father unknown, married for one day and one terrible night, and all that mattered at the moment was finding a place to rest for the night.

Now the houses were thinning out, with dark hedges hiding dark fields. The pavement was no more than a footpath with mud that oozed over the soles of her laced-up boots. The last time she had been along this road was a long time ago, when her father had hired a pony and trap for a day. Then the hedges were green, and the sun had shone down, and when the trap had swayed they had fallen against each other, laughing. Jenny blinked the rain away from her eyelashes as she saw the outline of a building looming upon her left.

It was a brick building, fallen into ruin, but it was at least a shelter so she went inside, stumbling over a pile of bricks in the entrance. Groping her way to the far wall she found a raised platform, forming a seat of sorts, and gratefully she sank down onto it.

She placed the brown paper parcel behind her back, raised her feet onto a wide stone, and with her arms held tightly round her shivering body, closed her eyes and began to will the next hours away.

It was deathly quiet, and now that her eyes had become used to the darkness she could see the doorway etched in a grey light.

She might have been a hundred miles from anywhere, and when at last it grew light, then she told herself that whatever was going to happen to her would begin. But first there was the night . . . .

Afterwards she remembered it as a long drawn-out nightmare, in which she dozed, to wake stiff and cramped, then forced herself to walk round and round the little shelter. She prayed; she listened to the silence, chivvied God up a bit when despair threatened to take over, then slept sitting bolt upright in the hour before the dawn.

When she stood up and stretched her aching limbs and went outside, she was just able to make out a sign over the doorway. James Clayton & Sons, Manufacturers of Heald Yarns. She bowed her head for a moment in grateful thanks to the unknown Mr Clayton and his sons who had built their tiny workroom of solid brick and topped it with a roof that kept off the rain.

To her surprise, the hunger had gone, leaving in its place an empty void where once her stomach had been. She was thirsty, not hungry, and the first thing she was going to do was to stop at the nearest cottage and ask for a drink of water. She could feel the rim of the cup held against her lips; she could feel the trickle of moisture down her throat, so she shook her head from side to side as if to shake the thoughts away, then she picked up the parcel and stepped outside . . .

When she reached the first huddle of cottages set back from the road it was still barely light, with no sign of life anywhere, so she walked on. The thirst was more of a dry ache in her throat now, and she wanted, as she had wanted the night before, to set as many miles between herself and the town as possible.

She had not known how desolate the countryside could look beneath a grey sky, with bare trees above her head and the muddy verge beneath her tramping feet flanked by ditches swollen with rain. She walked for what seemed miles past a dripping sodden wood with the trees thick and black in endless rows. She heard the clip-clop of horses's hooves behind her, and swayed into the shelter of the hedge, her head down, expecting it to pass. Then she lifted her head and stared, her mouth open with surprise as a man's voice called out to her.

'Want a ride, Miss? It's a fair way to the village if that's where tha's going to. Come on, then, I won't harm you. I've two at home like you, fast asleep in their beds if I know right. . . .'

The man had climbed down from the trap and waited for her. He was a thick-set, rough-looking man with a red face and a nose and chin that seemed to be straining to meet, leaving his mouth lurking somewhere in the hollow between them.

'Punch!' The thought came to Jenny even as she hobbled towards him, her feet swollen and ice-cold inside her boots, and her skirts with their mud-encrusted hems dragging as if they were lead-lined.

The carter peered down into her face, then when she managed to raise one foot onto the step, he put out a hand and half lifted her up. Going round to the other side of the trap, he climbed in, gathered up the reins and shouted:

'Giddy-up then, Flossie! Come on, old girl. Show us what tha's made of!'

The trap moved forward with a jerk so that Jenny fell against him. She straightened up and said she was sorry and he gave her a sideways look, openly weighing her up.

'Want dropping off at the next village, Miss?'

'No, the one after that, that is if you're going that far?'

'Malesbury?'

Jenny nodded. She had never heard the name before, but it would do. Any place would do that went in the opposite direction from the place she had left. She could not believe her luck in finding a lift like this. Why, at the rate they were going she could almost see the miles disappearing beneath the clippity-clop of the horse's hooves. If only she could stop shivering. . . . Sitting close to the man as she was she was conscious of the fact that he could feel her shaking, but he said nothing, just flicked at the horse now and again with his whip, his nose seeming to dip even lower towards his jutting chin.

'Nice place, Malesbury.'

'Yes.' Jenny clenched her teeth in a vain attempt to stop their chattering.

'Better when the sun shines like everywhere else.'

'Yes . . . oh yes. . . .'

It came to Jenny suddenly that she was, if she wasn't careful, beginning to feel sorry for herself. Too much had happened, too quickly. She was still wearing the black tape arm-band that Agnes had given her on the morning of the funeral. She touched it and wondered if she could slide it down her sleeve unobtrusively and drop it onto the road so that the wheels ran over it and ground it into the mud.

She was *glad* that Mr Waring was dead. She turned her head quickly as if the man by her side might have heard such wickedness spoken aloud, but he was staring straight ahead with a large dewdrop glistening on the end of his hooked nose.

She wasn't glad for Mr Waring's sake that he was dead, but she was glad for her own. Yes, that was it. She was glad because after that one night she had known she would have to get away. She hunched herself over the parcel on her lap. Suppose she was going to have a baby? Suppose she found a place and then they sent her away because she was going to . . . oh God . . . Jenny closed her eyes in a fervent prayer.

She opened them again as the road began to twist and turn, climbing upwards through an overhanging tunnel of trees.

'A short cut, Miss. Going this way means we cut Clay-bridge out and come down over the fell into Malesbury. I wouldn't attempt it in the dark, but it cuts miles off when tha knows the way.' He slowed the horse down as the road grew more stony, and then he was silent again.

Jenny saw a ridge of hills stretching away into the distance, purple hills wreathed in grey mist. She saw cows in a field, herded together, then they came out at the top of the hill with a long valley stretching below, dotted with isolated houses.

'Want me to drop you in the village street, Miss? Or if tha tells me exactly where it is tha's going I'll take you right there.'

The man's voice held a deep concern. He wasn't going

to ask no questions, not him, but if he was any judge of owt, this young lass was in some kind of trouble. From the looks of her she'd been walking a fair way afore he'd come across her, and from that black arm-band on her sleeve it looked as if she'd lost somebody not long back. Mother? Father? Nay, it was none of his business; he'd done his bit by making out he had been on his way to Malesbury when all the time his own destination had been miles back.

Soft in the head, his missus would say when he told her.

'Picking up gyppo women, then setting 'em down to do their beggin',' she'd say, but she would be wrong. This little lass weren't no gyppo, and that parcel on her knee weren't pegs. If what he suspected was right, that there parcel held all the bonny lass possessed. Running away more likely. But from where? From whom?

'Going to a place, Miss?' His curiosity and concern got the better of him as he asked the question, and when Jenny turned her dark eyes full on him and he saw the anxious worriting in them he wanted to tell old Flossie to whoa-up while he put his arm round her, just like she were one of his own and tell her to get whatever was troubling her off her chest.

But he couldn't do that. If he put out a hand to touch her he guessed she'd be down off his cart as quick as a flash. Aye, that she would.

Jenny nodded. 'Yes, I am going to a place, but I . . . I'm not quite sure where it is.' She looked straight ahead to the straggle of cottages that made up the main village street. 'If you drop me by those houses I'll make some enquiries, and get set on my way.' She lowered her head and did not speak again until the horse clip-clopped along the cobbles, then when he stopped, she jumped down and stood looking up at him.

'You've been very kind. I can't thank you enough,' she said, then she stood back on the narrow pavement and waited, so that there was nothing left for him to do but touch his cap, flick his whip and move on, muttering to himself and telling himself that if ever either of his two little lasses looked like that one did, it would break his heart – clean in two, that it would.

Jenny waited until the trap had turned a corner at the far end of the street, then she crossed over and began to walk down a winding lane going away from the village. There were more stone-built houses, and a butcher's shop with a carcass of a sheep in the window, a chandler's, and a shop that was just a house with the smell of baking bread making her feel suddenly weak and helpless with longing, so that she had to lean against a wall for support.

For a wild moment she wondered what would happen if she stepped inside and begged a crust. She actually felt her teeth sink into the warm bread, and she closed her eyes, chiding herself for her weakness before trudging on. She walked past a church with sloping gravestones and a weather-beaten porch, and she was tempted to cross over and sit down on the wooden bench, and just let something happen.

But she knew that life wasn't like that. You had to *make* something happen; you had to go on and hope that right round the next corner something good would happen. She had only started, and she wasn't going to give up yet.

The big houses should be starting to appear now. Jenny remembered from her infrequent visits to the country as a child that they were always a bit away from the village, set back from the road behind high walls. She walked on, her feet dragging now till she saw a farm with five chimneys, each one like a little castle with turrets etched in grey chunks against the sky.

There was a man in the yard carrying a bucket in each hand. He came out, and crossed the road to where hens clucked in a penned-in run on the other side of the lane. Jenny waited until he was close before she spoke:

'I wonder if you know of any houses round hereabouts where they might be taking on help?' She shifted the brown paper parcel from one arm to the other, pushed her tammy back from where it was slipping down her forehead and waited anxiously, wondering if the man were a farm labourer or even perhaps the owner? Perhaps she should have bobbed him a curtsey or at least have addressed him as 'sir'?

The man had heard her; she was sure of that, but he gave no sign, merely kept on across the lane, where he stopped by a gate, lowering one of the buckets to the ground before lifting the piece of rope tethering the gate to its stoop.

Then as he stepped into the field, turning round to replace the length of rope, he glared at Jenny from beneath wandering bushy eyebrows.

'Off!' he growled. 'Off with you! We don't want none of your sort round here!'

Jenny opened her mouth to tell him she wasn't begging, that she wasn't asking for something for nothing, then realizing the futility of argument, lowered her head and walked away, tears of anger stinging behind her eyelids.

'Always hold up your head,' Grandma Macartney had been fond of saying. 'There's none any better than you, Jenny, allus remember that!'

But even in her poorest days Grandma Macartney had always had a roof over her head, even when she had to stay inside for a whole winter when her boots were needed by one of her children. The tears rolled down Jenny's cheeks and she brushed them angrily away.

She walked past a tall red-bricked house, set well back. She hesitated, turned back and looked at the ivy covering every inch of the walls like a dark green cloak, and walked on. It was now just a case of putting one foot in front of the other, willing herself to keep on, of telling herself that her instinct would tell her when she had found the right place.

Then about half a mile further on she came to a pair of gates, with a straight drive leading to a house with large bay windows, with a high cedar tree standing sentinel on the lawn. The gates were open as if someone had recently driven a horse and trap out of them, as if the gravel had been sprayed by horses' hooves. Jenny took a deep breath and began to walk up the drive, past the house and round the back to a side door overlooking a paddock and down into a hollow behind a cluster of trees to what she guessed were the stables.

She hesitated, straightening the tammy on her head, leaning down to try to shake some of the clinging mud from her skirts, moistening her lips and setting her face into what she hoped was a pleasant expression. Then she lifted her hand and let the iron knocker fall back against the door.

It was opened almost immediately by a plump tiny woman with a strong fuzz of down on her veined cheeks, and light brown hair puffed out round her face in a cottage-loaf style.

'Fanny Barton?' The sigh of relief was replaced at once by a grimace of disgust. 'Nay, but you're not Fanny Barton, are you? I've been expecting her for this past hour, an' all she has to do is walk up from the village!'

Jenny held out a hand then took it back quickly in case the woman thought she was begging. What she had meant to ask for was a job, but what came out when she opened her mouth was a plaintive request for a drink:

'Please? May I have a drink of water?'

The door led into a stone passage, and leading off from that what was obviously the kitchen. Tantalising smells of baking bread made her clutch the doorpost for support, made her close her eyes against the longing, then the ground came up and hit her smack between the eyes.

It was only a little faint; she had never fainted in her life before, and she was conscious again almost as soon as she fell.

'I'm all right,' she said, struggling to get up, reaching for the parcel, 'it's just that . . . just that . . .'

Mrs Fanshawe, cook for twenty years at Cedar House,

had her own way of dealing with beggar women who came to the door asking for charity. Short of slamming the door in their faces she could see them off with a few well-chosen words, making it clear that if it was owt they wanted for nowt, then they were wasting their time. But this girl with her white face and her pleading anguished eyes was no beggar woman. A sound judge of character was Milly Fanshawe, always had been and always would be. With a strength that belied her tiny frame, she put an arm round Jenny's waist, and helped her into the house and down the passage.

She propped Jenny up against the end of a long scrubbed table, pulled a chair out from beneath it and pushed her down onto it.

'There, just catch your breath, love, and I'll get you a pot of warm tea, though from the look of you something a bit stronger might not come amiss. You're soaked to the bone. Put that parcel down on the floor, and here, let me draw the chair up to the fire. I dursn't sit you down in the rocking-chair, not with them wet things on, you'd soak the cushion through, the state you're in.'

Jenny did as she was told. She was too busy trying to stop shivering to do anything else. Then as Mrs Fanshawe passed her a pint pot of scalding hot tea she found to her embarrassment that the rim jittered against her teeth so much that the sound seemed to echo round the enormous room.

The kitchen of Cedar House was bigger than any room in any house she had been in before. There was a huge bread oven to the side of the fire, and a shiny brown teapot on the hob. Mrs Fanshawe passed over the sugar basin. 'Here, I'll do it for you, lass. How many? Three? Four? The last girl here took six and I told her, it was a wonder she could stir it round by the time she'd finished. But she's gone, same as they all do . . .' She put the glass sugar bowl down on the table and taking a second cup down from the dresser, poured out for herself. 'Nay, I haven't time to draw breath this morning, never mind sit me down with a pot of tea, but things is all behind upstairs so I might as well be hung for a sheep as a lamb, that's what I always say.'

'I always say that, too.' Jenny curled her stiff fingers round the pot of tea, and smiled, and it came to Mrs Fanshawe suddenly that she could like this shivering half-frozen young girl who could still smile when from the looks of her there hadn't been much to smile at for a long, long time.

'You looking for a place?' She wasn't one for beating about the bush, nor for looking a gift horse in the mouth, nor for letting the grass grow underneath her feet, and besides all that, miracles *did* happen. Not that she had known many, but if it wasn't providence bringing this little lass to the door on a day when she had no idea when she was coming or going, then her name wasn't Milly Fanshawe.

'How old are you, love?' That was important that was, because the girl who had left the day before, running back to her mother in disgrace for dropping the ash-can on the drawing-room carpet, had been thirteen years old, earning two shillings a week for living in. For penny-pinching and downright meanness the mistress, Mrs Bleasdale, would be hard to beat.

'Two shillings and all found!' she had screamed at poor little Daisy Best. 'Money doesn't grow on trees, you know. That carpet cost a small fortune, and what am I supposed to do with those holes? Burned right through to the backing they are!'

So Daisy had gone, just one more village girl running down the gravel path with tears streaming from her eyes, with a chip on her shoulder for the rest of her life.

Jenny lifted her eyes from the steaming cup. 'I'm seventeen. Eighteen in August.' She glanced down at the wedding ring on her left hand, drawing Mrs Fanshawe's astonished attention to it for the first time. 'My husband died last week, and when I couldn't find the rent they turned me out, so I thought . . . I thought the best thing was to try and find a living-in job.'

Mrs Fanshawe glanced at the parcel on the floor by the table leg. 'And your things?'

'What things?'

'Your bits and pieces of furniture? You know?'

'Nothing.' Jenny stared straight ahead, avoiding Mrs Fanshawe's eyes. 'We were renting a furnished room, you see.'

'Aye. Aye well. . . .' Mrs Fanshawe hesitated, but only for a minute. Fishy, she decided. Proper fishy, but with a dinner party coming up the next evening, and only herself and the daily cleaning woman, and Daisy Best back with her mother, beggars couldn't be choosers, and best strike while the iron was hot. 'Stop there then while I go through and have a word. I'm not promising nothing, but we are, as it happens, short of a parlour-maid, who's willing to turn a hand with the pots.'

'And the fires, and the hot-water jugs, not forgetting the bottles, plus the linen and the beds,' she muttered to herself as she climbed the stairs and pushed open the door at the top. But a sign was a sign, and what was meant to be was meant to be, and if that young lass knocking at the door hadn't been meant to be, then she would never believe in nothing no more.

Mrs Fanshawe walked down the long winding passage-way along the strip of grey carpet flanked by borders of brown linoleum to the drawing-room door. If she had been a Catholic, which she wasn't heaven forbid, she would have crossed herself devoutly before she knocked three times and waited for the summons to step inside.

Just five minutes later she was knocking at the same door, this time with Jenny by her side, a Jenny divested of coat and hat, with her face polished clean by one of Mrs Fanshawe's kitchen towels, and her boots rubbed over with a hastily found floor cloth.

'You may go, Mrs Fanshawe. You can leave this to me.'

Bertha Bleasdale motioned Jenny to stand in front of her with a wave of an imperious hand. She was forty years old, roughly the same age as Jenny's mother, but because of her pampered life she looked at least ten years younger. She had a small face, small eyes, an exceptionally small mouth and a large beaked nose, and many years ago her own mother had worked in the Bleasdale cotton mill, but this was a matter never referred to. As far as Bertha Bleasdale was concerned she felt she had come from a far more aristocratic lineage. If she had cut her finger she would not have been in the least surprised if the blood had run blue. Her accent was what Jenny thought of as 'cut-glass', and only when she was moved to anger did the Lancashire dialect creep in, and her careful vowels revert to their original flatness. She considered anyone not in possession of wealth as being of the 'lower orders' and she had a sharp fidgety way of darting her small eyes up and down when speaking to those she thought of as her inferiors.

'Your name?'

Jenny recognized Mrs Bleasdale's sort at once. 'Stuck-up,' Mollie would have called her. Stuck-up, and putting on airs because she thought she was better than the working classes. Quickly she reminded herself that she was in no position to take offence, and bobbed a small but respectful curtsey.

'Jenny Waring, ma'am.' Her married name came awkwardly to her lips and she hoped that the haughty woman sitting on the huge chesterfield had not noticed.

'Age?'

'Seventeen. Going on eighteen, ma'am.'

'Previous experience?'

Jenny shook her head. 'Not in service, ma'am.'

'What in then, Waring?'

Jenny flinched at the abrupt use of her surname, then reminded herself that if she was to be a parlour-maid it was said to be the normal form of address. She reminded herself also that if she crossed swords with this unattractive woman she would be out again in the cold and the rain, knocking on doors like a beggar woman. She answered in what she hoped was a suitably humble tone of voice.

'I worked in a shop, ma'am.' She went on quickly before Mrs Bleasdale could ask in what kind of shop: 'But I gave that up when I got married, and since my husband died I – it is necessary for me to find a living-in place.'

Bertha Bleasdale found it hard to conceal the triumph darting from her small pebble-cold eyes. This was more like it. This was no mamby-pamby girl who would run back to her mother on the slightest pretext of being hard done to. This young woman with her white face and desperate eyes had nowhere to run to, if she was any judge. And with no previous experience, she would not realize that what she would be expected to do in the big draughty house far exceeded the duties of a parlour-maid. But she must not let her satisfaction show because this girl was no fool either. That much was obvious.

'What took your husband off?' Mrs Bleasdale asked the question in ringing tones, completely unaware that the phraseology was at total variance with the refinement of her tortured vowels.

'A heart ailment, ma'am.'

'Mm . . .' Mrs Bleasdale's mind was made up. As far as she was concerned the interview was over, but it would never do to let this girl think it was as easy as that. She fingered the brooch at her throat with a hand made vulgar with a crusting of rings. 'This is not a very big establishment, Waring. Just my husband and myself, and our daughter, Sarah.' Jenny was quick to notice the softening of her hard features as she spoke her daughter's name. 'Miss Sarah is upstairs at the moment resting in her room. She injured her leg in a fall from a horse three years ago. Not that she's a cripple, or anything like. She just needs extra taking care of.'

116

'She has a personal maid, ma'am?'

'Indeed not!' The tiny pursed up mouth almost disappeared. How many times had she told Mr Bleasdale that for appearances' sake if nothing else their daughter ought to have a maid of her own, only to have him throw back his head and slap his knee in disgust. 'Nay, lass, what would we be doing with another female around the house just to brush our Sarah's hair and tidy her stockings away? We've got Miss Fielding comes four days a month to sew, and Mrs Fanshawe to cook, not forgetting that woman from the village dashing about with her dust-pans and polishes every day, and a string of Daisies. Tha'll be telling me I need a man to fasten me boot laces for me one of these days! We're ordinary folk, Bertha, who just happen to have come into money through the mill. No good acting like Lady Muck, lass. Why I remember your mother sitting out on her upstairs window-sill cleaning the outsides, *and* stoning her flags. Let's not get carried away.'

'I think our last parlour-maid's aprons and caps will fit you, Waring. I take it you have dark dresses of your own?'

Jenny looked down at the brown serge dress, its hems thickly encrusted with drying mud, and remembered the good navy, folded neatly into the brown soggy paper parcel.

'I mostly wore jumpers and skirts in the shop, but I have enough, ma'am.'

Mrs Bleasdale nodded. 'When Miss Fielding, our sewing woman, comes next week we will get her to make you a black silk for when we entertain, and we can deduct sixpence a week from your wages for the material. Shall we say two shillings and all found?'

The interview was over, and on her way back to the kitchen Jenny almost bumped into a grey thin little woman down on her knees polishing the brown strips of linoleum, with a coarse sacking apron tied round her middle.

'She's taken you on, love?' The woman sat back on her heels and brushed a strand of dust-coloured hair away from

117

her face. 'Mrs Fanshawe's been telling me about you.' She smiled a wide toothless smile that instantly turned her head into a grinning gargoyle. '*He's* all right, and Miss Sarah's all right, but that one in there, she's a bad bugger. Wouldn't give the skin off her rice pudding to her starving grandma begging on her knees for it. You watch out for her, chuck, skenning faggot that she is.'

Jenny nodded, half smiled, and glanced back down the long corridor towards the closed door of the drawing-room, provoking the kneeling figure into a tinny cackle of amusement. 'Nay, don't fash yourself, chuck. Yon woman's as deaf as a doorpost, though catch her letting on. Thinks she's somebody she does, though there's them as knows different.'

At the other side of the kitchen door the smell of roasting meat caught Jenny so that she actually clutched at her middle and felt the bile rise from her empty stomach up into her mouth.

'Here now, you're not going to faint again, lass?' Mrs Fanshawe thumped the rolling-pin down on the table and stared at Jenny's white face with anxious concern.

'I'm hungry, that's all.' Jenny stared wide-eyed at the soft mound of raw pastry, controlling an urge to break a piece off and stuff it into her mouth. 'Hungry, that's all.'

The rolling-pin clattered to the floor, as with a sweep of a floury hand, Mrs Fanshawe made space for a plate, on which she placed a thick wedge of freshly-baked bread. A pot of liquid honey was pushed alongside, and the teapot raised to pour hot brown liquid into a pot a quarter full of milk and sugar. Jenny crammed the bread into her mouth, closed her eyes, then forgetful of her manners, raised the pot to her lips and inadvertently slurped the tea.

'Excuse me,' she said automatically, and took another over-sized bite of the bread.

'You're sure you're not expecting, lass?' Mrs Fanshawe had to ask, because it wouldn't be the first time she had taken on a girl only to see her belly swell underneath her pinny, before she'd hardly had time to get used to things.

She *wanted* this girl to stay; she *liked* her already. There was an honesty about her, even though the country-woman guessed she was keeping her mouth shut about a lot of things. Mrs Fanshawe was sick and tired to her soul of training village girls then seeing them depart in tears, their spirits broken by the mistress's tongue, and she might be wrong – though she didn't think she was wrong – but she had formed the impression that this one had spirit. Aye, and spirit was needed to stand up to the mistress. She would have left long ago if it weren't for her husband back from the Boer War these three years with a gammy leg and a shattered lung that made his every breath a living torture. There wasn't all that many places where a cook could set off home when the evening meal was prepared, and the two facts had forged an uneasy truce between her and the lady of the house, with her sharp tongue and her complaining hoot of a voice.

'I'm hungry, that's all.' Jenny's reply was more fierce than she had intended it to be, and if she felt sick then it was because she was stuffing herself too fast. It *had* to be. She would know in a few days, anyway, and if that one terrible night had given her a baby, then she would kill herself. She would have to; there would be nothing else for it. She fought the urge to push her chair back and rush out into the yard round the back to vomit away the food now lying uneasily in her stomach. She carried the plate over to the stone sink.

'Nay, leave that.' Mrs Fanshawe looked up from trimming the edges of a pie as the cleaning woman came into the kitchen, wiping her hands on her sacking apron. 'Nellie. Take our new Daisy up and show her her room. Aye, and take a jug of water up with you, Nellie.' She flattened a spare piece of pastry and with a few deft flicks of a knife, formed it into a decorative flower. 'Come down when you're ready, lass. If I've got everything going in here I can show you how Mrs Bleasdale likes the table set for lunch.'

'Not that tha'll ever suit *her*,' said Nellie, turning on a tap and filling a wide-mouthed enamel jug to the brim. 'If tha presented her ladyship with the crown jewels she would say there was summat wrong with them, the old cow.'

'That's enough, Nellie,' Mrs Fanshawe said automatically, glazing the pie with cold milk and a sprinkling of sugar.

On her way down from the attic room, with her hair brushed as flat as it would go, then piled high to fit underneath the white frilled cap, Jenny fastened the strings of Daisy's apron into a bow at the back, and was turning to go down the back stairs when she heard a voice calling to her.

'Hello? Could you come in here a moment please?'

The girl framed in the doorway of her room was of such startling beauty that Jenny thought at first it must be a trick of light. A sudden shaft of pale sunshine from the high landing window touched red curls to brilliance as they fell round Sarah Bleasdale's shoulders over a loosely held cream wrapper. Now she could understand the pride that had softened Mrs Bleasdale's hard features when she spoke her daughter's name, and her first thought as she turned and walked towards the beautiful girl was to wonder how on earth someone as plain as Mrs Bleasdale had produced such an exquisite creature.

'Miss Sarah?'

'And you must be the new Daisy?'

'Waring, Miss. Jenny Waring.'

They smiled at each other, openly appraising. This girl, Jenny calculated, must be about eighteen or nineteen years old with a skin more transparent than pale, as delicate as a white rose, with eyes that glinted green beneath heavy eyelids, fringed with lashes as long as spider's legs. This girl would never have suffered lumpy purple chilblains disfiguring the backs of her legs, nor hands that chapped red with the slicing up of great slabs of horse meat. Everything about her was soft and clean, as delicately etched as a cameo, and beside her Jenny felt like a great red-faced uncouth peasant, in spite of the satisfactory reflection she had seen of herself not five minutes before, with the white cap pinned on top of her dark curls with a black velvet bow.

'Have you come from the village, Jenny?' Sarah Bleasdale moved back into the room, walking with a noticeable limp which she concealed by taking slow deliberate steps. 'Mama said there was a new girl coming this morning – though I thought she said she was to be a Fanny, not a Jenny?'

'I'm from the town, Miss.' Jenny stood with her hands folded in front of her in an instinctively servile gesture, her eyes taking in the softly draped room with its brown carpet and the leaping fire sending sparks off the brass fire-irons. She had never dreamed a bedroom could look like this, could smell like this, and feel like this, as if everything in it was seen and softened through a film of gauze.

'I see.' Sarah limped over to the dressing-table set in the window, sat down and lifted her hands underneath her hair, sweeping it up on top of her head. 'Do you think you could pass me the biggest of my combs, Jenny? I must get dressed. Mama worries if I'm not down before ten o'clock. If I am late she always thinks it's because I'm not well . . . oh, thank you, Jenny. Are you sure I'm not keeping you from anything? Daisy used to come up and do my hair about this time.' She handed the comb back to Jenny and sat like a child, admiring herself in the mirror as she waited to have her hair pinned and combed into place. 'I can't tell you how pleased Mama will be that you've come today. It's my betrothal party tomorrow evening. Five extra for dinner. I'm to accompany Mr Ibbotson on the piano. He always sings the same two songs. "Alice, Where Art Thou?" and "The Lost Chord". With *great* expression.'

She prattled on, and meeting the green eyes in the

mirror Jenny saw that Miss Sarah was holding a conversation with herself. She wasn't being over friendly with a domestic servant, or trying to make the new maid feel at home, she was addressing no one but herself, enchanting herself as she pouted and shrugged her shoulders, watching her own reaction to what she was saying. Miss Sarah was like a pretty child, a spoilt child who has been denied nothing from the minute she first opened those strangely limpid green eyes.

'Mr Ibbotson could have been an opera singer if he hadn't gone into law like his father and his grandfather. He acts when he sings, you know, like this. . . .' She flung out a white arm, and opened her mouth as if sustaining a long note as Jenny patted the last curl into place.

'There, Miss. Will that do?' Jenny turned, and for the first time saw a little brown dog asleep at the foot of the bed.

'My dress, Jenny. Button me into my dress before I go down. It's there on the bed. My fiancé is calling this morning, that's why I'm wearing this dress. He likes it because he says it matches my eyes. Do *you* think it matches my eyes, Jenny?' Then, without waiting for an answer: 'That's my fiancé there, in the silver frame on the table by the tallboy. He owns High Trees, the big farm over at the other side of the long meadows. Farms it all by himself ever since his father died, and his brother got killed in that awful war fighting the Boers. They used to hunt then but all the hunters have gone now.' She sighed and stuck out a leg. 'That's how I got this, jumping a hedge, with Paul urging me on when he should have known better. I ended up in the ditch with my horse on top of me. Paul shot Maybelle personally, they told me afterwards when they carried me back to the house. Poor Maybelle, she was a lovely horse, in spite of her legs not being all they should have been. Like mine are now.'

The light voice was prattling on, but Jenny was learning already that there was no need to listen. No answering remarks were needed, or even wanted, and Miss Sarah was too busy smoothing down the waist of her green velvet dress to notice that the new maid was staring at the photograph of a young man in full dress army uniform as if she could not believe the evidence of her eyes.

Paul Tunstall, the tall man with the shining fair hair and the silvery grey eyes, the arrogant teasing man coming twice into the shop in a week, laughing *at* her but not with her. Jenny bobbed a respectful curtsey and moved towards the door. Would he recognize her? And if he did would he give her away? Would Mrs Bleasdale send her away when she found that her new parlour-maid, Waring, in her fancy apron and frilled cap, had on occasions trundled the cat-meat cart round the streets herself? Not, as Jenny had intended her to surmise, served behind the counter of a clean decent shop, measuring ribbons along the rule set into the counter, and sending the change pinging along the overhead wires to the lady cashier in the cash-box.

She wasn't to find out that day; she soon realized there was no time to find anything out that day. With a sacking apron over her white starched frills she was set at the sink to wash the breakfast dishes, and the lunch dishes, the fine bone china teacups. To clean the silver, the *best* silver in readiness for the dinner party the following evening, to help Mrs Fanshawe prepare three different puddings, and stuff the turkey and the goose, and set them in their roasting dishes ready to go into the oven. To scrape the vegetables and cover them with water, polish the glasses, fold the starched damask napkins into mitre shapes, fetch the delicate egg-shell-thin coffee cups from the display cabinet in the dining-room and wash them in the sink with a towel laid in the bottom.

Her legs ached, her back ached, and when she served what Mrs Fanshawe said was a simple meal that evening, her hand trembled so much as she passed the gravy-boat that her new master, Mr Bleasdale, took it from her and gave her a wink.

'No need to get nervous, lass. Just take it steady and you'll be all right. Rome wasn't built in a day, tha knows.'

For a startled moment Jenny thought Mrs Bleasdale was going to correct her husband's slip into dialect. Her nose twitched and her pointed chin jerked upwards, but it was at Jenny she directed her spite.

'That will do, Waring, and tomorrow you will have to be quicker than this, *much* quicker, and I hope you can do something with your hands, they are enough to put people off their food. Try some starch powder or something.'

'Yes, ma'am.' Jenny left the room to rush back to the kitchen, shaking her hands as if she could shake the swollen chilblains away.

'Daisy always used to do the soup plates while she waited for them to ring for the pudding,' Mrs Fanshawe said kindly, spearing a navy-blue felt hat on top of the puffed out hair. 'I'm off now, and don't forget Miss Sarah's hot milk before she goes to bed. No skin to be seen, mind and a teaspoon of sugar.'

'And Mr and Mrs Bleasdale?' Jenny plunged her red hands into the hot water and soda and started on the soup spoons. 'What do they have last thing?'

'What *they* have comes out of a bottle,' said Mrs Fanshawe, taking a basket down from a peg behind the door and nodding an encouraging goodbye. 'Just make sure you get rid of the glasses before they come down in the morning, but I'll be here before then. All things being equal,' she added, closing the door behind her.

The dining-room bell jingled out before the cook's wide behind had waddled down the side path towards the paddock gate, and Jenny wiped her hands hastily, then picked up the tray with the apple pie and the jug of custard set out.

Oh no, there had been no time to worry about what Miss Sarah's fiancé's reaction would be when he recognized her tomorrow. Though Jenny knew what Mrs Bleasdale's reaction would be if he said something like, 'Ah, the girl from the cat-meat shop!'

She would probably faint dead away. 'Knowing *her*,' Jenny muttered, unconsciously imitating Nellie's withering tone.

7

Jenny's first glimpse of Paul Tunstall was as she carried in the huge tray of hors d'oeuvres, with the anchovies threaded together in basket-weave style, the olives layered to resemble fish scales, and the radishes and nuts splayed out like rays from the sun.

Jenny backed into the room, balancing the tray on one hip, hoping that her frilled cap would stay in place on the hair she had washed with green soft soap the night before. She had gone to bed long before it was dry, and had thanked God fervently for bringing her to this place, adding an impassioned plea not to let Paul Tunstall recognize her and give her away.

'Ah, the cat-meat girl!' she kept on imagining him saying, throwing back his fair head and laughing his uninhibited laugh. 'Jenny, the cat-meat girl. What on earth is she doing here?'

He was leaning over the back of Miss Sarah's chair, whispering in her ear in a teasing, loving gesture.

'Thank you, Waring.' Mrs Bleasdale was wearing a blue shiny dress cut low in front to show an ugly wrinkled cleavage. Ear-rings sparkled in her ears, and her hair was caught back at the front with an equally sparkling brooch.

Jenny kept her eyes down and her back to the loving couple framed by the long red curtains at the far window. 'Sir?' she said, and a thick-set man with a florid complexion and a leonine head covered with clustering black curly hair, reached out a hand and took a water biscuit topped with threaded anchovies.

Now was the time for her to turn around and offer the tray to Miss Sarah. Now was the time when recognition must surely come.

'Thank you, Jenny.' Miss Sarah's voice was soft with gentle understanding. 'This is our new Daisy,' she said, and the silver-light eyes of the man behind the chair stared straight into Jenny's wide and startled gaze.

For a moment Jenny's heart stopped beating, as holding her breath she waited for what must surely come.

But there was nothing in Paul Tunstall's eyes but a polite acceptance as he reached for an olive. 'Thank you, New Daisy,' he said, biting into it with his strong white teeth.

'Waring!' Mrs Bleasdale's voice startled Jenny so that she turned too quickly, caught her foot in the Bengal tiger rug, tried desperately to regain her balance, and impeded by the weight of the heavy tray, fell full length, upturning the hors d'oeuvres onto the carpet.

Radishes bounced in all directions, fishy biscuits lay face downwards on the dog-rose pattern on the green carpet and right in front of Jenny's nose a squashed olive embedded itself on the whiskery jaw of the Bengal tiger.

Mrs Bleasdale leaped to her feet, small eyes darting malevolent shafts of fury as Jenny crawled about replacing the ruined food. Although her anger was held fiercely under control Jenny could feel it reaching out, made all the more terrible by its enforced silence.

'Take it away, Waring.' Her voice was toneless, and as Jenny struggled to her feet with the tray, the man with the florid complexion walked to the door and held it open for her.

'You missed this,' he whispered, depositing a mangled biscuit on the tray, then he added: 'Don't worry, lass. It's not the end of the world, not by no means.'

'That would be Mr Ibbotson.' Mrs Fanshawe, hot and

flustered with the effort of having everything ready at the same time, took a well-crisped goose from the oven and poked at the glaze with an exploratory finger. 'He's the biggest noise there is round here. Justice of the Peace and God knows what else. If he's on your side it won't matter. A proper gentleman he is, not a jumped-up 'un, like her. Come on, love, there's too much to do to worrit yourself. It's all her fault expecting the two of us to see to everything. Oh, I know Nellie overheard her ranting and raving to him about wanting a butler, but what good would that have done? It's another pair of hands in the kitchen what's wanted, and someone to help with the serving when she wants to show off.'

'She'll tell me to go tomorrow.' Jenny stared at the enormous soup tureen waiting for the thick vegetable soup to be poured into it, and imagined herself hurling it into a silken lap as she passed it round the table. Mrs Bleasdale had told her during the long hectic frantic day's preparations that formal dinners at Cedar House were served à la Russe.

'That means passed round, Waring,' she had said. 'Like they do down in London.'

'Bugger London!' Mrs Fanshawe had remarked, her behind stuck up in the air as she basted the joints. 'Be telling us to call everything by their French names next. Blanc-Mange à la Vanille to follow. Silly old faggot!'

'She'll tell me to go tomorrow,' Jenny's mind kept repeating as she presented Mr Bleasdale with the goose to carve, then dashed back to the kitchen for the vegetable dishes. She knew that she had learned quickly, but there was a terrible moment when she had to be reminded in ice-cold tones to fetch the gravy-boat, and another when the Nougat Almond Cake almost shattered its towering dome as she pushed open the heavy dining-room door.

When it was all over and Mrs Fanshawe had gone on her way, explaining that she'd stayed far longer than she should as it was, Jenny fastened the coarse pinafore over the starched frills of the white best apron, and stared with dismay at the pile of dishes crowding every single surface of the kitchen.

Her hands stung as she plunged them into the hot water laced with washing soda; her eyes stung as she fought back the tears. It didn't help when a voice she guessed must belong to the kindly Mr Ibbotson floated down the long passageway booming out 'The Lost Chord' with a roaring dramatic intensity.

'It may be that Death's bright Angel will speak in that chord again. It may be that only in Heaven I shall hear that grand Amen!'

Jenny reached for a cluster of soup spoons and thrust them into the water. Well, that made sense. *Her* grand Amen would come when everyone had gone home. Perhaps Mrs Bleasdale would not even wait until tomorrow. Maybe like Agnes she would close the door and leave her to walk away into the dark winter's night, clutching the pathetic brown paper parcel of her belongings. . . .

It had all been too sudden. There were moments when she could not believe she was the same girl who had trundled that loathsome cart round the back streets, stood for hours behind the counter of the little poky shop, married Bob Waring, been savaged by him on her wedding night, because that was the right word for it. *Savaged.* Prayed with Agnes round the bed of old Mr Waring, stood outside her own front door and heard Harry Howarth yelling and shouting at her mother. Found this place . . . oh, dear God. All that in the space of a few weeks. . . .

'Ah, ha! The girl with the laughing eyes!'

Jenny whirled around, dripping washing-up water all over Nellie's clean floor. 'Oh, sir. You frightened the life out of me.' She turned back so as to say what must be said without looking at him.

'I'm grateful that you didn't let on about having seen me before.'

'Why?' There was the same teasing smile in the deep

voice. 'Why, Jenny? Does Mrs B think you dropped in here from nowhere?'

A knife was scoured vigorously. 'No, sir, but I never told her I worked in a cat-meat shop.'

'You didn't?'

'No, sir.'

'Then where *did* you say you worked, bright-eyed Jenny?'

'I let her think something like in lingerie, sir.'

'*Corsets*, Jenny?'

There was no mistaking the chuckle in Paul Tunstall's voice, and Jenny bent her head lower over the sink, wondering if blushing spread right round to the back of the neck.

'Tell me something, Jenny.' Paul moved to the front of the table so that she felt him behind her, sensed that if he stretched out a hand he could touch her. She stiffened and picked up a fluted finger-bowl from the side.

'Did the meticulous Mrs B not ask you for a reference?'

'No, sir.' Jenny rinsed a second bowl and willed him to go away. 'I think she was in a bit of a spot because the new girl, the one after Daisy, hadn't turned up.'

'And how then, did *you* come to be wandering so far from home? Come on now, Jenny. You owe me the truth, now. Miss Sarah has taken a fancy to you, and if you're to be taking care of her, then things must be straight between you and me, don't you agree? For instance . . . you weren't wearing a wedding ring the last time I saw you, I'd swear to that. What did you go and do? Marry the little man with the weasel face lurking in the shadows of that abominable shop? And if so, where is he now? Jenny? Where is he *now*?'

From the drawing-room Mr Ibbotson's ripe deep voice soared into song once more. 'One year back this even, and thou wert by my side,' he lamented.

'Come on. No more lies. Just the truth, Jenny, the absolute truth.'

He wasn't prepared for what he saw when she wiped her hands on a towel, laid it down again and turned to face him. The bonny laughing look he had remembered from the day this girl faced him in the dark interior of the grimy shop had disappeared, leaving in its place an expression of haunting sadness, made all the more melancholy by the plaintive song sung now in a baritone whisper.

'I married a man I had known for a long time, sir. I married him because I had to get away from home when my step-father – when he tried to do something. The man I married was a good man, a Chapel man, with a voice like that, sir, that one we can hear now. But my husband was also a cruel man with a twisted mind, and I found that out the day I married him.' She held her head up, tilting her chin, heedless now of the blush she knew was creeping up from her throat. If telling Miss Sarah's man the truth was the only way she would be allowed to stay here, then the truth she would tell, and in some way, some strange way she could not understand, it was as if she was standing outside herself, hearing herself confess. As though there was a single spotlight on her on a stage, with the audience rapt and attentive before her. Like the times Harry Howarth had ranted and raved and she had stood up to him. Like that; aye, just like that.

'He, my husband, fell down in the street on the way home from work the next day, struck his head on a stoop and died. . . .'

'You're making all this up, Jenny. You have to be.'

'No, I'm not, sir. An' the day after the funeral I went to my mother's house, thinking mebbe I could go back there to live, but I never got no further than the front door. I heard my step-father going on again, and I knew I would rather die than live there. So I went back to my husband's house, but his sister had put my things outside and locked the door, so I walked, then got a lift in a trap, and found this place, an' there's only one thing I've left out, and that is that when my step-father tried it on with me,

I went for him with the poker and nearly finished him off.'

There were tears glistening in her brown eyes, so that they were bright again the way he remembered them, but she brushed them angrily away with the back of a reddened hand, turned her back on him once again and continued with the washing-up.

'Now, sir. Are you going to tell Mrs Bleasdale all that?' Her voice trembled. 'Because if you do she'll have me out of here quick, and if you don't, then I'll work hard and look after your Miss Sarah for you. . . .'

'I'm going back, Jenny.' Paul was Captain Paul Tunstall at that moment, speaking to his men, sure of himself, and aware of their vulnerability. 'I have not heard a single word of what has been said in here, and if Miss Sarah asks me where I've been I'll say I went to look for the Alice that Mr Ibbotson is still singing about. Right?'

'Yes, sir.' Jenny whispered the words, but he had gone.

'Where have you been, Paul?' Sarah Bleasdale's beautiful eyes were wistful as she acknowledged the polite applause, and nodded acceptance of Ben Ibbotson's thanks for accompanying him so sensitively. She knew she ought not to act so possessively, her mama had warned her about that, but she still found it hard to believe that this eligible man had asked her to be his wife. Since coming back from the war and settling down at High Trees, living alone, apart from the servants, Paul Tunstall had been in great demand socially for miles around. Mama acted as though they were of equal standing in the county, but Sarah knew different. Paul, with his inherited wealth and his determination to bring the house and the farmlands back to their former glory, with his off-hand arrogance and his way of laughing at things not meant to be laughed at, had set hearts fluttering for miles around. And yet he had chosen her. Why, she asked herself, sometimes waking up in the night to stare into the darkness? Why?

'Out,' he said, in reply to her whispered question, helping her up from the piano stool and leading her over to the high-winged chair by the window. 'I don't care for men singing, especially ballads,' he whispered in her ear. 'Marching songs with a tankard of ale held in their fists, but not love-sick songs, especially about a mythical Alice who wasn't worth the bother.'

There, he was making her laugh again, teasing her out of her petulance. Sarah leaned her head back against the brocaded chair showing the long lovely line of her throat, and Pootsy, the little Pekinese, scrambled up onto her lap.

Paul got up from the arm of her chair and walked over to talk to her father, saying something that made Mr Bleasdale slap a fat knee in protest while his face exploded into laughter. It was no good, Paul refused to take anything seriously. He had been like that for as long as she could remember. Long ago when she was a little girl and he had come home from Cambridge for the long summer vacation, striding about, with a dog always at his heels, his Norfolk jacket covered in hairs, and his breeches torn at the knees.

'You ought to come out with the hounds instead of just hacking about,' he had said the year before he joined the army. 'You'd learn what riding was then. You're not bad, you know. For a girl.'

Sarah glanced down at the long skirt of her velvet dress, hiding the ugly caliper on her leg, seeing in her mind's eye the hedge coming up to meet her, her horse hesitating for just too long before. . . .

'Are you all right, dear?'

Mrs Ibbotson came to sit beside her, her smooth serene face anxious beneath its cloud of ash-grey hair. 'My husband does tend to go right through his repertoire, especially when he is accompanied by such a sympathetic pianist. He hasn't tired you too much, my dear?'

'No, I enjoyed playing for him, truly.' Sarah smiled

reassurance, and even as she smiled, her eyes followed the tall handsome man she was to marry round the room. She remembered the way he had proposed to her soon after he came home for good from the army; the way he had put his arms round her and held her close so that the sharp little insignia on his uniform jacket had pricked against her face. She recalled the look of horror on his face when he first noticed her ungainly limp, and heard with remembered shame her mother telling him that in a way she held him responsible for encouraging her daughter to jump a horse that was never intended to do more than canter down the country lanes.

Oh yes, her mother had smiled as she said it, but Paul had tightened his mouth, and looked at her mother as if he could kill her. And the next week he had proposed.

Now the hunters at High Trees had been sold, the local pack had split up, as farming the land took priority, and Paul supervised the running of his lands with a seriousness that surprised all who had known him before.

'When is the wedding to be?' Mrs Ibbotson's own eyes were following Paul's smiling progress round the room with a speculative gaze. 'Sometime in the summer, dear?'

'The first week in May.' Sarah clenched her hands in the folds of her skirt, tense without knowing why. 'The invitations go out next week.'

'Plenty of time to decide what to wear.' Mrs Ibbotson smiled and walked over to talk clothes with Mrs Bleasdale and Mrs Entwistle, a small plump woman with the bones of her stays showing through the tight silk of her beruffled black dress.

The company did not stay late. The Entwistles and the Ibbotsons lived no more than a short distance away, and Paul Tunstall thought nothing of taking the short cut to High Trees over the dark fields, then along the river path, skirting the bluebell wood, and entering his own lands by climbing the five-barred gate into the ploughed field.

Jenny, her face beneath the frilled cap creased into lines of a terrible anxiety, handed out cloaks and hats in the hall, avoiding Mrs Bleasdale's cold eyes, and Paul Tunstall's mischievous wink.

Miss Sarah went straight upstairs, holding onto the banister rail, placing her good leg firmly on each step, then dragging the injured one stiffly behind her. Mr Bleasdale told Jenny that he would see to the lamps, and she went back into the kitchen to await the scene she knew must surely come.

Everything had been tidied away, the big iron pan set ready for the next morning's breakfast porridge, the stone floor washed over, and the fire banked down for the night. All done to Mrs Fanshawe's explicit instructions, so that all Jenny wanted to do now was to climb the back stairs to her room and drop into her bed, close her eyes and sleep. It seemed to her that if she slept for a week she would still not have rested enough. She had only remembered just in time to remove the sacking apron before going out into the hall, and it was the first thing Mrs Bleasdale saw lying over the back of a chair when she swept into the kitchen, nose first. Her small eyes glinted dangerously.

'What's this?' she asked, picking up the coarse apron and holding it out in front of her as if the very sight of it had mortally offended her.

'One of Nellie's aprons, ma'am. Mrs Fanshawe told me to be sure to fasten it round me before I did the pots, and the floor.'

'The dishes, Waring. Not the pots.'

'Sorry, ma'am.'

Bertha Bleasdale felt the evening had gone off rather well. The food had been praised, and seeing Mr Ibbotson standing there with one hand on the piano as he sang to Sarah's accompaniment had made her swell almost visibly with pride. Never had she thought the day would come when the Ibbotsons would grace her drawing-room. Never. It might be true that Mr Bleasdale had the mill, but it wasn't the same as having a profession. Mr Ibbotson was a solicitor and a company director, a gentleman who thought nothing of spending over a hundred pounds on a painting, even though it had been done by a Dutch artist at that. Mr Ibbotson had shares, and belonged to a club in Manchester, and sometimes wore a grey top hat. He went down to London too, staying in Mayfair, though he always said he was glad to get back to where there was air you could breathe and a wind that whistled instead of sighed.

She drew herself up to her full height of five feet one, and putting all thoughts of Mr Ibbotson firmly behind her, fixed the girl standing in front of her with a malevolent eye.

'What have you to say, Waring?'

'About tripping and spilling the food off the tray, ma'am?'

'About being *careless*, Waring! Apart from the shame and the embarrassment of what happened, I hope you realize that the stains in the drawing-room carpet will never come off? Do you realize why that tiger rug was there in the first place?' She thumped with a jewelled hand on the wide table. 'To cover burn marks caused by Daisy Best dropping hot ashes onto it! What's wrong with you girls? Is it because your feet's so big that you keep tripping over them?' She glanced down at the pointed tips of her satin slippers peeping from beneath her taffeta dress. 'And that dress is too tight for you, Waring. It shows your shape.'

Jenny shifted her weight from one foot to the other. She was so tired that she almost wished Mrs Bleasdale would get on with it and give her the sack if that was what she intended to do.

'This dress was made for Daisy, ma'am.' She spoke without thinking, sticking up for herself as usual, stupidly forgetting in her exhaustion that the only way she could hope to keep her place was to kowtow to this unpleasant woman. Sticking up for yourself got you nowhere, and as

Mrs Fanshawe had warned her, she knew what side her bread was buttered on, if she had any sense.

'You cheeky girl!' Mrs Bleasdale pounded the table again. 'You come creeping to my door, from goodness knows where, then when you get taken on without as much as a reference from nobody – on *trust*, Waring, you have the nerve to answer me back!' Her eyes, slightly crossed, like pig's eyes, Jenny thought, glowed like twin black coals. 'Not a word. Not a single word of apology for what you did to my carpet, and I saw you making eyes at Mr Ibbotson when he opened the door for you, so don't think I didn't. A man like that, why, you're not fit to get down on your knees and chew his shoelaces!' She stalked majestically to the door. 'You can go now and get them marks off my carpet, and if there's as much as a single spot in the morning then you go straight upstairs and pack your things and go.' She turned to deliver her parting shot. 'Back to where you come from, and in my opinion that's the gutter!'

Jenny waited until the door had swung to, then sitting down on one of the hard upright chairs, she dropped her face into her hands. She was too tired and too angry to cry, and when the door opened once again, she stared at her mistress's spiteful little face with a completely blank expression, before struggling to her feet in anticipation of another tirade.

'An' you can use a candle, Waring. Mr Bleasdale has seen to the gas in there, and I don't want you dripping taper wax all over everything.'

'Yes, ma'am.' Jenny choked on the words, but they had to be said. 'I'm sorry, ma'am. I wasn't careful enough, but I'll know next time.'

'If there *is* a next time, Waring. Don't go counting no chickens, you hear me?'

Wearily Jenny pushed the big black kettle back over the still glowing coals, reached for a pail under the sink, and found dry cloths and a bar of soap. Then, when the water was hot enough, she held the candlestick high, and carried the pail of soapy water through into the drawing-room. It wasn't easy to see what she was doing in the flickering light, but she rubbed with the soapy cloth then dried with the clean one until she was reasonably certain that the sticky marks had disappeared.

Dizzy with tiredness she washed in the kitchen to save carrying water all the way upstairs, just her hands and face for once, and never mind the rest. If she got to sleep right away she could have almost five hours' rest, and that should be enough for anybody, she told herself hopefully.

She was creeping along the landing towards the flight of stairs, leading to her attic room, when she heard her name being called in Miss Sarah's soft and rather breathless voice:

'Jenny? Can you come in here a minute?'

Sarah was in bed with her green velvet gown thrown anyhow over a chair, and the ugly contraption of leather and iron propped against the stool of her dressing-table. There was a special light fixed to the bed-end so that once in bed she could put it out herself, but it was on now, shining down into the lovely oval face with the emerald green eyes staring anxiously at Jenny.

'You won't go away, will you, Jenny? I heard Mama shouting downstairs. She always shouts at the servants, that's why they never stay for long. She, Mama, is not used to servants, she wasn't brought up with them, but she doesn't mean it, not really.' As she pushed herself up in the bed the glorious red-gold hair tumbled down over her shoulders. 'Please don't go, Jenny. I like you. You're different from the others. I want us to be friends.'

Jenny glanced behind as if expecting Mrs Bleasdale to appear. 'You mustn't say that, Miss Sarah. I can never be your friend. It wouldn't be right, and besides it's not up to me whether I go or stay. Your mother is the one to decide, you know that.'

The green eyes glinted feverishly. 'Do what she tells you, Jenny. Do everything she says and don't answer back.

Promise? You can go when I get married, but please, please, stay till then. I *need* someone to talk to, Jenny. Oh, I'm older than you, I know, but you're the first person, the very first person I find I can talk to. Papa is kind, but when he isn't at the mill he's working on his papers here, and Mama doesn't know how frightened I am.'

Jenny moved closer to the bed. 'Of what, Miss Sarah?'

'Of getting married, Jenny.' She glanced at the wide gold band on Jenny's left hand. 'You've been married, even if it was only for a short while, and there are things . . .' She looked over to where the caliper stood propped against the embroidered stool. 'He's never seen . . . he doesn't realize.' Tears suddenly filled her eyes and flowed down the smooth cheeks. 'He, Paul, he makes a joke of everything, but will he be able to make a joke of that?'

'Oh, Miss Sarah.' Jenny put the candlestick down on the bedside table, and forgetting her place entirely, came to the bed and took Sarah's hand in her own, and even in the moment of compassion she noticed the difference between them. Sarah's hands were milk-white and smooth, with the nails buffered like pearls, whilst her fingers were puffed out with chilblains, and rough from the harsh soda water.

'I'll stay if she'll let me, Miss Sarah. I have to stay, because I have nowhere else to go.' She smiled into the older girl's anguished face. 'Needs must, Miss Sarah, needs bloody must.'

She used the swear word deliberately, and sighed with relief as it had the desired effect. Like a child who is given her own way, the tears stopped and the dimples came and went at the corners of Sarah's mouth as she smiled.

'Oh, Jenny. You were meant to come here, you know that, don't you?' she said.

Up in her room Jenny lay back and stared up at the sloping ceiling. It was a funny thing but Miss Sarah didn't know her fiancé at all. Laugh he might do on occasions, but underneath he could be as soft and understanding as the next one. He had proved that, hadn't he?

'Please God, don't let Mr Waring have given me a baby,' she whispered, her hand on her stomach, then before she could say her usual prayer was fast asleep.

8

'Mrs Bleasdale. I can assure you that the motor car being delivered to me next week will take Sarah quite safely to Lytham St Annes for our honeymoon. For heaven's sakes, Mrs Bleasdale! It has *brakes*, and that's more than you can say for a horse!'

'How dare you try to tell me that a horse doesn't have brakes, Mr Tunstall! Hasn't my child suffered enough through you encouraging her to jump long before she was ready? And now you want to take her in one of those loud explosive things that are scaring decent folks off the roads! I won't allow it!'

'*You* won't allow it, Mrs Bleasdale?'

Paul's voice was quiet and controlled, but Jenny, polishing the hall table outside the drawing-room door, heard it as clearly as if it had been the crack of a whip-lash.

Nellie had sent word she was staying at home for a week to nurse her elderly mother who had fallen downstairs, leaving Jenny to add the cleaning of the big house to all her other duties.

There was to be no baby as a result of her brief marriage, and when she thought about Bob Waring now it was to find she had almost forgotten his face. In the two months she had been at Cedar House, she had neither asked for, nor been given any time off, and she was waiting for the right time to approach her mistress with a request that she might be allowed to pay a visit to the town to see her mother.

But this morning was obviously not the time.

'She's still my daughter, Mr Tunstall! An' when she's married to you, then she's *still* my daughter! It's not a bit of good you pretending to yourself that you're marrying a normal girl, because Sarah needs caring for, an' resting, not wrapping up in a silly veil to keep her face from the dust flying up from one of them contraptions. I say again, if you can't take Sarah away decently in a carriage, or even on the train from Preston – I have no objection to that – then she's not going, and that's my final word!'

'We'll see about that, Mrs Bleasdale!'

The drawing-room door was banged open as Paul flung himself out. His usually pleasant expression was distorted with anger, and his right hand clenched his riding-crop as if he held it ready to lash out at the nearest object in his way. Jenny shrank back against the wall as Mrs Bleasdale's voice rang out like a clarion call.

'For two pins I'll stop the wedding! I can, you know, you young varmint! Sarah will listen to me rather than you, make no mistake about that! You might be able to talk her into most things, but when it comes to what matters it's me what she'll listen to. You persist in driving her in that contraption you're getting and I'll stop the wedding, see if I don't!'

Ignoring Jenny standing with a tin of Mansion polish in one hand and a duster in the other, Paul turned suddenly and strode back into the room.

'Oh, no you won't do that, Mrs Bleasdale. Not now half the county has got invitations, and you've had a fine new dress sent up from London. Besides, if *I* don't marry Sarah, then who will?'

Jenny gasped, and ran down the hall, through the swing door and into the kitchen. She could not believe she had heard Mr Paul say what he had just said. Not him. Arrogant he might be, and rude, downright rude on occasions, teasing and making fun all the time, but he was never cruel. And that last remark had been real cruel. Inferring that nobody would marry poor Miss Sarah with her damaged leg but him.

'The mistress is carrying on something terrible,' she told Mrs Fanshawe, who was busy lifting the fish-kettle onto the range. 'She says she will call the wedding off if Mr Paul insists on driving Miss Sarah away in his new motor car.'

'Not her.' Mrs Fanshawe passed a long-handled knife to Jenny. 'Give that a bit of a sharpen on the back step, love. She's cock-a-hoop on account of her daughter marrying into the Tunstall family. He was the youngest by a long chalk, was Mr Paul. He has a married sister down south married to a lord, and a brother living in foreign parts, not forgetting the poor lad killed in South Africa. His mother died when he was away fighting, and his father not long after, and Mr Paul came back with nowt in his fingers – no profession tha' knows. He was a bit wild when he was away at Cambridge, they say, then going straight in the army didn't give him much of a chance to make owt of himself. But Mr Paul has more than brass to his name. He's got breeding, like them horses in his stables. That's more than what you can say for her ladyship.'

After Jenny had sharpened the knife she went out into the garden to bring the washing in. It was freak weather for late April. Hot and sultry, with bluebells juicily blue over the fence where the garden backed onto a wooded copse. There were cool ferns and cushions of moss, and it was all so different from the grey streets and the little houses with rows of washing blowing up and catching the soot-blackened walls.

And yet she knew she had to go back, and soon, to see what was happening in the dusty house where her mother dragged herself wearily about, weeping as if her insides were a well that would never run dry.

'Jenny Waring! Stop dreaming, and talk to me.'

She turned round to see Paul Tunstall standing behind her, his mouth set in a grim line and his eyes narrowed in anger. He held his riding whip in one hand, swishing it against the beige cord of his breeches.

'Oh! Yes, Mr Tunstall?' Jenny smiled at him. She had become used to him seeking her out when he came to the house. He made her laugh, and yet today there was no laughter in the silver-light eyes. He was looking at her as if she was on an equal footing with him, as if she were a friend he had come to confide in. He motioned with the whip to a felled tree trunk, sat down himself and patted a place beside him.

She glanced back at the house. 'I'll be in bother if the mistress catches me.'

He grimaced. 'To hell with the mistress, Jenny. You heard what went on just now. Why did Miss Sarah not tell me yesterday that she was going with Mrs Entwistle to buy yet more dresses and fancy hats? I'd never have come over had I known.' He spoke with none of his usual flippancy. 'Miss Sarah talks to you, Jenny. She confides in you, and don't deny it because she tells me. You're probably the only true friend she has, the only friend she is allowed to have with that snake of a mother swallowing her whole as if she were a frightened rabbit.'

'You ought not to be talking to me like this, sir. Not with me being just a servant and everything. It's not right.' Jenny glanced at him nervously, then back to the house.

'Blast what's right and proper!' Paul put a brown hand on her arm, gripping so that she felt the nails dig into her flesh. 'When you've been where I've been and seen what I've seen you don't bother about what's right and what's proper! You're a *girl*, like Sarah, aren't you? Made of flesh and blood, and with thoughts of your own? I had a scout out there during the war. He followed me across the veld and when he spoke to me he called me "Baas". He was as black as coal and he could neither read nor write, but he was my *friend*, Jenny Waring. His Zulu talk was hard for me to understand, but he saved my life that black boy. He stepped in front of me when a Boer scout raised his rifle, then he died there in my arms. And the ground was too hard for me to bury him, Jenny, so I had to leave him there to be pecked to a bloody mess by the birds. And you talk to me about what is right and proper!'

The fair eyebrows were drawn angrily together. 'You've got to make Miss Sarah understand that she must stand up to her mother. She *has* to, because even when we're married we're still no more than a pony trot away. She hardly ever starts a conversation with me that isn't a repetition of what her mother says, what her mother thinks. Has she no mind of her own, Jenny Waring?'

Jenny was so conscious of the hand on her arm that she had to look away towards the bluebell copse to stop herself from staring fixedly at it. The physical contact was sending shivers of a frightening response through her. She could feel the violence in him, sense the despair, and in spite of what he had just said she knew that the world was still divided into 'them' and 'us', with no possible point of contact between them.

'I will speak with Miss Sarah,' she said softly. 'I will put it to her carefully that her mother – that the sun doesn't rise and set on what her mother thinks. But she, Miss Sarah, is very young in her ways, if you will forgive me for saying so, sir. She has had a very sheltered upbringing, and since her accident she relies on other people to think for her.' Jenny hesitated, picking her words with care. 'That doesn't mean she can't think for herself, but here, in this house, it's hard to assert yourself. Once you've taken her away, things will be different.'

'They'd better be.' Paul took his hand away and stood up so that she was staring down at his shiny leather riding boots. 'You are a wise lass, Jenny Waring. So very wise for your age, and very very sweet. Do you know that?'

He walked away from her, and it was a few minutes before Jenny raised her head, and the first thing she did was to push back her sleeve and stare down at the marks on her arm where his strong fingers had been. He was the first man to have touched her since Bob Waring, and then the violence had made her want to scream. This time she wanted to cry. For some reason she wanted to leave the basket of washing on the grass, climb the low fence over into the shade of the little wood, and throw herself down and weep until she was drained and empty, filled with nothing but a languorous silence she did not understand.

'Dear God, forgive me,' she whispered, not knowing for what she was asking to be forgiven.

'You can have a weekday off after the wedding, Waring,' Mrs Bleasdale said when Jenny asked to be allowed to pay a visit to the town. 'You have Sunday afternoons now, and one evening. You girls are all the same, no sense of duty, that's what it is.'

'But I need a full day to get there and back, ma'am.' Jenny stood her ground, knowing even as she did so that it was no good. The whole of the village was coming to the ceremony in the old dark church, according to what Mrs Fanshawe had said. Mrs Fanshawe herself was to be allowed to go, sitting at the back where she could creep out and back to the house in readiness for the guests' arrival. She had sewn new pieces of lace at the neck and wrists of her Sunday best dress, and had helped Jenny to renovate a dress belonging to Miss Sarah, a stiff silk that could stand by itself.

'But it's upstairs with you quick and into your black and your cap and apron,' she warned. 'By rights you should be stopping here with Nellie to see that those hired girls coming from Preston don't make off with anything. How we're to get done in time I can't think. I'll have to do the fancies two days before, but we'll have to whip the cream for the meringues on the day . . . and the trifles. Oh God, help us if it's not just right. I don't trust that new gas cooker, you know where you are with a fire-oven, but with beef and chicken and a whole ham to glaze . . . oh, God help us, Jenny, she must think we've got four hands each or summat.'

'We'll manage, Mrs Fanshawe, you'll see.' Jenny answered her glibly, but when the wedding day finally arrived she felt she could have stretched herself out and slept on the clothes line in the back garden.

The house shone with polish, rubbed into the furniture to the accompaniment of Nellie's loud grumbles; there was a new carpet in the drawing-room to replace the one with the burns, and the Bengal tiger rug had been replaced in its original place in Mr Bleasdale's study. Jenny went to bed at midnight the day before and got up again at four, creeping down to the kitchen to check that nothing had gone off after the previous day's feverish activity, and to lay the long tables set out in the drawing-room.

There were flowers to be picked to twine between the dishes, and at five o'clock she went out into the sleeping garden where the morning was turning blue and the stars paled in the brightening sky. It was going to be a lovely day and in seven hours from now Miss Sarah would be married, and this stillness, this quiet, was what she needed to come to terms with that fact. Jenny's fingers trailed down the bark of a tree, and she leaned her forehead against its cool roughness, grateful for what seemed to be its understanding.

'Oh, God, hide my thoughts from everyone, even from myself,' she prayed. 'Show me that what I feel for him, for the man I am to watch being married today is just utter and stupid foolishness. Tell me that the closeness I feel of mind and spirit when he talks with me is all my imagination. Send me someone of my own to love, if that is what this craving means, and send him to me soon!'

Mrs Fanshawe opened the back door, and appeared round the side of the house, tousled and frantic, her white cap slipping down over her worried forehead.

'Dreaming again, Jenny? There's not time for that

today. Miss Sarah's awake and wants her early tea. Come on, love, we haven't even made a hole in what has to be done yet.'

The moment of anguished truth was over, and somehow the long day had to be got through before Jenny could find comfort in the solace of her little room at the top of the house, reading far into the night by the candle flame, taking her to an escape into the realms of make-believe.

'I can't do it, Jenny!'

'Can't do what, Miss Sarah?'

'Go with Papa in the carriage to church and get married. It's no use, you'll have to go downstairs and tell them, make them understand.'

Sarah was standing in her room, supporting herself with one hand on the back of a chair as Jenny laced her into her stays. She was almost ready, with her red-gold hair dressed high, secured on top of her head by a wreath of orange-blossom in readiness for the long flowing veil. Tiny emerald ear-rings swung from the lobes of her ears, and round her neck Jenny had fastened the emerald necklace with a single dropped stone in the centre, the present from the bridegroom-to-be.

'Don't talk daft, Miss Sarah, you know you can't back out now. Every bride feels like this on her wedding day. It's nerves, that's all. Here, hold your breath a minute then it's on with your petticoats and your dress.'

'Were you like this, Jenny? Were you afraid on your wedding day?'

'Oh, my wedding day. . . .' Jenny fastened the last hook and raising her head saw her face reflected in the dressing-table mirror. Hot and flushed, with her dark curly hair unruly beneath her cap, with her eyes wide with the rush of it all. Damp stains under her arms, and hardly time to have a quick wash before she changed into the silk dress lying over the little bed in her room. She remembered herself coming downstairs, unbride-like in her serviceable serge, with Agnes saying not a word and Bob Waring with that strange smile playing round his thin lips.

'I was just so glad to be getting away from home I only remember feeling gratitude,' she said. 'Not a bit like this, Miss, with your mother and father waiting down there to see you in your beautiful dress, and half the county waiting in the church. No, you can't compare.'

And that was the understatement of the year, she told herself wryly as she slipped the flowing white chiffon dress from its hanger and started to undo the long row of buttons down the back of the bodice.

Sarah put out her hands as if she would physically ward off Jenny's approach with the dress. 'I'm so afraid, Jenny. You don't know, you won't believe me.' The large green eyes filled with tears and a hand crept up to the wreath of flowers as if she would tear them away.

Jenny laid the dress carefully over a velvet buttoned chair, and moved quickly forward. 'Now, sit down, Miss. And this is no time for crying. Do you want to walk down the aisle with your eyes all red and your face as green as the stones in that necklace? What is it you're afraid of? Come on, tell me.' She glanced at the small gilt clock on the mantelpiece. 'They'll just have to wait then, that's all.'

The words were hardly said before the door opened and Mrs Bleasdale swept in, magnificent in plum-coloured silk, her sallow complexion more muddy than usual with the competition from the harshly violent shade.

'Sarah! Love, I'm just off to the church with the Ibbotsons. Why aren't you ready?' She turned on Jenny. 'This is all your fault, Waring. I told you exactly the time to be up here to dress Miss Sarah. Can't you be trusted to remember anything?'

'I'm sorry, ma'am.' Jenny moved to stand in front of the weeping girl, praying the tears would go unnoticed. 'Five minutes now, then we'll be ready. Just five minutes, that's all.'

'She's crying!' Mrs Bleasdale's voice was loud in accusation. 'Oh, my God, what is she crying for? Not on her wedding day with everybody waiting.' She pushed Jenny aside rudely and kneeling down on the carpet, heedless of the magnificent gown, tried to draw the weeping girl into her arms.

'Don't you want to leave home, sweetheart? Is it all too much for you?' She held out a hand behind her and anticipating her need, Jenny took a lace-edged handkerchief from the embroidered case on the dressing-table and passed it to her.

'There, there, love. Mama understands, but you're only going just across the fields, and you're to have your own pony and trap so you'll be able to come home every day. It's not as if you were going to live miles away.'

'It's not that, Mama.' Sarah's voice was a wail of desperation, a cry for help, torn from her in pain. The tears flowed even faster. 'It's not leaving home I'm afraid of. It's something else.'

'Shall I go, ma'am?'

Jenny spoke quietly, but Mrs Bleasdale waved an imperious hand.

'Stop where you are, but close the door, and look in my purse there for the smelling salts.' She lowered her voice. 'Now then, Sarah, you can tell Mama. Whatever it is you can tell her.'

'I'd rather tell Jenny.'

Sarah's head came up so that the emeralds in her ears swung back, flashing bright green in the sunlight streaming through the window. 'If you'll go away I'll tell Jenny.'

So Paul was wrong. His bride to be *could* stick up to her mother after all. Jenny flinched from the hatred and anger in Mrs Bleasdale's eyes as she swept past her out of the room without another word.

'She knows there isn't time to argue.' Sarah dabbed at her eyes with the scrap of cambric and lace. 'But she'll never forgive you, you know that, don't you?'

Jenny held out the dress, realizing that for some indefinable reason the battle was won, and obediently Sarah held up her arms to receive it.

'That wasn't very kind, Miss Sarah.' She lowered the froth of chiffon over the layered petticoats, then with fingers that trembled with the rush of it all started to push the tiny pearl buttons through the exquisitely-fashioned loops.

'I know, Jenny, but when I saw Mama in that hideous colour, with her face all pinched with worry, I knew I couldn't let her down. It would *kill* her if she had to tell everyone to go away now with all that food prepared and everything. I know she shouts and expects too much of the servants she hires, that is why she can never keep them. That is why Daisy Best went and Fanny Barton didn't come. Mrs Fanshawe only stays because Mama lets her go home every evening to her sick husband. Besides, Mama knows she would never get another cook as good.'

Now the veil. Jenny began to pin its filmy cloud just behind the top-knot of red-gold curls, securing it with hair-pins so that it looked as if the wreath of orange-blossom was holding it in place. There was a shorter circular veil attached which she pulled down over Sarah's face so that the trembling mouth and tear-drenched eyes were given a breath-taking luminous beauty.

'There, Miss Sarah! Your flowers are down in the hall, and when Mr Paul sees you looking like that he'll be so proud of you. *I'm* proud of you,' she added, her own throat tight with unexpected emotion.

'Thank you, Jenny.' Sarah put out a hand and gripped Jenny's workworn fingers. 'And if I hold tight to Papa's arm my limp won't show. It won't show, not with this dress being so full, will it, Jenny?'

'You could hide a couple of dolly legs underneath that dress, Miss Sarah, and nobody would be the wiser.'

Sarah laughed and the sound was good to hear, but before she went out onto the landing, the trembling was in her voice once again.

'I did not tell you what it is I am afraid of, Jenny. I was going to before Mama came in, but it wouldn't have been fair. It's something I shouldn't have given a thought to. That's what Mama would have said.'

Jenny, one hand on the bedroom door handle, stayed where she was. They were waiting downstairs, the church bells were ringing out over the valley, and Mr Paul would be there, the sunlight glinting on his fair head as he waited for his bride. But this was important. This had to be said.

'I know what it is, Miss Sarah. It's *intercourse* you're afraid of, isn't it?'

The indrawn breath behind the film of veil was answer enough.

'It is nothing,' Jenny said in a firm voice. 'Mr Paul is kind, and he loves you. I've watched him with you and I know he will be gentle and loving. Marriage between two people who love each other is wonderful, Miss Sarah. You have my word for that.'

Then as Sarah walked to the top of the stairs, one hand firmly on the banister rail, the beautiful dress flowing like a river of cobwebby lace behind her, Jenny turned and flew up the short flight of stairs to her own room.

Tearing at the buttons on her sweat-stained working dress, she dropped it round her ankles and stepped out of it. Sarah's half-ashamed admission had brought it all back to her. The sharp clawing fingers of Bob Waring on the night of her own wedding, the bite of his teeth in her shoulder, the probing of his tongue, and the frantic way he had torn into her, using her as if she were a kept woman.

Jenny sloshed cold water over her burning face, then reached for the silk dress lying across her narrow bed. She did not know how she knew, but oh God, she did know, that with Paul Tunstall it would be different.

He was strong and he was ruthless, but in his actual strength lay his gentleness. She had seen him one day hold a bird with a broken wing in his hands, and it had come to her that it was the same compassion he felt for Miss Sarah. His voice would be low, and his movements slow and unhurried; her long hair would lie across the pillow like a lick of flame, and he would wind it round his fingers.

Some day *she* would meet a man she could love, but with Paul Tunstall as a yardstick, where would she find him? Where, if she travelled the length and breadth of the country? She flew downstairs to find that Mrs Bleasdale was still waiting for her carriage in the hall, tweaking Sarah's veil unnecessarily into place, and reducing her daughter to a new state of nervousness as she bewailed the fact that they were going to be late. At least ten minutes late, and then what would everyone think?

'Waring! What are you doing using the front stairs, and where do you think you're going? Where is your cap and apron, girl, and just *who* do you think you are?'

Jenny bobbed her little curtsey, conscious of Mr Bleasdale's sympathetic glance in her direction, but knowing he would say nothing.

'Mrs Fanshawe said I might go to the ceremony with her if we took the short cut across the meadow and sat at the back so we could creep out before the end. . . .' Her voice faltered and died away.

'Then Mrs Fanshawe has another think coming!' The flowers on Mrs Bleasdale's wide hat nodded with indignation. 'You can go right back up there and put your best uniform on, Waring. Do you think I am going to leave my house and all the wedding presents in the care of those two Preston girls? I wasn't born yesterday you know. I know what goes on.'

'Mama. . . .' Sarah's hands were shaking so much that the posy she held quivered as if in a sudden breeze. 'The dining-room door is open. They will hear you, and then what will they think?'

'They're paid *not* to think!'

Mrs Bleasdale swept to the door as the jingling sound of harness announced the arrival of her carriage.

'And try not to stoop as you walk, Sarah. Slowly . . . like I said.'

'Yes, Mama.'

Sarah turned to speak to Jenny, but with disappointment stinging behind her eyelids, mingled with a kind of shamed relief that she was after all going to be spared the ordeal of going to the ceremony, Jenny ran back upstairs, to change once more.

She did not remember having exchanged more than four sentences with Mr Bleasdale since coming to Cedar House, apart from the time he had come into his study and caught her with a leather-bound book in her hands.

'Fond of reading, lass?' he had asked.

Then when she had bobbed politely and made for the door he had called her back.

'If you only take one at a time, and don't turn the pages down at the corner or anything, I don't mind you borrowing,' he'd said, then smiled as she thanked him breathlessly. 'Nay, lass, it's time somebody read these books. I don't get the time nowadays, and they're there to be read. What's that one, then?'

'Tennyson, sir.' Jenny ran her fingers over the leather-tooled bindings and the marbled facings. 'He writes like music. You can hear his words singing when you read them aloud under your breath.'

Jenny had flipped over the tissue covering the line drawing of the poet at the beginning. 'He's got such a dreaming face, sir, don't you think?'

'Well, bugger me!' Mr Bleasdale had said, and had told his friend Mr Ibbotson about the new maid who had held a book in her hands as if it were a precious piece of porcelain.

'An unusual girl that,' Ben Ibbotson had said. 'Thought so the first time I set eyes on her. Where does she come from?'

'Nay, where do any of them come from, Ben? I might as

well tell you I often watch them and think "there but for the grace of God goes our Sarah". Liking Tennyson! There's a caution, what?'

Jenny was starting on the clearing away when her employer came over to her, more beetle-like than ever in his frock coat and high winged collar.

'You've done very well, lass, and now it's all over why don't you have a day off next week? I'll square it with the mistress. I'm taking her over to see her sister at Salmesbury on Wednesday, anyroad, so how about picking on that day? Where was it you said you come from?'

'Blackburn, sir.' Jenny piled a set of glass trifle dishes together. 'I could get there and back in the day if I went with Farmer Collins on his wagon. He takes his eggs and butter that day for his stall on the market. He could bring me back too, if I met him at the place where he stables his horse. It's not far from where I used to work.'

Too late she realized she had said too much and waited with head bowed for the inevitable question. But Mr Bleasdale was not interested in the whys and means, and patting her on her shoulder walked away, making for the stairs and his bedroom to wrench at the stiff collar and ponder on the strangeness of a servant girl for whom a poet made words sing.

9

The summer sunshine was wan in the grey narrow streets as Jenny walked from the market place to her mother's house. The rag-and-bone man jogged his horse and cart along with the empty bottles rattling beside him, and a cobbler stood at his shop door, swinging his hammer by its long wooden handle.

It was strange, but Jenny knew she was no longer afraid of coming face to face with her step-father again. It was only months since she had stumbled away from the town in the dark of a winter's night, but it might have been years. It was not him she had come to see, but her mother, she told herself as she walked down the familiar street and stood for a moment outside the house where the paint had long since peeled from the front door, and the step stayed unmopped from one week to another.

She opened the door, unconsciously squaring her shoulders and stepped inside. The sour smell of neglect made her wrinkle her nose in disgust.

'Mam? It's me!' she called out, and pushed aside the curtain separating the parlour from the living-room at the back.

And it was worse, far worse than she remembered. The grate was empty and the grey ashes spilled across the hearth in dusty neglect. Harry Howarth lolled in his chair, unshaven, with his collarless shirt unbuttoned over a hairy matted chest, and Mollie crouched rather than sat in a chair opposite to him, her hair slipping from its top-knot, her eyes sunk deep into the pads of flesh pushing them up into blood-shot slits.

'Jenny!' She started to get up from the chair, then fell back, dissolving into a shaking torrent of tears.

'The bloody prodigal returns!' Harry Howarth made no attempt to rise, merely glowered at Jenny from beneath lowering black eyebrows.

Jenny put the basket of eggs and the seed cake Mrs Fanshawe had kept in a tin since the wedding down on the table, and lifting her arms unpinned her hat and unbuttoned her short jacket.

'Don't cry, Mam.' It was funny saying that, the first words since they had last met, realizing that she must have said them over a hundred times with as little effect as they were having now. 'You knew I would be coming to see you as soon as I could get away.' She went to kneel by her mother's chair, and smelt again the sour-sweet smell of rancid neglect coming from the fat little woman's body, worse now than she ever remembered it. 'Why didn't you write back to me? Three times I've written and never a word. What's wrong? There is something wrong, isn't there?'

Before the house had been unclean, now it was dirty, filthy, with dust lying thick on the cut-rug, and the steel fender looking as if it had never known the touch of a piece of emery paper. She moved her head from side to side. Was she seeing it like this because she was used to furniture that gleamed dark from the shine of polish? Had she forgotten that windows could be dulled as if a fog lay thick outside, that a sink could be piled with unwashed pots?

'Dishes, Waring!' As if from another world, another existence, she heard Mrs Bleasdale's raucous voice.

'What's *wrong*?' she asked again.

'I'm going out.' Harry Howarth lumbered to his feet, took his dirty white muffler from behind the door, winding it round his neck and lurching from the room as if already, at that early hour, he was in the throes of drink.

'Nay, he's not drunk. I only wish he were.' Mollie groped in the pocket of her skirt for a frayed piece of rag and held it to her streaming eyes. 'He's hungry, that's what he is, same as me, but he'll get taken on down on the market same as he always does on a Wednesday, putting up the stalls and fetching the stuff from the warehouses. He only does casual work now, Jenny, and what bit he gives me just keeps body and soul together, that's all.'

'But why?' Jenny got up and unhooked her mother's apron from the same peg where her step-father's scarf had been. 'He's well enough to work in a proper job, isn't he? An' you can't mean you're hungry, Mam, not really *hungry*?'

'Only because we had nowt for breakfast. We had fish and chips last night from the shop.' Mollie moved her head round to indicate the untidy sink. 'He gets paid on a day-to-day basis now, and where it goes I don't rightly know.'

'He spends it on drink!' Jenny rolled up her sleeves, and kneeling down by the fireplace, started to rake out the ashes. 'You don't have to tell me!'

'But he doesn't. I swear it!' Her mother's voice was a wail as she rocked herself backwards and forwards. 'What little he gets he gives me. I know it. And he sits there, night after night, stopping in, not speaking, staring at nothing.'

'Do you mean he's going off his chump?' Jenny carried the overflowing shovel outside into the yard, and came back with it piled with coal. 'There's coal in the shed, Mam. Why are you sitting without a fire? How do you expect to boil a kettle when there's no fire? Mam! What has that man been doing to you?'

But it was no use. It never had been any use asking questions when her mother cried as she was crying now. Great rivers of tears ran from her swollen eyes, dripping from her quivering chins, as with her mouth wide open she sobbed and sobbed. Jenny got the fire going, filled the kettle and swung it over the flames, then broke two eggs into the congealing fat in the bottom of the frying pan.

It was no good bothering about niceties, she told herself. 'First things first,' as Mrs Fanshawe was always saying.

'Now, Mam, come on.' She pulled a piece of bread from the end of the toasting fork, and laid the fried eggs on top of it. 'Get this down and when the kettle boils we'll have a pot of tea. When I've washed two pots that is. Mam! What have you been doing to get in a state like this? I think it's time I came home to live again.'

'Will you? Would you, Jenny?' Mollie stopped chewing for long enough to ask the question, the tears drying on her cheeks as she wolfed the food down. 'Things might be different if you were back at home.'

But it was the Jenny she was now, not the Jenny she had once been who answered. 'No, Mam. I won't ever live in the same house as him again. An' you know that with me here, things would be worse. Mam, it's just like I told you in the letters, only better. You can smell the country the minute you open your eyes in the morning, and when the sky is blue it's a proper blue, not with the sun struggling to get through a hazy mist of grey, then being shredded to nothing by the tall mill chimneys. Mam, it's hard work and little thanks for it, but everywhere you look there's green, not like the green in the park where if you pull a piece of grass the soot comes off on your fingers.'

Mollie's eyes filled again. 'I *know* about the country, Jenny. I worked in a big house remember, where there were ten maids, and a butler to open the door, and an under-cook and two kitchen maids. And I might have been there still, but for . . . but for . . .' Mollie choked on a sob and a mouthful of food. 'Over t'other side of Preston it was.' She stopped and bent her head to her plate again, saying too much and determined not to say any more.

'Tell me about him, Mam. About my father. No, don't look like that. I've been married remember, and I understand. Maybe I understand more than you think. I don't blame you, Mam. I know what men can be like, the only difference I can see is that you had a baby and I didn't. You were *raped*, Mam. You couldn't help it.'

And so was I, she added to herself, but I had a ring on my finger to make it nice and legal, that was the only difference.

'How dare you use that word? A daughter of mine, using words like that!' Mollie pushed her plate away, changed her mind and pulled it back again, plying her knife and fork with furious indignation. 'You've changed, our Jenny. You've come back home thinking you can say what you like. You should have stayed up Park Road with Mr Waring's sister; at least you'd have been with a decent family. Good Chapel folks the Warings, an' I thought you were settled for life there. Oh, Jenny, why do you have to be always acting *different*? I know they say his sister is one on her own, but to move away so soon after the funeral. I still can't make reason out of it.'

There was no point in telling her mother the truth. Jenny started to clear the table. It sometimes seemed to her that her whole life was a careful evasion of the truth. That day in the kitchen with Paul Tunstall, she had said she had told him everything about herself. But even that wasn't true either. Sordid as her story was, she had still missed out the most shameful thing of all – that she didn't know the name of her own father.

'Who was he, Mam?' Suddenly it seemed to be the most mportant thing to know. 'At least if you can't tell me who, tell me something about him. Anything! The colour of his eyes, the way he stood, whether he even knows that I exist. There must be *something* you can tell me, because I have to know.'

Mollie slid the chair back and got up from the table. Her plump face was a quivering, sobbing mask of misery as she groped her way towards the foot of the stairs, a hand held in front of her as if she was blind.

'I'm going for a lie down, but I'll tell you somethin' first, madam! You're like him, just like him the way you want your own way and demand to get it. But you'll get no more out of me, trying to rake up something that's over and done with. An' I'll tell you something else. I'm glad Jack's no longer here to listen to you going on about him. What sort of a man is it that *pays* to have a girl sent away, and sets her up with furniture, just to have her married and living anywhere but near to him?' She started slowly up the stairs, pulling herself up with the rail as if she was twice her age.

Jenny held the greasy curtain to one side with her hand, feeling the blood rush to her face as she shouted after her mother.

'But he couldn't marry you, how could he? Men like him don't marry people like us. They pick their own sort.' She swallowed hard as she remembered Paul Tunstall helping Miss Sarah into the carriage as the guests clustered round waving them off on their honeymoon. It had seemed for a moment that his eyes had met hers over the fancy hats and the fluttering handkerchiefs, a moment of recognition, but dear God, recognition of what? 'They live in their world, Mam, and we live in ours, always have done and always will do, you know that!'

She rolled up her sleeves, and taking the kettle from the hob, poured a stream of hot water into the tin bowl, then swished a bar of hard soap round in it before starting on the washing-up, and all the while her mind was leaping ahead as she planned what she was going to do next.

The grate first, that was if she could find the tin of black lead and the brushes. Then the steel parts of the fender to be rubbed up with emery paper. The cut-rug out in the yard and beaten till the dust flew, and the dresser polished with vinegar water. She moved with quick short steps from slopstone to fire, from fire to table, scrubbing, sweeping, polishing, till the sweat ran down her forehead and into her eyes. Appalled at what she found, and ashamed because living at home and working at the shop had left her with little more than Sundays to do what she was doing now.

She emptied her purse onto the table and counted the meagre pile of pennies and sixpences, then changing her mind, she pulled on her jacket again and went up to the corner shop. At least Harry Howarth couldn't spend food, she told herself as she replenished her mother's cupboard, wondering where he had gone and praying that she herself would have left the house before his return.

'I'll come back,' she told her weeping mother. 'I'll make Mrs Bleasdale let me save my half days so that I can come again. I'm getting her measure now, Mam. She knows she's getting more than her money's worth out of me, and she's no fool. She's a hard-faced woman, but she's no fool.'

As she turned the corner she glanced back down the little street and saw Mollie standing on the doorstep, fat and unkempt, with her hair coming down and her arms folded over her bulging stomach.

'Did I ever live there?' she asked herself as she hurried down to the market place. 'How could I *ever* have lived there?'

Then ashamed of her thoughts she crossed the street, dodging the wheels of a coal cart with the sacks piled high and the driver hunched over the shafts as he urged his horse over the cobbles.

'Miss? Miss? You're the lass what used to live down there? That's right, isn't it?'

Jenny paused, stared at the woman with the raddled pock-marked face barring her way and tried to walk on. She knew what the woman was, there had been plenty of her sort living in the area round the cat-meat shop. Feverish grasping women with tatty bits of fur round their scraggy necks and rouge dotted on their cheeks, accosting decent men on their way home from work.

Bob Waring had told her about them, warned her to

look the other way when she saw them as if they were possessed of the evil eye.

'Night-women, Miss Macartney,' he had said as they walked home from the Mission Hall together. 'Creatures not fit to be on God's good earth. Should be put down like dogs if I had my way.'

And this one was actually speaking to her, calling her by name, putting out a claw-like hand and fastening it over Jenny's arm.

'You married Mr Waring who used to work at the iron foundry. That's right, isn't it?'

Jenny tried to shake off the clutching hand, but the fingers dug in deeper.

'You couldn't possibly have known Mr Waring,' she heard herself say. She looked round but nobody seemed to be taking the slightest notice of what was happening. 'Now let me pass. I'm late.'

The woman smiled, and for the first time Jenny was forced to look into her eyes. Strange brown eyes flecked with gold, fringed with long black eyelashes. At one time, she told herself even as she panicked to get away, at one time this woman must have been pretty, beautiful even, but now the teeth showing between the rouged lips were broken and uneven, so that the smile was more like a grimace.

'I have to go,' she said more gently. 'My husband is dead. There is nothing he can do for you now.'

'That's what I want to tell you.' The woman lowered her voice. 'Nay, lass, what did you want with marrying a man like him? A good girl like you?' She peered up into Jenny's face with the once brilliant eyes narrowed into menacing slits. 'It was what I did for him, more like, but even *he* didn't deserve what he got.'

Jenny's heart skipped a beat then began to hammer in her chest. 'What do you mean, what he got?'

'Harry Howarth.' The voice was no more than a whisper now. 'I know all about you, Miss. I've made it my business to know, and if I was you I'd keep well away from your step-father. Go back to where you come from and leave well alone.'

Jenny stared into the twisted face in stupefaction for a moment. 'Tell me what you're trying to say. Look, I'm meeting someone, and if I'm not there he will go without me. Tell me?'

The thin face jutted forward. 'I'll tell you all right. I live in the street by the iron foundry, and I was looking through me curtains one night when I saw your step-father talking to Mr Waring.' She gave the mirthless smile again. 'I'm often looking out when they come out of the foundry because there's more than one of them knocks at my door, see? And what did I see that night but big Harry running away from summat lying in the street, on the flags, just outside my house, and do you know what that was?' She nodded twice. 'Your Mr Waring, love, lying there dead.'

Jenny closed her eyes, and as her eyes closed her ears seemed to close too, so that the street sounds of wheels on cobbles, clip-clop of horses' hooves, a child bowling a hoop along the pavement, a baby crying in a high-pitched wail, all receded as if a thick wet blanket had been thrown over them, shutting out every noise but the pounding of her heart.

'You mean you saw my step-father actually . . . actually *hit* Mr Waring?'

'Nay. I didn't say that now, did I? But he's having to pay for what he did, and that's right and fair, isn't it? You wouldn't like to see him up in court branded as a murderer, would you, love? Not now you've got yourself a fine job. Out in the country, did you say?' She released her grip on Jenny's arm to push her in the chest with a finger. 'And no need to look at me like that. You never know what you might come to if need's must.'

'Don't say that!' Jenny broke away and started to run, holding up her skirts with one hand, heedless of the faces turning after her with lifting eyebrows and incredulous looks of astonishment. She ran and ran until her rasping breath was a sore in her side, turning into a narrow alley-way lined with carts, the cobble-stones slippery with cabbage leaves and mounds of rotting vegetation.

'Eh, Miss! Where d'you think you're going?'

One of the market men, his coarse apron stained with dirt, stepped forward holding out his arms. 'Give us a kiss, bonny lass!'

He was teasing; Jenny knew he was teasing, but fresh from the encounter with the night woman, and the things she had said hammering in her brain, it seemed to her as if the whole world had suddenly turned evil. She twisted away from the man's light grasp, turned and saw that the alley-way behind her was deserted in the hour before the temporary stalls were taken down.

'All right, lass?' The market man had dropped his bantering tone and was staring at her with concern. 'Somebody after you?'

Jenny shook her head, too out of breath to speak, then stumbled on, leaving him to take off his flat cap and scratch at a thick thatch of greying hair.

'Tha'll kill thyself dashing like that!' he shouted after her, but Jenny ran on, tammy slipping from her head, clutching at it with one hand, and holding up her skirt with the other.

And the farmer was there, ready for off, sitting in his seat with the reins held loosely, beaming when he saw her, and reaching down to hoist her up beside him.

'Had a good day, then, lass?'

She nodded, staring straight ahead, trying to appear normal, and telling herself that nothing would ever be normal again.

Her thoughts whirled round and round in her head, like a moth caught in a street lamp. . . . Harry Howarth had murdered Mr Waring. He had waited outside the foundry and accosted him as he walked to the tram stop on his way home from work. Asked him for money, no doubt, when her wages were no longer there for him to steal from the knife drawer. Threatened him, then killed him. And run away thinking no one had seen him. But, oh God, someone *had* seen him, and that woman, that dreadful woman with the piercing eyes and the rouge dotted doll-like on her high cheekbones, she was blackmailing him.

That was why the little house had smelt of poverty, why her step-father had curbed his tongue and left the minute she got there. Why there was barely enough money for food, and why her mother sat weeping, not understanding.

'By gum, but it's good to get away from the town and get some proper air up your nostrils.'

The farmer's trap swayed as they jogged along towards the road leading to the first of the outlying villages. It was a warm evening, with the air gentle, and the soft sky wistful above the rows of houses and the chimney-pots. The sun was still high in the western sky, but the day was drawing to a close, and as they clop-clopped towards home Jenny stared at the mare's satin coat, and heard again the night-woman's voice.

'I know what I know, and you never know what you might come to.'

The beauty of the summer evening seemed to be mocking at her. It was pressing all around her, stifling her with its loveliness. She was being suffocated, and there was no escape. . . .

'Glad to be getting back, then?' The farmer's ruddy face was set into lines of content, and even the horse lifted her head as they left the town behind. Soon they saw men in heavy boots with handkerchiefs tied round sunburned necks, making their way home from the fields, and a girl in a blue print dress swung a milk-can from a hand as she walked along.

'Nearly there now.'

Jenny climbed down from the trap, thanked the farmer, and set off to walk across the fields to Cedar House. Now the sun had almost gone, and the valley was filled with the quiet sounds of evening, full of gentle light. She climbed a stile, and saw, coming towards her, the tall broad figure of Mr Ibbotson, his hat in his hand and his head held high as he walked with his long strides towards his red-brick house set back from the road with its chimneys etched sharp against the misty blue sky.

'Good evening, Jenny. Read any more Tennyson lately?' He stood before her in the narrow lane, smiling, his eyes kind beneath the dark curling eyebrows. 'What would *he* have said about a day like this?'

'I don't know, sir.' Jenny dropped her little curtsey and wished he would disappear as quickly as he had come. One more minute and he would have passed the stile, but now she had to smile at him and be polite and pray that he would not notice that in her anxious state she barely knew what he was saying.

Ben Ibbotson, pleased with the way his own day had gone, and at peace with the world, with a glass of fine port waiting for him after his evening meal, struck an attitude and recited in a booming voice:

'And was the day of my delight as pure and perfect as I say? The very source and fount of day is dashed with wandering isles of night.'

'Would that do, Jenny? Or is a Rossetti sonnet more to your taste? How about this one?'

Putting a hand inside the buttons of his waistcoat he recited:

'My heart is like a singing bird, whose nest is in a watered shoot.' He stared up at the sky searching his memory, shook his big head and laughed out loud, the laughter stopping abruptly as he noticed for the first time Jenny's pallor and the agitated way she was staring at him with dark eyes wide.

'What's the matter, lass? Mrs Bleasdale been giving you hell?' He patted Jenny's shoulder. 'Her bark's worse than her bite, lass, and she won't be herself not till she gets that girl of hers back from Lytham. You've spirit enough to stand up for yourself, haven't you? More pluck than the other lasses she's had working there, I'd stake my life on that.'

'Sir?' Jenny was biting her lip as she tried to remember what Mrs Fanshawe had told her about this big impressive man who Mrs Bleasdale was always so proud to entertain. 'Sir? Are you a solicitor? You know? Do you have dealings with the law?'

'You could say that, lass.' Ben Ibbotson swayed on his feet, toying with the gold watch-chain draped across his waistcoat. He was enjoying this unexpected encounter with the Bleasdale's parlour-maid who crept up the back stairs to her room with a book underneath her arm. There was something about her; something far different than the usual run of village girls who came into service the day they left school. There was intelligence in the expressive brown eyes, an awareness, and her skin was the delicate cream of a wild rose, with a bloom on it so that if he'd been a younger man he would have stretched out a hand and run a finger lightly down the rounded cheek.

'What have you been up to, lass? Robbing a bank?'

'It's blackmail, sir.' The words rushed out, tumbling over themselves as Jenny tried to be coherent. 'I've been to see my mother and step-father, and I think – I'm almost sure – that someone is blackmailing them.' Her lip quivered. 'At least, blackmailing my step-father.'

'What for, Jenny. Have you any reason for thinking he's done something, this step-father of yours, that would warrant a blackmailer thinking it was worth his while?'

'I think he may have killed someone, sir.'

The watch-chain dropped as Ben Ibbotson's fingers released it. 'You only *think*, Jenny? Have you any proof?'

'No, sir, but he could have.' Her head drooped as she blurted out the shame of it. 'He drinks, sir.'

'And you don't like him?'

'I hate and loathe him, sir. That's why I got married. To get away. You see?'

Mr Ibbotson did not see, he did not see at all, but he tried.

'When was this . . . this murder supposed to have taken place?'

'In February, sir.'

'And you've no proof?'

'No, sir.'

'Hmm . . .'

Ben Ibbotson, before he had taken up the directorship of his Company, and before he had become interested in politics, had often sat behind his desk, toying with the watch-chain as he listened to young girls like this Jenny lass telling him fanciful stories of what had happened to them, or happened to someone they knew, half of it lies and the other half fantasy. And yet, and yet . . .

'Look, lass. When is your half day off? Your next half day off?'

'It won't be for another week, sir. The day before Miss Sarah comes back from her honeymoon.'

'That makes it a week tomorrow then. A Thursday?'

'Yes, sir.'

'Then I'll tell you what. I'll be at home that day, so what say you come round to the house about three? Then you can tell me all about it, slowly, and then perhaps we'll both of us understand. Right?'

'Oh, yes, sir.' Jenny bobbed a curtsey, but the big man was walking away, swinging his hat in his hand as he resumed his evening walk, shaking his head a little.

Somehow his mood of euphoria had dissolved into nothing, sinking like the sun. Not a man given to fanciful notions, he stopped carrying his hat and replaced it on his head, tapping it into place with the flat of a big hand. At the bend in the lane he turned and saw young Jenny walking slowly now, her head bent, dragging her feet like an old woman of the roads.

'There's more in this than meets the eye,' he told himself, as sighing, he turned into the long drive bordered with rhododendron bushes, their pink and white blossoms brown now and scattered untidily on the gravel path.

'Come Thursday and we'll see,' he muttered, then arranged his face into a suitably blank expression with which to greet his wife.

10

'Now then, lass. Let's start from the beginning, shall we?'

Jenny sat facing Mr Ibbotson across the width of his leather-topped desk. It had rained for three days, and a passing cart in the lane had splashed her skirt with mud. In spite of the loan of Mrs Fanshawe's umbrella the dampness had curled her hair into a riot of dark waves, and her cheeks glowed bright pink with the rush of getting away from Cedar House in time.

'You say you think your mother's husband is being blackmailed? That was what you said, wasn't it?'

Jenny was very grateful that the important man had spared some of his busy time to see her, but she sensed that he was having great difficulty in taking her seriously. He was playing with a fountain pen, scribbling wavy lines on the writing pad in front of him, and as he spoke to her his glance was going through the tall heavily-curtained windows to the dripping green of the trees outside.

'I went to see my mother,' she began, sitting forward in the leather chair and speaking clearly and slowly. 'My step-father, Harry Howarth, was there, and I expected him to jump up and rant at me when I went in.' She nodded her head. 'I wasn't afraid of him, not this time, but I knew what to expect. He doesn't like me, you see.'

'And he didn't rant that day, lass?'

'No. He got up and went out, and my mother told me that he was doing casual work. Down at the town that time, because it was market day.'

'Go on.'

'She, my mother, told me that although he is earning money he never brings much home lately, and when I said it would be because he was drinking it away as usual, she said he never drank now, that he sits in his chair and broods.'

'And she can't ask him straight out why?'

Jenny's eyes opened wide. 'You can't ask Harry Howarth anything straight out, sir. He flies into rages when he's questioned, and my mother is all for peace at any price. He *dominates* her, sir.'

'And you, Jenny? Did he dominate you when you lived at home?'

'He tried to, sir, but the last time he came at me I went for him with the poker, that was why I left home and got married.'

Ben Ibbotson threw the pen down with an impatient gesture, which Jenny completely misunderstood. His impatience was not because she was taking too long to get to the point of her story, but because he found the idea of this lovely vital young girl with the intelligent dark eyes mixed up with a drunken bully, totally abhorrent. He could see, in his mind's eye, exactly the kind of home she had come from. Dark and cheerless, with a front door that opened onto the street, and a primitive lavatory out in the back, and a poker handy in the hearth for when a man crazed with drink made sexual advances at her.

'Your husband?' he asked quietly.

The dark eyes clouded and Jenny lowered her head so that all he could see was the crown of curls pinned up on top of her head. 'He was a Chapel man, living with his sister and his father. His first wife had died with their baby, and I felt sorry for him.'

'But you did not love him?'

'No!' The denial seemed torn from her. 'I thought I might have been able to, but he . . . he frightened me.'

'When he took you to bed, Jenny?'

172

The voice was gentle, but the question was asked with authority.

'I have to know, lass. I have to get a clear picture, right?'

'Yes. He was violent, sir, but the next morning he went off to work as usual, and when he did not come home at the usual time, we waited, his sister Agnes and me, and then the police came and said he had been found dead in the street outside the iron foundry where he worked as a clerk.'

'And the cause of death?'

'It came out that he must have taken a dizzy turn – his heart was faulty – and fallen with his head on an iron stoop. The row of houses used to be farm labourers' cottages a long while ago, and . . .' Her voice faltered.

'I see. And that was that. So how did you come to ask for work at Cedar House?'

'She turned me out from her father's house. Bob's sister Agnes. She put my clothes out and wouldn't let me in. And last week was the first chance I had of going back to see my mother, and it was like I said. Then when I was walking down to the market place I met this woman.'

'Known to you?'

Jenny's upward glance was indignant. 'No, sir. She was a night-woman, and she stopped me in the street and told me that she lived in one of the tiny cottages by the foundry, and that she had seen my step-father running away from a man lying on the pavement outside.'

'She went to help him?'

'No, sir, but she went outside and recognized him. She hinted that he had been one of her . . . one of her customers. So she wouldn't want to get involved.'

'And you believe her?'

For a full minute there was no sound in the oak-panelled room but the rain, blown to fury now and dashing against the window panes.

'I believed her.'

Mr Ibbotson ran a hand through his thick hair. 'And you think this woman is blackmailing your step-father?'

173

'She said he was paying for what he did.'

There. It was told, and Jenny let out a deep sigh and sat back in her chair. For the last few nights she had hardly slept, tossing and turning in her bed in the attic room, asking herself over and over whether she was doing right, whether she ought to go again and confront Harry Howarth with what she had found out. But every time her mother's white face came before her, the tears running down the plump cheeks as she sat rocking herself backwards and forwards in the squalor of the small living-room.

'He wouldn't have meant to, sir. He's not that bad, but I think he went to meet my husband to ask for money. He would miss it, you see, sir. It wasn't much, but he would miss it.'

Ben picked up his pen again. It wasn't a pretty story, and he doubted whether the verdict would have been brought without further enquiries, but blackmail wasn't pretty either. He looked straight at Jenny.

'Your mother's name, lass?'

'Mollie Howarth, sir, but before she married my step-father her name was Mollie Macartney. She met him, Jack Macartney, when she was in service, sir, then when they married they went to live in the town.'

She gave the address, then waited expectantly for the next question, but to her astonishment Mr Ibbotson's face turned a deathly white. She actually saw the high colour leave his cheeks, leaving it grey-tinged as the hand holding the pen shook visibly. He pushed his chair back abruptly, got up and walked over to the window, standing with his back to her, holding onto the long red plush curtains as if he needed their support.

'Sir? Are you ill?' Jenny moved to go to him, but he turned and waved her back to her chair.

'That's all. That's all for now.' He tottered rather than walked to the door, holding it open, and as she stepped out into the wide hall, he muttered that he would see to things, that she must say nothing and do nothing.

'I understand, sir.' Jenny picked up Mrs Fanshawe's umbrella from the porch and lifted a face anxious with worry. 'I'm sorry, sir. You *are* ill, sir. Please let me fetch Mrs Ibbotson. You've got a chill, see, you're shivering. Let me ...'

'Just go, lass.'

To her amazement it seemed as if tears stood in the big man's eyes. He took the umbrella from her, unfurled it, then as he handed it over, touched her cheek lightly with a finger, trailing it down to the corner of her mouth.

'Goodbye, Jenny. I'll go. . . . I'll go and see your mother. Leave it with me.'

The heavy front door closed behind her as she stepped out into the rain-swept front curving drive, and it seemed to her as if the tall rhododendron bushes were closing in on her as she made her way out into the lane.

'I thought you told me to bring tea in, Ben?' Elaine Ibbotson hovered in the hallway with a tray held before her. 'You know it's Mary's afternoon off and I'd be getting it myself. You might at least have warned me that Jenny Waring was going.'

Her husband stared at her as if she were a total stranger; as if he had never seen her in his life before. Without saying a word he brushed past her rudely and went back into his study, slamming the door almost in her face.

Elaine Ibbotson was a woman who above all things craved peace. Childless and frequently lonely, married to a man who was married to his work and his manly interests, she would normally, used to his moods, have taken the tray back to the kitchen and said nothing. But not this time.

Setting the tray down on the hall table, she took a deep breath, opened the study door, and confronted the man who was sitting at his desk, his head buried in his hands, his broad shoulders hunched as if an intolerable burden had suddenly been set upon them.

'I saw you!' She closed the door behind her and approached the desk. 'I saw you touch that girl's cheek.' She sat down in the chair Jenny had just left. 'Oh, Ben, it's not starting again, not after all this time?'

'Get out!' His voice came muffled as he answered her without taking his hands from his face.

She clasped her hands together to stop them trembling, but what she had to say she was going to say.

'Oh, Ben, it's been over ten years now since the last time, and I thought . . . Ben! She's a servant girl! She works at the house of your friend! You can't humiliate me like this. When you told me she was in some kind of trouble and wanted advice, I thought it was the usual kind of trouble. I worked out that you were going to get her into that Home at Preston till she had her baby, but it's not that, is it? She's young, Ben, and you're old enough to be . . .'

'I said get out!' Ben leaped to his feet, picked up the heavy ink-stand and brandished it above his head. His eyes were wide and staring, and for a moment she thought he was going to smash it into her face. Then, as she got up from the chair and almost ran from the room, she heard him slam it back onto the desk.

'You're wrong, woman!' he shouted. 'You don't know how bloody wrong you are! Now leave me alone, for heaven's sake. Just leave me alone!'

When Paul Tunstall caught up with Jenny not a hundred yards past the Ibbotsons' red-brick house, she was so surprised to see him, so full of what had just happened, so sure that he was still in Lytham on his honeymoon, that it seemed as if her mind had blanked out for a few seconds.

'Here!' He stood before her, amused, impatient. 'What have you been up to, Jenny Waring? Pinching the silver from Mr Ibbotson's table?'

'You're not coming home till tomorrow.' She found she could not look at him because she was not prepared for seeing him, and once again there was the strange sense of unspoken intimacy between them, as if all that had gone before and all that was to be was as nothing compared to this vital moment snatched from time.

He laughed. 'Well, there's a welcome for you! It used to be the same when I was in the army; a day of extra leave and everybody got flummoxed. Not much fun honeymooning in the rain, Jenny, lass.'

Jenny was silent. He had no right to speak to her like this. It was wrong; it was against the laws of them and us; it was stepping over the dividing line, like Mr Ibbotson touching her cheek in that unexpected intimate way.

'Why have you been to the Ibbotsons'? To take a message from Sarah's mother?'

'No, to see Mr Ibbotson on private business.'

The words were out before Jenny had time to realize that a nod at his assumption would hardly have been classed as a lie.

Paul tightened his mouth and swished with his riding crop at the hedge, sending a shower of raindrops from it. 'Does Mrs Bleasdale know that you have sneaked out of the house to see Mr Ibbotson on private business?'

Jenny forgot her place for long enough to let her indignation show. 'I did not sneak out of the house, sir! I came out of the back door and walked down the drive underneath Mrs Fanshawe's umbrella.'

'And did you tell Mrs Fanshawe where you were going?'

'No.'

'What did you tell her, then?'

'I said I was stepping out to get a breath of fresh air after being cooped up in the kitchen all morning helping her to prepare for you and Miss Sarah coming home *tomorrow*.'

The ploy of trying to change the subject failed to work. Paul's grey eyes flashed angrily, and for a moment it seemed as if he would actually strike her.

'Hah! So you deceived her as well! And what did the mighty Mr Ibbotson do, Jenny? Recite poetry to you, then seal his words with a kiss?'

Jenny could do nothing about the blush. The unexpected challenge brought the touch of Ben Ibbotson's hand on her face, a finger trailing tenderly down her cheek, so much to mind that her face flamed. She felt the hated blush creep up from her throat and suffuse her cheeks in bright revealing colour. She felt guilty without having any cause to feel guilty and the shame of it made her quick temper flare.

'He's not like that, sir! Mr Ibbotson is a gentleman! He's not the sort to take advantage of a girl like me. I won't have you speak to me like this!'

Almost she stamped her foot; instead she stepped back straight into a puddle so that the muddy rain water splashed up round her ankles.

'Listen to me, Jenny.' Paul Tunstall's voice had dropped its bantering angry tone. For a brief moment she saw him as she knew he really was. Kind, considerate, and filled with a compassion for anyone young, defenceless and helpless. 'I don't tittle-tattle, I leave that to the women, but take it from me, Jenny, there is a dark side to our esteemed Justice of the Peace, though I must admit he does seem to have been behaving himself of late. He has taken advantage, as you so rightly say, on quite a few occasions. They say there's more than one bastard running around the countryside with its head topped with a mop of the Ibbotson black curls; you go home and ask Mrs Fanshawe. She'll tell you, if you won't listen to me. I forbid you ever to creep out and see him again. For your own sake, Jenny. For your own sake, love!'

He was staring at her with a scorn and derision that belied his words, but Jenny ignored the unexpected endearment, and turning her back on him started to walk back down the lane.

'You can't forbid me to do anything, sir, and I certainly will see Mr Ibbotson again, and alone, because what we have to talk about is private and nothing to do with anyone else at all!'

There, she had done it again. Spoken her thoughts and

forgotten her place, and besides she did not care, and for another thing he was wrong. There had been nothing suggestive in the way Mr Ibbotson had treated her, she knew men and they were all alike. Her mother had told her just that many, many times. Jenny hurried along the lane with the hedges dripping greenly either side of her. But *did* she know men? She had been proved wrong about Bob Waring, hadn't she? Dreadfully, dreadfully wrong. She shuddered. But talking to a solicitor was like talking to a doctor. Surely? And yet, was that the reason why Mr Ibbotson had suddenly changed and turned pale, walking over to the window as if he was gasping for air? Had he, in reality, been fighting for control over a passion that threatened to engulf him?

Jenny's vivid imagination, bolstered with the reading of Mrs Fanshawe's *News of the World* and what Matthew Arnold had called the 'popular publications with their generous instincts', interspersed with her devouring of the classics, took wings, until, as she turned into the drive of Cedar House, her sense of humour and innate sense of the ridiculous brought her down to earth again. Mr Paul Tunstall was wrong, so wrong that it was laughable, and that is what she would do if she wasn't so worried. Laugh in his face.

She had barely had time to shake the drops from the black umbrella before Mrs Fanshawe was beside her.

'Thank heaven you're back, Jenny. Nellie's gone home in one of her sulks, and Miss Sarah's stopping to dinner, and all when I'd planned plain eating tonight on account of them supposed to be coming tomorrow.'

The fuzz of fine down on the cook's round cheeks seemed to be standing out with indignation. 'Words they've had, Jenny, already. Shouting her head off the mistress was, and Miss Sarah crying, and her not back hardly from her honeymoon.' Mrs Fanshawe almost pushed Jenny towards the pile of vegetables ready by the sink. 'Mr Paul's gone off in a worse sulk even than Nellie. Striding off down the lane in a temper. He said as they were coming tomorrow to dinner anyway, he thought it right that his wife should go back to the farm with him. Sent the trap back with the boy, and walked off into the rain.'

'I saw him.' Jenny tied her apron strings round her back. 'Wet through with the rain pouring down his face. No wonder he looked mad.'

'Mad?' Mrs Fanshawe slapped a mound of pastry down onto the table and shook the white enamel flour shaker over it. 'It's his new wife what's mad if you ask me. It's not that poor lass's leg what's crippled, it's her *mind*. And Mr Paul will soon find out that he has married her mother as well. Silly young girl, having her first meal at home with her mother when she knows she doesn't live here now.' She took a china pie funnel from the dresser and wriggled it down into the dish of meat and onions. 'He won't stand for it, not Mr Paul. Forced into that marriage he was, with her going on and on about it being his fault Miss Sarah fell off her horse. Proper wild he was when he were a lad. Girls and horses, though not in that order. Something must have happened to him out in the war to calm him down, though it's there, just waiting to boil over if she goes too far. Silly old faggot!' The pastry was given a whacking thump with the rolling-pin, then turned over and whacked again.

She glared as the bell over the door jangled into life. 'She knows it's your half day, Jenny, and still she rings. It's a ring through her nose she wants, the stupid old cow.'

To Jenny's surprise Sarah was alone in the drawing-room when she knocked at the door and went in.

'Jenny!' Sarah remained where she was, sitting in the middle of the brocaded sofa, but she held out her hands in welcome. 'Oh, it's good to be home again, Jenny! You can't think what it was like sitting in those rooms at the hotel day after day watching it rain on the sea. Nothing but grey everywhere, not even a little ship. Nothing, and to think the sun had shone for weeks before we went away.

My . . . my husband felt the same way, I know. He was dying to get back to the farm and see what a mess they had made of things. He didn't even change before he was out in the stables.'

She was chattering as usual, friendly and kind, her lovely red-gold hair a bright splash of vivid colour against the pale green upholstery. A beautiful child back from a holiday, Jenny thought, as she stood by the door with her hands folded in front of her. Not a wife back from her honeymoon, happy to be in her first home, going round touching things and ordering a special meal for the two of them. And she had been weeping, there was no doubt about that.

'Mother has gone upstairs with a headache. She is lying down for a while, and I wanted to ask you. . . .' She glanced towards the door, and instinctively Jenny put the flat of her hand against it to show that it was closed.

'Yes, Miss Sarah?'

'I wanted to ask you, if Mother can get another girl in your place, not until of course, would you be prepared to come and work at High Trees for me?' She smiled gently and touched the stuff of her lilac-shaded silk gown. 'My . . . Mr Paul, he thinks you would be a help to me. A *companion*. There wouldn't be any kitchen work, Jenny. He has old Mrs Ellis for that, but it would just be perhaps waiting at table on occasions when we entertain. It's too much for the others, oh, and seeing to my clothes and going out with me in the trap. I *hated* that car, Jenny. My hair! No matter how much I tied it round, it still got mussed.' The beautiful green eyes were suddenly wistful. 'I'm used to being with Mother, you see, Jenny, and my days are going to be so long over there.'

She gazed out of the window as if, Jenny thought, High Trees was an ocean's width away, and not merely across the fields and over the stone bridge to the other side of the valley.

'May I have time to think it over, Miss Sarah?'

The green eyes widened in disappointed surprise. 'Why, yes, if you wish, Jenny. Take as long as you like. Take till next week.'

Jenny closed the door on Sarah's bowed head, then leaned against its dark wood for a moment. To live and work at High Trees, with the gentle Miss Sarah to care for. To be part of a companionship more lovely and perfect than any relationship she had ever known; to bridge for the first time the solitude she knew now had always been a part of her. To see *him* every day, to move in the light she always felt was around him, to hear his teasing laughter and be warmed by it, even as she accepted it was not for her.

She walked back to the kitchen, finished her task, ran upstairs to change into her best cap and apron, waited on a satisfied mother, a father who obviously felt something was wrong, a stony-faced husband with his fair hair still clinging wetly to his head, and a wife who chattered gaily as if nothing was amiss.

At last the clearing away was done, twilight came, and she went up to her room, leaving Mrs Bleasdale alone in the drawing-room playing an irritable game of patience with herself, whilst her husband pored over his account books in his study.

Jenny pushed up the window and leaned far outside. He was there, over the fields, not far, and yet a million miles away. She could see lamplight glowing in cottage windows over the dark fields, and right away, over the hem of the sky, was the sea she had only read about, moving darkly now with snatches of foam. She saw herself running along the sands with him, the rain and the wind buffeting their cheeks, hitting like sharp knives. She thought of how it would be, sheltered away in the green fastness of High Trees, with Miss Sarah treating her as a friend and the door banging back as he came in from the fields, laughing, teasing, impatient, intolerant, talking to his wife, but meeting her own eyes now and again with that strange flicker of recognition.

It needed an effort to leave the window and her dreams, but at last Jenny pulled down the blind and stumbling over to the bed, lit her candle.

The room was ugly and small and hot, but it was the nicest room she had ever had. She was shelled in her own solitude there with the candlelight flickering on the bare walls, and her book of the moment, *The Poetical Works of Lord Byron*, on the table beside her bed.

No shouting from the other side of a thin wall. After Harry Howarth's drunken raving Mrs Bleasdale's tantrums were no more than a pleasant storm in a comfortable teacup.

Mr Ibbotson was going to see to things. He had said so, and she was so tired, so filled with emotion, that if the guttering candle would last out she would read until all the strange happenings of the day receded into nothing.

'I saw thee smile – the sapphire's blaze beside thee ceased to shine; It could not match the living rays that filled that glance of thine.'

And not for the first time she was comforted by words, by the singing truth of them.

Paul Tunstall's silver-grey eyes – like Byron's blaze of light – as far removed from her as the stars paling now in the clear after-the-rain sky.

Jenny closed her eyes, crossed her hands dramatically over her calico chest. And slept.

I I

When Jenny opened the door two weeks later and saw Ben
Ibbotson standing there, she knew it was she he had come
to see and not her mistress. Nobody called on anyone in
these parts without first leaving a card, or sending a letter
to make formal arrangements. But she observed the rules
by bobbing her little curtsey, and explaining that Mrs
Bleasdale was out across the fields visiting her daughter.

'It's you I've come to see, lass.'

He was looking at her with that same mixture of tenderness and compassion, and as Paul Tunstall's warning
flashed in her mind, she felt her face flame as she stepped
aside, holding the door open for him to pass.

Where was she to receive him? Certainly not in the
kitchen, and equally not in the drawing-room, but even
as she hesitated, overcome with embarrassment, the big
man strode down the hall and walked into the drawing-
room, leaving her with no choice but to follow.

'Close the door, lass. You've not told nobody about any
of this?'

Jenny shook her head. 'No, sir. Not a soul.'

She would have preferred to stand, but Mr Ibbotson
seated himself on the chesterfield, and patted a place beside
him, and nervously she sat down, pleating the frill of her
apron round and round in her fingers, wondering if Mrs
Fanshawe had seen what was happening, and was even
now standing in the kitchen with her mouth a wide round
O of surprise.

'I went to see your mother.' He sighed, shaking his big head from side to side. 'She was in a state of great distress, as you explained, and your step-father was there also, and although I disliked him intensely, I made no bones about it and told them both what I had found.'

'What was that, sir?' Jenny sensed the reluctance and the distaste in Mr Ibbotson's attitude, but her heart was pounding away as she tried to wait patiently for what he was obviously forcing himself to say.

'I told Harry Howarth that I had been and looked up the case of your husband's untimely death in the coroner's files, and the medical report was clear on the fact that Bob Waring suffered a heart condition which could have caused his death at any time. It was a miracle he had lived to the age he had, apparently, as one of the valves of his heart was completely closed.' He waved a large hand in front of his face. 'No need for me to go into any more detail than that, but his days were numbered, lass.'

'So Harry Howarth was paying money out for nothing?'

'Not entirely. He admitted what had taken place, and admitted also that the woman finding your husband lying outside her house was blackmailing him.' A fist almost as big as a side of ham was thumped down on a pin-striped knee. 'What a man, Jenny! What a foul-mouthed brute of an apology for a man, your step-father is! And I'll tell you something, lass. I wouldn't have raised a finger to help him if it hadn't been for your mother.'

Jenny's face was anxious beneath her white cap. 'What did she say when you brought it all out into the open? What did she do?'

'She wept. She wept so much I can't rightly remember her saying a single word, but I got that man to promise that he would never give the woman blackmailing him another penny. I told her if she threatened him again, *when* she threatened him again, to say that he was in touch with the law, who know how to deal with blackmailers.'

'So that's that, sir.'

'Aye, that's that.'

The air was charged with emotion, the same indefinable emotion that had filled Ben Ibbotson's study on the rainswept afternoon. Jenny blinked away tears of relief, and tried to stammer her thanks.

'How can I thank you, sir? I came to you merely for advice, and you took time from your busy life to go in person and sort things out.' Her head drooped. 'I can never thank you enough for that.' To her dismay her voice choked on a sob. 'It's kindness, sir. I can stand anything, but kindness gets me, and what you did was more than kind, it was wonderful.'

She lifted her head to see him staring at her with such sadness that her heart turned over.

'You are only a child,' he said softly, 'and what I want you to do now is to put what has passed behind you, if you can. What I want is for you to be happy. To be *glad*, Jenny lass, and if I could see that it would be thanks enough. Not many stories like yours have happy endings, but I'd like to think . . . dear God, I would like to think. . . .'

He took Jenny's hand and held it between his own, and for a moment she had an irresistible urge to lift his hands and lay them each side of her face. And it wasn't a bit like Paul Tunstall had said: there was no passion, no lust, just that rare moment of knowing that two people as far apart as circumstances could make them, were as one, close in a way that no poet with his singing words could explain.

'Waring!' Mrs Bleasdale had come into the room, had been driven up to the house without either of them hearing. Her face was a comical mixture of shock, dismay, and pride at seeing the great man sitting there in her drawing-room.

'You'll have tea, Mr Ibbotson? Waring! As quickly as you can! I'm surprised that you haven't already. . . .' She glanced round the room for the non-existent tray as Jenny made her escape, to run back to the kitchen hot and flustered to tell Mrs Fanshawe that her mistress would never ever forgive her for this.

'I must apologize, ma'am.' Ben Ibbotson stood, towering over her, holding his hat in his hand.

Mrs Bleasdale unfastened her hat and puffed up her hair in front of the oval gilt-framed mirror over the mantelpiece. Her smile, when she turned, was gracious and womanly-wise, even as her mind teemed with the implication of what she had just seen.

Her uninvited visitor was ill at ease; she could sense that by the way he stood waiting for her to sit down, refusing to meet her eyes. And she wasn't going to help him, not her, and what was more, *he* wasn't going to help her, either. The small mouth champed on nothing, and the small eyes darted from side to side as she considered the implications.

'How is Sarah? I see her piano is still here.' Mr Ibbotson nodded towards the window. 'I cannot imagine Sarah without her piano. Did she not wish to take it with her?'

Mrs Bleasdale sat down. 'Sarah comes here to play most days, Mr Ibbotson. Paul is out in the fields with the wagons; he is hoping for a good harvest at the end of this summer. Who would have thought he would take to farming like he has?'

'Who indeed, ma'am. Last year his haystacks were as neat as rows of drilling soldiers.'

'Trust you, Mr Ibbotson, to come up with just the right description. You have a way with words, you know.' She wagged a roguish finger.

Ben sat down opposite to her. What on earth was he to tell this garrulous woman? He could read her like a book. One side of her playing the gracious hostess, and the other ferreting round in her mind for an explanation of why her parlour-maid had been seen sharing the sofa with the husband of one of her friends. He waited until Jenny had brought in the tray, set it down without looking at him, before leaving the room.

'I've been doing some unofficial legal work for your maid.' He balanced the fluted cup and saucer on a broad expanse of knee. 'Confidential of course.' He forced himself to look secretive.

'To do with her husband? She clams up, our Sarah says, when the subject of her marriage comes up. Has she come into money, then, or am I not supposed to ask that?' The question was put with a roguish smile.

Ben willed an eyelid down into a knowledgeable wink. 'No money, Mrs Bleasdale, just a legal formality, that was all. All over now.' He put the cup and saucer down on the sofa table and stood up. 'Now if you will excuse me, and will forgive my unpardonable rudeness in calling when you were away . . .' He bent his head over the cluster of rings on her fingers. 'I believe we are having the pleasure of your company Thursday week?'

Mrs Bleasdale sat for a long time after Ben Ibbotson had gone, drumming her fingers on the arm of her chair, deciding what to do. It would be gratifying to ring for Waring and force her to explain, but *would* she explain? And if she refused point blank, then there would be nothing left but dismissal, and, oh God, the boredom of interviewing yet one more village girl, all slack mouth and blank eyes. Of listening to Mrs Fanshawe's grumbles about a girl who didn't know a saucepan lid from a ladle, who fell over her feet, and came into the room with her cap slipping over her eyes, awestruck and dumb in company.

Strangely enough she believed Ben Ibbotson. He was too much a man of the world to spit, if not on his doorstep, then on the step of his friend's house, and if Jenny was not coming into money then there would be no question of her leaving.

And all right, admit it, she did not want her latest parlour-maid to leave. No girl had ever worked round the house so unobtrusively, doing jobs no trained parlour-maid would lower herself to do. Jenny Waring was bright, and willing and in a peculiar way lent 'tone' to the household, and more than one of Mrs Bleasdale's friends had complimented her on her choice of a maid.

'So helpful, Bertha. So clean and tidy. Where did she come from? She doesn't look as if she was born with a straw in her mouth.'

Besides, if she had a showdown with Waring, the girl would pack her bags and hare off to High Trees. Sarah had more or less admitted that she would like Jenny for herself, and if that happened, and Sarah felt her obvious loneliness a little less, then she would not need her mother so much.

And if Sarah did not need her . . . Mrs Bleasdale got up from her chair and went to take the small pack of patience cards from the bureau . . . if Sarah did not need her then her life would have no meaning.

She shuffled the cards, her face a mask of quivering despair.

After the blaze of summer the early autumn turned out to be the wettest anyone could remember. Day after day wild ragged clouds drifted over the valley, the turned earth at High Trees and the choked ditches spilled over until the fields ran like lakes.

Sarah was forced to forgo her daily visit to her mother, and when Jenny trudged her way over to the farm for extra milk one afternoon in October, Sarah blushed bright pink and confided that she thought – that she was almost sure – she might be going to have a baby.

'Mother says it will be another month before I can be sure, but I *know*, Jenny. I can't tell you how, but I feel different, here.' She laid a white hand over the ruffled frills of her lavender house-gown, and leaned her head back against the sofa cushions. 'I haven't bothered getting dressed today, because I can't go out, not in this weather, and Paul has been out all day laying a hedge with the men.' She put a languid hand to her forehead. 'My head aches so, Jenny, and my leg always pains me when it rains.

Why won't you come and live here? Mother gets furious with Paul because he leaves me alone so much. It's horrid lying here and seeing nothing but the sodden garden. Why don't you take off your cloak and sit and talk to me? I'm *bored*, Jenny. Paul says why don't I find something to do, but what *is* there to do here? I hate farming, Jenny. Everything smells so, and even Pootsy sleeps all day. She put out a hand and stroked the little dog's head, and Jenny looked away as she saw the red leather collar half hidden by the Pekinese's long hair.

How long ago since Paul Tunstall came into the cat-meat shop, his fair hair gleaming, and his teasing voice questioning her: 'First choice red, and second choice blue.'

Now she avoided him, knowing that he realized she was avoiding him, telling herself that there was nothing they could say to each other. Ever.

'I can't leave your mother, you know that.' She stood in the doorway, dripping rain she was sure, onto the polished floor. 'She took me on untrained, Miss Sarah, you know that.'

'Only because she was in a spot.' Sarah's mouth drooped sulkily. 'I love my mother dearly, but she has no idea of how to treat servants.' The brilliant green eyes widened. 'Not that I think of you as a servant, Jenny. If you came here you would be my *companion*. You could read to me, and mend my clothes. Paul says we have to be careful till the farm picks up again. He talks as if he was *poor*!'

Jenny glanced round the big pleasant room with the fire burning in the red-brick grate and the fire-irons burnished so that the flames struck little sparks off them. She laughed out loud.

'Poor, Miss Sarah? Poor is not having enough to eat. Poor is snuffing a candle out because you can't afford another, and poor is having to stay in because your boots need mending. That's what poor means.'

Sarah's green eyes widened. 'Stay with me for a while

and tell me about being poor, Jenny. I'll send a message over with one of the boys. Mother will understand.'

'Your mother is having the Ibbotsons to dinner, and Mrs Fanshawe needs the milk for an egg custard to go with the last of the plums for a pie. And I have a thousand and one things to do, Miss Sarah.'

Jenny tried to be firm and forthright, but it was difficult with the lovely girl lying there on the sofa, the lavender of her gown and the red blaze of her hair making a picture that appealed to Jenny's frustrated appreciation of beauty. Miss Sarah was a gentle affectionate *child*, a hundred years younger than she felt herself, and the thought of the coming baby filled her own heart with longing.

'I must go, Miss Sarah, but when the rains stop and you come over to see your mother, I'll read to you if it is possible.' She smiled. 'Why don't you read yourself, Miss Sarah? Why don't you have your piano brought over or ask Mr Paul to buy you another one? Then you would not be lonely, would you?'

'I thought you would understand. Of all people, Jenny Waring, I thought you would understand.' Sarah lifted the little dog till the top of its head rested underneath her chin. 'Very well, then. Come and say goodbye to Pootsy. If you won't be nice to me, then you can at least be nice to him.'

Reluctantly Jenny walked forward, off the polished surround, onto the carpet, over to the sofa. Trying not to show her unwillingness she touched the dog's wet black nose with her finger, then stepped back with a smothered cry as the sharp pointed teeth nipped her hand.

'Oh, you naughty boy!' Sarah turned the dog round so that its squashed face was inches from her own. 'It didn't hurt, did it, Jenny? He was only playing. You were only playing, weren't you Pootsy?'

'Goodbye, Miss Sarah.' Jenny left the room, hiding her injured finger in the folds of her cloak. It was true, she thought as she picked up the big jug of milk and started off across the fields. She had not been 'nice' to Miss Sarah, and if she faced herself truthfully she knew exactly why she had not been nice.

Miss Sarah's baby was living proof of Paul Tunstall's love for his wife, and all her dreaming, all her pretending in the little attic bedroom, was nothing more than that. Just dreams. She started to walk quickly, found that the milk was slopping over the edges of the big jug, then forced herself to walk more slowly. She was watching it carefully, holding it steadily when a voice behind her startled her so much that if she had not clutched the jug to her tightly she would have lost every drop.

'Jenny?' Paul Tunstall seemed to have materialized from nowhere, appearing from a gap in the hedge, his fair hair plastered to his head, his jacket black wet, and pieces of sacking tied round his knees with string like a man of the fields.

'What have you done to your finger, Jenny?'

Without a word he came to her, and looking down she saw with surprise that her forefinger dripped blood.

'Pootsy found out that I did not like him.' She held on to the jug, but before she knew what he was about to do, he took it from her, set it down on the path, lifted her finger to his mouth and sucked the blood away, his eyes never leaving her face.

'Now. We will walk to the barn together and you will tell me why you refuse to come to the farm.' He picked up the jug with one hand, steadied her with the other until she pulled at him, her eyes pleading.

'Please don't come any further, sir.'

'Then tell me why you won't come to the farm.'

'Because I can't leave the place I already have. Because I'm happy there.'

'You're lying. You haven't looked happy for a long time. You look terrible.'

She met his eyes. 'So do you, sir. So do you!'

He stared at her unsmiling. Her eyes were the brightest,

the most candid, the most arresting he had ever seen. There was implicit truth in their depths, and something else. A hunger, a loneliness, a needing. She called to him this girl, as distinctly as if she shouted his name aloud. With a swift movement he pulled her up against him.

His mouth covered hers with a gentle exploring sweetness. She tasted of apricots ripening in the sun, and her mouth was soft and yielding, so that the blood leaped in his veins. He pulled her closer still, lost to reason, drowning in her sweetness, till with a strength he would never have dreamed she possessed, she broke free and pushed him from her.

'Miss Sarah!' She almost shouted the name, her dark eyes wide and terrified. 'She's your wife! You must never ... never!'

Trembling as if she was taken by fever, Jenny stooped, picked up the jug, only to feel his hand gripping her arm.

'My wife is a *child*, Jenny! A child who will never grow up. Oh, my God, you must know that.'

She looked up into his angry face, saw the passion in his eyes and knew it was mirrored in her own. And the shame and anger made her cry aloud.

'But not too much of a child to be having your baby. Sir.'

He crumpled before her. Before he swayed and buried his face in his hands she saw the shock and utter disbelief. She faltered, and put out a hand towards him, a hand which he knocked away with a fierce downward motion.

'Sarah is having a child?'

Jenny closed her eyes in horror. 'You mean you did not know, sir?'

'Her mother knows?'

She nodded, unable to do more.

'Oh, God in heaven! She told her mother *that*? Before *me*?'

As she moved away he stumbled after her; as she opened the gate and stepped out into the lane, still he followed, numbed with despair, wanting her nearness, and yet making no move to touch her again.

'You must go back, sir.' Jenny's voice was full of aching concern. 'You must forgive me for speaking out of turn, and you must forgive Miss Sarah for keeping her secret until she was sure.'

They stood either side of the gate, and when he put out a hand and pushed the hood of her cloak away from her face, when he touched her hair, she knew he was seeking comfort and made no move to stop him.

'Go home, sir,' she said gently, and as Paul walked away from her, weaving from side to side like a drunken man, she watched him go, heard a noise behind her and turned to see Ben Ibbotson there in the lane astride his horse, a huge champing chestnut as overweight and unpredictable as his rider.

The big man slithered easily from the horse and faced her.

'What is going on between you and him?' The handsome florid face was dark with a terrible anger, and there was a scathing derision in the furious gaze.

'Nothing, sir.' Jenny faced him squarely. 'I had been to the farm for extra milk and Mr Paul walked back across the fields with me. That was all.'

She was fighting to keep her voice normal, calling on all her acting ability, widening her eyes in innocence even as she detested herself for the role she was playing.

He had been going to strike me, she told herself in amazement as without another word Mr Ibbotson remounted, pulled at the reins and cantered away. He would have struck out at me with his riding crop, I am sure of that.

Mr Ben Ibbotson was turning out to be not the man she had first thought him to be, and it could be, oh it could be that Paul had been right about him, because the blazing fire in the big man's eyes could have been jealousy.

Jenny turned into the drive of Cedar House, holding the jug of milk with both hands, feeling that the past thirty-five minutes away had lasted for a lifetime.

'You've taken your time, lass.'

Mrs Fanshawe grumbled round the kitchen, doing three things at once, being far too busy to notice that Mrs Bleasdale's parlour-maid was staring straight ahead with eyes that looked far beyond the present, with eyes clouded with a bewildered despair.

12

When Ben Ibbotson had stabled his horse, taken off his riding boots in the back porch, and stumped through into the house, the thunderous anger still set his features into a fierce scowl.

His wife was waiting for him, standing in front of the wide fireplace, nervously fingering the long gold chain of her locket, her eyes troubled.

'Where have you been, Ben?'

He threw his riding crop down on the sofa, surprised to find that it was still in his hand. 'Exercising Copper after the rain. Why?'

'Oh, nothing.'

He turned towards the door. 'I'll be in my study till it's time to get changed for dinner. I don't want tea.' He walked over to the hand-carved table and taking a key from his waistcoat pocket, unlocked the stand of cut-glass decanters. 'Have a glass sent in. This weather's getting me down. I feel like something stronger.'

'Why, Ben?'

'Why what?'

'Why do you need something stronger?'

He looked at her properly for the first time since coming in. She was pale, and the fingers twisting the gold chain were trembling.

'Sit down, Ben.' Her voice was low even as it rang with authority. 'I have something to say to you.' She turned and stared down into the fire, keeping her back to him. 'From my bedroom window, Ben, it is possible to see right to the bend in the lane.'

'And?'

'I wasn't spying, Ben. I do not spy or even pry, but I saw you, Ben. I saw you talking to that girl from the Bleasdale house, that Jenny Waring. You had arranged to meet her, hadn't you, Ben? In spite of what you said about her coming here on business, you have been lying to me, haven't you?' She turned to face him. 'It's starting again, isn't it, Ben? With a girl young enough to be your daughter?

She had expected him to be angry. He always was angry when he was cornered, so angry that in the end she sometimes found herself apologizing, but not this time. Not this time.

'I repeat, Ben. Jenny Waring is young enough to be your daughter. Almost young enough to be your granddaughter?'

With a sound that was more like a moan than an exclamation, he came to her, held her by the elbows and forced her to look into his face. All effort at control vanished, he hissed the words through clenched teeth.

'But she *is* my daughter, you silly bitch, you stupid interfering bloody excuse for a woman! You can't give me children, and she is *mine*! And I must never claim her. Never! Never!'

He let go of her abruptly, staggered over to the sofa and sat down, dropping his face into his hands, his whole body racked by shaking unmanly sobs. He cried as she had never seen a man cry before, in great gasps and shuddering sobs, the tears trickling through his fingers and running down into his shirt cuffs.

And when the mist before her eyes had cleared, Elaine Ibbotson knew that she had never loved her husband as much as she did at that moment. Kneeling down by his side, she pulled him close, stroking his thick black hair, murmuring endearments, hushing him into a semblance of composure.

'It was the maidservant who was sent away? Seventeen, eighteen or more years ago?'

'I had forgotten. Oh, forgive me, God, but I had forgotten, and then she came to me . . . oh God. If this comes out I am finished. You know that, lass?'

The face upturned to her was tortured and ravaged with despair. 'I *want* to claim her, can't you see? She is all I ever wanted, lass. Good and honest and a part of me. But I must never . . .'

'Never, Ben.' His wife was the stronger now. She knew it, and he could feel her strength. 'That is the cross you have to bear. For my sake as well as yours, dearest.' She glanced round her wildly. 'We would have to move. We would be the laughing stock. You know that? This must be our secret, yours and mine. For ever.'

Then she rocked him in her arms, as if he were a child, the child she would never have, this wonderful, artistic, passionate man, hers now for the first time in their marriage.

'Hush, my love,' she whispered, and drew him to her again.

By the time December came, and the fields were so sodden that drilling would be impossible until the spring, Sarah had, on her mother's advice, moved into a separate bedroom.

'No decent man touches his wife when she's in your condition, and if that sickness doesn't stop then I think you should come home, pet. Just till the baby comes.'

'But I can't. . . .' Sarah, pale and peaky, nevertheless took her mother's advice about sleeping alone, and spent her days lying on the sofa at the farm, her lame leg covered with a mohair rug.

Jenny went back to see her mother the week before Christmas, and found Harry Howarth, his big frame shrivelled to a shadow, with the wildness of his eyes the only thing alive as he muttered vaguely and incomprehensibly to himself.

The little house still reeked of poverty and neglect, but

when Jenny asked her mother how they were managing, Mollie evaded meeting her eyes.

'We manage,' was all she would say, 'but he's not the same. It's as if he's living in another place. Sometimes I think he's a bit . . .' She touched her forehead. 'He has these nightmares, and they seem to last him through the day.' She dabbed her eyes. 'I used to want you to come back but not now. It takes me all my time looking after him. I couldn't stand his bother, and nowadays he doesn't make none. You can see for yourself.'

Troubled in spirit Jenny went back to the country, wondering how she had ever left it, even for a day. There was a certain solace to be found in the bleak bare branches of the trees as they made a pattern of black lace against the perpetually grey skies, and there was her room and her books, and the big warm kitchen range to sit by listening to Mrs Fanshawe grumbling about all the extra work that Christmas brought.

In January Sarah moved into Cedar House, and now Paul Tunstall came and went like a stranger visiting. The dripping fields slumbered dark and silent, and the sixty-foot cedar tree grew from a great heap of rotted leaves outside the drawing-room window, where Sarah lay on the brocade chesterfield, watching her mother play patience and wasting the long hours away.

One dark afternoon when it should have been Jenny's half day, she took a book from the library shelf and went to read to the languid girl, lying still and thinking herself into invalidism.

That day it was a Wordsworth sonnet chosen at random from the brown leather volume of his poetical works, and as she read Jenny felt she had stepped outside herself as the musical flow of the words held her in their spell.

'Nuns fret not at their convent's narrow room; and hermits are contented with their cells; and students with their pensive citadels. Maids at the wheel, the weaver at his loom . . .'

'Have you ever been in a cotton mill, Jenny?'

Used to frustrating interruptions, Jenny laid the book aside. 'Yes, once. My father took me, but I held tightly to his hand and would not go right inside.'

'Why?'

Jenny smiled at the memory. 'Because of the noise, Miss Sarah. It was like nothing I can describe, all clanging and shifting machinery, with the weavers standing at their looms, standing on cold stone floors running with damp. Their fingers moved amongst the cotton threads with such skill and speed, and the cotton fluff caught in their hair like dandelion heads.'

'I've never been in a mill, Jenny.' Sarah shifted her position and the dog at her feet raised a tousled head in protest. 'That must seem strange to you when my father owns one.' She sighed. 'I never wanted to go into one though. It all sounds too dreadful for words. Is it true that *children* work there?'

'Not so much now, Miss, but they used to do. Nine- and ten-year-olds standing on boxes because they could not reach the looms. Brushing down they called it, for five and threepence a week. Working such long hours that they never saw the light during the winter months. Some of them so tired and exhausted that their fathers carried them home through the dark streets and put them to bed just as they were without undressing them.'

'My child will never have to do that.' Sarah patted her thickening waist with a complacent soft white hand.

'No, Miss Sarah. Your child will never have to do that.'

Jenny picked up the book, closed it and got up to take it into the library. When Miss Sarah was in this idle petulant mood she could be very trying. Boredom made her say unconsciously cruel things, and sometimes Jenny had heard her being so offhand with Paul Tunstall that she had felt an urge to cover her ears and moan softly to herself.

'Oh, he doesn't deserve it,' she would whisper. 'He doesn't deserve it.'

'My father says that his weavers don't know any better.'

Were the green eyes full of malice, or was she deliberately being provocative? Jenny didn't know, but her chin went up.

'Don't know any better than what, Miss Sarah?'

'Than the hard life. They just lump it, he said, and make their own lives. "Mek shift and fadge." That's how they talk, isn't it?'

'Some of them, Miss. Some of them only went to school as half-timers. Would you like me to talk broad to you, Miss? Just for a laugh?'

Sarah missed the sarcasm completely. 'No thank you, but I can believe you could. I've heard you change your accent lots of times, Jenny Waring. You talk one way to Mrs Fanshawe and another when you are talking to me. Did you know that?'

Jenny blushed. 'That's because I have an "ear" for sounds, Miss. I can't help reproducing what I hear.'

'Now you're cross.' Sarah stuck out her bottom lip. 'Oh, what a stupid conversation, Jenny. I'm so *bored* I could die!'

She stretched her arms above her head only to bring them down sharply as her mother came into the room, long nose twitching when she found Jenny there.

Sarah pouted. 'I forgot about lifting my arms, Mama. Jenny thinks I should be at home with my husband, don't you, Jenny?'

'Waring thinks *what*?'

Jenny almost dropped the heavy book so great was her surprise. She had known Miss Sarah was out to make mischief, and now she had done it. Good and proper. Bored almost out of her mind she had obviously decided to stir up trouble then lie back and enjoy the result. It was cruel and flagrantly obvious.

The green of Sarah's beautiful eyes deepened. 'Jenny thinks I ought not be here. She thinks a wife's place is with her husband, especially when she is expecting his child. Don't you, Jenny?'

It was time the gas-lamps were lit. Darkness came quickly at that time of the year when the light came filtered through the great tree outside, but the glow from the blazing fire had given Jenny all the light she needed for her reading.

Now the large room was grey-tinged, with shifting shadows, with Mrs Bleasdale's face a white mask of anger as she waited to hear what her parlour-maid had to say.

It was exactly like the times Harry Howarth had waited for Jenny to come in, waited and hunched over her, willing her to a defiance more tantalizing because it was controlled.

Jenny took a deep breath. 'Yes, ma'am, I *do* think that Miss Sarah's place is over at the farm. Especially at this most important time. It has nothing to do with me, but since you ask, yes, that is what I think.'

'Oh, you do, do you?' Mrs Bleasdale's pointed nose quivered with rage. 'You come here, turning up on my doorstep, like a waif and stray, with no references, and I take you in and feed and clothe you, and you wheedle your way into my daughter's affections, then try to tell her what she should do, and what she should not do.' She forgot her vow about biding her time. '*And* you entertain *my* friends in this room, just as if you were the lady of the house.'

'Mr Ibbotson came to see *me*, ma'am. He walked in here and I had no choice but to follow.'

'Aye, to sit on my sofa with him holding hands!'

'Mama!' Sarah sat up suddenly, disturbing Pootsy who let out an indignant yelp. 'What do you mean? Jenny isn't like that.'

'Oh, isn't she? Private business, yah!' Mrs Bleasdale forgot to be a lady as she rounded on Jenny. 'There's one thing you were never taught to do, Waring, and that was to keep your place. An' your place was in the kitchen peeling the tatties, and your place was waiting at table, an' your place now this minute is upstairs packing your things, and crawling back into the gutter where you come from!'

'Yes, ma'am.' Jenny put the book down on the sofa table,

then without glancing at Sarah left the room. She was so agitated that she forgot to use the back stairs, so shaken with anger and the injustice of it all that she hardly knew what she was doing.

It was like a book where two pages had stuck together so that you had to read the same words all over again. First Agnes Waring shouting at her through the closed door, telling her to go away, and now Mrs Bleasdale doing exactly the same . . . and oh God, even the weather was the same, cold and dark, and when she stepped outside the door there would be nothing this time but the unlit muddy lane, and the miles of walking before she could find shelter.

And where could she go? Where would she find another place this time? Everybody was angry with her. Mr Ibbotson who had wanted to take his whip to her, Paul Tunstall because she had stirred up trouble about the baby without meaning to, and even Miss Sarah who was not quite the guileless child she had seemed to be. . . .

Jenny's dragging feet reached the first landing, then as she stepped off the carpet onto the uncarpeted bit that led to her own flight of stairs, she heard loud voices down in the hall below.

'All right then, ma'am, not tonight, but tomorrow morning, I'm coming over for Sarah in the car and taking her back to the farm with me, where she belongs. What sort of a man do you take me for? A mamby-pamby milksop who visits his own wife because she hasn't got the guts to nip her umbilical cord?'

Jenny crept back, and leaning over the banisters, saw Paul Tunstall facing his mother-in-law, a woman whose temper was still up, who looked as if she could have thrown herself on her son-in-law and torn him to shreds with her sharp white teeth.

'She's stopping right here, milad. With her mother who knows how to look after her. She ought not to be having a baby if you want me to speak out. She's not strong enough to be having a baby. You're all the same. . . .'

'Madam!' Jenny's hands gripped the rail as the drawing-room door opened, revealing Miss Sarah with her glorious hair hanging down her back, and her eyes wide and terrified.

'Go upstairs and ask Jenny to pack some of your things.' Paul's voice was low and firm. 'I have the car outside, and the rain has stopped, and you'll come to no harm if you wrap up.' He turned to his mother-in-law. 'I didn't want it to be like this. I wanted you to listen to reason, but you didn't give me a chance. Now we'll have it my way. For a change. Sarah?'

Like a child who looks first to her mother for guidance, Sarah held out a pleading hand. 'Mama?'

Before Jenny could draw back, Paul came to the foot of the stairs.

'Jenny? I know you are there. See that Miss Sarah has what she needs for the night. I'm standing it no more.' He glared at Mrs Bleasdale and folded his arms.

Slowly, pulling herself up with the banister rail, Sarah climbed the wide stairs, as white as a little frightened ghost, her lame leg taking each stair stiffly, the little dog at her heels.

'Sarah!' Mrs Bleasdale's strident voice spiralled suddenly after her. 'Sarah?'

The cry was that of an enraged wild animal, all semblance of ladylike behaviour vanished. Sarah turned swiftly, found the dog beneath her stumbling feet, and before Jenny could move to help, fell headlong down the stairs to lie in a heap of lilac frills in the hall below.

Jenny reached her as Paul Tunstall gathered his wife up into his arms. For a moment he glanced back towards the door, then he walked steadily and slowly up the stairs, across the landing and into the white and gold bedroom, where he laid the unconscious girl down on her bed.

'I'll fetch Doctor Barnes. . . .' His voice was ragged with despair as he bent over his wife, pushing the mass of hair back from her forehead. 'Look after her, Jenny.'

'Mama?' Sarah opened her eyes, then closed them again, but not before Paul had heard.

And watching him go, hearing his footsteps in the hall and the banging of the front door, Jenny could not have said, at that moment, just where her pity lay.

With the still silent girl on the bed, with her husband driving his car like a maniac down the gravel path and out into the winding lane, or with the middle-aged woman, rubbing her daughter's hands, and moaning softly to herself as she crouched on her knees by the bed.

During the night Sarah lost the baby in a fevered tossing of blood-soaked sheets. Jenny worked with Mrs Bleasdale, sponging, soothing, carrying soiled linen down to the wash-house, arms bruised from the terrified girl's frantic clinging.

When the dawn came and Sarah slept at last, they faced each other, exhausted, grey-faced, *equal* in both mind and spirit for the moment, all their defences down.

'You can stay, Waring.' Bertha Bleasdale curled her fingers round the cup of tea handed to her, holding it like a common woman from the streets, reminding Jenny of the way her own mother drank.

Sarah woke as they were tiptoeing from the room, and held out her arms to her mother.

'Oh, Mama. I don't want to go back to the farm. I . . . I don't like being married.'

She was a child again, crying to creep back into the womb, wanting her mother's love beyond all else. Mrs Bleasdale rushed back to the bed and pulled the weeping girl back into the shelter of her arms.

'Then you don't have to be married, little love. You don't ever have to go back there again. . . .'

Jenny closed the bedroom door behind her, smiled a tired reassurance at a Mr Bleasdale committing the un-pardonable sin of being seen on the landing in his dressing-gown, and climbed the short flight of stairs to her own little room.

There was no doubt in her mind this time as to where her pity lay.

In spite of the intense cold, she pushed up her window and leaned out into a morning where the air was as sharp as needles on her upturned face.

Over the dark winter fields the man she pitied from the depths of her heart waited alone, waited to be told that his wife was never going back. Ever.

13

By a cruel stroke of what was first supposed to have been luck, Sarah's headlong fall down the flight of stairs had hurt her good right leg, leaving the bad leg untouched. So that normally she would have been left with nothing more than a slightly twisted knee.

But relying, as she had for years, on the strength of her good leg, using it as a lever and a crutch, now when she got out of bed and tried to walk she was found to be more crippled than ever.

'It's all that man's fault,' Mrs Bleasdale stormed. 'Scaring her out of her wits and making her fall. Everything that has happened to her has been his fault. You must send him away, Waring, the next time he calls. Tell him we don't want his presents or his presence in this house.' She sniffed. 'Tell him we want *nothing* from him, not now, or ever!'

It was pitiful to see the lovely girl pulling herself round the drawing-room by the furniture, struggling to get up from the sofa, allowing herself to be carried upstairs by Wilson the gardener, her red-gold hair a vivid splash of colour against the man's dark grey working jacket.

Jenny found her one day, a month after the fall, writing a letter with her small writing desk on her lap, and Pootsy stretched out in sleep over her feet.

'I want you to take this to Paul.' She whispered the request even though Mrs Bleasdale was out on one of her rare visits to friends for afternoon tea. 'I must tell him in my own words why I can't go back to High Trees. I must ask him to forgive me for what I have done to him.' She raised tear-wet eyes. 'It wasn't because of him I fell. *You* know that, Jenny.'

'She'll kill me if she finds out, Miss Sarah.' Jenny held out her hand for the letter, pushing it down deep in the placket pocket of her long black skirt. 'She nearly sent me packing then, remember? This time she'll mean it, an' I'll never find a job as soft as this, now that Mrs Fanshawe's got another girl in the kitchen. Look at my hands.' She held them out, admiring their whiteness, remembering how swollen they used to be with the ugly chilblains that had a year ago made the winters almost unbearable.

'I look like a lady now, Miss Sarah. I've even started wearing cotton gloves when I clean the silver. My own mam wouldn't recognize me.'

'Take the letter tomorrow when it's your half day. You can be there and back before you're missed. And don't wait for a reply, Jenny. I don't want to be involved. It makes my head ache just to *think* about being involved.' Sarah sighed deeply, and patted the sofa for Pootsy to jump up beside her. 'I could not bear it if things got complicated again.'

'But they *are* complicated, Miss Sarah.' Jenny bit her tongue. She would never learn. Always speaking out of turn instead of merely dropping her little curtsey and obeying without question.

Sarah shook her head from side to side. 'Don't start that again, Jenny. You don't know how ill I feel. You're never ill, so how could you know?'

'I'll go tomorrow, Miss Sarah.' Jenny walked to the door, closing it gently behind her before running swiftly up to her own room to conceal the letter beneath the pile of underclothes in the top drawer of the little chest which just fitted beneath the angle of the sloping roof. It would never do for Mrs Bleasdale to come back and hear the crackle of paper as she served their evening meal. And hear it she would with her ears as sharp as a grey squirrel's.

*

With her shoulders hunched against the cold wind, and her hair tied up in a scarf, with wild ragged clouds scudding across the sombre sky, Jenny set off to walk across the fields to High Trees. The choked ditches spilled over onto the narrow field path where puddles shifted and glistened in the reflected sky. The old farmhouse was cloaked in dripping ivy, and Jenny felt nervous and exhilarated at one and the same time, knowing she would be seeing Paul Tunstall again.

She opened the porch door, stepped round a pair of muddy boots, and lifted the iron knocker, letting it fall against the big front door.

It was answered after a long wait by a bent and gnarled old woman with a humped back that pushed her face almost onto her chest.

'Who are *you*?' She peered at Jenny through reddened eyes. 'We don't want nothing, thank you. Did you not see the notice on the gate?'

'I have a letter for Mr Tunstall.' Jenny stared past her into the big oak-panelled hall, bare of furniture, with a wide staircase leading to a window set high in the wall.

'A letter from who?' The old woman made to close the door. 'He's out, anyroad. Has been since first thing this morning, and don't ask me when he'll be back because I don't know that neither.'

A foxhound, grizzled with age, lolloped down the hall, thumping its tail at the sight of her. Jenny raised her voice.

'I've been sent with a letter from Cedar House. May I come in, please?'

The tone she used was one of authority, and grumbling and muttering, the old woman stood aside to let her pass.

'In there, then. Second door on the right, and don't blame me if you have a long wait. Stops out all hours he does, then comes back and expects his food to be hot. No wonder there's only me left, and I'm going next week. There's no cause for nobody to put up with him the way he is. His father would turn in his grave if he saw the way he carried on, drinking and stopping up all night. There's better folks than me would have gone long ago, but I knew Mr Paul afore he was breeched, and a right scallywag he was even then.'

Nodding her head in a curt gesture of thanks Jenny opened the door pointed out to her. She was even *behaving* like a lady now, refusing to listen to servants' gossip, successfully hiding the fact that her knees were trembling, and her heart beating in her chest like a tom-tom drum. She pulled off the scarf and patted her high-piled hair before unbuttoning her coat and walking over to the large bay window.

Outside the tall windows bare trees bent gaunt branches to the ground, and the whole scene was one of winter desolation and uncared-for neglect. She turned around and as she had done in her mother's little house, drew in a breath of dismay as she saw the dust lying thick on the dark furniture, the unswept carpet, and the fire-irons scattered anywhere on the ash-strewn hearth of the enormous fireplace.

In her mother's house she had rolled up her sleeves and set to; now she could do nothing but wait for the master of the house to come home. She glanced at the sofa from where Miss Sarah had confided that she was going to have a baby, and with a pang realized how lonely and spoilt the girl must have been.

This was a man's room, a room that had not known a woman's touch for a long time, and there by the fire was the high-backed chair where Paul would sit when he came in from the fields, his long grasshopper legs stretched out across the hearth.

The walls at each side of the fireplace were lined with books, and Jenny moved over to them and ran her finger across the bindings, wondering if she dare take one down and lose herself in the turning of the printed pages. She was actually picking one out, the anticipation quelling her nervousness and calming her down, so that when she heard a noise behind her she turned quite naturally and faced Paul Tunstall.

The change in him was so great that her dismay was audible. With a hand to her mouth she stared at the man who had once, a long, long time ago, a whole lifetime ago, walked into the cat-meat shop like a prince with golden hair and eyes that teased with a twinkling silver-grey light.

Now his hair seemed to have changed colour, to have faded to a dull brown, and the eyes were like Harry Howarth's eyes when he was too drunk to be sober, but too sober to be properly drunk.

'Jenny Waring? What have they sent you to tell me now? That my wife is dead? She would do that, wouldn't she, that mother of hers . . . after of course . . . long long after they had buried her.' He threw himself down into the chair by the fire, rolled a log into the flames and kicked it into position with the sole of his muddy boots.

' "Sarah . . . the daughter of John and Bertha Bleasdale." That's what they'd put on her gravestone. Wouldn't they?'

Jenny held out the letter. There was no point in talking to a man when he was like this. Far from unlessoned in the ways of drinking men, Jenny knew neither to agree nor to contradict, so she merely stood with the envelope in her hand, waiting for him to take it from her.

'And who, may I ask, has had the courtesy to write me a letter, Jenny? Mr Mill himself, or his wife, Mrs Long-nose?' He laughed, a sly laugh that ended as an unmanly giggle. 'Don't you think that is funny, dark-eyed Jenny, or are you disgusted with me, like those two foolish girls from the kitchen who went to be shop assistants in Preston?'

'The letter is from Miss Sarah. From your wife.' Jenny placed it on the small round smoking table to the left of his chair. 'She doesn't expect a reply, sir, so if you will excuse me I'll be getting back, it's going to go dark early this afternoon and I . . .'

'Sit down!' Paul shouted the command at the top of his voice, so that instinctively Jenny glanced towards the door

'Deaf, love. Deaf as a post, and daft as a brush, and don't look at me like that, pretty Jenny. I wouldn't hurt you, not lovely Jenny with the honest eyes and the virtuous ways. Sit down I say!'

He tore the envelope open, took out the letter and began to read, his lips moving like a child with his first capitals. There was stubble on his chin, and his carelessly tied cravat was spotted with food stains. Jenny sat down on the edge of the sofa, pity welling in her like a great dam, wanting to comfort and knowing that any words of comfort would have been waved away with a sweep of his hand.

'All women become like their mothers, that is their tragedy. Do you know that, Jenny, love? Or are dear Oscar's works banned from the library-for-show at Cedar House?' Paul crumpled the letter in one hand then hurled it into the fire. 'She's not coming back, or did you know that already? And who could blame her?' He waved an arm. 'All gone, Jenny, and that old crone in the kitchen is going next week. She would prefer the workhouse to living with me. What do you make of that?'

Jenny looked down at the unswept carpet, lifted her eyes and stared the unshaven man in the face. 'Miss Sarah is ill, sir. Since her fall she finds the greatest difficulty in walking. She needs nursing care, full-time nursing care. Could *you* give her that?'

He gave her a baleful glance from beneath lowered eyebrows. 'And would she come if I could, Jenny? Would she come back to me if I engaged a specialist from Harley Street to wait on her every imagined ill? Would she?'

'No, sir.' Jenny gripped her hands tightly together. 'And who could blame her?' She nodded towards the unswept hearth. 'This room's like a pigsty, sir. And you . . . do you want to know who it is you remind me of?' She took a deep breath. She had done it now, and no mistake. 'You remind me of my step-father, lolling there in that chair fuddled with the drink. You're sorry for yourself, that's what you are, sir. You are wallowing in self-pity, and you disappoint me, sir. I know you can't do much out there, not till the rains stop, but what's to become of the farm in the spring? What's happened to the men? Have they gone too? Have you sent them away with your snivelling ways? I saw no one when I came up through the fields. I saw nothing but waste and a terrible damp neglect. Is that what you would have your wife come back to? Is it?'

What Paul Tunstall said in a flat expressionless voice was the last thing she would have expected him to say. Anger she had anticipated, abuse even, but not this.

'Then why don't *you* come and look after me, pretty Jenny? Why don't you move in here next week, when that senile nattering doddering old has-been moves out?' His mouth twisted into a bitter smile. 'Or has Sarah's mother cast her evil witch's spell on you also?' His expression changed abruptly. 'Jenny, love. I *need* you. I've needed you for a long time.' He stared into the fire. 'Do you know how long it is since I heard laughter in this house? There was still the smell of death in these rooms when I came back from South Africa. I wasn't meant to be a farmer, Jenny. God knows *what* I was meant to be, but it wasn't a farmer. Then when I tried to work the farm I found I enjoyed it; for a while there were doors slamming as the men rushed into the kitchen for their mid-day meal then out again. There were hooves crunching on the gravel and the smell of scrubbing soap in the hall.' He shook his head from side to side. 'And do you know what? My wife *hated* it. Right from the very beginning she hated marriage and all that went with it. She said the house was as cold as a tomb.' He got up and reached for a decanter of port, lifted it, and shook it so that the fire caught the sparkle of the dark red liquid.

'Port in the afternoon. That would make a good title for a poem, don't you think, Jenny?' He filled a small glass, raised it to his lips and tossed the drink back as if it had been water.

'Did you have any lunch, sir?' Jenny knew she was

speaking out of turn, forgetting her place once more, then reminded herself that she had spoken out of turn to this man from the first meeting. There was so much emotion rampaging through her blood stream that every time she saw him, or talked with him it, was as if no barriers of class or upbringing had ever existed between them. She said what came into her head, and that was that.

'I can't remember.' Paul refilled the glass and drank it down again, half smiling at her, swinging the decanter between the fingers of his hand.

'Then you'll be sick, sir.' Jenny got up from the sofa, buttoned up her long coat, and draped the scarf round her head, crossing it at the front so that the ends hung down behind her back. 'You must know I can't come and work for you here. You must *know* that.'

Paul's smile held more than a suspicion of a leer. 'Because I kissed you, Jenny love? Because of one innocent harmless little kiss?' He came towards her, and she backed away so swiftly that he threw his head back and laughed, a laugh that ended as abruptly as it began.

'You need have no fear, virtuous Jenny. I asked you to be my housekeeper not my mistress.'

Bright colour flamed in her cheeks. She took in his bleary eyes, filled with scorn, his easy lithe body, thinner than it had been, and his thick hair tumbling over his forehead.

'Don't look so affronted, Jenny,' he was saying. 'You need have no fear. I've never raped a girl in my life, do you know that? Pleasured many, but never forced. . . .' He staggered and would have fallen but for the sofa behind him.

'Goodbye, sir.' Jenny moved on trembling legs towards the door, opened it, and turning round saw him holding the glass between his knees as he refilled it from the decanter. He didn't even raise his head, then as she stepped out into the freezing cold of the hall, his voice bellowed after her.

'Next week, Jenny! Don't desert me, Jenny. You're my

one bright star, did you know that? My one bright bloody star!'

'She knows where you've been, Jenny.'

Mrs Fanshawe's cheeks were flushed from the heat of fire-oven as she spooned fat over a leg of mutton spiked with rosemary. 'She wanted you for something and I heard her scream like a stuck pig when Miss Sarah told her you'd gone over to the farm.'

Jenny, her mind still fixed on Paul Tunstall crouched over the dusty decanter, drinking port in the afternoon, shouting after her with a terrible ragged aching despair in his voice, blinked in disbelief.

'But she wouldn't. . . . Miss Sarah asked me specially to take a letter. She was scared to death herself of her mother finding out.'

The meat dish was pushed back into position and the door with its burnished steel fitment closed gently. 'Slowly does it, Jenny, for a roast. I know there's some what would differ but every tub's welcome to stand on its own bottom, and I say long and slow, every time.'

Mrs Fanshawe took a jar of dried mint down from the high cupboard, shook some out into a jug and sprinkled sugar over it. 'Miss Sarah would just, Jenny. You've not known her as long as what I have. All flarchy and flowery over anybody new, making out they're her friend, then along comes someone fresh and she would cut your throat as soon as look at you.'

'But . . . how do you mean, someone fresh?'

'That music mistress who came in the front just as you went out the back this afternoon. Nellie had a good listen afore she went off, and then I heard what when on as she was being shown out.' The fuzz seemed to stand out on the cook's downy cheeks as she tried a falsetto imitation of Mrs Bleasdale's high-pitched voice:

'Then we can expect you next week, Miss Cronshawe. I'll have you met at the station.'

'But Miss Sarah doesn't need a music *teacher*. She's past that stage, surely?' Jenny slowly dragged off the scarf and walked over to warm her hands on the brown teapot on the table. 'Miss Sarah plays so well. I don't understand.'

Mrs Fanshawe lifted the kettle from the hob and poured boiling water over the sugared mint. 'This new one is to be a *companion*, from what Nellie heard with her ear up against the door panel. She will hear Miss Sarah play the piano, and read to her and be her *companion*. You've heard of them, haven't you? Too snotty-nosed to be with us in the kitchen and not quite snotty-nosed to be one of *them*. You *know*.'

Jenny poured herself a mug of lukewarm tea, then grimaced and put it down again as she tasted it. 'Then where does that leave me, Mrs Fanshawe? I've been the one doing the companioning for Miss Sarah these past weeks. I thought she liked it that way.'

The vinegar bottle was lifted from the cruet-stand on the dresser. 'There's nowt like the smell of mint, even when it's not straight out of the garden.' Mrs Fanshawe tipped in exactly the right amount of vinegar into the jug then gave Jenny her undivided attention.

'Look, love. I've got right fond of you since you came here, an' I can't forget what you looked like that morning. Starved to the bone, and right down. As down as you could get I reckon, but I want to tell you summat about Miss Sarah. I kept me mouth shut because I could see you was taken with her, and she was taken with you, and with her getting married soon after and everything, I thought mebbe things would right themselves.' She pulled at a stray hair on her small rounded chin. 'She's allus been the same, love. Spoilt rotten with her mother, aye and with looks that could have got her anywhere, if it hadn't been for that leg of hers. Loyalty?' She sniffed. 'Miss Sarah doesn't know the meaning of the word. She's fickle, Jenny, an' I'll tell you something for nowt. It won't be long afore she's tired of Miss Fancypants and her music and her

London accent. Then she'll be out on her ears, with the mistress looking round for something or somebody else to pacify her daughter who's never grown up.' The hair was proving difficult. 'Aye, and Mr Tunstall found out quick enough that tha' doesn't need to look at even the fanciest mantelpiece when tha's poking the fire.'

'Mrs Fanshawe!' Jenny's eyes flew wide, then she jumped as if suddenly prodded in the back, as the bell from the drawing-room jangled from its fastening on the wall.

'That's her.' The cook nodded towards the kitchen door. 'Best look sharp, love, an' . . . an' try not to be hurt. She can't help herself, love. It's Miss Sarah's mind what's twisted as well as her leg.'

Jenny knocked at the drawing-room door, waited for the summons to enter, then stood with her eyes downcast and her hands folded in front of her, refusing to look at the girl on the sofa with the little brown dog snuggled underneath her chin.

'Where have you been, Waring?'

'It's my half day off, ma'am.' Jenny studied the pattern on the carpet.

'I said where have you been?'

'You *know* where I've been, ma'am.'

'I want to hear you tell me, Waring.'

Jenny sighed. 'I went across to High Trees, ma'am.' She raised her head and looked straight at the lovely girl watching her with narrowed green eyes from the sofa. The eyes were calculating slits, and the message in them was obvious:

'Don't tell her about the letter, please!' they were saying.

For a moment Jenny hesitated, biting her lip. For a brief moment she was wishing she was back in the street, where at least you knew where you stood with folks. They did not grow women like Miss Sarah down the street. She frowned, and in that moment, the pity she had always known was waiting there inside her to get the better of her, intervened.

What sort of a person would *she* be if she was condemned

to sitting about, with two damaged legs stretched out useless in front of her? Never to run across a meadow yellow with buttercups, never even to walk down a muddy lane with the rain and the wind on her face? And Miss Sarah was afraid of her mother; she had seen that fear more than once, as she was seeing it now, and though she knew in her heart it was compounded of a mixture of love and terror, she wanted none of it.

'Why did you go to High Trees, Jenny?'

'I went about a job, ma'am. I heard that Mr Tunstall wanted a housekeeper, so I went to apply.'

There, it was said, and once again she had burned her bridges and her boats, and she might as well be hung for a sheep as a lamb. 'Mr Tunstall said I can start next week, ma'am,' she finished.

Even the girl on the sofa showed her amazement. There they were, the two of them, mother and daughter staring at her with eyes wide and mouths agape. Mrs Bleasdale was the first to recover.

'Then you can go upstairs, Waring, right this minute and get your things. There's no call to wait till next week.' The hawk-like nose seemed to protrude more than ever, to grow pinched and sharp with rage. 'You little scheming varmint, you! Get out of my house this minute, and don't think I don't know what you're up to, you little whore!'

'Mama!' The voice from the sofa was soft with reproach, but there was no telling the truth from that lovely mouth. Mrs Fanshawe had been right. Loyalty was an unknown quantity in Miss Sarah's vocabulary. There was nothing but derision in the green eyes, tinged maybe with the slightest touch of shame. Jenny could feel a certain pity for the Fanny Bests and the Miss Cronshawes who would bask in Miss Sarah's approval for the time it took for her to tire of them, then be sent on their way.

And when Miss Sarah grew tired of anyone, she realized, they might as well be dead.

*

Jenny made a parcel of her things, leaving the parlour-maid's uniform on her bed. She held the tiny cameo brooch given to her by Mr Bleasdale at Christmas in her hand, then casting pride aside pinned it firmly to the neck of her blouse.

It was quite dark now, but after the rain the sky was a clear washed navy blue, and the garden and the fields beyond were tinged with the silver of the full moon.

The lie about going to High Trees farm had been impulsive, brought out on the spur of the moment to save Miss Sarah from her mother's anger. Home was where Jenny knew she should be going. Back to the town, catching the horse-bus in the next village if she hurried, back to her weeping mother and the man who intentionally or not had killed Bob Waring. Trying to find a job without a reference to recommend her, leaning out of her bedroom window at night and smelling soot and the choking fumes of countless chimneys instead of the fresh country air. Hearing not the melancholy hooting of owls, but the wail of tom cats and the muffled oaths of the night-soil men as they went about their unenviable task.

Jenny tiptoed softly down the back stairs, hugged Mrs Fanshawe briefly, kissed her downy cheek, wished the new girl good luck, and stepped outside into the quiet garden, sleeping its winter sleep beneath the pale stars in the night sky.

Then, picking up her long skirts with one hand, and clutching the parcel firmly with the other, she turned her back on the road leading to the village and the chance of a ride into town, and climbed the stile leading to the fields beyond which lay the tall red-brick chimneys of Paul Tunstall's farm.

He was lying in a stupor on the sofa in the living-room, and for a frightened moment she thought he had stopped breathing. Jenny left him there, and found the old woman dozing by the kitchen fire, an empty pot of stout beside her on the floor, and nothing in the huge walk-in pantry but a slab of hard cheese, a hunk of stale bread and a massive jar of home-made pickles.

Calmly she set about making tea and toast, moving from fire to table and table to fire as if she had lived there all her life, and when the old woman woke up she explained that from now on she would be living in, that Mr Tunstall had hired her as his housekeeper.

'Then I can go tomorrow.' The old eyes had lost their sparkle long ago, and watched Jenny as if through a shrouded mist. 'Me sister needs me what with her being crippled with the rheumatics. She lost her husband in the war.'

Jenny's dark eyebrows drew together in a puzzled frown. 'In South Africa?'

'Nay, miss. The Crimean lot. He was a regular and one of the first out.'

'But that's fifty years ago!'

'Is it? Strange, it only seems like yesterday. Died he did, not with the fighting but with drinking dirty water from a hole in the ground. My sister reckons it must have been on the day she was putting flowers in the church for the Harvest Festival. Never believed in nothing since then. Is he . . .?' She turned her misty gaze towards the door.

'Asleep,' Jenny said firmly, 'and now if you will take me upstairs and show me a room where I can put my things I'll make up the bed then come down and give Mr Tunstall his supper.'

'He won't eat nowt.'

'We'll see about that.' Jenny held out a hand to help the old woman up from her chair. 'And don't you worry about him when you're with your sister. I'll see to him. I'm used to dealing with awkward customers.'

When she looked at it properly the next morning, the room was shabby. The jug and basin on the wash-hand stand were threaded with a network of brown cracks and the wallpaper, a design of pink and grey flowers, had the look of long-washed muslin. But there was a wardrobe, the first wardrobe she had ever owned, standing against a wall, flanked by a chest with dull brass fittings matched by the brass bed-ends. Even the Warings' house back in Park Road had only had cold lino on the floor. Jenny stared down at the faded carpet with housewifely pleasure, and holding the candlestick high turned and surveyed the simple room before closing the door gently behind her.

Then she went downstairs, and going into the living-room made up the fire and sat in the winged chair waiting for Paul to wake up.

She had come as his housekeeper, and housekeepers did not sit in the master's room like this. But even though she knew this, there was still that strange intimacy between them, she could sense it even as he lay in a sleep so deep he might have been in a coma.

Jenny moved the chair so that when he awoke the first thing he would see would be her sitting there. She wanted to see the gladness on his face.

14

Spring came early that year. The fields dried out and prim-
rose clumps lifted their rain-washed pale, yellow faces to the
softly clouded sky. The men came up from the village and
the newly-drilled fields basked in watery sunshine.

The shabby farmhouse shone with polish, and when Paul
came in from the stables or the meadow, he ate with Jenny
at the big scrubbed table in the kitchen.

For the first few weeks she had shot the bolt on her
bedroom door, despising herself for doing so, but soon their
relationship developed to one of friendliness, teasing
laughing friendliness, with both of them so tired at the end
of the day that sometimes they were too tired to talk.

She was so full of housewifely pride that one day she
took a broom and swept out the hay-shed, tut-tutting when
a hay truss burst its bindings and the hay scattered in the
March wind.

Paul caught her at it, and shooed her back to the house,
pulling at her kerchief so that her dark hair tumbled down,
cascading over her shoulders in a riot of waves. Her cheeks
were flushed, and suddenly he put out a hand and gently
touched her face. She stood quite still as he lowered his
head and kissed her closed mouth without touching her.

For a moment he saw the terror flare in her eyes, then
their bodies fused together and they were kissing as if each
must drink from the other or die.

'Jenny,' he whispered, and she felt him shaking against
her before he let her go violently and left her, striding from

her, from the house, with his broad shoulders hunched against the wind, walking like a man possessed.

He came to her that night, and when he saw her sitting by her dressing-table brushing her hair, with a thin cotton wrapper slipping from her throat, he lifted her and carried her over to the high bed.

'I'm not going to hurt you.' His heart-beats were choking him as he tore at his clothes, and when they were both naked he held her closely and brushed the heavy hair away from her forehead.

She was trembling so violently that just before he entered her he spoke softly, looking deep into her dark eyes.

'I'm not going to hurt you. . . .' He repeated it over and again, his hands caressing, his lips at her throat. Then incredibly she was as aroused as him. She wound her legs round him, drew him deep into her as her eyes closed in passion.

Her long hair tangled on the pillow as biting her lips she turned her head from side to side, and in the last unbearable moments she cried his name aloud, then was still.

'I love you,' she said as he lay exhausted, his limbs heavy and his eyelids drooping in sleep. With an effort he raised his head and looked at her face stilled with love, the dark eyes slumberous and the damp hair curling over her forehead.

'You won't be afraid any more?' He smiled, and her answering smile was so tender it pierced like a pain.

'I *love* you,' she said again, then he kissed her and settled his head sleepily against her breasts.

Jenny had never known such happiness could be. She had never known such optimism, even when her intelligence told her she was living in an unstable state of limbo. The warmth in the spring days went with her mood, and she stayed at the farm, having the provisions brought up by one of the field workers. It seemed to make sense to her that if she stayed put nothing and nobody could touch her.

She lived for the present, for each unclouded day. She learned to milk the cows and to mix the swill for the pigs. She wore her hair in two long plaits, and her face took on a sun-kissed look which brought out the colour and depth of her dark eyes.

Paul Tunstall called her Mrs Waring when the men were around; bossed her and hurried her from one task to another, so that sometimes a man would give her a sympathetic wink, as if he sympathized and wondered how she put up with such treatment.

She would take the lunch out to the hay-shed, great slabs of home-baked bread and dripping, and she gave silent thanks to Mrs Fanshawe every day as she remembered the way she did things, and followed her methods, improvising as she went along.

It didn't seem to occur to Paul that she could have done with help around the house, and if he had offered, Jenny knew she would have refused.

Their moments alone together were sweet and full of teasing laughter, and when he came to her room at night, her arms and her lips were ready for him so that their joy in each other increased to the fringe of anguish.

'I love you, love you, love you,' she would whisper and he would hold her closer and call her his pretty Jenny, and he would smell of hay and earth and horses, not drink, so that she gloried in him, and drew him to her again.

But Cedar House was still across the fields. . . . Jenny could see the top of the sixty-foot-high tree when she climbed a grassy ridge and shaded her eyes against the sun. Miss Sarah was there, no, not Miss Sarah – Mrs Tunstall, and one day the pink balloon that was her happiness must burst. She knew that as surely as one spring-like day followed another.

It came one day when she was completely unaware of what was happening, when she was setting a batch of bread to rise in the kitchen, covering the baking tins with clean towels and putting them on top of the fire-ovens to catch the warmth from the meat simmering slowly inside.

Paul was sitting astride his horse down in the far meadow, staring with satisfaction at the neatly drilled furrows, willing the tender green shoots to grow even faster. He could see the men working on the sloping exposed rafters of the stables, his mind at peace, his every sense dulled into complacency by the warmth of the late April day.

He started at the sound of hooves behind him and turned in his saddle to see Ben Ibbotson astride his horse Copper, watching him from beneath lowered brows.

'Forgive my trespassing, sir.' Polite as ever, Ben raised his cap an inch above his black head. 'But I've stayed away as long as I could.' He pointed with his whip to the spread of fields. 'Should be a good harvest at the end of the summer.' He nodded at the elderly foxhound panting in the shade. 'Ever thought of starting a new pack, Tunstall? It would be like the old days, would it not?'

Paul smiled and shook his head. 'Too busy farming, sir. My hunting days are over, and I've no regrets.' He was hatless, his hair the colour of pale barley, but the grey eyes were wary, as if he knew this was no polite social call.

'Care to come up to the farm for a tankard of beer? It's uncommon warm for the time of the year. I could do to slake my thirst, and you look a mite hot, sir, if you don't mind me saying so.'

The big man shifted in his saddle. He had kept his promise to his wife to let matters be, but it was no good; there were matters that could not let be, and his long expertise as a solicitor and a magistrate had taught him diplomacy, or so he thought.

'How is Jenny Waring?'

The question took the man smiling at him with complete surprise.

'Mrs Waring, sir?'

Ben nodded. 'Aye. The little maid from the Bleasdale place. I believe she's settled in well as your housekeeper?'

The inference was slight, but Paul caught the emphasis

on the last word. The light eyes sparked with irritation. 'She's very well, sir. As you will see for yourself if you come up to the house.'

'She's a good lass, Tunstall, a bright lass with spirit, a cut above the normal run of servants. You agree there?'

'I agree there.' Paul steadied his horse, a sensitive mare who seemed to sense his irritation. He had a sudden urge to forego his manners and canter away back down the wood path, hearing the horse's hooves on the hard ground and the twigs breaking, but he sat still watching the older man and waiting for what he would say next.

'Do you think it fair to ruin the reputation of a girl like that by having her living-in alone with you?'

Paul could not believe the evidence of his own ears. It would have been rank interference for the man to have queried his apparent neglect of his wife, Sarah, but to talk women's talk about a girl from the lower orders ... To his dismay Paul heard his mind form the pompous phrase. He twitched at the reins causing his horse to rear and whinny nervously.

'And what business is it of yours, sir, may I ask? Why should you concern yourself with the reputation of a girl like that?' Paul felt his temper rise, then to his astonishment he saw that Ben Ibbotson's own face had darkened with a terrible anger.

'Have you seduced her, man? Have you? I can't believe you've been alone with a bonny lass like that and not got up to some of your old ways. She deserves better than you. You a married man who can't keep his wife where she should be, or did that last accident the poor girl had make her into a liability?'

Paul pulled at the reins, turning suddenly and urging his horse into a trot. It pulled at the bit, but he forced it into a canter, then a gallop, whipping it on as his anger took possession of him. He heard the thunder of hooves behind him as he entered the wood. He heard the trees bowing as their branches tossed in the slight wind, then he was out of the closeness of the wood and into a clearing. He put his horse into a trot, then stopped, wheeling round to face his pursuer.

The two men faced each other with eyes blazing. It was ludicrous, it was unbelievable, but it was happening. Paul spoke through clenched teeth.

'I repeat. What has Jenny's reputation got to do with *you*, sir? If you were a younger man I'd have you down off your horse and beat the truth out of you.' The image of Jenny coming from the solicitor's house in the rain, troubled and upset, flashed in front of his eyes. 'Perhaps your concern is because the cap fits. Is it? Is it, then?'

To his amazement Ben Ibbotson seemed to crumple in his saddle as his anger evaporated into one deep sigh. Then he raised his head and taking off his riding hat looked straight into Paul's eyes.

'Don't you *know*, Tunstall? Can't you guess? In all your wildest dreams, can't you *see*?'

The normally ruddy face had a greenish cast, but as Paul stared at him there was something . . . the droop of the dark curly head, the wide-set eyes beneath well-defined black eyebrows, the set of the shoulders. . . .

Paul found he was shaking with shock, and even as he despised himself for his weakness, was unable to still the trembling of his hands on the reins.

'It's true, Tunstall. Jenny Waring is my daughter. I discovered the truth when she came innocently to me about some trouble with her mother.' Ben looked very strange as he lifted his head. His dark eyes were wandering and seemed to register nothing, but his voice was firm. 'It was a chance in a million that our paths could cross, but then was it?' He shook his big head from side to side. 'It's said we pay for what we do, eventually, and God knows I got away with it lightly eighteen years ago. Just one more servant girl sent away in disgrace, even though my conscience was eased by the fact that there was some poor chump willing to marry her.' He lifted his chin. 'And I don't need to tell you what I've said must be a secret between us. The most important secret you've ever been asked to keep.'

Paul blew out his breath, then his face tightened. 'And you want to try to order Jenny's life without ever claiming her. Am I right?'

Now they were speaking as man to man, the same language, the gentleman's code of honour at stake, understanding each other all too well.

'How can I claim her, Tunstall? Think what that would mean! Ruin for me as well as my wife. Good God, man. I'm up for Alderman in the autumn. I've already overstepped myself by keeping something dark I never should have – a near murder, no less. Think what a thing like that would do to my wife, to Elaine. Think of the gossip and the scandal. I can't do that to her. You know that!'

'And Jenny?' Paul's voice was low.

Ben's colour was coming back, but he still looked as if he could drop from his horse at any moment. 'Especially Jenny, Tunstall. Think what it would do to her, knowing she had a father who had no wish to recognize her as his daughter. Already she senses a closeness between us, but she must never know. Never! Never! Have I your word? As a gentleman?'

Feeling as though it must surely all be a dream. Paul accepted the outstretched hand, and there beneath a pale blue sky with drifts of cloud wisping across it, they shook solemnly.

'But you did not come merely to unburden your soul, did you?' Paul felt his impatience giving way. 'You haven't made your confession just to feel better, have you, sir?'

'No.' Ben Ibbotson was the lawyer again, the man who could take heart-break and mould it into ways and means. Paul saw him struggle with his emotions, then begin to speak as if he was addressing a client from behind his desk.

'I've been making enquiries about Jenny's ... about her mother. She's in bad straits, Tunstall. Her husband,

Jenny's step-father, has lost his reason, with good cause, though I won't go into that. Suffice to say that his damned Irish conscience has finally caught up with him.' A small pulse throbbed on his temple. 'I can arrange for him to be certified, easily, and I can also arrange for his wife to be paid a certain sum monthly, thus assuaging my own conscience,' he added wryly.

'In return for what?' Paul narrowed his eyes, admiring the older man's apparent return to normality.

'In return for your promise that you will send Jenny back home. Back to her mother, back to the town, before you ruin her, Tunstall. Dammit, man, do you intend to *marry* her?'

Paul expression was answer enough. 'How could I marry her when I'm married already?'

'There's always divorce.' Ben watched him carefully. 'You could send her away for a while, for the while it took to get your divorce, then send for her. You're living apart from your wife; it would be all too easy for you to spend a night or so in Manchester and provide the necessary evidence?'

'Divorce Sarah?' Paul looked startled. 'Her mother would never agree to that.'

'You would not be divorcing her mother.'

'Same thing. No, sir. Having a tragically deserted sick daughter in the house is a far cry from a divorcee. It suits Mama this way. I am therefore able to provide for her daughter without ever seeing her. Mama has got her daughter off her hands and still keeps her, if you see what I mean.'

Ben sat up straight in his saddle. 'So unless you want to ruin Jenny Waring's life, you will do as I say.'

'Which is?'

'Send her away, man. She's young. She'll meet someone else. Bound to with looks like that.'

'Which could mean *you* will never see her again. Have you thought of that, sir?'

Ben lifted his eyes to the floating clouds. 'Aye, Tunstall. I've thought about that. I have thought about nothing else for days. But I've given her nothing, all her life. I've given her nothing, and now I've got a chance to set her right again, and if setting her right means never seeing her again, then I'm prepared to do that.'

He lifted his cap, pulled at his reins and turned to ride away. 'Think it over, Tunstall, and I'll meet you here same place next week. Right?'

Paul rode back to the farm with his brain in a ferment of worry. The unbelievable interview with Ben Ibbotson had filled his mind with a jumble of mingled despair and a terrible aching sadness. He wondered how he would be able to face Jenny naturally, and when she held up her face for his kiss, holding her flour-dusted hands well away from his jacket, he turned away without even touching her.

'I'm going out again,' he said. 'No, I'm not hungry, or thirsty. You carry on without me.'

And holding her hands to her breast, Jenny followed him to the door and watched him mount his horse and canter away across the perimeter of the big field. She watched until he disappeared into the trees, and she knew that her bright promise of unending happiness was ending. Her eyes filled with tears as she walked slowly back into the kitchen to the smell of bread baking, and the sound of the clock ticking away on the cream-washed wall.

She had always known that her life at the farm was in no way resolved, but she had wanted it to last for a little longer, even for ever.

Jenny covered her face with her floury hands and wept. . . .

That night when it grew dark and the curtains were drawn against the night air that Jenny's mother had impressed on her was treacherous, they sat wrapped in silence, with Paul brooding into his second glass of whisky, and Jenny supposedly busy at her mending.

He came to her room and used her body as if it were a

drug, then when it was over he lay against her breasts like a child seeking comfort from its mother.

'I love you,' she whispered, and even as she said the words she accepted a fact she had not wanted to accept before. Not once had he told her he loved *her*, and when he had slept a little he took her savagely again, using her as if she were a prostitute. Jenny knew after that it was all over.

In the morning, after a silent breakfast during which he seemed to be avoiding her eyes, he rode out to the fields, and unable to curb her restlessness any longer, Jenny followed him over the stubble field.

She saw him standing on the high ridge, the place where she had stood on more than one occasion, shading his eyes against the morning sun as he stared over the fields towards Cedar House. There was such desolation in his stance that, feeling like an intruder on some private grief, she moved to hide beneath a wide oak tree, and when he turned the anguish on his face was more than she could bear.

Something had happened the day before; she knew that as clearly as if he had told her himself. Something to do with Miss Sarah and the house sheltering behind the high spread branches of the tall cedar tree. Jenny picked up her skirts and ran swiftly back to the farm, forcing herself to remember Paul's face as he had lifted the unconscious girl into his arms after her fall down the stairs. Reliving the moment when he had strode from the house, torment etched in every line of his tall figure.

All dreams ended. She knew that, and this one had gone on for longer than she dared to hope. She could not expect a man like Paul Tunstall to shut himself away with a girl from a cat-meat shop for the rest of his life.

She ran upstairs to her room and started to pile her clothes on the bed. If she hurried she could get a ride into the village on the cart that came with the mid-weekly produce, and if she did that, she would free Paul from the embarrassment of telling her that he had grown tired of her, that he had remembered at last he was a married man.

Jenny bundled the few things together, and remembered the times she had refused when he had wanted to buy her dresses and silk stockings and fine lawn nightgowns.

'That would make me feel like your mistress. Sir,' she had added for devilment, and he had swung her off her feet, holding her so that he could laugh into her outraged face.

'Oh, Jenny . . . lovely little Jenny, what a paradox you are! One minute like a Methodist maiden, all blushes and puritanical ways, and the next . . .'

And he had slowly lowered her, holding her close against him so that she could feel his desire, hard with longing against her thighs.

And now it was over. But never, never would she give him the chance to tell her so.

She turned the corner of the street just as the Black Maria with its high black sides moved away from the front of the house. She found her mother weeping in the arms of a neighbour, who stared at Jenny with hostile eyes.

'So you've come back then? And not before time. Went for her, he did, with the carving knife, and it took three of them to get him into the strait-jacket, foaming at the mouth and swearing words I never thought to hear in my born days. See, now Mrs Howarth, your lass is back.' She glanced at the parcel tied with string. 'You're all right now, love. See, look who's here!'

She left Jenny alone with her mother, and as Mollie raised a face bloated and swollen with weeping, Jenny held out her arms and pulled the shaking quivering little woman close.

It was all so dreadful, the smell, the filth, the shabby poverty, that she suddenly felt she could never bear it. She had been away for not much more than a year, but in that year she had changed. Now she had been where the grass grew green, and where cleanliness and warmth and light were taken for granted. There she had felt that on certain days she could have put up her hands and touched the sky. Now the woman she had become, recoiled from the dreadful drabness of what once had been her home.

'Don't cry, Mam,' she whispered, as she had whispered so many times before.

As undoubtedly she would whisper again in the future stretching before her into a terrible eternity.

15

That summer in the street where Jenny lived no birds sang. There was no hint of green to soothe the eye, and in front of each little house a semi-circle of mopped flagstones proclaimed its inside cleanliness.

'Look at her step and tha'll know what it's like inside,' was a maxim that held good, and now that Jenny was back, her mother's house would have passed the acid test along with the rest.

Down Jenny's street the gutters were paper-strewn, and they were choked with filth. Old paint blistered in the sunshine, and Mollie would often take a chair outside to sit on the flags and gossip with her neighbours.

Inside the house Jenny dreamed of the hay fields on Paul Tunstall's farm. She could close her eyes and see the golden crop rippling in the warm August sunshine. Paul Tunstall was all of her dreams, his clear grey eyes vivid against the tan of his thin face, his barley pale hair bleached by the sun. She could see him pushing it back from his forehead with the gesture she remembered so well. The ache in her body was a grinding cramp as she recalled his touch, and the more she tried to forget, the more she remembered.

True to his promise, Ben Ibbotson sent two pounds a month, delivered regularly by the postman, and whilst Mollie accepted it as her rightful due, Jenny shrank from her bland acceptance of it.

'He won't miss it. Not him.' Mollie had regained some

of her bounce since the day the Black Maria had taken Harry Howarth out of her life for ever. 'Made of brass his sort are. You saw yourself in the paper last week how he's been promoted to the bench of Aldermen for Preston. He's a public figure, he is, one of them philanderers what gives to charity.'

'*Philanthropists*, Mam.' Jenny's face was anxious and worried beneath the cloud of dark hair. 'I know he's noted for what he does to help people in need; they'll likely build a statue to him when he's dead, but that doesn't mean he has to give you money. Why pick on you? I know he came to do what he could that time, and my guess is he kept my step-father out of prison, but two pounds a month is a lot of money. I can't make it out.'

Mollie's usually placid face wore a stubborn look. She chunnered to herself as she sat at the table waiting for Jenny to mix her mid-morning pot of cocoa. Far better to say nowt than say summat she might regret. And yet, dear God in His Heaven, there was none as blind as them what didn't want to see. She could only suppose that the truth was so unbelievable that never in a million years would it have occurred to this suddenly matured and grown-up independent daughter of hers. If Mr Ibbotson had not said he would stop the money if she ever said as much as a word, she might be tempted. . . . As it was, things were perhaps better all round.

She watched Jenny mix the cocoa powder to a thin paste with sugar and a drop of milk before pouring the boiling water into it, and in a rare moment of perception she saw how the fresh pink colour had faded from Jenny's cheeks, and how her downcast eyes seemed to be shuttered in sadness, making her look far older than her years.

'Besides, love, how could we manage without the money? Now they've put the rent up to five and sixpence a week, and I've upped the burial insurance to fourpence, not forgetting the price of a hundredweight of coal, what would we *do*?' She buried her nose in the steaming pot of cocoa and when she raised her eyes Jenny was not surprised to see that they were moist with the threat of tears.

'Mam, don't cry,' she said automatically. 'What are you crying for now?'

Mollie sniffed and groped in her skirt pocket for a handkerchief. 'I'm crying because you won't tell me nothing. Me, your own mother!' Her chins quivered pathetically. 'You come back home without a reference, then wonder why you can't get taken on anywhere. Why can't you write to that Mr Bleasdale what owns the mill up Hollynook way? Why can't you write and ask that farmer chap for one?' Her eyes brimmed over. 'He didn't do nothing at you, did he?'

'No, Mam!' Jenny shouted the denial. 'I've told you and told you that I won't ask him for anything. It's a matter of pride.'

'Pride!' Mollie dismissed that quality with a loud snort. 'I'm glad I've got none then, otherwise we'd starve.' She turned off the tears as abruptly as if she had grown a tap from her forehead. 'Then what about Bob Waring then?'

'Bob Waring?' Jenny shouted the name as if it were an obscene word.

'Aye, him.' Mollie set her pot down on the table with a jerkiness that spilled splashes of cocoa over the clean cloth. 'You *were* his wife, Jenny, even if it were only for a short time. He was still your husband, and don't tell me he hadn't got a tidy bit put by. His first wife had property I heard. Why don't you write to that sister of his, and just mention the way we're placed? I bet her brother would turn in his grave if he knew how she treated you, especially with him being a praying man. An' why don't you go to Chapel no more? Bob Waring owes you something; I'd have the law on his sister if I was you.'

'Mam!' Jenny shouted it like an explosion. 'Bob Waring owes me nothing! Being married to a man for a day and a night doesn't guarantee a meal ticket for a lifetime. I wouldn't communicate with Agnes Waring or *beg* from

236

her, not if I died from starvation. She turned me out, Mam! It was a dark cold night and she locked me out! That's where all her praying got her! She's evil, Mam! Like he was ... sanctimonious on the top and rotten inside.' Jenny walked quickly to the stone slopstone and poured the cocoa away. 'What sort of a girl do you think I am?'

'I don't rightly know, Jenny.' The chins did their quivering little dance once again. 'You seem to get the wrong side of everybody somehow. You speak your mind when you should be keeping your mouth shut, then you wonder why you land up in trouble. You've a streak in you that I can't fathom. Why you have to be different I don't know.'

She applied the handkerchief to her streaming eyes again, knowing full well why her daughter was 'different' and knowing equally that she was treading a difficult road if she said more. 'There's bad blood in you somewhere,' she said, getting up from her chair and snivelling her way upstairs.

Jenny watched her go, waited until the curtain at the foot of the stairs had fallen back into place, then took her mother's cocoa pot over to the slopstone.

'I love you, Mam,' she muttered, facing a truth she had kept hidden inside her for a long time. 'I love you, but I don't *like* you. God forgive me for even thinking it, but I don't like you, not one little bit.'

That day they sat down to a meal of boiled onions sprinkled with salt, mopping up the colourless liquid with hunks of bread, and the next day the money came from Ben Ibbotson.

For the first time there was a note enclosed, addressed to Jenny. It was written in the big man's decisive writing, kept short and to the point.

'Dear Jenny Waring. I hope you are well. The harvesting is well under way at the farm and I thought you would be interested to know that Miss Sarah is back with Mr Tunstall again. He fetched her in the trap one day, and has engaged a day nurse for her, and another for during the night. Once a week he takes her over to see her mother and leaves her there for the day, bringing her back in the evening. I thought you might like to know this. Yours sincerely, B. Ibbotson.'

Jenny folded the letter and put it away in the pocket of her skirt. Then she went upstairs and sat on the edge of her bed staring at the wall.

Mr Ibbotson had wanted her to know that Miss Sarah was back. In the strange way he seemed to have involved himself in her life and her welfare, he had *wanted* her to know. He had guessed maybe that the dream lingered where she imagined herself going back some day, and he had known that with Miss Sarah there it would be impossible.

He had guessed how it had been between her and Paul, and he was telling her in a subtle way that she had done the right thing by coming away. He was *paying* her to stay away. He was sitting behind his desk in the study, dark with the green shade of trees outside, and he was playing at being God. And her simple little mother downstairs thought he was a philanthropist!

Stung into action, Jenny poured cold water into the bowl on her washstand, an addition to her room she had insisted upon since coming home, and swilled her face, rubbing it with a rough towel till it shone. She pinned her straw boater on top of her high-piled hair, took out a clean pair of white cotton gloves from a drawer, bit hard at her lips to give them colour, and was ready.

It was a four-mile walk to the iron foundry in Dartwell Street where Bob Waring had worked since leaving school at thirteen, but rather than ask Mollie for a penny of Ben Ibbotson's money, Jenny decided to pass the tram stops, where people risked life and limb by dodging through the traffic to climb aboard. She was going to do something she never thought she would have the nerve to do. Her mother had maybe been right in saying that Bob owed her something. Jenny nodded her head twice, so that a

238

small boy swinging from a rope tied to the arm of a lamp-post stared at her strangely.

She was going to march right into that foundry place and ask to be taken on. Yes, she was, and if they tried to turn her away she would remind them of the long years her husband had worked there with such dedication that he had gone in on the morning after his wedding. She would remind them of how he had died almost on their doorstep, hurrying home late as usual, long after the other clerks had gone, and if they still would not listen she would say:

'Nearly twenty years pen pushing for you, and what did he get for it? A bunch of flowers to lay on his grave!'

She nodded again and turned into a street where a trio of babies not long out of their nappies played bare-bottomed in the gutters. Old pointed faces on tiny bodies, impetigo scabs on little chins, legs already bowed with rickets. Noisy, restless children who, if they had been well fed from birth might have looked completely different.

Only one in five fronts mopped daily with that wide semi-circular frontage heralding the desperately sought for cleanliness inside. One window with a tower of bright red and yellow cocoa tins to make do for the absence of curtains, and another shining out from its neighbours with lace curtains starched and dipped in dolly blue, fronted by a geranium in a brass pot.

Jenny walked on, feeling her cotton blouse sticking to her back as the sun rose higher in the hazy sky, wishing that, just for one day, she could wave some magic wand and transport the dreary women and their numerous offspring away from the filth of the streets out to the country where the sky was a clear blue, where streams trickled lazily over round grey stones.

She lifted her head and walked on with her swinging long stride, her face rosy beneath the round straw hat, her vitality restored now that she was doing something positive.

'I'll make them take me on, I'll *make* 'em!' she muttered fiercely.

239

Young Mr Hargreaves, Mr Will to the employees at the small privately owned iron foundry, looked up from his desk to see his only lady clerk, Miss Warburton, standing discreetly in the doorway.

'Yes, Miss Warburton?'

He tried not to look as impatient as he felt. Already that morning he had been informed by the foreman down on the shop floor that two orders would have to be delayed. His father had insisted on coming into the office as usual for the three hours he worked each day, and with his memory failing at seventy-nine, had still argued the toss about a procedure he knew nothing about.

At fifty-four Mr Will still felt there were days when he was still treated by his father as if he were still wet round the ears, and it was only his affection for the doddering old man that stopped him from giving the old worriter the rough edge of his tongue.

'There's a young lady in the outer office, sir.'

Mr Will thought that Miss Warburton looked uncommonly surprised, but then with her grey hair scragged back like that she *always* looked surprised.

'She says she is Mr Waring's widow, sir. Mr Bob Waring. You know, sir, the man who dropped dead in the street outside. . . .'

'I know, Miss Warburton. I remember.' He took off his spectacles and laid them down on his blotter. 'Did she say what she wanted?'

'No, sir, she says she wants to see you privately. On personal business.'

Mr Will picked up the spectacles and put them on again. 'Then send her in, lass. Oh, and see we're not disturbed for the next ten minutes or so.' He frowned. 'It's the least we can do, considering . . . nasty business that was . . . real nasty.'

'Yes, sir.' Miss Warburton seemed about to say something else then changed her mind and left the glass-fronted office.

'Her feathers are up, I wonder why?' Mr Will began

to write, then threw his pen down and stared at the door.

And nobody in their right senses could ever have called Mr Will Hargreaves a fanciful man, but when Jenny came through the door with her face alight with eagerness, her cheeks as red as polished apples, and her dark hair shining beneath the ridiculous straw boater, he was immediately transported up and out of his drab surroundings.

This girl was summer. She was cool green water in a cove; she was as fresh and quick as those remembered droves of minute darting fish, like a packet of gleaming pins spilled into the water. She was beautiful, so beautiful that for a long moment he could only stare and wish that he were thirty years younger.

He took off the spectacles and saw the way his clerk Thomas Eccles was actually standing up on the rung of his stool down in the main office to see better. Mr Will gave him a look, then coughed.

'Mrs Waring? This is indeed a surprise. What can I do for you?'

'I hope you can give me a job, Mr Hargreaves.'

Jenny had not meant to blurt it out like that. She had meant to lead up to her reason for being there, gently. First she had been going to say how her husband had always appreciated working for Mr Hargreaves Senior, and for Mr Hargreaves Junior, not come straight to the point as rudely as that. She bowed her head, and stood as she had learned to stand in front of Mrs Bleasdale, with her hands folded together in front of her.

'A job, Mrs Waring?' Jenny heard the amusement in Mr Hargreaves's deep voice, and bit her lip.

'Come and sit down, lass.' She felt better when she recognized the kindness and moved forward to sit down on the small hard chair indicated to her by a sweep of the hand.

'What kind of a job had you in mind, Mrs Waring?' Mr Will leaned back in his swivel chair and smiled. 'I can't see you on the shop floor, somehow!'

Jenny smiled back, shaking her head so that the black velvet ribbons fastened to the back of her hat did a little dance. Mr Will stared at the sight, enchanted.

'I write a good hand, Mr Hargreaves, a *very* good hand. I'm quick at figures, and . . . and I get on well with people. I used to work in a shop,' she added, crossing her fingers in case this kindly man asked her what kind of shop.

'Do you typewrite?'

'No, sir. But I could learn,' she added desperately. 'I pick things up quick as a flash.'

It was in that moment that Mr Hargreaves, father of four girls not all that much older than the lovely creature sitting across from him, saw and recognized the desperation in her dark brown eyes. He tried to bring to mind the almost forgotten little man who had occupied one of the stools down in the office for years, and surprised himself by the unbidden thought of that pious crawling young-old man holding this exquisite girl in his arms.

'It was a terrible thing that happened.' He leaned forward, clasping both hands on the blotting pad. 'My father and I, we had neither of us ever guessed that your husband was in such delicate health. He was always so conscientious, so hard working, so wedded to his job.'

'Yes.' Jenny seemed to shake off the memory of her dead husband with an involuntary shudder. 'He always spoke well of you, sir.'

Mr Will rubbed his chin thoughtfully. 'And he . . . Mr Waring, he left you well provided for?'

'No, he left me nothing.'

Jenny touched the cameo brooch at the neck of her blouse as if seeking reassurance. 'His sister and I, we didn't see eye to eye. I left my husband's house almost immediately after his death, and since then we've had no communication.'

'Ahem . . .' Mr Will was at a loss. It was he who was doing the interviewing, damn it, he was the boss, and yet somehow this young lass had taken him, Mr Hargreaves,

242

man of means, keen Mason, dutiful husband and father, Church Warden of St Phillip's, and made him feel it was his bounden duty to help her. He took a spotlessly white handkerchief from his breast pocket and breathed on his spectacles before rubbing the lenses with a thoughtful circular movement. Character, that was what it was. Personality. An extra indefinable something that he only wished one of his daughters possessed. Why, with a disposition like this, they could have – he would have been willing to pay for them to see the stars. As it was, they seemed content to sit with their embroidery tittle-tattling with their mother, docile, obedient, obviously destined never to give their father a moment's bother. He sighed.

'And you've had no experience other than as a shop assistant?'

Jenny's glance was direct and disconcerting. 'I have worked as a parlour-maid, and helped on a farm.'

Mr Will tried not to gulp his surprise. 'References?'

'None, sir. I left my last place in a hurry.'

'May I ask why?'

'Private reasons, sir.'

'Oh, I see.'

And strangely he *did* see. This girl would draw trouble, man trouble to her like a magnet. And yet why Bob Waring? Why in God's name had she chosen a man like that to marry?

'I'm afraid there's nothing I can offer you, Mrs Waring. I'm very sorry, but as you can see, we are only a small firm. We only deal in small parts, and the administration side is run by just a handful of clerks, myself, my father on occasions, and Miss Warburton – the lady who showed you in.' He smiled a rueful smile, and waited for Jenny to accept his decision and go.

To his amazement she pulled the chair forward, leaned across the desk, and for a wild moment he thought she was going to take his hands in hers.

'Mr Hargreaves, sir. Please, listen. I'm not cut out for

begging, but I'm begging you now. I've tried and tried to get a job without a reference, and it's no good. I seem to put the women who've interviewed me off, and the men, well, I can see them fingering their moustaches and wondering how easy I would be.' Jenny held up a hand. 'Don't be shocked, sir. You are a family man, a good man. I know a lot about you through my husband, and when he died you said if there was anything you could do to help . . . well, now there is. You can repay all those years he spent working for you by giving me a chance. Anything! Making tea, sweeping the floor, anything! I have to work, sir. Working is as important to me as breathing. I can't live on charity. I can't!'

Trapped, Mr Will stood up and stared down into the office. In spite of the normal frustrations in running a small business, things had been looking up lately. Only last week he had taken on two more apprentices, and only last evening Thomas Eccles had stayed on late to catch up with some ledger work. He fingered his muttonchop whiskers, then he walked back to his desk, extracted a foolscap sheet of scribbled words and figures, and passed it to Jenny.

'Very well then, lass. Against my better judgement I'm going to give you a trial. Take this to Miss Warburton, ask her to show you a desk and stool and copy this out in fair writing. Neat figures and legible writing. Then bring it back to me.'

Jenny took the paper, bowed her head in thanks, and walked with her light step out of the office, leaving Mr Will raising his eyes ceilingwards as he called himself the softest chump in Christendom.

Jenny walked home so quickly that she was almost running. Now the black colour of the building, the pavements, the streets, seemed to be bouncing a white light back at her. The ashes of age had fallen from the people's faces, and the grand poetic landscape of the surrounding moors had infringed the streets so that there was space to breathe. She was on the man before she recognized him;

she was turning into her own street, the news that she had found a job bursting in her throat, the words trembling on her lips.

'Paul!' She stopped, and the colour drained from her face, leaving her white and still as a small pale ghost. 'Oh, Paul! I never thought to see . . .'

He drew her by the arm round the corner of the cobbled back, then with both his hands gripping hers, he said:

'Oh, Jenny, Jenny love. I had to see you. I tried and tried, but I had to come.'

The heat from her body brought little beads of perspiration on her upper lip, but she could not withdraw her hands to wipe them away. He was holding on to her as if he was drowning.

'But how . . .?' She stared up into his face, seeing the line of strain beneath his tanned skin, then she blinked and smiled. 'Oh, Paul, it's good to see you, so good.'

He shook her hands gently. 'I left the horse and trap at the Bay Horse, then I walked.' He let go her hands and slid his own up her arms to rest on her shoulders. 'You had told me how it was where you lived, but I never dreamed, I never imagined . . .'

'That it would be so awful?'

Their faces were almost touching. To people passing within a few yards at the entrance to the back, they were merely a pair of lovers saying a fond farewell, but to them both it was as if they were making love. His eyes were taking her, and she gazed deep, as though she was responding. His mouth was sweet as her own lips parted for the kiss that did not need to be.

'I love you, Jenny,' he whispered, and she closed her eyes against the sweet anguish of hearing it for the first time. 'I love you, and I can't go on living without you. You are all I need.' He raised a hand slowly and as if in a dream, ran a finger softly down her cheek, and heedless of time and place, she turned her mouth and caught the finger between her teeth.

245

He shuddered and swayed towards her, then the grey remembered eyes opened wide as she stepped back.

'Paul! Your wife? Miss Sarah? I know she's back with you because a letter came from Mr Ibbotson this morning. How did that happen? How did you persuade her to come back to the farm?'

He reached for her again, but she resisted. 'I have to know, darling. You have to tell me.'

The unexpected endearment, said so softly, brought unmanly tears to his eyes, and as he blinked them away angrily Jenny saw the depth of his anguish.

'Paul?'

He shook his head wearily from side to side. 'I wish I could tell you that it was of her own accord, but her dear mama has suffered a slight stroke, and with her upstairs out of the way I went with Mr Ibbotson and persuaded my wife that forgetting the obvious reasons, and taking into consideration only the practical ones, it was her duty to relieve the burden on the work staff of Cedar House and return to me.'

'That sounds like Mr Ibbotson's legal phraseology, Paul.' Jenny half smiled. 'He seems to concern himself with other people's problems to an unwarranted degree.' She put her head on one side and smiled mischievously. 'Now I am talking like him. It must be catching.' Then she grew serious again. 'How is it with Miss Sarah, Paul?'

He stared down at the cobbles of the steep back, kicking disgustedly at their greasy surface. 'She hardly moves from her couch, Jenny. She grows plump and the little Pootsy grows plump, and every Sunday I carry her out to the carriage and take her over to Cedar House where her mother is brought downstairs where they loll and commune the day away.'

'And will Mrs Bleasdale recover?'

'They say she is far from the invalid she pretends to be, even now, but like mother like daughter, I think they have

246

both found that invalidism brings its own power, given the money to indulge in it.'

'Paul! That's cynical.' Jenny realized that as always between them there was a stepping out of class. She was speaking to him as an equal, and he was treating her the same. He was talking to her as naturally as if, like his wife, she had grown up with never a need to dirty her hands, with a maid to brush her hair, and a handy man to clean and polish her boots. He was handsome and filled with the vitality of life; he loved her and wanted her as much as she wanted him.

And it could never be.

'We must not meet again, Paul.' It was as if the woman she had grown to be was chiding the romantic, poetry-loving girl she had once been. 'You must not come again, an' I must never ever be tempted to come out to the village. Paul! Don't be angry. I've got a job in an office. Not scrubbing or cutting cat-meat up, but *writing*, Paul! Sitting on a stool and writing in big fat ledgers. . . .' She spread her arms wide to show him, her face bright with excitement. Then as suddenly she dropped her arms to her sides. 'An' don't go thinking I am happy, Paul Tunstall, because I am far from that.' She turned and put out the tip of her tongue at a small girl watching them from the street, her face tight with the fascination of realizing there was something 'going on', her small feet itching to run home and tell her mam about the fancy man Jenny from the bottom house was talking to down the back.

'See what I mean, Paul? That is all that child has to do. There are no fields for her to run wild in, no trees to climb. I hate it here, Paul, I know now that I always hated it, an' I'll tell you something else. Some day I am going to get out. I am going to save, even if it's only twopence a week, an' I'll get a cottage to rent in the country. I will, and don't tell me I can come back with you, because I couldn't let you be making love to me upstairs while Miss Sarah and that night nurse you've got for her were in the downstairs room.' She shook his arm gently. 'We've got to forget each other, Paul. You've got to go on, and I've got to go on, because life isn't all roses, not for some folks it isn't.'

'Jenny!'

She heard him call after her, but before he could stretch out a hand to hold her she was running away from him, feeling the tears gush from her eyes as she ran. Wiping them away with the flat of her hand. On down the street and opening the front door with such force that it banged back against the plaster, causing Mollie to call out from the back living-room:

'That you, Jenny?'

'Yes, Mam, it's me.'

She stood quite still for a while in the unused parlour, her hands gripping the back of the horse-hair sofa, her chest tight and hurting with the tears she knew she must not shed. She had sent him away; she had done the right thing, and oh, dear God, and sweet loving Jesus, if this was what doing the right thing made you feel like, then the next time she came on this earth it was going to be as a bad bugger. The baddest bugger of them all.

16

Although Thomas Eccles had left school at thirteen and gone straight into Hargreaves's foundry, to a white collar job, as his parents proudly boasted, he had always resented their assumption of his cleverness.

'Clever lads stop on at school, and then go on to take degrees and things. Where is it going to get me adding figures and making invoices out? I'm twenty-one now, and if I'd served my apprenticeship down in the shop I'd be finished now. I'd have done me seven years.'

'And been what?' Mr Eccles lowered his evening paper a fraction. 'A machine minder, that's what, lad. A fancy name so they could get cheap labour out of you, then pushed out when the slump came, an' mark my words there's going to be one. Why, these big firms will swallow a little midden like Hargreaves's whole!'

'Then I will still be out of work, the only difference will be that I'll be an out of work pen-pusher.'

'Tha can pen-push anywhere.' Mr Eccles ruffled the pages in dismissal. 'Why don't you write to them lot at the Town Hall? Now that *would* be a step in the right direction.'

'We didn't want to see you coming home with mucky hands and oily overalls, lad. We only wanted the best for you.' His mother added her weight to the argument, an argument that had gone on regularly for more years than Thomas cared to remember.

He was stuck, and he knew it, and what was he? A nobody, laughed at by the lads going in their dirt straight from work to the football match, to watch the Rovers. Mrs Bradley's meat pies in grubby hands and beer bottles shoved deep in pockets. He was different all right, and without the brass to enjoy being different. And until young Mrs Waring had come to work in the dusty office he had been ready to pack it in. But not now. She had worked there for two whole months before he summoned up the courage to ask her to go out with him.

'Nights are drawing in, Mrs Waring.' He waited outside until she came out, buttoning her coat up to her throat, and pulling on her darned fabric gloves.

Jenny smiled at him. She was always smiling, even when that po-faced Mrs Warburton kept bringing work back for her to do again. Had it in for her from the very beginning, Miss Warburton had, and no wonder. Her with her sharp weasel face and red blotchy neck and Jenny with her springy step and that smile . . . oh God, that smile . . .

'But we're having a lovely back end, Mrs Waring.'

He fell into step beside her. 'May I call you Jenny, Mrs Waring? It seems a bit daft you saying Mr Eccles and me saying Mrs Waring when we're away from the office.'

She turned her head, teasing him. 'All right then, Thomas, and yes, it is a lovely back end. We've had a proper Indian summer.'

'I'm thinking of going to Blackpool for the day on Sunday, Jenny.'

She walked quickly, passing the tram stop as if it did not exist, and yet he knew where she lived. Right the other side of the town and only a penny tram ticket to the Boulevard. He took a deep breath to steady his nerves.

'Would you care to come with me, Mrs Waring? Jenny?'

She stopped right where she was, staring at him, while home-going foundry workers, jostled against them on the narrow pavement.

'To the *sea*, Thomas? Do you know, I have never seen the sea.'

'Go on, you're having me on.'

She started walking again, but he could feel her excitement reaching out to him. 'No, it's true. My father used to take me perhaps twice a year out to the country, but I've never been as far as the sea.'

'Then you'll come?'

Now the excitement had gone and her voice was flat but firm. 'No, Thomas, I won't come. I can't.'

He had passed the street where normally he turned off, but what did that matter? If he said the right words; if he played his cards right . . .

'It would be on me, Jenny. I live at home, you see, and I'm not that short. We could take sandwiches for dinner, then just have a cup of tea or something before we came back. Go on, say yes. This weather seems set in for a bit, seems a pity to waste it. We could go to Morecambe if you like. They have a lovely sunset there right over the Bay, and you can walk for miles on the sands.'

He was going to be late home for his tea, and his mother would be worried, but he did not care. This lovely girl striding along beside him had given herself away when he had mentioned the sea, and if he kept pegging away . . .

'Just friendly, Jenny, that's all. Nobody would think nothing. We wouldn't tell them at the office.' He coughed, a little nervous cough. 'You could meet me at the station if it's fine, and if it rains, well just don't turn up. I will understand.'

Silence for the next hundred yards or so, then suddenly Jenny stopped again, facing him on the pavement, smiling, marvelling at the prospect of walking on the sands, seeing the sun go down in a wide expanse of uncluttered sky.

'Thank you, Thomas Eccles,' she said. 'I'll come with you to the sea, and *I'll* bring the sandwiches. Thank you very much.'

Her mother had perked up when she was told about the **outing.**

'Do you good, love, bring some of the roses back to your cheeks,' she said, and she stood on the doorstep, blowzy with sleep in the corners of her eyes, waving Jenny off.

And Thomas knew that for the rest of his life he would remember the look on Jenny's face when she saw the Irish Sea, rippling dark green, shaded with blue in the autumn sunshine. She was as wide-eyed as a child, for once inarticulate, as they walked away from the centre, along the wide sweep of the promenade, out to the sand-dunes and the springy turf, to sit down and stare out at the hazy shimmering sea, lost in wonder.

A rain cloud came over, silvered at the edges, then rolled away. Gulls swooped from nowhere, calling plaintively. They watched a small rowing boat close in to shore, so close they could hear the creaking of the oars.

'If only we didn't have to go back.' Jenny unpinned her hat, shook her hair loose and lay back, unconsciously provocative, closing her eyes. 'To think that people actually *live* here! Oh, Thomas, how can we bear to live where we do? How can we bear the muck and the grey drabness of everything? And it all comes down to money, Thomas Eccles, you know that, don't you? But then I expect winter brings unemployment to a lot of the folks here. Like the farm workers in the country. Wages control their lives, like ours. Oh, why do we have to live in the mucky streets. Why?'

But Thomas was not listening. He could see the way her long black eyelashes lay on her cheeks; he could see the soft swell of her breasts against the tightly buttoned grey serge of her jacket, and he could see the tender hollow of her throat.

Leaning over her, he muttered thickly: 'Oh, Jenny. I do love you. I have loved you since that first day.' The words burst from him eagerly with no accounting for their practicability. Then suddenly his mouth was on hers, a close-lipped hard kiss as he covered her with his trembling body, only to move away suddenly as her total lack of

252

response shocked him to his senses quicker than if she had surrendered.

He sat up and drooped in despair, hanging his hands between his knees. 'Now I've gone and spoilt everything. I made up my mind I wasn't even going to hold your hand. I was going to let you see how different I was, but I'm not, am I? I'm no better than an ignorant lout what takes a lass out just for what he can get, all groping hands and wet lips, an' I wanted to, I was going to ask you to marry me, Jenny.'

She sat up, and he saw to his amazement that she wasn't angry or even embarrassed. She was just looking at him with such sadness in her dark eyes that he had to take a hold on himself to prevent himself from making a muck-up of things once again.

'I am not cross with you, Thomas, honest.' She stared down into her lap. 'You haven't kissed many girls before, have you?'

He frowned, refusing to lift his head and meet her eyes. 'None passionately like that, Mrs Waring. *Jenny*. But then I've never felt like this before, all screwed up inside me, with a proper pain when I look at you. I dream about you, Jenny. I go to bed thinking of you and when I wake up in the morning I am still thinking of you. I want to marry you and take care of you.' He lifted his head, his eyes filled with anguish. 'I get the feeling that you've never been properly looked after. I can feel it here.' He thumped his chest. 'I want to *marry* you, Jenny, not kiss you in the sand-dunes. I want to cherish you and work for you, an' I will, Jenny. I'm going to apply for another job at the Town Hall where there's a chance for promotion, or a railway clerk where you can get on if you move.' The words poured from him eagerly. 'I could apply to be moved to the sea or the country, Jenny. There's stations there, and all this would be ours. . . .' He swept an arm to encompass the wide sweep of the far horizon. 'I can do it, Jenny. You'll see.'

Jenny laid a hand on his arm, but he forced himself to

sit quite still, not taking advantage of her nearness. She was so beautiful with her hair loose like that, and her cheeks glowing pink with the sun and the wind, he could scarcely bear to look at her.

'Thomas? You don't know anything about me, and I don't know anything about you, except that you are sweet and kind.' She shook her head sadly. 'I am what – three years younger than you? Right, but, Thomas, I am fifty years older in experience. Listen to me. I've been married, oh only for a day and a night, but it happened, and I have lived with a man, as his *wife*. You understand?'

'I don't care.' He was mumbling like a small boy, then in an access of confidence he said: 'I would still want to marry you if you had been married seven times, and lived with a different man every day of the week. I'm not shocked.'

'I was not trying to shock you, Thomas. Just telling you. Showing you that so much has happened to me that I am not ready to be loved.' She sighed. 'Maybe I won't ever be ready to be loved . . . oh, dear Thomas Eccles, it's as though I am *waiting* for something, and till I know what it is, I am no use to anybody. Does that make sense?'

She was smiling again, and this time he did take advantage of her change of mood. 'Let's eat them sandwiches then. What's in them? Potted meat?'

Like a couple of children they took off their boots and stockings, to wander over the sands to the water's edge. Jenny was enchanted by the sand ripples left by the tide, intoxicated by the smell of seaweed, and when, as the afternoon was dying, they walked down a lane fringed with white-washed cottages, she told Thomas that some day, somehow, she was going to live in a little house like that.

'With me?' His grey eyes crinkled at the corners, and unfettered by his tweed cap, his brown hair flopped forward over his forehead. 'All right, all right . . . don't blame me for trying.'

When they went reluctantly to catch their train the

western horizon had lost the brilliant blaze of sundowning colour. Soon the moon would climb high in the heavens, and out on the sand-dunes there would be no sound but the rhythmic swish of the waves.

'We'll come again,' Thomas told Jenny. 'Perhaps not till next year, but we'll come again.'

He was uplifted on a wave of euphoria, so tired that he could have stayed awake for ever as the thoughts chased round in his head, round and round, each one more optimistic than the last. Next week he would write that letter to the Town Hall. He would stop kidding himself that he ought to have been an engineer. He would take a correspondence course on business management; he would learn to typewrite; he would go to night school and learn to do shorthand. He would grow a moustache.

Then Jenny Waring would marry him. By the gum but she would be glad to, when she saw the kind of man he had become.

The first thing Jenny noticed when she got back home was the smell of smoke. She wrinkled her nose. Tobacco smoke.

'Mam? Have you taken to smoking a pipe?' She asked the question lightly, smiling still with the remembrance of the day at the sea, but to her surprise Mollie turned on her in swift retaliation.

'Don't talk daft, Jenny. Anyroad, you've a nose on you like a ferret, always had. You're always going on about smells, you are.'

Puzzled, but not unduly so, Jenny went outside to empty the debris of crumbs from the cloth bag into the midden, came back in, lit a candle and went upstairs to take off her hat and short jacket and put them away behind the curtain that served as a wardrobe.

The candle was on its last, so holding her hand round its spluttering flame she went into her mother's room for a new one, and as she lit the fresh candle from the flame of the old, she noticed that the thin cotton spread on the double bed was rucked up as if it had been hastily pulled back over the pillows. Two pillows, with the indentations of two heads clearly showing.

And even up here there was still that unmistakable smell of pipe smoke, stale smoke, because Mollie could never bear to see a window open.

Slowly Jenny went back downstairs.

'Did anyone come when I was out, Mam?' She wished the words unsaid the minute she had said them, but it was too late, and as she saw the way her mother's doughy complexion flamed with anger she wished the floor beneath her would open up and swallow her whole.

Mollie was too guilty to take her usual refuge in tears, too taken aback to blurt out anything but the truth.

'Aye, somebody has been, madam! John Renshawe from number sixteen. He often comes in during the day if you must know. He's lonely since his wife was took off with the cough, and that lad of his isn't much help. Always at the billiard hall or out on the road of a Sunday.'

Jenny sat down, her legs suddenly weak. 'I'm sorry, Mam. I didn't mean to pry. It's nothing to do with me.'

Mollie stood in front of the fire, arms folded over her pendulous breasts, chin quivering with an injustice she was making for herself. 'Aye, you're right at that. It has nowt to do with you. No more than it had nowt to do with me when you went off and got married without caring what was going to happen to me shut in here with that madman.' Her mouth stayed wide open as her eyes gushed the ever-ready tears. 'Do you know how old I am, Jenny? I'm thirty-nine, that's all, still young enough for a man to lust after me, and don't act as though you don't know what that word means! You've never thought fit to tell me just why you left that farm and came back here in a hurry, but it wasn't on account of me. Nothing's on account of me, an' I'll tell you something else. When Mr Renshawe gets that lad off his hands I am going to suggest to him that he moves in here with me, and if he asks me to marry him I will, but if he doesn't then folks can wag their tongues as much as they like, an' see if I care! Just see if I care!'

'Mam!' Jenny sighed a deep shuddering sigh. 'I'm . . . I'm glad you've found a friend. You deserve what happiness you can get after what you went through with Harry Howarth, and it's true. I had never thought that you were still a reasonably young woman. You're my mam, and I never thought . . .' She spread her hands wide, but Mollie ignored her apology.

'Friend? Did you say friend? You've always had a sarcastic tongue on you, Jenny, comes of all that book reading, twisting words and making double meaning out of them. Women like me don't have men as *friends*. You know that. When a man sets his cap at my sort it's for one thing and one only, and if she lets him then he comes again. *Friend!* I suppose you'll be telling me next that the lad you've been on that outing with today is your friend!'

'I am going up to bed, Mam. It's Monday tomorrow, an' I like Mr Renshawe, I do, really. He always speaks to me when he sees me in the street.'

'Well, ta very much.' Mollie lifted the corner of her apron and wiped her eyes. 'Thanks for them kind words.'

Had her mother worn her apron as she lay on the bed with Mr Renshawe in the front room? Had she made the noises Jenny had so often heard her make when she lay in that same bed with Harry Howarth, and with Jack? And with the unknown man who was her father?

Was that really what it was all about? Would that shy young man on the sand-dunes have done the same if she had let him? It had certainly been lust for her that had made Bob Waring propose marriage, and what of Paul?

Jenny crawled into bed and pulled the covers over her face. Oh, but she could be sick when she thought about sex in connection with her mother. Why, her mother wasn't even particular about herself. She would never change the sheets on her bed, if Jenny did not do it for her, and yet . . .

1   257

'Oh, Paul. Oh, Paul. . . .' The tears came as she remembered his loving and the way he had looked at her the last time they met. It wasn't sex that had accounted for that lost bereft look on his face, it was love. . . . But then the two were synonymous. Surely?

There *was* beauty. There had been beauty today, and even now where the sea was, and where the fields were, there would be bats on the wing, owls with round staring eyes, and quiet lanes winding like silver ribbons in the moonlight.

It was all there, out there, waiting for her, she knew it; she had to know it, otherwise how could she hope to exist?

17

Just once in the year Thomas Eccles's mother had two
fires going in the house at once, and that was on Christmas
Day. The usual fire in the living-room and the other in the
front parlour. And what did it matter if the parlour fire
smoked and choked and refused to get going? There was
always the fat from the goose spread with a knife over
newspaper, rolled up into small parcels and shoved underneath the uncooperative slabs of shiny black coal.

Thomas knew that the fire this year was for his benefit,
his and Jenny's. Proper courting couples always sat in the
parlour when they had parents as understanding as his,
and they had taken to Jenny, really taken to her. After
the shock of the idea of their son courting a married woman
had worn off.

'But she's not a married woman. She's a widow,' he had
tried to explain, but his mother had sniffed so hard that
the whole of her nose had twitched sideways.

'She's been married, therefore she's not a . . .' She hesitated, not able to bring herself to say the word virgin in
front of her only son. '. . . she's not a young girl. Oh, you
know what I mean!'

For a wild moment Thomas wondered what his mother
would say if he told her that Jenny Waring had not only
been married, but had actually lived in with a man, as his
mistress. There was one thing he knew for certain, there'd
be no fire in the parlour this Christmas morning. Not on
account of Jenny, anyway.

'Are you sure her mother won't feel it, being on her own today?' Mrs Eccles fiddled with the ornaments on top of the never used piano. 'It doesn't seem right, leaving her alone. There'll be plenty of everything to go round.'

Thomas shook his head so that the soft unruliness of his brown hair flopped over his high forehead. 'She's got a friend going in.'

'Oh, well.' His mother gave a last satisfied glance round the over-furnished room, moved the brass pot holding the aspidistra plant an inch to the right, and went on, 'Your father said he would have finished his round at twelve. Who would be a milk roundsman on Christmas Day?'

Thomas walked over to the window, and lifting the dolly-creamed net curtain at one corner, stared out into the street. Jenny had refused to let him fetch her, and in a way he was glad. It embarrassed him going down there and seeing that man always sitting in the rocking-chair by the fire. Having to pretend it was natural, when all the time he knew that Jenny's mother had a husband out Liverpool way in a loonybin. He wondered what his mother would think to that?

He still could not believe that Jenny Waring was his girl. It had been hard going, but now that he worked at the Town Hall and finished an hour sooner, he had been able to position himself outside the foundry every night, waiting for her.

Waiting for Jenny. Always, it seemed, waiting for Jenny.

At first she had seemed to be irritated by his persistence, but his skin was tough enough to stand any amount of coolness, and gradually she had come to accept that he would be there. Especially on dark nights when she could walk along with her hand tucked into the pocket of his overcoat.

He turned and glanced over to where, at the far end of the mantelpiece, his present to Jenny waited, wrapped carefully in paper and tied with string. He wished it had been a ring, but he wasn't going to rush things, not chance his arm. If patience was a virtue then he was sprouting ruddy wings right between his shoulders.

He saw her then, walking down the quiet street, tall and lovely, swinging along in the way she had, making eyes turn towards her, and mouths that had not meant to smile turn up at the corners as if the very sight of her brightened their day. Oh, but she was special, and far above him, in spite of what she had told him about being illegitimate. He hesitated over the word even though he was only saying it in his mind. And he pushed to the back of his mind the anxious worriting, the uninformed doubts he had about whether it would have to come out on the wedding certificate.

That was another thing his mother must never find out about. Or his easy-going father, for that matter. Born the wrong side of the blanket, was the way they would put it, and he still squirmed when he remembered his father advising him to keep himself pure till he married the lass of his dreams.

He was at the door before Jenny had lifted her hand to the knocker, drawing her in, helping her off with her coat, shouting through to the back room:

'Jenny's here, Mam. Jenny's here!'

He could not take his eyes off her as they ate their Christmas dinner. He saw his father watching him, but nothing mattered, nothing but the fact that his Jenny was there, her very presence round their table giving weight to the fact that she was *almost* one of the family. The familiar cramping pain spread through his insides, and he knew that once again he was waiting. Waiting for the time when they could be alone in the front parlour, sitting side by side on the horse-hair sofa, with Jenny's head on his shoulder, and his arm holding her close.

When he gave her the present, her face was very still as she unwrapped the paper and took the rolled gold locket from the tissue inside. 'It's not one that opens.' Thomas felt he ought to get that in quick before she tried to open it and felt disappointed. 'It's just for show, but some day when we're . . .' He bit his lower lip, he was going too fast. 'Some day I will buy you a proper one. They gave me a shilling a week rise before we shut up for Christmas, and I didn't expect that, not with only being there such a short time.'

Jenny turned her face to his and closed her eyes as his firm hard kiss descended on her lips. Descended was a funny word to use about a kiss, but it was the right one. He had, on occasions, brought a blood blister up on her lip – it was as if his teeth got in the way – she tried hard to relax, tried with all her mind to will herself into feeling something, anything. Even repugnance, but it was no good. Thomas's kisses were to be endured, and nothing else.

She opened her eyes when the long hard kiss ended, and stared into the loving face suspended just above her own. She could see the adoration in his long-lashed brown eyes and wished with all her heart that it was mirrored in her own. Thomas Eccles would have been so easy to love, so right, so comfortable; he was perfect husband material, gentle, kind, earnest . . . oh, dear God, so very very earnest. There wasn't a single thing about him she disliked, but equally there was nothing that she loved.

'I do love you, Jenny.' The brown eyes swam with emotion.

'Oh, Thomas,' she said, and turned her head away so that the next fierce kiss missed its mark, and his eyes filled with reproach.

'Do you love *me*?' His leg was trembling against her own, and his hand sliding down her arm clutched her fingers with a convulsive urgency.

Jenny felt at least a hundred years old. 'I am very fond of you, Thomas,' she said slowly and with truth. 'Very, very fond.'

To her dismay he pulled her close so that she could hear his heart hammering as the desperate hardness of his kiss descended again. For a moment it was Bob Waring all over again, forcing her, biting, heaving, then as the kiss ended she saw that love, frustrated desperate longing, was the only motivation behind Thomas's despair. And immediately a sense of shame and a deep feeling of regret filled her.

'Thomas, listen to me.' Jenny pulled his head down on to her shoulder and tangled her fingers in his hair. 'Love cannot be *willed*. Once I loved a man desperately. I ached with the loving of him, and I gave myself to him, because myself was all I had to give. But he never said he loved me, and I was so . . . so obsessed it didn't seem to matter. If he had asked me to die for him I would have done so gladly, but never once, not even in the middle of the night, did he say that he loved me.' She was still for a moment. 'Then, when it was too late he came to me and told me that he loved me, and I sent him away.'

Thomas's voice came muffled. 'What are you trying to tell me, Jenny? That I should send you away?' She felt his head shake from side to side. 'Oh, no, I would never do that. I would wait, as you waited, and then when you knew I would ask you to marry me, an' if you married me still without knowing, I wouldn't care. That's how much I love you, Jenny Waring.'

The two gas fittings above the cluttered mantelpiece bathed them in an unromantic light, a spray of holly was tucked behind the oval mirror, and the aspidistra plant pot sat in a red crêpe paper frill. The fire glowed in the grate, living up to its one day of glory, and from the back room the clatter of crockery told them that Mrs Eccles was setting out the high tea of tinned salmon, thin bread, and butter, and Christmas cake.

It was all more than she deserved, Jenny told herself, smoothing her skirt and tidying her hair before going through. And she was not the sort of girl who would waste her life pining and mooning for a man who had a wife of his own. Yearning, unrequited love was all right for the girls in the magazines that Nellie had devoured with such

eagerness at Cedar House. No, in *her* book life was for
getting on with. All she needed was time, and more than
that – all she needed was to wake up just one single day
when Paul Tunstall's face was not there, his eyes teasing,
and the tender catch in his voice when he spoke her name.

If she bided her time, he would go away.

When she got home it was to see the burly figure of John
Renshawe sitting by the fire across from her mother, his
feet in carpet slippers and his pipe going nicely. Both faces
turned to her in unflattering surprise.

'You're back early.' Mollie glanced at the clock on the
mantelpiece. 'Thomas not coming in?'

'I didn't ask him.' Jenny nodded politely to Mr Renshawe
and wished him a Merry Christmas, and wished at the
same time that she could see him just once without being
reminded of him going upstairs to the big double bed with
her mother.

He was almost completely bald, with a large face surrounding a nose so small that it looked as if a child had
rolled a tiny ball of clay and thrown it, so that it stuck
there beneath the round watery eyes. His hands as he got
up and knocked his pipe out on the bars of the grate were
the size of knuckle-ended hams, and his shoulders had a
permanent stoop about them.

'I'll go up then.' He spoke directly to Mollie, but avoided
Jenny's eyes. 'It's best for you to tell her.'

'Tell me what, Mam?' Jenny stood there beside the
dresser, the cold from outside still with her, pinching her
nose and tinging her cheeks to red. She lowered her voice.
'Why is he going up our stairs? Does he think he lives here
now?'

Mollie pushed herself up from her chair, using her hands
on the arms, like a woman twice her age. She reached up
and took an envelope from behind the clock. 'That came
soon after you'd gone out.' She handed it to Jenny.

The telegram was briefly worded, saying that Harry

Howarth had died peacefully in his sleep, and that instructions regarding his funeral would be welcome. It was signed with regret by the superintendent of the asylum.

Slowly Jenny handed it back. She took off her hat and coat and sat down in the chair still warm from Mr Renshawe's considerable behind.

She felt nothing; she despised herself for feeling nothing, not even relief, but her mother, dry-eyed for a change, narrowed her pale eyes and rocked herself backwards and forwards silently.

'Well?' she said at last. 'Why don't you tell me I've wasted no time?' She jerked her head towards the curtain at the foot of the stairs.

Jenny felt nothing but a spreading aching weariness. 'You mean Mr Renshawe has moved in for good?'

'Aye, I do. His son went off to join the regulars, and we see no point in paying two rents. He's fetching his best bits here, and the rest he'll send to the sale room, they won't fetch much, but it'll be better than nowt.'

'Are you going to marry him, Mam?'

'Aye.' Mollie nodded, her eyes still narrowed into defiant slits. 'Aye, come the New Year and we'll be wed. He's got a steady job down at the paper mill, there's no cause to wait.'

'Then you won't need Mr Ibbotson's money no more.'

It was the last thing Jenny had dreamed of saying, or wanted to say, but there it was, said on its own, no taking it back, and proving to herself how she had hated the monthly handouts from the man she still thought of with respect.

And now the inevitable happened. Mollie's lower lip trembled, her eyes swam as she groped in her pocket for the ever-grubby handkerchief.

'Trust you to think of that first, our Jenny. Not a word of sorrow about your step-father's passing, and not a word to me about Mr Renshawe's goodness in taking over.' She mopped fiercely at the falling tears. 'An' he *is* a good

265

man, Jenny. Jack was a good 'un, Harry was a bad 'un, but now I've got a good 'un again. He even went upstairs right away so I could tell you meself. He's had it rough with that son of his and I'm not seeing him start all over again with his step-daughter!'

'His step-daughter?' Jenny heard her own voice rise on a note bordering on hysteria. Oh, God, dear God, in another minute she would be laughing, and if she laughed then she would deserve all the things her mother was thinking about her. Jack Macartney who she had loved and believed to be her father, Harry Howarth who never in a million years could she have thought of as her father, and now John Renshawe, all sitting in the same chair and sharing the same bed with her mother, whose only way of getting out of an awkward situation was to cry.

'Stop crying, Mam. *Please* stop crying.' Jenny got up from the chair so quickly that it rocked on its runners as if it had a life of its own. The fire was almost out, Christmas was almost over, and in that one day it seemed as if the rest of her life had been mapped in for her. In Indian ink to make it permanent.

'Thomas Eccles asked me to marry him today, Mam.' She said it to comfort, to stop the flow of tears, to soothe, to stem the flow that all her life had stopped dead any communication there might have been between herself and the sloppy snivelling woman with wobbling chins and swollen cushiony eyelids.

'An' you're going to?' The turn of the invisible tap as the tears ceased in mid-flow.

Jenny knelt down by her mother's chair. 'I don't know, Mam. You like him, don't you?'

Mollie's head came forward in a vehement nod. 'I just think I do like him. You'd not do better, not if you searched the whole world over.' She put out a hand and in a completely uncharacteristic gesture of affection, touched Jenny's cheek. 'It's not that I want you to go, love, but well, John has had a bellyful with that lad of his, and I

266

want a bit of peace this time. I want peace more than I can ever say.'

'And it was my fault that there was always trouble when . . . with Harry?'

The hand was immediately withdrawn. 'You can be awkward, Jenny. You set yourself up as different, an' you're not. You was born in the streets and you'll likely as not die in the streets.' She felt for the handkerchief again. 'Jack filled your head with book learning, and you was clever at school, but where has it got you, love? It's sometimes much more comfortable to be ignorant.'

'Oh, Mam. . . .' Jenny smiled at the unaccustomed touch of humour. 'I don't *want* to be different. All I ever wanted was to be . . .'

'What then?'

But Jenny couldn't answer. When she went up to bed, to lie with her head underneath the blankets as the sound of voices, murmured voices, seeped through the thin walls, there was still no answer.

All she knew was that she would have to go away again, and if going away meant marrying Thomas Eccles, then it would be like a wheel turning full circle again. The pressures were there, almost the same pressures, even though the drama of Harry Howarth's bullying violence had been exchanged for John Renshawe's mild unwilling acceptance of her.

And Thomas was no Bob Waring. Thomas would cherish her till death did them part. Her mother had been right. She was awkward, awkward and wicked not to be grateful, and stupid and crazy to want something different.

Then as she tossed and turned, closing her ears to the sounds from her mother's bedroom, Paul Tunstall's face was there again.

'Oh, God, tell me what to do,' she prayed, then childishly she added: 'Give me a sign. If you are there in your heaven, then give me a sign!'

18

Jenny was to marry Thomas at Easter, and they were to live with his mother and father until a house could be found for them to rent. Jenny's mother and Mr Renshawe had married in January, quietly and with the minimum of fuss, and in his own undemanding way John Renshawe had stepped into Mollie's first husband's shoes, wiping away the burly shadow of Harry Howarth as if he had never existed.

Jenny endured Thomas's kisses, told herself that when they were married and his frustrated passion was assuaged, things might improve. She was very matter of fact about it, very controlled as she tried to fit herself into the groove that life seemed to have planned for her. She kept away from her mother and the new husband as much as was possible, spending long hours at Thomas's house, growing fond of his parents as they grew fonder of her.

There were times when she saw Mrs Eccles watching her, as if there was something she could not quite put her finger on.

'Do you love my son? Really love him?' Mrs Eccles might have said if she had been born into a class where feelings were talked about and sometimes analysed. But to talk of loving was out of the question, and as for that 'other thing', well, Fanny Eccles would rather have died than broach the subject.

But she could not help noticing that Jenny seemed quite content to sit with them of an evening, and that when

Thomas came in from seeing her home there was nothing about him to suggest they had lingered in some shop doorway, or round a corner for a bit of a kiss and a cuddle.

'They're like an old married couple,' she told her husband. 'I can't make it out.'

Herbert Eccles shook his head at his wife's anxious face. 'You have me beat, Fanny. Cheese and flippin' rice, you would be out of your mind with worriting if you fancied they was up to something! Women are never satisfied!'

His wife tightened her lips. 'I just don't want my lad to get hurt, that's all. An' one of these days I have a feeling that lass is going to hurt him so bad he'll feel the skies have fallen in on him. An' if that happens, I'll . . . I'll *murder* her! I'll swing for her, that I will!'

Herbert Eccles gazed in astonishment at his wife's normally placid face screwed now into lines of fierce determination.

'All mothers of only sons talk that way about their lad's intended,' he mumbled.

He went back to reading the report of the Rover's last football match, then found he had read it right through without taking in a single word.

'Even a tub has to stand on its own bottom. Remember one thing, love. Our Thomas is a grown man,' he said.

But even to his own ears, the words had a hollow ring.

Thomas called for Jenny early one Sunday morning on a day that could have passed for spring. White tufted clouds drifted over the rows of chimney-pots, and pale sunshine lingered in patches down the narrow little streets.

They were to go to Chapel for the first time together, and Jenny was ready, neat and subdued in her long brown coat, with a velvet hat of lighter brown pinned firmly into her upswept hair.

'I look as if I am going to be interviewed for the post of under-parlourmaid, all ready to curtsey and say "yes, Ma'am, no Ma'am, three bags full Ma'am" and you . . .'

Her eyes twinkled. 'You, Thomas, look as if your mother has spent an hour pressing you with her flat iron.'

Her eyes took in the grey suit, just too short in the sleeves, and the trouser bottoms, showing too much of his highly polished boots. 'You look as if you are applying for the post as under-butler.'

She turned away to fasten the buttons of her gloves, knowing that new clothes for Thomas were out of the question now that he was saving every penny for the day they would be married.

They were going back to the seaside for their honeymoon, to the place where, on that Indian summer's day, he had first told her that he loved her. So long ago, so very long ago. And yet, as far as she was concerned, nothing had changed. Nothing at all.

Sighing, she picked up her Bible from the table, and jerked her head towards the curtain at the foot of the stairs.

'Getting dressed,' she said defensively, knowing she was on the defensive, and despising herself for it. 'They always lie in of a Sunday.'

'Oh, aye.' Thomas nodded. 'Aye, well, that's what Sundays are for, lying in.' He smiled at Jenny. 'Ready then, love?'

The loud knock at the door startled them as they walked in single file through the parlour, through the narrow passage left by the back of the sofa and the large mahogany sideboard.

Jenny jumped as violently as if she had suddenly been prodded in the back.

'Who on earth?' She opened the front door, and the hand not holding the Bible flew to her mouth as the blood drained from her cheeks.

'Paul?'

'Jenny?'

Paul Tunstall regarded her gravely. It had been a long hard ride from the village, with the trap swaying from side to side on the rutted roads, with him rehearsing in his mind a dozen times exactly what he was going to say. And now he could only stare at the white-faced girl regarding him with dark eyes that were giving her away as surely as if she had thrown herself into his arms. He swallowed hard as his gaze took in the young man hovering behind her, and unconsciously his mouth tightened.

He spoke quietly. 'It's Mr Ibbotson, Jenny. He has suffered a heart seizure, and the doctor fears he won't last much longer.' He lifted his hand in the gesture she knew so well. 'He wants to see you, Jenny.'

He went on, his eyes never leaving her face. 'I've left the horse and trap at the Bay Horse, but if you come with me now, we can be there before noon. *Will* you come, Jenny?'

'We was just going to Chapel.'

Thomas heard himself interrupt rudely, but there was a gnawing pain in his insides because they were ignoring him, the both of them, staring at each other as if he did not exist. Talking to each other as if they were in a world of their own with everything and everyone else faded away. And he knew, he knew inside him, that this was the man, the farmer chap that Jenny clammed up about when he tried to ask her questions. And, oh God, he was everything that he, Thomas knew, he was not, and never would be. Without trying, this tall fair man was that. One of the uppercrust who would spit at you as soon as look, with his face lightly tanned even in flamin' March, with his casual clothes, making Thomas feel a country gobbin going to a funeral.

'We was just going out,' he said again, ungrammatically, and not caring, his cheeks red as he tried to assert himself. Knowing all the time it was no use.

Jenny turned round, and with a pang of terrible anguish Thomas saw that she was looking at him as if he was not really there. With her eyes dazed and unseeing, as if already she had gone far away from him.

'Who was that knocking fit to wake the dead?'

Mollie came through the parlour, her thick flannel blouse buttoned wrongly, so that a left-over piece dangled at the bottom edge, her pale eyes like two bleached currants in the white dough of her face. Her hair slipped from its slovenly bun, and she looked as if she had done no more than wipe her face with a damp flannel on getting out of bed.

When she saw Paul, her expression changed into one of servility as she wiped dry hands on the inevitable apron.

'Oh, sir. Beggin' your pardon. Why don't you ask the gentleman in, Jenny? We can't have him standing on the step like this.'

Thomas winced as he heard Jenny speak as if her voice came from a far distant place. He knew then that he might just as well have been invisible.

'He has come to ask me to go with him to see Mr Ibbotson. Mr Ben Ibbotson.'

Jenny's manner might have been dream-like, but there was nothing dream-like about the way Mollie suddenly clutched at her throat as if she were choking. Her words came out in a croak:

'Mr Ibbotson? Why should she want to go and see him?' The chins began to quiver as Paul addressed her directly, still keeping his voice low.

'He is dying, ma'am, and knowing he is dying, has made a last request to see your daughter.' He glanced impatiently up the deserted Sunday morning street. 'Have you any objections to her going with me right this minute? I promise to bring her back before, *well* before it goes dark.'

The tears gathered in Mollie's bulbous eyes. 'Do you *want* to go, Jenny?' She looked from one to the other, twisting her hands together, as if lathering them with invisible soap. 'Do as you think fit of course.' She chewed on her bottom lip. 'Aye, then, perhaps under the circumstances . . .'

'Then we will go now.' Paul nodded at the quivering plump little woman, nodded in Thomas's direction, then held out his arm to Jenny. Moving like a machine, she took it and stepped over the doorstep into the street.

She turned round before they had taken more than a few steps, as if much against her will she had suddenly remembered something. A something of not all that much importance.

'Oh, Thomas. I am sorry.'

That was all, but in those few words Thomas Eccles read his dismissal. He had no idea what it was all about; no idea why Jenny's mother was now drowning in her tears, but he knew that the man taking Jenny away from him was the man who had stopped her from belonging to him entirely.

'What's the matter, lass? Come on in. You don't want folks to see you upsetting yourself on the doorstep.'

John Renshawe was there, tucking his shirt lap into his trousers, his bald head inclined solicitously towards his wife. 'Come in now. There's nowt a pot of tea won't put right.'

'I'd best be going, then.' Thomas moved over the step, shiny and clean in his Sunday best, going home because he could not think of anything else to do.

Knowing that even as he went, his going was unnoticed, and meant nothing to anyone.

They were in the trap, with Paul's hands loosely on the reins, when Jenny asked the question for at least the third time.

'Why me, Paul? Why should Mr Ibbotson ask to see me?'

'Don't you know, love?'

She turned and saw his profile, every line etched on her memory. The firm chin, the thin hollowed cheeks, the pulse jerking by the jaw line. She felt a sudden griping pain low down in her stomach.

'No, I don't know, Paul. Should I?'

The streets leading to the outskirts of the town were very quiet that soft and balmy Sunday morning. Blinds drawn in upstairs windows told of mill workers still abed, enjoying their once-weekly lie-in before Monday morning brought the merciless grind of their monotonous lives round once again. Not even the first touch of pale sunshine had tempted them from the cushioned comfort of their feathered mattresses.

'Paul?' Jenny put out a hand and touched his arm at the same time as he turned to face her, his silver-light eyes so kind, so full of compassion that her heart turned over in her breast.

'He is your father, love. That is why he cannot die without seeing you. Because he is your father.'

'Oh . . . oh, no!' Jenny whispered the denial, whimpered it, and immediately Paul's arm came round her, holding her close against his shoulder.

'I have known for a long time, sweetheart. Jenny, my dearest love. But it was a secret I had to keep. For your sake as much as his. That was why he *interfered* so much; that what why he once threatened to horsewhip me.'

She shook her head from side to side. 'And that was why he sent money to my mother. And when I was worried nearly out of my mind at the way things were, that was why he took over and sorted things out. Oh, Paul, and that was why I felt a strange closeness whenever I saw him.'

She lifted her head and he saw her cheeks wet with tears. Her dark eyes suddenly flashed fire.

'Paul! Turn the trap round! I won't go. I don't want to see him.' She twisted away from him in her agitation. 'It's too late. Much too late. He . . . my mother . . . oh, Paul, he sent her away. He paid her off and sent her away. He had got her into trouble, and all he wanted was to be rid of her. I can't forgive him for that!'

At once the invisible gap closed, the ruthless gap closing

ranks between one class and another. Paul flicked the reins and urged the horse to trot faster.

'She was a servant girl, Jenny, and he was a married man, a man rising to the top of his profession. What else could he do?'

Jenny tried to take the reins from him, then felt herself pinned back against the seat, as Paul's arm came across her.

'It takes two, Jenny love. It takes *two*. And stay still if you don't want us thrown out of this confounded thing. I would have brought the car, but it's stabled like a horse with a broken leg. They say horses will be off the roads before too long, but I have my doubts. . . .'

He was so controlled, so much the master that Jenny's exasperation caused her to beat with her fists against his steel-like grip of her.

'Bugger the car! And bugger the horse!' she shouted. 'What can you know about what happens to a girl when she has a baby out of wedlock? Is that what you would have done with me if I'd fallen? Paid me off and sent me away?'

She saw the colour flare in his face, but his composure never faltered.

'From what I was told, there was a man willing to marry your mother; there was the house in the town for them to go to, and also from what I heard, your mother was happy with the settlement Mr Ibbotson arranged for her.' He stared straight ahead. 'She has married again, I see. For the third time?'

There was insolence in his tone, a studied insolence that made Jenny want to claw with her nails at his face, to scream and demand to be let down from the swaying trap.

Then as if she were holding a book with its pages ruffling over from the back, she saw in her mind's eye the tousled bed in the back room with a clear imprint of a head on the second pillow. She heard her mother's moans as she lay with Harry Howarth, and she remembered Jack Macartney telling her to go outside and play on Sunday afternoons.

She stopped fighting, accepted a clean white kerchief and mopped her face with it.

Paul nodded twice. 'That's better. And now you've calmed down, love, do you really see Mr Ibbotson as a wild seducer of innocent women? The good he has done far outweighs the bad, surely?' He flicked the whip against the horse's glossy back, and they drove the next mile in silence, leaving the cobbled streets behind.

'You told me once he had a reputation . . .?' Jenny's tone was reproachful and not a little sulky. 'Have you forgotten that?'

Paul grinned. 'I was provoked, love, if you remember?' For a moment their eyes met before he sighed and stared straight ahead once again. 'Don't play the part of a prude, Jenny. It doesn't become you. Besides, are we to bicker all the way? We've a way to go yet. Are we not to be on speaking terms when we arrive?'

'Oh, Paul.' Her face gentled again with the love she felt for this man who could incite her to anger, tears, then laughter, all in the space of minutes. This man she had never thought to see again. In any minute now, she told herself, she was going to forget why she was here with him, and just let the happiness take over. She fiddled with the buttons on her gloves. 'It takes some getting used to, finding out about my father. I'd given up dreaming that one day I would find him. It didn't seem to matter any more.'

'And now?'

'Now I feel so strange.' She put up a hand and touched her hair, the dark wings of hair showing at the sides of the velvet go-to-Chapel hat. 'My hair is like his. It is, isn't it? And my eyes?' She ran a finger down her cheek. 'And I am tall, so much taller than the girls I knew at school, an' I like reading aloud, an' acting. How strange that I should be, should have so many things like him and yet I never knew him.'

Paul glanced briefly at her, then swiftly turned back

again. There it was – there was the reason he could never forget this lovely, vital, bright girl sitting by his side. She was meant to be happy; she had always been meant to be happy, and now there she was, behaving like a child, claiming her father in her heart, accepting the truth, and in a strange way, glorying in it.

'And now he is dying,' she whispered, as her head drooped forward. 'Now it is too late.'

'It was always too late, love. You know that, and Mr Ibbotson knew it. Time and circumstances made it all the way it had to be.'

He jerked at the reins as they drove up on over the hills, then down to the sun-drenched valley spread below. Now the road was flanked by patchwork fields; now they drove through a little wood, with trees making a waving pattern against the sky, past red-brick houses set back from the road, and isolated cottages.

'What will I say to him, Paul?' Jenny's mood of brief exhilaration disappeared as swiftly as it had come. 'Will he . . . is he well enough to talk to me?'

'To see you will be enough.' He put out a hand and touched her knee. 'That is all *I* have, dear love. Just this one unexpected bonus of seeing you.' His voice was harsh. 'If you only knew how it was for me, Jenny. If you knew how many times I have asked myself why virtue does not bring its own reward. Whoever said that was a fool, an insensitive, unthinking, goddamned fool!'

'Miss Sarah?' Jenny stared away from him as if the hedges on her side of the trap held a fascinated interest for her.

'The same. No, worse than the same. Oh, Jenny, love. Christmas was the worst. We were there on Christmas Day, over at Cedar House. Sarah, her mother, the nurse and me, with my father-in-law skulking in his study as usual.'

Paul drove the trap into the side of the road as a farm cart lumbered by. 'If I could have saddled a horse and got away, I would have ridden it hard to come to you. They were talking amongst themselves as if I was not there, anyway.' He lowered his voice. 'Would you have welcomed me, Jenny?'

The heartbreak in her voice matched his own. 'I was sitting with Thomas in his mother's parlour. I am to marry Thomas soon, Paul.'

'The young man with you when I knocked at the door?'

She nodded. 'He is so kind and good. And he *loves* me! I will make him a good wife, I will. I know I will!'

'And you love him?'

She clutched the side of the trap as its sudden swaying threw her against its edge. 'He wants to *marry* me, Paul! I can't spend the rest of my life thinking about you! I won't!' She stole a glance at him. 'Not even though seeing you like this has set me back a bit.'

He saw that she was trying to smile, trying to tease, and a great weight of melancholy settled on his chest, till her next words made the reins jump against his wrists.

'Would *you* marry me, Paul? If you were free, would *you* marry me?'

They were coming to the village now, but he made no answer. Not until they were turning into Ben Ibbotson's drive did he speak again.

'Yes, I would marry you, Jenny Waring. I would marry you were I free, so fast you wouldn't have time to catch your breath. And I would burst with pride at having you belonging to me. Does that answer your question?'

The maid who opened the door had eyes swollen and red from weeping. When Paul asked if they might come in, she stood back to let them pass, her shoulders shaking with sobs.

'The master?' Paul asked the question softly, but Jenny knew the answer before it came.

'Gone, sir. An hour back, all on his own. There was nobody with him. He was all by himself.' She lifted her apron to her streaming eyes.

'And your mistress?'

The weeping girl jerked her head towards the stairs. 'Up in her room, sir. The doctor give her something afore he left just now. Oh, sir, I can't believe it. I just can't believe it.'

A slight noise on the stairway made them stare upwards as Elaine Ibbotson came slowly down, trailing a hand on the banister rail. Grey of face, grey of hair, but dry-eyed, with her head erect, there was an almost unbearable dignity in her bearing.

'Oh, ma'am. The doctor said you was to lie down.' The maid stepped forward with a helping hand, only to have it gently tapped away.

'That will do, Mary.' Mrs Ibbotson turned to Jenny. 'I am sure you would like to see him, my dear, and then I would like to talk to you.' She turned to Paul. 'Will you call for her in an hour, please?'

'I'll wait at the gate,' Jenny whispered, then as Paul hesitated, she nodded towards the door. 'It's right. It's what she wants,' she whispered.

'Is there anything I can do? Anything at all?' Paul stood for a moment in the open door, his tall figure etched against the bright morning.

'Thank you, nothing.' Mrs Ibbotson inclined her head, then motioned Jenny to follow her. 'In here, dear. We had his bed brought down to his study when the stairs got too much for him. . . .' For the first time her voice faltered, then as Jenny stepped inside the study, she closed the door quietly, leaving her alone.

Slowly Jenny walked towards the bed set in the big bay window. The long red curtains had been drawn, but someone had lit candles and set them high on top of the bookshelves. Tall, white candles which burned with a steady unflickering flame, throwing the room into dark deep shadows.

Mr Ibbotson lay with his face uncovered, his big face drained of its fresh colour by death, frozen into a mask as shiny white as the candles.

It was not him. He was not there. Jenny went to stand close, then slowly put out a hand and touched the still face. It was like touching a slab of cold marble, and she withdrew it quickly, then sank to her knees.

'Father?' She whispered the word softly. 'Oh, my father, I wish . . . oh, I wish things had been different, then I could have grown up with you, an' loved you. . . . I could have loved you so much.' The tears ran down her cheeks. 'An' please, if you've gone anywhere where you can listen to me now, I'm telling you that I'll never forget you. I'll always remember the kind things you did, but I wish . . . I wish with all my heart that just once I could have told you that I loved you. Because, you know, it's funny, but I did love you. Right from that first time when you winked at me when I spilled on Mrs Bleasdale's best carpet.' She heard her voice choke on a sob. 'We could have been lovely together, you and me, because there's a lot of you in me. An' you knew that, didn't you?'

Then with a theatrical gesture that Ben Ibbotson himself would have applauded, a gesture that had been so essentially a part of him and now was a part of his daughter, Jenny laid her lips against the waxed forehead.

'Goodbye, Father,' she said softly. 'Goodbye.'

Mrs Ibbotson was waiting for her in the dark hall. At least by the swiftness of her appearance, Jenny guessed that she had been waiting. The drug given to her by the doctor was obviously taking effect as she swayed where she stood. Her voice came thick and blurred.

'In here, my dear. I won't . . . it won't take a minute to say what I have to say.'

'You ought to be lying down, ma'am. Please . . .'

Mrs Ibbotson obeyed like a child, allowing Jenny to guide her over to the sofa. 'Very well, then, but I have to ask you to make me a promise. A promise you might find very hard to keep.' She raised a hand to her forehead. 'For my sake, and for . . . for my husband's sake, I want you to swear that you will never tell a soul about . . . about your relationship to him.'

Jenny started to speak, but was silenced by a raised finger.

'Mr Tunstall knows, only because my husband confessed that in a moment of anger he had broken his word to me and blurted out the truth. But he is the only one, and if there was one man in the world I could trust to keep a secret, it is Paul Tunstall.'

'The maid?' Jenny glanced towards the closed door.

'No. She was used to . . . to people coming to see my husband. He was a very generous man, Jenny, helping where he could. Mary has got used to people coming to him with their problems, but now . . .' She closed her eyes. 'I fear all that must stop. His generosity outgrew his purse-strings.'

'So you knew he was sending money to my mother?' Jenny kept her voice low. 'He told you that?'

Without opening her eyes, Mrs Ibbotson nodded. The drug was taking effect. She could fight it off no longer, and Jenny could see that she hovered on the verge of merciful sleep.

'My mother has married again, so there's no need . . .'

Again the barely perceptible nod. 'And you, Jenny?'

If the woman on the sofa had been able to open her heavy eyelids she would have recoiled from the expression in the dark eyes. She would have seen her husband's eyes flash fire as they had done so often when his temper flared.

'I stake no claim, Mrs Ibbotson. As far as I am concerned, things are as they have always been. I said my goodbye just now, an' . . . an' I'm grateful to you for letting me come.' Jenny lowered her head. 'I wish I could have spoken to him, but he owes me nothing, nothing but the fact that I am here. An' *you* owe me nothing. Not now or ever!'

Mrs Ibbotson's mouth was having difficulty in stretching itself round the words. 'My life here – the left-over life that I still have to live – it would be unbearable if it were known . . .'

'I *promise*!' Jenny started to back away.

'You may go then, Jenny.'

She had been given her place, and knowing and accepting it, Jenny walked to the door, opened it, then closed it softly behind her.

There was no sound anywhere in the big house, no sound outside in the spring-lit garden as she let herself out of the front door. Paul had said he would be back for her in an hour, and she was grateful for the chance to walk a little, to grieve a small private grief, and to say a second goodbye to the place to which she knew she would never be returning.

Paul's farm was on the right, over the fields and through the little wood. Jenny left the road and walked slowly, the burning sense of resentment washed clean. The desire to weep was gone, and she was filled with a strange lethargy, a closing in of the spirit, where there was no energy left even to think. Only to be.

She came out of the little wood, and crossing a field, climbed the hillock where during the long summer she had often stood, shading her eyes against the sun and looking over to the tall cedar tree sheltering the house where, at that time, Paul's wife languished her days away.

She tried to imagine what he would be doing in the rambling house. Would he be watching the gilded clock on the high mantelshelf, waiting for the time to make his excuses and drive to the Ibbotsons' house to fetch her? Would he be holding his head high in the mannerism that had always given him away? Hurt and diminished, but determined not to show it? Would Miss Sarah be chattering to her mother, excluding him, watching him now and again with her green eyes assessing, secure now in her hold over him, wrapped in her invalidism and somehow revelling in the power it gave her?

Slowly retracing her steps to the road, Jenny sat herself down on one of a huge pair of boulders flanking the Ibbotsons' gate, and prepared to wait.

'But I don't want you to go out again, Paul! It's Sunday, and all the time you were eating lunch I knew you were planning to go out again. I could see you watching the window as if you couldn't bear to be cooped up in here with me.'

Sarah's green eyes watched him carefully over the head of the little brown dog, snuggled up to her chin. 'Mama will be up in her room for another two hours at least, and you know my father won't come out of his study till teatime. Then nurse will come, and we will have to go home, and you'll be out in the fields till it grows too dark for you to see.' She pouted her lips like a child about to burst into tears.

Trying not to glance at the clock on the mantelshelf, Paul went to sit beside her. 'I *have* to go out, Sarah. Why don't you try to sleep? I promise I'll be back as quickly as possible.'

Sarah thrust the little dog away from her with such fury that it gave a sharp yelp of surprise, then scrambled back on to the sofa to lie at the foot with its head buried deep in its paws.

Paul sighed, making no attempt to touch his wife, knowing that if he did his hand would be knocked away with the same swift show of temper.

Two spots of red burned in Sarah's usually pale face, high up on the cheekbones, making the green eyes sparkle like polished emeralds.

'I feel ill! I sometimes feel as if I might die! I *could* die, and you wouldn't care! All you think about is the farm. You never stop to think what it's like for me, and since Mama was ill she only thinks about herself. And my leg . . . the pain I suffer! There isn't one day, not one single day when I have no pain. Or one night, and what do the doctors do? They do nothing! I might as well be dead.'

Paul buried his face for a moment in his hands. Oh, dear God, but it was all true. Every word Sarah said was the damnable truth. She *was* in more or less continual pain, and he did leave her alone too much, but he was only human. He was, wasn't he? And who but a saint could stand the never ending whining, the reproach, the sheer obstinacy of her refusal to do anything, anything at all? But he could try. Once more he could try.

'Nurse says there is no reason why you can't sit at the piano and play, or even walk slowly round the room. Or work at some stitching, or read. Anything! It's the doing nothing that's getting at you, Sarah. Can't you see?'

The sound she made was half-way between a scream and a moan. He could almost see the hysteria rising, knew that in another moment he would have to grip her hands tight to prevent her from raking her nails down his face as she had done many times before. When she was like this her voice came out high in staccato jerks, without pause for breath, and once, but only once, he had slapped her, believing quite wrongly as it happened that the slap might have brought her to her senses. The memory of her screams would always be there, ringing in his ears, and the memory of her throwing herself on the floor, to crawl, when there was no need to crawl, over to the fire where she had threatened to thrust a hand into the leaping flames.

'If I have no legs, then I might as well have no hands!' she had screamed, and the horror of what she was about to do had stayed his own hands for a terrifying unforgettable moment, before he could gather her up in his arms and carry her back to the sofa.

'If you leave me again today . . .' Her voice was starting its familiar hysterical stuttering. 'If you leave me now, Paul, I promise you that for the rest of your life you'll regret it . . . I mean it! Go on! Go on, just try me, and see!'

And down the lane Jenny would be waiting for him. In the silly velvet hat, with her chin held high, and the tears, if tears there had been, wiped from her eyes. And she was going to marry that lad, that unfinished lad with his namby-pamby face and the brown hair falling over his forehead.

And there was nothing he could do about it. Nothing.

'It will take me just three minutes to go round the back and have a word with Wilson,' Paul told his wife. 'I will send him on the errand I had to do, and then perhaps when I come back, you will play for me? That's fair, isn't it?'

He tried to make his voice light, even as his words had their desired effect. Sarah caught her breath for a moment, watching him warily, then realizing she had won, relaxed amongst her cushions.

'I don't feel like playing, but you can read to me,' she said, scooping the dog up again, and widening the green eyes innocently. 'You have a lovely voice, Paul, but not when you are angry with me. I can't bear it when you are angry with me, it makes me feel ill, so very ill.'

'Three minutes, five at the most.' Paul patted his wife's shoulder, then left her quickly, before the enormity of what he was about to do had time to sink in. This was how it had to be. He would never see Jenny again; she would marry that boy, and forget him. As he must forget her. Dear God, as he *must* forget her.

'Mr Tunstall said . . .' Wilson took off his cap and scratched his head. 'He said as how I was to tell you *exactly*. He said that his wife needs him, *has* need of him, he will not be able to take you back to town. He said as how you would understand.'

The weather-beaten face was contorted with the effort of getting the message right. It had nowt to do with him, but he had guessed from Mr Paul's expression that it was important, so important that he had been made to repeat it twice. He had heard Miss Sarah carrying on as he walked past the window, and disgust had made him spit out of the side of his mouth at the spectacle of a young lass like that acting as she had always done when she could not get her own way.

'By the gum,' he had chunnered to himself. 'If my missus ever carried on like that I'd have leathered the living daylights out of her long ago. That was what Miss Sarah had been asking for for years. Someone strong enough to clout her one, even though she *were* half wick. An' she weren't half as bad as what she made out. Not her. He'd seen her with his own eyes walking, stiff-legged it were true, but *walking* when she thought Mr Paul were out of the way. Bye, but there were bad blood somewhere, even though she had a face like a ruddy angel straight down from heaven.'

'He said as how you would understand,' he repeated, then felt his throat tighten with pity as the Jenny lass nodded and thanked him politely before allowing herself to be helped up into the trap.

Wilson touched his cap and took up the reins, muttering into the checked muffler wound twice round his scraggy neck. By the gum, but he *hoped* as how there *had* been something going on between Mr Paul and this little lass. Comfort was what both of them were crying out for, and if they had got it from each other, then good luck to both of 'em. And if that made him into a dirty old man, then that was what he was.

'Giddyup there!' he said, and started the trap swaying along the winding road leading away from the village.

And when Jenny told Thomas she could never marry him he put his head down and cried.

'I've known all along,' he sobbed, 'and when that chap turned up, I knew for sure. Are you going to him, then?'

'I will never see him again, Thomas.' Jenny's voice was gentle, and he could see the way her face was stiff with the hurting of it. 'That is all over, but to marry you would be wrong.' She laid a hand on his arm. 'Some day you will meet another girl, Thomas, a girl who will love you the way you deserve to be loved.' She looked away from him. 'In a way I feel I've used you, Thomas, but now I've got to stand on me own two feet, an' I've made a start.' She gave him a little shake. 'I've got a room, just one room to begin with, but it's a start. Thomas, would you believe me when I tell you that Miss Warburton is leaving the foundry office?'

In spite of his misery a shadow of interest passed over Thomas's woebegone face. 'But Miss Warburton's been there for ever. She were there when the old man were in charge.'

Jenny nodded. 'She's come into some money, and she's leaving and going to live with her friend in a cottage in the Lake District. There! What do you think about that?'

'And you've got her job?'

'More or less, Thomas. I'm going to night school to learn typewriting, and any day now I'll be like Miss Warburton, just like her, with me blouses throttling me, and me hair scragged back. I'm going to be a business woman, Thomas. You never know, one fine day I might be the first lady Town Clerk, then I'll be bossing *you* around. What do you make of that?'

He pushed the lock of soft brown hair back from his forehead. 'But can you afford to live on your own, Jenny? Even in one room? Why don't you stop at home just till you get on your feet? It's not nice for a girl of your age to live alone. Folks might think . . .'

'I don't give a damn what folks think. They can think what they like. Bothering about what folks think gets you nowhere.'

Jenny tilted her chin. As if she were ready to take on the whole world, Thomas told himself, then when she had gone he wept some more, and when his mother told him she had seen it coming, he rounded on her with uncharacteristic fury.

'You never liked her,' he shouted unfairly. 'Just because

you thought she was a cut above, you never liked her!'

'That's not true, son!' His mother's eyes filled with tears at the lie. 'I allus made her welcome, you know that.'

'Let him be,' Mr Eccles told his wife. 'He's hurt that bad he has to lash out at somebody, and thy back's broad enough, lass. Just let him be.'

19

The summer months in the little room at the top of the old house in a street near the centre of the town dragged on in a haze of heat and discomfort.

It was really part of a converted attic, half of it used as a store room for the family on the second floor who ran a family business of making matchboxes, where even the youngest child, a boy of four years of age, sat for hours glueing and sticking the pieces together.

The only daylight the child saw was through the grimed windows looking down onto a cluttered courtyard, and some Sundays Jenny would take him to the Corporation Park, sitting alone on a bench whilst he scrambled up and down a grassy bank, and ate the bread she had brought to feed the ducks on the pond at the top of the Broad Walk.

She was very thin those days, very quiet, very business-like in her dark skirts and high-necked blouses, and achingly lonely as she pored over her books in the summer evenings when the Technical School was closed, aware that she was striving for a place in a man's world, but deter-mined to succeed.

She was 'Mrs Waring' to the men in the foundry, and she would look up from her desk at times and see them in their dirt-ingrained overalls, helping the rivets to fly until the buzzer went at half-past five, most of them earning no more than a pound a week, even with overtime, whilst the little firm grew and expanded, and the shareholders pocketed their ten per cent, never questioning their rights to it, or stopping for a minute to think how it had been earned.

'Stick to your own job, Jenny,' Mr Will told her one day when she tried to bring the subject of the men's wages up with him. 'All right, so Jim Bates's wife has given birth to her sixth child, but what is that to do with me? Don't they realize that they have to feed every mouth they're responsible for? Control's what's needed, more self-control.'

'But when they are cold and there's no coal, where else can they keep warm but in bed?'

Jenny spoke without thinking, then blushed to the roots of her dark hair as the implication of what she had said dawned on her.

'You talk like a man,' her mother had told her only the week before. 'Bothering your head about things what don't concern you.' Mollie had sniffed, secure now in a marriage that was giving her the security she craved as a plant craved water. 'Why don't you get yourself a young man? Mrs Cross over the street hinted last week that you might be turning out to be one of them unnatural women, freaks of nature or summat, though I don't rightly understand. Why did you have to send that nice young lad away? You could have been married by now, with a little 'un on the way instead of living all by yourself and doing nowt as far as I can see, but read.'

And oh, but she wasn't an unnatural woman. Jenny knew that. If only her mother knew the times she lay in her bed, listening to the slamming of doors on the floors below, hearing the sound of squabbling, and sometimes even the sound of laughter.

Lonely was what she was, not perverted. Achingly lonely for the touch of a man's hand on her. Worse than lonely because she had known the way it could be. And loving a man as she still loved Paul Tunstall wasn't a fluttering of the heart and a flushing of the cheeks like it said in stories. It was a grinding cramp low down in her, as though her guts were twisted with fear, like when you looked down from a high place and felt the fear tighten between your legs. It was real and painful, physically painful, and there was nothing she could do about it, not unless she was like the night-woman who lived in the basement, and got her satisfaction that way.

Just after Christmas that year the snow came, turning the grim courtyard with its empty cartons and mounds of accumulated filth and rubbish into a sparkling white fairy grotto. Sitting by her window one Sunday afternoon, before the light fell, Jenny heard the footsteps on the narrow staircase, heard the soft knocking at the door, and discarding the shawl she had taken to wearing to save building the fire up too high, opened the door to see Thomas standing there.

She was so glad to see him that she almost dragged him inside. Her voice had a singing lightness as she bustled to swing the kettle over the coals, with a deft flick of the poker taken from its stand.

'Thomas! Oh, but it is nice to see you. Why haven't you been before? Sit down. Go on, take the chair and I'll sit on the bed. Oh, but you *do* look well! Your face is fatter, and you've got more colour in your cheeks. Oh, but it is nice to see a friend. I'm right glad you came. I really am.'

Thomas took off his cap, and doing as he was told, for the simple reason that he would always do as he was told, came forward and sat himself down in the straight-backed chair by the fire.

'You look well too, Jenny,' he said, not meaning it. He twisted the cap round and round in his fingers. It wasn't that she looked ill, more as if her features had been sharpened, making her high-piled hair seem too heavy for her head. She was all eyes, and hair, and her waist pulled in by the band of her long skirt, well, he was sure he could have spanned it with his hands.

'Tell me all you've been doing,' she was saying, setting out cups and saucers on the small table over by the window.

291

'I've looked out for you so many times, and hoped I'd see you. Down on the market, and in the park of a Sunday. How is your mother? And your father? Oh, but I *liked* your father. He was such a matter-of-fact kind of man. I don't suppose much has ever bothered him, has it?'

'Jenny!'

Thomas spoke more loudly than he had intended to, because any minute now she could be going to say something she might regret. He knew Jenny Waring, and he wouldn't put it past her to take it upon herself to suggest off her own bat that they started up again together. An' at one time, right up to last summer, he would have been over the moon. But his mother had been right, after all. Jenny wasn't cut out for the likes of him, and never had been, not when he thought of Dolly, waiting downstairs now in the passage, till he saw the way the land lay.

'I'm getting married soon,' he blurted out. 'To a girl what stands the market with her mother. They have a fancy goods shop, just a house like, regular, then the stall twice a week.'

Jenny whirled round to face him, and her face was alight with pleasure. It *was*, Thomas told himself, with relief and then again, was it? She was that deep she could just be acting, and she was good at that. Too clever for him by half, not like Dolly who hung on his every word as if they were spun from gold.

'She's downstairs now,' he said, jerking his head towards the door. 'It was her, as a matter of fact, who wanted to come and see you.' He looked sheepish. 'I went on that much at first about you, and she wants to have everything straight afore we wed.'

'You mean your Dolly doesn't want to think you are still hankering over me?' There was a hint of laughter in Jenny's voice, and Thomas got to his feet, shuffling them on the shabby strip of carpet like a schoolboy caught out in some misdemeanour.

'Aye, well, mebbe.'

'Bring her up then and let's have a look at her.' Jenny calmly set another cup and saucer out. 'Oh, and Thomas. I'm glad for you, right glad, honest.'

She pulled the chair back to the window again after they'd gone. Thomas oozing pride, and his Dolly clinging to his arm, her round face aglow with love beneath the frizz of light brown hair. She was right for Thomas. Jenny had known that at first glance. Adoring, simple, Dolly would make him a good wife, and fit into his family with the ease of a foot slipping into a comfortable shoe.

Jenny hoped they would come again as they had promised to. But she doubted it. When she had suggested as much, Dolly's little mouth had set firm. Sure of her love she might be, but in her code it wasn't done for a man to be friends with his past love. Besides, surely there was something odd about a girl living all on her own like that when her mother was still alive? Girls got married from their parents' house, decently, the way she was going to do, and even if they never got married, then they still stopped on till they got to be thirty or so with all their chances gone. And then they turned into spinsters and pretended they had never wanted a man anyway.

Oh, yes. Jenny had read all that in Dolly's open countenance, and the knowledge left a small pain somehow. She sat on watching the snow fall until it grew dark, imagining how it might have been if she could have been considered a kind of aunt to Thomas's children. Sewing feather stitch round small flannel petticoats, and threading ribbon through eyelet holes worked into cotton dresses. . . .

Then she gave herself a good mental shake-up, drew down the blind, and put a taper to the fire to light the gas. She had a few more figures to quote to Mr Will the next time she had a chance, and she hoped it would be the next day. Jenny drew a paper-backed sheaf of forms towards her, and began to read:

'In the textile trades of the United Kingdom for the

previous year, forty-eight of the adult men earned less than twenty-two shillings a week.' A shilling *more* than the men employed in the foundry.

'He undercuts them,' she muttered to herself. 'Mr Will might be a good man in some ways, but he's not playing it right. He classes them as unskilled when they're not. I don't know how he manages that, but he does. He even foxes the Unions, and if he gets black-listed then it will all be his own fault.'

'Then *you'll* be out of a job yourself,' she said aloud, then catching herself speaking aloud to the emptiness of the little room, she dropped her head onto her hands, and stayed there for a few minutes, the gas-light making a halo round her dark curly hair.

She went to bed early that night, then woke to hear a sliding rushing sound as the unexpected thaw brought the snow slithering from the roofs. By the time she opened the front door onto the street the whole of the cobbled lane was a quagmire of grey slush, patterned with the water-filled imprints of clogs where mill workers had struggled towards the mills as the early hooters blared.

It was not the day to prod Mr Will's social conscience, Jenny decided as he came into the office sneezing into an outsized white handkerchief.

'You ought to be in bed, sir,' Jenny told him as she carried the letters through into his little glass-walled office. 'You ought not to have come out on a day like this.'

'Hah!' Mr Will glanced balefully at her from beneath puffed eyelids. 'If I were one of the men down there on the shop floor, then I might be able to take a day or two off to nurse a cold.' He sneezed again. 'And it might not be unreasonable to suppose that the firm would manage without me. But in *my* position, because of *my* responsibility, I am hard put to it to take an hour off, let alone a day!' He sneezed again. 'Now, how do you reconcile that with your social conscience? Does that turn me into the ogre you've been trying to make me out to be?'

'You may have a point, sir. Just a tiny one, but a point all the same.' Jenny smiled at him, knowing just how far she could go with her teasing of this man, this self-made man who seemed to have forgotten that he had once confided to her his own humble beginnings. She went from the room, back straight, but not ram-rod straight as Miss Warburton's had been. That good lady, Jenny knew, would have recoiled in horror if she could hear the way the new lady clerk sometimes spoke to her employer.

And to tell the truth Jenny surprised even herself at times. She put the empty folder down on her desk and went to the window overlooking the street. Was she able to talk like that to Mr Will because knowing Paul Tunstall, *living* with him, had taught her that the dividing line between THEM and US was not as impenetrable as she had once thought it to be?

Or was it because the part of her that was all her father was somehow inherent in her make-up?

She sighed and rubbed at the pane of glass, steamed up now from the heat rising from the new length of piping installed recently in the office. The thin sleet of the early morning had changed to heavy rain, bouncing up from the cobblestones and flooding the gutters till they ran like streams.

Like the little gurgling stream at the bottom of Paul's garden, where the grassy bank sloped down, a bank that in another few weeks would be a carpet of snowdrops, tiny nodding white heads that miraculously had survived the long, harsh winter.

That was the worst of the countryside. Each season brought its memories, and with the remembering came the longing. Turning, she saw that through the wide pane of glass Mr Will's eyes were on her, and reminding herself that she was not being paid to dream, she sat down at her desk, and drew a sheaf of invoices towards her.

By the end of the week the continuous rain had swollen

the little stream at the bottom of Paul Tunstall's garden so that it rose and overflowed the grassy bank, leaving it awash.

The fields were flooded to a depth of six inches in places, and still it rained. For over a week now Sarah Tunstall had been unable to visit her mother at Cedar House, and for two days the day nurse had been unable to make her way over the flooded meadow land to the farm. Only the night nurse remained, and worn out with her charge's petulance and never ceasing demands, she had left her in her usual place on the sofa in front of the living-room fire, and retired upstairs to her room for what she considered to be a well-earned rest.

Down the long stone passageway in the kitchen, the resident cook, the lunch dishes cleared away and the joint sizzling slowly in the oven for the evening meal, kicked off her shoes, and put her head back for a nap. With Paul down in the stables, the house settled into the dark afternoon with nothing but the occasional clink of a cinder into the ashpan to break the silence.

Sarah too slept for a while, then she opened her eyes and saw that although it was barely three o'clock the room was as shrouded in darkness as if darkness had already fallen. The rain had stopped, but outside the sky hung so low that it seemed to be pressing in at the window, grey, thick and sodden with gloom.

It was like the end of the world. It might just as well have been the end of the world, and when the little dog Pootsy, sensing she was awake, crept up and tried to lick her face, Sarah knocked him away from her so that he fell onto the carpet whimpering with fright.

Sarah stretched out a hand for the brass bell on the small table by her side, then drew it back again. If the nurse came down she would only draw the curtains, light the lamps and throw a log on the fire, rubbing her hands and remarking on the awfulness of the day, and suggest a nice game of cards before tea was brought in.

Nothing would *happen*. Nothing ever happened. Even the scenes she made with Paul had lost their excitement. Now when she shouted and screamed he just got up and walked away.

'I'll come back when you've finished,' he had said, quite calmly after lunch, leaving nurse to put a damp cloth on her forehead and spoon some of the dark-tasting medicine through her clenched teeth.

Sarah's green eyes narrowed into menacing slits.

'She must never be left alone,' he had told the nurse. But that was when there were two of them. Now there was only one, and every time Sarah had opened her eyes in the bed which had turned the dining-room into a bedroom, the night nurse had been there, dutiful and vigilant, sitting in her chair by the fire, a book slipping from her knees.

Paul would be very angry if he found out that the nurse, worn out from lack of sleep, had crept upstairs for an hour. And he would be even angrier if something happened whilst she was neglecting her duties.

Sarah pushed the rug from her legs and holding onto the back of the sofa stood upright. Yes, she hadn't been imagining it, the leg injured in the fall downstairs at Cedar House *was* getting stronger. The iron caliper still held the left leg rigid, but the other one bore her weight. She tested it gingerly and reached for the stick looped over the end of the sofa.

Her eyes darted feverishly round the room, as her heart began to beat in heavy thuds. Now, what could she do that would make Paul have to send the nurse packing? Oh, God, but she was tired of her cheerfulness, sick to death of seeing the round red cushions of her cheeks wobble as she laughed.

But what to *do*? She could throw herself down on the floor by the door, so that it would look as if she had been trying to get help. But if the nurse found her first she would only lead her back to the sofa, then Paul would want to know why she had not rung the bell. Sarah's eyes glittered.

He didn't miss a trick, not Paul Tunstall, the eligible man she had married who spent his days working in the fields or with the horses, like a farm labourer.

No, it would have to be something more drastic than that.

For a moment she stared at the fire, her mind as clear as if she was working out an intricate mathematical problem. . . . She could perhaps pull a log from the fire with her stick on to the thick rug so that it caught alight. She could be back on the sofa ringing the bell and screaming. But that would not bring Paul in from the stables. With the window tight shut against the winter's day, he would not hear, and it was him she wanted to punish. Him she wanted to punish for leaving her alone, for looking at her with those silver-light eyes. For being so patient, so good, because it was his duty.

Now her breathing was rapid as her mind darted from one possibility to another, and all the time the darkness was crowding in, the dampness seeping through the window, the sky itself coming lower and lower, grey, soft, clinging, like a wet shroud.

She could not remember the last time she had opened a door for herself, but now, with the stick looped over an arm she found she could manage. The dog slipped through behind her, but she did not see. All that mattered was that she got out of the house somehow, away from walls pressing in on her, down the passage, one dragging step after another, her soft slippers making no sound as she drew closer to the heavy front door.

She stood for a moment in the porch, shivering in her velvet dress as the cold tore into her like a knife, blowing her red-gold hair round her pale face. The dank mist swirled up from the river, hiding the fields and hedges, but over there, not too far over there was the cedar tree standing sentinel over her mother's house.

For a moment Sarah thought she heard her mother's voice, strident and piercing, but always softened and gentled with love when she spoke to her daughter. For a moment sanity came back to her, so that she groped behind her for the door handle, only to see the dog rush past her skirts to a glorious freedom he knew awaited him in the fields over the stepping-stones across the bubbling stream.

But there were no stepping-stones. The little stream was a rushing torrent, and as his front paws gave way beneath him he slithered down the waterlogged bank out of control.

'Pootsy!' Sarah saw the dog disappear, and without stopping to think took an unsteady step after him.

For a split second the right leg took her weight, then when she tried to bring her other stiff leg forward, she fell, the stick careering away from her, its rubber tip failing to grip the slippery bank.

Over and over she rolled, down the few feet of flooded grass into the stream, striking her head on a flat stone hidden by the onrush of water.

The freezing cold water brought her swiftly to her senses, and she raised her head, knowing even in her terror that if she could raise herself and scream for help, someone would hear. There was no way she could bring herself to a kneeling position, once she was down she was there until someone lifted her up, but she could survive if only someone heard.

And the dog, the stupid, fear-crazed little dog, was thrashing round her, its brown eyes dilated with fear. Sarah put out a hand towards it, then drew it back hastily as she felt the sharp teeth sink into her wrist.

And it was the unexpected pain that severed the last remnants of her slipping sanity. Now when she opened her mouth to scream no sound came. The ice-cold water dragged at her velvet skirt, the mist closed in, and the swirling water filled her mouth as her head fell forward. Gasping and spluttering she raised her head again, screamed a soundless scream, then as though the effort was too much allowed her head to droop forward as the water filled her ears, her mouth and lungs, taking her into an oblivion she could never have stage-managed even during one of the worst of her flights of hysteria.

Jenny read the report in the paper that Friday evening. 'Wife of Gentleman Farmer drowns in three feet of water' it said. Then it went on to say that foul play was not suspected, and described how Mr Paul Tunstall had found his wife when her little dog had appeared in the stables, soaking wet and shivering with fright.

The paper dropped to the floor as Jenny covered her face with her hands. Her first thought was for Paul. Her first instinct was to go to him, to soothe, to comfort, to tell him that she was there if he needed her, to close his eyes against the horror as she held him close to her. But then commonsense took over, and she told herself that she must do nothing. She reminded herself of the long months since they met, told herself that too much had happened, made herself be still.

'There's something happened to that little lass at the office,' Mr Will told his wife the following week. 'She does her work just the same. I've never known a better clerk. I reckon we could go away this summer and leave her to run the office. She knows it all, she's like a sponge soaking up everything I tell her, but she's eating her heart out about something, I'm sure of that.'

'Man trouble?'

He knocked out his pipe against the bars of the grate in their spacious drawing-room. 'Aye. Bound to be with looks like that. But I can't say owt, can I? She's not a child. In some ways she's older than me, lass. But there's something very wrong, and there's nowt I can do but just let her get on with it.'

'It'll work right,' his wife said. 'Things have a way of doing that if you just let be. We all have to work our own salvations out. I firmly believe that.'

And her own salvation having been worked out most comfortably, she bent her head over her sewing and dismissed the problems of her husband's lady clerk from her mind.

The grassy bank in front of Paul's farm was bright with primroses before he came to find Jenny.

So often she had imagined how it would be if he came. So often had she imagined herself opening the door and seeing him standing there, feeling his arms go round her, and hearing his broken words of love.

But when it happened she just put out a hand and drew him inside, saying nothing until he was sitting by the fire, standing in front of him, waiting for him to speak.

'Jenny?'

'Yes. I'm here, Paul. I'm listening.'

She was very pale, very composed, so much thinner than he remembered. Older, and with a dignity about her that cancelled out the years between them so that he felt that all he wanted to do was to draw her to him, bury his face in the stuff of her skirt and cry.

'I'll never know, Jenny.' His voice was no more than a whisper. 'To my dying day I will never know if she intended to kill herself. That's what I can't come to terms with. That's what's eating at me.'

He raised his head, and she saw the anguish in the silver-light eyes. 'She was always threatening to do something, for ever blaming me for the way she was, and oh, Jenny, the way she was was terrible.'

He moved his head from side to side in a lost bewildered way. 'She . . . she would never have done that though. I keep telling myself that. Never have gone outside. I didn't know she could *walk* that far, Jenny. And it was cold . . . oh God, but it was cold. And wet. I keep going over it in my mind. Over and over. Why did she drown when there was no need to drown? Could I have stopped it? If it hadn't been for the floods, the day nurse would have been there, and it wouldn't have happened.'

He rubbed a hand across his forehead. 'I am no hypocrite, Jenny. There were times when I wished her dead. It's true. She *hated* me, Jenny. But to die like that, in three feet of muddy water. Oh, God, I wake in the night and see her hair floating round her dead face. I see her stick lying on the bit of path, and now when I see the stream, no more than a trickle over the stepping-stones, and the bank bright with primroses, I still can't believe it.' His eyes sought hers. 'Her parents have sold Cedar House and moved away. Her mother blamed me, Jenny. At the funeral she cursed me and said I had driven her daughter to it. And I keep asking myself. Had I? Or did Sarah even mean to die, or was she just getting at me, one last time, one terrible last time?'

'Paul! You must stop!' Jenny sank to her knees by the side of his chair, looking into his face but not touching, not stretching out even a finger towards him. Her dark eyes were bright with tears. 'You will destroy yourself if you don't stop, an' Paul, oh love, have you ever thought that may have been what she was trying to do?'

'Not that way!' He almost shouted at her. 'Not that way, Jenny! Not her. She always made sure that the hurts she inflicted on herself were little hurts. Never, never, would she have chosen that way!'

She could bear his distress, his pain no longer. Reaching out she pulled him close, and when she felt his arm go round her she put up a hand and stroked his hair, the thick barley pale hair she remembered so well.

'I am going to make a pot of tea, Paul. A comforting, soothing pot of tea, then you are going to tell me all about the farm. About the crops you have sown, about the horses, about the house and the dogs . . .' Her voice faltered.

'The night nurse took Pootsy away. I never wanted to see it again.' He was speaking in a more normal tone of voice now, and she pushed him gently from her and went to set the kettle over the leaping flames of the fire.

And they sat there in the tiny room till the light faded, without kissing, without even touching each other again.

MAGGIE CRAIG

Marie Joseph

From the natural successor to Catherine Cookson

At the turn of the century, the north of England was a hard, bleak world. A world where the only things in plenty were work and poverty – where joy and love were words in someone else's book. A world where men were resigned and women oppressed. It was here that Maggie Craig was born.

Strong-willed and spirited, as rebellious as she was beautiful, Maggie Craig flew in the face of the harshness of her life – and found a man she truly loved. But that passion was to cost her dearly all her life . . .

Then when he got up to go, she went with him to the door, looking up into his face, waiting for the words that only he could say.

He took her face between his hands, holding her so that she saw the love in his eyes. 'Jenny . . . oh, my own sweet Jenny. Not now. Not just yet, but I will come for you. When the . . . when the roses are in bloom, I will come for you. Will you be waiting? Will you, Jenny?'

Suddenly he smiled and there was a hint of the teasing laughter in his voice. 'What have you done with him, the other one? The boy who you were going to marry? When I went to your mother's house and she told me you were living alone I almost wept for joy. Do you know that?'

'There'll be no more weeping when the roses come into bloom,' Jenny said, lifting her mouth for his kiss. 'I promise you that, Paul. No more weeping. I'll see to that.'